THE IMPERIALIST

broadview editions
series editor: L.W. Conolly

Photograph from *Putnam's Reader V* (October 1908-March 1909) 502.
Courtesy of the Metropolitan Toronto Reference Library.

THE IMPERIALIST

Sara Jeannette Duncan

edited by Misao Dean

broadview editions

Library and Archives Canada Cataloguing in Publication

Duncan, Sara Jeannette, 1861–1922.
    The imperialist / Sara Jeannette Duncan; edited by Misao Dean.

(Broadview editions)
Includes bibliographical references.
ISBN 1-55111-540-9

    I. Dean, Misao   II. Title.   III. Series.

PS8455.O85I5 2005   C813'.4   C2005-902264-7

Broadview Editions
The Broadview Editions series represents the ever-changing canon of literature in English by bringing together texts long regarded as classics with valuable lesser-known works.

Advisory editor for this volume: Jennie Rubio

Broadview Press Ltd. is an independent, international publishing house, incorporated in 1985. Broadview believes in shared ownership, both with its employees and with the general public; since the year 2000 Broadview shares have traded publicly on the Toronto Venture Exchange under the symbol BDP.

We welcome comments and suggestions regarding any aspect of our publications — please feel free to contact us at the addresses below or at broadview@broadviewpress.com.

North America
Post Office Box 1243, Peterborough, Ontario, Canada K9J 7H5
Post Office Box 1015, 3576 California Road, Orchard Park, NY, USA 14127
Tel: (705) 743-8990; Fax: (705) 743-8353;
email: customerservice@broadviewpress.com

UK, Ireland, and continental Europe
NBN Plymbridge, Estover Road, Plymouth PL6 7PY UK
Tel: 44 (0) 1752 202301   Fax: 44 (0) 1752 202331
Fax Order Line: 44 (0) 1752 202333
Customer Service: cservs@nbnplymbridge.com Orders: orders@nbnplymbridge.com

Australia and New Zealand
UNIREPS, University of New South Wales
Sydney, NSW, 2052 Australia
Tel: 61 2 9664 0999; Fax: 61 2 9664 5420
email: info.press@unsw.edu.au

www.broadviewpress.com

Broadview Press Ltd. gratefully acknowledges the financial support of the Government of Canada through the Book Publishing Industry Development Program for our publishing activities.

Typesetting and assembly: True to Type Inc., Mississauga, Canada.

PRINTED IN CANADA

Contents

Acknowledgements

When Don LePan finished his graduate work and told us all he was going to start a publishing company, we thought this was a short term plan. But strangely, he didn't go bankrupt—who knew? Thanks for suggesting this project, Don, and for your amazing energy and achievement in Canadian publishing.

The professional and hard-working Interlibrary Loan department of the McPherson Library at the University of Victoria have done much to make this project possible, as have the office staff in the English Department (Diana Rutherford, Jenny Jessa, and Darlene Hollingsworth). Thanks. My research in the A.P. Watt Papers at the University of North Carolina at Chapel Hill was funded by a University of Victoria Internal Research Grant. I would also like to acknowledge John Roscoe, Jessica Posgate and Weldon Hunter, three graduate students in the English Department at the University of Victoria who have at various times compared texts, proofread, go-fered, and otherwise supported this project.

Love and thanks always to Gerry, my sounding board, back-up child-care provider, hand-holder, legal representative and dear husband.

Introduction

When *The Imperialist* was first published it appeared in four countries on three continents in the space of six months. Its audience, and its aesthetic, was international; its politics global. Yet when the book was republished in 1971 as part of the New Canadian Library series it was interpreted solely within a Canadian context, as part of an effort to recover the historical grounding of the celebratory nationalism of the 1970s. *The Imperialist* was seen from this perspective as both an attempt to represent the uniqueness of Canadian character and setting, and as an articulation of a nineteenth-century form of Canadian nationalism. Feminist critics of the 1980s and 1990s focussed on the novel's representation of gender, while more recent interpretations of the book retrieve the novel from its nationalist critical context and present it as a postcolonial novel that interrogates the very category of the postcolonial. This edition introduces *The Imperialist* as an important Edwardian novel, as well as an innovative Canadian one: its ironic tone, its graceful style, and its analysis of race, nation, and gender in the context of the waning British Empire make for challenging and enjoyable reading.

Sara Jeannette Duncan, the author of *The Imperialist*, was one of Canada's earliest literary successes on the international stage. Born in 1861 in Brantford, Upper Canada (later Ontario), Duncan graduated from the local high school and trained as a teacher. But her career in teaching was a short one; her first publications appeared in the Toronto *Globe* when she was nineteen, suggesting that writing was always her goal. In 1884 she travelled to the New Orleans' Cotton Centennial as a freelancer, and her articles in the *Globe*, the *Washington Post*, and the London *Advertiser*, published under the pseudonym "Garth," were so successful that she was offered a regular column when she returned to Canada in the spring of 1885. Her subsequent career in journalism was studded with achievements: by the age of twenty-seven, Duncan had written editorials and managed the Current Literature department for the *Washington Post*, become the first woman journalist to work in the editorial office of the Toronto *Globe*, and covered Parliament for the *Montreal Star*.

In 1888, Duncan resigned from her job at the *Star* to begin a round-the-world trip with fellow journalist Lily Lewis. Following the lead of the popular "stunt journalists" of her day, she intended her "unconventional" trip to furnish material for her first book. Duncan and Lewis began by riding the newly-completed railway from Montreal to Vancouver, continuing on by steamship to Japan, China, Singapore, Calcutta, and Egypt before pausing in London to complete revisions to the manuscript. The resulting book, *A Social Departure: How Orthodocia and I Went around the World by Ourselves*, was serialised in the *Ladies' Pictorial* and published by Chatto and Windus in 1890. The book was an instant success, and Duncan was launched on a career as an author that would include twenty-two books published in London and New York, as well as stories, articles, and editorials published in magazines and newspapers in Canada, the US, Britain, Australia, and India.

In retrospect, Duncan's journalistic career was an admirable apprenticeship for her fiction. Duncan's columns for the Toronto *Globe* and the *Montreal Star*, published under the pseudonym "Garth Grafton," are a grab-bag of "delicious scraps": a pastiche of news items gleaned from other publications, personal reflections, and advice. They deal with such diverse topics as life insurance for women, mass-produced interior decor, and the popularity of gilt-hair pins. Like her early fiction, they feature a narrative voice that is "risible but serious, a fresh, clever and cultivated woman's disposition"[1] and commonly use dialogue as a way of exploring subjects. On a more serious note, "Women's World" included interviews with prominent women like the Mohawk poet Pauline Johnson and Dr. Alice McGillivray, one of Canada's first female physicians, and discussed the new literary realism and its attraction for women readers. Under her own signature Duncan also wrote a column for the Toronto literary periodical *The Week*, edited by the prominent intellectual Goldwin Smith. In it she discussed Canadian literature, education for women, and the little rituals of Toronto society. On the dampening effect of colonialism on the growth of the arts in Canada, she wrote in a September 1886 column: "Our enforced political humility is the distinguishing characteristic of every phase of our national life. We are ignored, and we ignore ourselves." She condemned Ontarians as a "camp of the Philistines" and cited newspapers as proof: "Politics and vituperation, temperance and vituperation, religion and vituperation; these three dietetic articles, the vitu-

---

1   Rae Goodwin, "The Early Journalism of Sara Jeannette Duncan, with a Chapter of Biography" (MA thesis, University of Toronto, 1964), 93.

perative sauce invariably accompanying, form the exclusive journalistic pabulum of three-quarters of the people of Ontario." No matter what the topic, be it copyright law, contemporary trends in interior decor, or women's suffrage, her writing is lively and irreverent, "always diametrically opposed to Victorian narrowness and the cultural degeneracy of which she so frequently complains," observes Rae Goodwin.[1]

Duncan met Everard Charles Cotes, a British civil servant working at the Calcutta Museum, in India in 1889, and married him when she returned to India in 1890. Despite plans to move to England in 1894, the couple remained based in India where Cotes became a successful journalist, editor of the *Indian Daily News* from 1894 to 1897, and later, Managing Director of the Eastern News Agency. Duncan never lived in Canada permanently again, though she continued to visit her family in Brantford; she and Cotes maintained homes in Delhi, Simla, and Calcutta, with extended stays in London, and visits to New York and Toronto.

Marriage did not dampen Duncan's ambition or her output. She suggested in an interview in 1895 that her move to India had actually facilitated her writing career: "One's housekeeping is done in a quarter of an hour in the morning.... And there is such abundance of material in Anglo-Indian life—it is full of such picturesque incidence, such tragic chance."[2] She maintained a steady schedule of writing and publishing, working every morning until she had three or four hundred words completed on her current project. She continued this schedule even when she was under treatment for tuberculosis in 1900; she completed a book of sketches, *The Crow's Nest* (1901),[3] while recovering in the fresh air of her Simla garden. Despite her frequent travels between Canada, England, and various homes in India, she maintained personal connections with many of the important Canadians of her day; these included George Ross (who she met when she was a teacher in Brantford), Goldwin Smith (editor of *The Week* in Toronto), Hamilton-born novelist and editor Jean Newton McIlwraith, and prominent journalist and editor John Willison. She corresponded with J.L. Garvin at the *Observer* in London, and with her literary

---

1 Goodwin, "The Early Journalism of Sara Jeannette Duncan," 94.

2 G.B. Burgin, "A Chat with Sara Jeannette Duncan," *The Idler*, VII (August 1895): 117.

3 This book was published under the name *On the Other Side of the Latch* in England.

agents, A.P. Watt and sons A.S. Watt and Hansard Watt. She played hostess to E.M. Forster when he visited Simla and Delhi in 1912[1] and pursued acquaintances with US novelists W.D. Howells and with Henry James, whose work she greatly admired.

These friendships signal the artistic and literary context for Duncan's writing. Like Howells, Duncan was interested in what she saw as the unique ways that British culture developed and changed in North America, and in her novels she developed characters as representative national "types."[2] In novels like *The Simple Adventures of a Memsahib* (1893) and *Set in Authority* (1906) she extended this analysis to India, drawing on the works of Rudyard Kipling to create fictional types like the memsahib, or the heroic colonial administrator. Like Henry James, she often placed her colonial characters in conflict with representatives of "old Europe" and focussed on the complex internal life of characters faced with an ethical dilemma. This inner life is represented in a significant evolution of style, from the witty and "delightful" tone of her journalism and travel writing to the complex, dense, and ironic narrative voice that many critics saw as directly influenced by James' later work. However, Duncan's contacts in the London literary community and her frequent extended stays in England suggest other influences, most especially those of the literary *fin de siècle* and popular Edwardian novelists. Duncan was interested in the new dialogue about gender prompted by suffrage and social reform movements; she read "scandalous" authors like George Egerton (Mary Chavelita Dunne) and Robert Barr and commented on the "New Woman" of the 1890s. She was fascinated by visual art (several of her novels feature painters as characters), and like Oscar Wilde and other "magic picture" novelists, represented art as a revelation of moral truth.[3] While she depicts the advent of modernity in her female characters (who shop in department

---

1 See Mary Lago and P.N. Furbank, *Selected Letters of E.M. Forster* (London: Arrow Books, 1983), 153, 159-60.
2 See Thomas Tausky, "The American Girls of W.D. Howells and Sara Jeannette Duncan," *Journal of Canadian Fiction*, 13 (1975): 146-58; and Misao Dean, "Canadian Nationality in the Early International Novels of Sara Jeannette Duncan," *Journal of Canadian Studies*, 20:2 (September 1985): 132-49 and *A Different Point of View* (Montreal: McGill-Queen's UP, 1991).
3 See Kathryn Ready, "Sara Jeannette Duncan's *A Daughter of Today*: Nineteenth-Century Canadian Literary Feminism and the fin-de-siècle Magic-Picture Story," *Canadian Literature*, 173 (Summer 2002): 95-112.

stores, decorate their homes with mass-produced goods, and travel on the outside of double-decker buses), like other Edwardian novelists she rejects the self-interest and commercialism of consumer culture by representing art as the ideal antithesis of the commodity.[1] And, like Kipling, whom she characterized as the inescapable forerunner of any novelist writing about India, she was interested in the future of England and the Empire in an era of weakening British influence and burgeoning local nationalisms.

The Imperialist was Duncan's fourteenth novel, and the only one set entirely in Canada. Written for the most part in India, over a decade after she had left Canada for good, the novel still seems realistic rather than nostalgic to most readers: both "warm with remembered affection,"[2] and characterised by a "precision of detail that often seems documentary."[3] Family members confirm that the setting of the novel contains many autobiographical elements,[4] with the character of John Murchison based on her father, Charles Duncan, and the loving and stimulating family home modelled on her own upbringing at 96 West Street in Brantford. Duncan admitted in a letter to Archibald MacMechan[5] that the ebullient Dr. Drummond is a fictional portrait of the minister in her own church, Dr. William Cochrane, a "tremendous Presbyterian" who became, like his fictional counterpart, Moderator of the Presbyterian Church of Canada. The autobiographical sources of the novel suggest the way that the "realism" of the novel is based in part on the representation of observed material detail. Like the "local color" realists of the late Nineteenth Century in the US, such as Hamlin Garland and W.D. Howells, Duncan strove in *The Imperialist* to create "a literature based on personal observation and experience"[6] that is faithful to the details of ordinary life in a particular time and place.

---

1 Janice Fiamengo, "'Susceptible to no common translation': Language and Idealism in Sara Jeannette Duncan's *The Imperialist*," *Canadian Literature*, 160 (Spring 1999): 123.
2 Clara Thomas, "Canadian Social Mythologies in Sara Jeannette Duncan's *The Imperialist*," *Journal of Canadian Studies*, 12:2 (1977): 39. See also Marian Fowler, *Redney: A Life of Sara Jeannette Duncan* (Toronto: Anansi, 1983); and Joseph Zezulka, *"The Imperialist*: Imperialism, Provincialism, and Point of View," in John Moss, ed., *Beginnings: A Critical Anthology* (Toronto: NC Press, 1980), 142-91.
3 Thomas, "Canadian Social Mythologies," 39.
4 See Goodwin, "The Early Journalism of Sara Jeannette Duncan."
5 See Appendix A.3.
6 Zezulka, *"The Imperialist*: Imperialism, Provincialism and Point of View," 143.

But Duncan wrote at a time when realism was not necessarily either popular or approved. In fact, by the late 1880s, realism in literature had become a controversial topic, and many of the journals for which Duncan wrote throughout the 1880s and 1890s waged a "realism war." At issue was whether realism could be art. Some claimed that realistic fiction was merely a mechanical reflection of everyday life, "requiring only a concentration of one's attention upon the details of one's neighbour's daily life, an accurate transcription thereof, and a great deal of assurance," as Duncan herself wrote in the columns of *The Week*.[1] More seriously, critics attacked realism because it seemed to neglect a public duty to morally uplift or educate its readers. Realist novels represented immoral scenes and actions without explicitly condemning them, and realist plotlines often concluded without the traditional ending in which the evildoers were punished and the good characters rewarded. Because realist novels emphasized the individuality or uniqueness of particular places or people they seemed to some readers to be merely sensationalist, focussing on the extreme, the unusual, and the unique at the expense of what W.D. Howells called "the more smiling aspects"[2] of life. The defenders of romance argued that, unlike realist fiction, it strove to instruct and uplift readers by idealising its heroes and exaggerating the consequences of evil, and to refine the taste of the uneducated with elegant and ornamental language. They believed that the grand emotions of romantic fiction expanded the scope of feeling for those condemned to live prosaic and commonplace urban lives, an argument that Duncan also found persuasive.[3]

The partisans of the "realism war" felt there was more at stake than just literary technique. For them, realism offered a way of viewing the world that was political and ideological as well as aesthetic. In an age when conservatives idealised monarchy and feared the mob, realism focussed on the middle and lower classes, and implicitly challenged the status quo. Its opponents attacked realism as "literary democracy" and accused W.D. Howells, the champion of US realism, of advocating a "communistic"

---

1 "Saunterings," 3 March 1887.
2 W.D. Howells, "Dostoyevsky and the More Smiling Aspects of Life." *Harper's*, 73 (1886): 641.
3 See "Saunterings," *The Week*, 13 January 1887; and Carole Gerson, *A Purer Taste: Reading and Writing in Nineteenth Century Canada* (Toronto: U of Toronto P, 1989), 61-62.

literature that "must inevitably degrade the taste, lower the standards of art, and prove fatal to all elevation of mind and noble ambition."[1] Romance seemed to them to encode the values of a stable, hierarchically organized society with classes clearly demarcated and the route of culture clearly marked. In contrast, realism seemed to represent the voice of the newly enfranchised masses, led by a middle class that celebrated its own philistinism.

Duncan was one of the few early defenders of literary realism in Canada. She argued that "life should be represented [in novels] as it is and not as we would like it to be, regardless of probabilities."[2] This focus on "life as it is" would require not just careful observation and reportage, but a renovation of plot and character. The role of the heroine in the novel needed to be updated; no longer the "painted pivot of the merry-go-round," characterised solely by her "ebon locks" and "rosebud mouth," the heroine of the realist novel should reflect the changing social status of women, Duncan argued. "The novel of to-day is a reflection of our present social state. The women who enter into its composition are but intelligent agents in this reflection, and show themselves as they are, not as a false ideal would have them" she wrote in her column in *The Week*.[3] The hero in Duncan's novels may be an idealist, but as Francis Zichy points out, "he is not to be a knight of romance, capable of superhuman feats, or a romantic villain heroically at odds with normal decencies, but rather a believable citizen of a society presented in recognizable detail."[4] However, as readers of *The Imperialist* discovered, Duncan did not fully reject the literary conventions known in her time as "romance." Her endorsement of realism is always qualified by her acknowledgement that representation always involves selection, according to aesthetic, ideological, or other criteria. Chief among these criteria, for Duncan, is "art": "literature should at its best be true not only to the objects upon and about which it constructs itself, but faithful also to all the delicate attractions and repulsions which enter so intimately into the highest art."[5] Another of these criteria is an unchanging realm of absolute value, associated with

---

1 Louisa Murray, quoted in Gerson, *A Purer Taste*, 58.

2 *Montreal Star*, 17 January 1888.

3 See Appendix A.2.

4 Francis Zichy, "Portrait of the Idealist as Politician: The Individual and Society in *The Imperialist*," *English Studies in Canada*, 10:3 (September 1984): 333.

5 *Montreal Star*, 5 December 1887.

the mode of romance: "In literature, as elsewhere, certain fundamental principles do not change. We must have truth of one sort or another—truth to certain values in the ideal, truth to certain actualities in the real."[1] Somehow, Duncan suggests, novels must be true to both "the ideal," an abstract realm of values whose mode is romance, and to "the real," the material realm perceived as modern, global, and ever-changing, whose mode is realism, while rendering both according to the dictates of "art."

Critic Glenn Willmott suggests a way that Canadian novelists worked to reconcile the two sides of the "realism war," and his comments are particularly relevant to *The Imperialist*. Willmott argues that the characteristic form of the early Canadian novel is a version of the *Bildungsroman*,[2] featuring a virtuous, sympathetic hero with ties to the "old world," in conflict with the values and practices of a particularised Canadian society. The "unchanging" values of romance are self-consciously associated with England or Scotland and attached to a hero who stands for the persistence of these values in the New World, while the Canadian setting itself signals fidelity to "the real" for its audience. "The real and the 'distinctively and characteristically Canadian' are the same thing" in such novels; and "realism is a descent into Canadian national particularity."[3] By choosing to write about Canada at all, realist novelists signalled their commitment to representing the culture and the material circumstances of life around them "realistically." At the same time, Canadian novelists incorporated the values of romance by depicting heroines and heroes educated in a tradition of cultural continuity with Europe, a tradition they defend as setting an ideal standard of moral responsibility. In *The Imperialist* the "ideal" is constructed "inescapably in the light of a transfigured imperialism" represented by the hero, Lorne Murchison, "and the 'actual' or 'real' marked by Canadian historical particularities—regions, races, classes, genders, languages—to which the new ideals must adapt or correspond."[4]

Willmott's identification of "the real" in *The Imperialist* with "Canadian historical particularities" seems particularly just.

---

1   "Saunterings," *The Week*, 4 November 1886.
2   A novel that has as its main theme the formative years or spiritual education of one person.
3   Glenn Willmott, *Unreal Country: Modernity in the Canadian Novel in English* (Montreal: McGill-Queen's UP, 2002), 22.
4   Willmott, *Unreal Country*, 22.

Many popular "romances" from the late nineteenth and early twentieth centuries by Canadian authors such as May Agnes Fleming, Gilbert Parker, Amelia Fytche, and Robert Barr, are set in such locations as the US south, the far North, Paris, and London, and render their locations in less than convincing detail. In contrast, Duncan reiterates the material details of life in Elgin with a keen sense of the way that domestic practices and consumer behavior signal class and status in small towns. The fashion of wearing evening gowns with three-quarter sleeves and square necks; the rag rug in Mrs. Murchison's spare room; the reluctance of the Elgin housewives to "traipse" home from the market with anything that looks inconvenient (or has feet attached); the remarkable adaptability of Canadian feet to American shoes: all of these details are rendered exactly, with a sense of the way that they indicate class, gender, and cultural norms. Duncan saw this kind of writing as appealing specifically to the feminine reader, and played up the details of domestic life with this in mind: "With regard to woman's taste in fiction, we would hardly like to confess how dear the commonplace is to every petticoated one of us.... The ordinary details of humdrum life and circumstance, pen-painted by an artist with sympathies keen enough to detect the mysterious throbbing of life that is inner and under, fascinate us like our own photographs."[1] In *The Imperialist* the details of a particularised Canadian setting and specifically Canadian social practices are represented as both enabling and defeating the hero's growth toward maturity, signalling both the unique character of Lorne's home community and its inextricable connection to global trade.

The detailed portrait of domestic life in Canada, along with its analysis of religion and class, was judged by reviewers of the time to be one of the chief strengths of *The Imperialist*. Jean Graham, writing in *Saturday Night* in 1904, judged the novel "photographic in its fidelity to local conditions and types.... Elgin, the town described, is said to be Brantford, but it might be Guelph or Stratford or Goderich. We all know the Murchisons, the family circle into which [Duncan] so warmly welcomes us; in fact, I know I have had tea at the Murchisons, where 'the chicken salad gleamed at one end of the table and the scalloped oysters smoked delicious at the other.'"[2] Contemporary critics have tended to see the

---

1 "Other People and I," *The Globe*, 17 June 1885.

2 J[ean] G[raham], *Saturday Night*, 4 June 1904. See Appendix C.5.

portrait of the Murchison family and the detailed description of Duncan's family home as tinged with nostalgia,[1] as indeed it must be: childhood memories exist as much in space as in time, as Gaston Bachelard has written, and they only become specific when located in the remembered window-nooks and cosy corners of a childhood home.[2] Duncan carried the seeds of Brantford goldenrod with her to India, where, as she said, "the warm scent of it" reminded her that "youth and its affections are not lost, but only on the other side of the world!"[3]

The "transfigured imperialism" that motivates Lorne Murchison's political career needs some explanation. For present-day readers the term "imperialism" is likely to suggest the military and economic exploitation of non-industrialised countries by Europe and North America. But for late nineteenth-century Canadians, "Imperialism" (or as it was called among its supporters, "The Idea") was "that movement for the closer union of the British Empire through economic and military co-operation and through political changes that would give the dominions influence over imperial policy."[4] Canadian supporters of "The Idea" proposed the re-creation of the Empire as a federation of independent states with a common economic and foreign policy, and a single military force. They argued that the British Colonial Office should be disbanded in favour of an elected Imperial Parliament with representatives from all of the self-governing colonies of the former Empire. They felt that the economic depression of the late nineteenth century could be remedied by creating a sort of free trade zone, or in the language of the times, a *Zollverein*,[5] that would encompass all of the colonies and former colonies of the British Empire, and thus provide secure access to British markets for Canadian agricultural products and resources like lumber and coal. Their Imperialism was a form of Canadian nationalism, which saw increased ties among the countries of the Empire as a

---

1 See Fowler, *Redney*; and Jon Kertzer, "Destiny into Chance: S.J. Duncan's *The Imperialist* and the Perils of Nation-Building," *Studies in Canadian Literature*, 24:2 (1999): 1-34.

2 Gaston Bachelard, *The Poetics of Space* (New York: Orion, 1964), 9-10.

3 See Appendix A.4.

4 Carl Berger, *The Sense of Power* (Toronto: U of Toronto P, 1970), 3.

5 This term, derived from German, originally signified a free-trade union between certain states of the German empire in the early nineteenth century.

means to increase Canada's voice in foreign affairs and a way to promote Canadian economic growth and stability.

Canadian Imperialists took their inspiration from a particular interpretation of Canadian history.[1] They saw Canadian support for the British Empire as deriving from the historical emigration of the Loyalists from the American Colonies during and after the American Revolutionary War. They believed that the Loyalist emigration signalled a commitment to the persistence of "British values" from the beginning of Canada, values like social stability, tradition, free speech, intellectual liberalism, and support for the monarchy. The succeeding generations of Canadian Imperialists saw these values threatened by the growing materialism of US society as well as by the social chaos and mob rule that accompanied and succeeded the Revolution in the US. In response, they argued that a continued connection to British institutions and culture would protect Canada against the spread of US mob culture, while a formal military and political connection would provide a strong arm to oppose the external threat of US power in territorial and economic disputes. Without it, they believed, Canada might be forced to "annex" itself to the US in order to ensure its economic prosperity, or might lose significant parts of its territory to US expansionism.

Canadian Imperialists frequently opposed industrialisation and promoted a kind of attachment to the land that was also associated with the romantic idea of the nation. They believed that farmers were the basis of a healthy society, because the nature and demands of their work promoted physical and mental health. In addition, because the lives of farmers were governed by the actual conditions of the landscape and the seasons in a particular place and time, they were most closely in touch with the geography that made the nation, and were themselves moulded by it. For these reasons, Imperialists idealised farmers, and in *The Imperialist* Lorne argues that preference trade will give priority to their economic health. In his election speech Lorne Murchison states that the Imperialists "stand for the wheat-belt and the stockyard, the forest and the mine, as the basic interests of the country. We stand for the principles that make for nation-building by the slow sweet

---

1   For more information about Imperialism in Canada, see Berger, *The Sense of Power.*

processes of the earth, cultivating the individual rooted man who draws his essence and his tissues from the soil, and so ... forms the character of the commonwealth, the foundation of the State." His views are shared in a more directly practical way by his father, who argues that the growth of manufacturing is dependent upon a healthy demand for manufactured goods among farmers, and that an economic policy that benefits farmers must eventually benefit the economy as whole.

However, this vision of the autonomous romantic nation vitally linked to a unique landscape comes up against the "reality" of Canada's dependence upon foreign markets, the linking of the Canadian economy and culture to other cultures and economies in a globalised world. As Harold Innis pointed out in his monumental study, *The Fur Trade in Canada*, the mercantilist economic structure typical of colonies (whereby the colonies trade unprocessed raw materials, "staples," for manufactured goods) is both a response to and a technology of continued interdependence of nations, of globalisation. Immigrants "who have become accustomed to the cultural traits of their civilization" rely on export trade to provide the goods that facilitate "adjustments to the new environment without serious loss"[1] of cultural values or standards of living. The continuance of cultural traditions is tied to the continuance of the trade relationships: "The methods by which the cultural traits of a civilization may persist with the least possible depreciation involve an appreciable dependence on the peoples of the homeland."[2] This cultural dependence and continuity provides Lorne with the "large ideas" by which he justifies his support for Imperialism, even as it limits his ability to conceive of a fully independent Canada.

Throughout the nineteenth century, support for Imperialism in Canada was associated with the Conservative Party of John A. MacDonald. As Duncan points out in her article "Imperial Sentiment in Canada,"[3] the Conservative Party claimed to be

> composed in part of the old United Empire Loyalists, who crossed the line with their families from Massachusetts more than a century ago to avoid taking up arms against King

---

1 Harold Innis, *The Fur Trade in Canada* (New Haven: Yale UP, 1962), 384.

2 Innis, *The Fur Trade*, 383.

3 See Appendix B.3.

George, and to continue to live under the British flag. This has always given a great accent to the loyal professions of Canadian Conservatives and has combined with the aristocratic and monarchical traditions claimed by the party everywhere to establish them very conspicuously.

But by the turn of the twentieth century, the Liberals were claiming the lead in promoting closer ties between Britain and Canada. The MacDonald government had instituted the "National Policy," whose three main initiatives of tariff protection for Canadian manufactured goods, the building of the trans-national railroad, and the encouragement of immigration to the Canadian West, attempted to create a more self-sufficient national economy. But by 1895, "the new industries began to flicker out, exhausted by their own competition in a narrow market" according to Duncan; MacDonald's attempt to create a national economy had failed to change Canada's dependence on external markets, and a generalised economic depression had its effects on Canadian business. Imperialists argued that Canada should try to gain secure access to British markets for Canadian agricultural products, particularly grain, and they received cautious support for this idea from the Liberals under the leadership of Wilfrid Laurier. The electoral victory of a Laurier government in 1896 gave supporters of a United Empire hope that the federal government would back up its professions of loyalty to the British with solid economic measures.

While in opposition, Laurier's Liberals had favoured closer ties with the US as a way to stimulate the export economy. Canada and the US had signed a "reciprocity treaty" in 1854 that created free trade in some goods. However, the US had refused to renew the treaty in 1866, amid some aggressive rhetoric about England's role in the US Civil War. Attempts by successive Canadian governments to renegotiate the treaty were rejected, and with the McKinley Bill of 1890 (which imposed import tariffs on a range of goods, including agricultural products), US trade protectionism became a persistent irritant in Canada/US relations. Goldwin Smith, the Toronto intellectual and editor of *The Week*, was a strong advocate for what he called "Commercial Union," a proposal for the economic union of Canada with the United States. In his book *Canada and the Canadian Question* (1891) he argued that the National Policy benefited only a small group of Tory manufacturers at the expense of farmers, miners, loggers, and fishers, and that attempts to secure access to the British market were misguided.

Let any one scan the economical map of the North American continent with its adjacent waters, mark its northern zone abounding in minerals, in bituminous coal, in lumber, in fish, as well as in special farm products, brought in the north to hardier perfection, all of which the southern people have need: then let him look to its southern regions, the natural products of which as well as the manufactures produced in its wealthy centres of industry are needed by the people of the northern zone: he will see that the continent is an economic whole, and that to run a Customs line athwart it and try to sever its members from each other is to wage a desperate war against nature.[1]

Smith claimed that his plan for "Commercial Union" would not involve any loss of Canadian sovereignty, but his opponents were unconvinced. Canadians like G.M. Grant and George Parkin wrote reviews critical of Smith's book, disputing its figures and attacking its idea of what was "natural" for Canada.

A key element in the Canadian debate over Imperialism was whether Britain was willing or able to respond to Canadian overtures for closer ties. As Lorne Murchison discovers in *The Imperialist*, the British were facing a significant economic depression; in 1903 Henry Campbell-Bannerman, leader of the opposition Liberal Party, gave a speech in which he quoted a study by "Mr. Rowntree and Mr. Charles Booth" that suggested that twelve million Britons were so poor as to be malnourished.[2] However, advocacy of "Imperial Preference Trade," a scheme to promote economic ties within the Empire by giving tariff preference to grain and other products imported from colonies and former colonies of England, was politically dangerous. Britain had strong populist opposition to tariffs of any kind on agricultural products, a result of the cruel and punishing "Corn Laws" designed to favour English landowners at the expense of the poor during the eighteenth and early nineteenth centuries. "Free trade" and "Free Food" were the rallying cries of the British Liberals, and they represented Imperial Preference as a measure that would increase poverty and want among the already suffering urban poor in England.

---

1 Goldwin Smith, *Canada and the Canadian Question* (Toronto: Hunter Rose, 1891).
2 John Wilson, *C.B.: A Life of Sir Henry Campbell-Bannerman* (London: Constable, 1973), 410.

When Joseph Chamberlain, the Colonial Secretary and a strong advocate of Imperial Federation, gave a series of speeches in the spring of 1903 advocating not only Imperial Preference for agricultural goods, but also a common military and foreign policy, he split the Cabinet of the Balfour government, and by the fall he had been forced to resign.

Chamberlain's tariff scheme was not created in a vacuum; it was part of an agenda of "national efficiency"[1] promoted by social reformers George Bernard Shaw and Beatrice and Sidney Webb, which called for social welfare spending to create a healthy "efficient" working class. They saw the Empire as a resource that could be administered in order to benefit the poor of England. Chamberlain planned to use the revenue from his tariff proposal to finance an old-age pension; his scheme was lauded as "a classic piece of social imperialism."[2] However, because Chamberlain proposed to abandon the traditionally progressive policy of free trade, the alliance between Liberals, Conservatives, and Fabian Socialists that the Webbs had promoted could not fully support it; the proposed party of National Efficiency split, just as Balfour's cabinet had done. The Webb's plan to promote progressive social spending was "effectively wrecked."

The themes of imperial identity and "the condition of England" were major preoccupations of the Edwardian novel in Britain. As Anthea Trodd points out, "imperialism was the dominant national ideology of the Edwardian period";[3] but the Empire itself was under attack both within and without, by liberal English politicians who doubted the morality of using military force in the colonies, and by local nationalisms in places like India. Kipling's *Kim* (1901) and Forster's *Howards End* (1910) are well-known examples of Edwardian novels that addressed the notion of imperial identity in the context of the waning British Empire. In addition, many argued that the Empire was no longer an economic advantage to Britain because it seemed to cost more to maintain than it contributed to the economy. Jonathan Rose reports in *The Edwardian Temperament* that "Edwardian newspapers were filled with apprehensive reports on the challenge of

---

1   Jonathan Rose, *The Edwardian Temperament, 1895-1919* (Athens, OH: Ohio UP, 1986), 132.

2   Rose, *The Edwardian Temperament*, 132.

3   Anthea Trodd, *A Reader's Guide to Edwardian Literature* (Calgary: U of Calgary P, 1991), 15.

American competition"[1] and assertions that "Britain, once the world's first commercial power, was being overtaken by the United States and Germany."[2] As in *The Imperialist*, "this relative decline was widely attributed to the wretchedness of the [British] working classes,"[3] just as Lorne attributes the conservatism and fear of British politicians to the "hungry twelve millions" of the British poor.

Laurier demonstrated his willingness to enter into preferential trade agreements at the Colonial Conference of 1902 when he proposed to extend preferential treatment to some British imports in Canada in exchange for exemption from British tariffs on Canadian grain. But his government was opposed to the idea of a common military and foreign policy, and during his tenure as Prime Minister relations with Britain were rocky. The British sided with the Americans in a dispute over the Alaska Boundary that dragged on from 1898 to 1903, and when the British went to war in South Africa in 1899, the Cabinet was deeply divided over whether to send Canadian troops to support them. The Liberal Party eventually gave up on the idea of Imperial Preference, embracing a policy of Unrestricted Reciprocity with the United States in the election of 1911, which they lost, largely due to opposition from Canadian Conservatives fearful of US domination.

★ ★ ★ ★ ★

The Imperialist was written and revised between 1902 and 1904, during the period when Joseph Chamberlain was championing the cause of Imperial Federation both within and without the British Cabinet, and the novel accurately represents the course of the public debate. British readers of *The Imperialist* immediately identified the character of Wallingham as Chamberlain, and considered its political theme drawn from the pages of the evening news.[4] Canadian readers recognized Lorne's election speech as an eloquent statement of the Imperialist case, as put by its advocates; Mr. Winter's reply, articulated in Chapter 28, sums up many of the arguments that its opponents relied upon to

---

1 Rose, *The Edwardian Temperament*, 120.
2 Rose, *The Edwardian Temperament*, 117.
3 Rose, *The Edwardian Temperament*, 117.
4 See especially the review in the *Times Literary Supplement*, Appendix C.2.

defeat it, while stopping short of advocating outright the alternative: closer economic and cultural ties with the US. Reviewers were split on the success of this strategy, with many complaining that portions of the book seemed to be drawn from a political pamphlet, even while they praised the lively characterisation and the realistic domestic detail. The reviews were unanimous, however, in their view that the novel as well as the novelist supported Imperialism.

Recent critics have been less willing to categorise the narrative voice of the novel as unambiguously supportive of Lorne's Imperialism, and indeed the attitude of the narrative to its subject was the central enigma addressed by critics in the 1970s and 1980s. Northrop Frye began the debate in his "Conclusion" to the *Literary History of Canada* in 1965 when he singled out *The Imperialist* as an exception to his assertion that most early Canadian literature is "rhetoric" designed to persuade readers of political or moral positions. In contrast, he suggested, Duncan's narrator is "a voice of genuine detachment, sympathetic but not defensive either of the group or of herself, concerned primarily to understand and to make the reader see."[1] Claude Bissell agrees in his introduction to the New Canadian Library edition of the novel published in 1971; he argues that the narrator "is not making a statement, nor is she parading her own convictions."[2] Michael Peterman wrote in 1976 that "balance is the ordering principle of the novel"[3] and Joseph Zezulka agreed in his 1978 article "Passionate Provincials: Imperialism, Regionalism and Point of View" when he suggested that Canadian authors like Duncan, Stephen Leacock, and Robertson Davies balance sympathy and critique when they adopt "provincialism" as both a point of view on the world and a target of their wit. (Victorian novels of provincial life, like George Eliot's *Middlemarch*, might also be considered in this light.) Yet Carole Gerson remarked in 1976 that "Duncan's personal attitude toward her characters remains strangely vague"[4] and Peter Allen found "Duncan's narrative voice" to be "the chief

---

1 Northrop Frye, "Conclusion," *The Literary History of Canada*, ed. Carl F. Klinck (Toronto: U of Toronto P, 1965), 839.
2 Claude Bissell, "Introduction," *The Imperialist* (Toronto: McClelland and Stewart, 1971), ix.
3 Michael Peterman, "Humour and Balance in *The Imperialist*," *Journal of Canadian Studies*, 11:2 (May 1976): 56.
4 Carole Gerson, "Duncan's Web," *Canadian Literature*, 63 (Winter 1975): 79.

puzzle" in reading the novel: because "she alternates between an ironic and an objective mode of reporting, and we cannot always be sure how to take her."[1] Along with Thomas Tausky (in *Sara Jeannette Duncan: Novelist of Empire*), Allen's modernist bias allows him to judge Duncan's "narrative uncertainty" to be a substantial flaw in the novel. However, Ajay Heble identifies narrative interventions in the text that "serve to restrict and limit meaning" in order to stabilise the "reader's attitude toward Lorne and toward the imperial idea he represents."[2] The criticism comes full circle to again suggest that the novel approves Lorne's ideas, even if it depicts him as too young and idealistic to sell them to a self-interested and politically savvy voter. In "Destiny into Chance: S.J. Duncan's *The Imperialist* and the perils of nation building"[3] Jon Kertzer contextualises the concepts of nation and empire in contemporary political thought, and suggests that the instabilities inherent in the concept of nation itself are exposed, rather than resolved, by *The Imperialist*.

Feminist approaches to the novel take a slightly different perspective. Early critics were motivated to recover Duncan's biography and her achievements as a woman writer: Rae Goodwin pioneered in this field, and Marian Fowler published a popular biography. Subsequent critics focussed on the female characters and on the representation of Imperial relations through the metaphor of heterosexual marriage. Catherine Ross shows how the novel creates a space for a new kind of heroine by parodying the heroine of the romance novel. She sees Dora Milburn as a stereotypical passive heroine ironically mocked by the narrator, and argues that while Advena Murchison is a more active alternative, her love story also reproduces the clichés of romance. Elizabeth Thompson builds on this analysis by focussing on Advena as a Canadian version of the "New Woman," a figure common in British *fin-de-siècle* writing and explored in more detail in Duncan's earlier novel, *A Daughter of Today* (1894). Subsequent critics have been interested in the ways that the political ideas of the book are worked out as family relationships.[4] All of the marriages

---

1 Peter Allen, "Narrative Uncertainty in *The Imperialist*," *Studies in Canadian Literature*, 9:1 (1984): 43.

2 Heble, "This Little Outpost of Empire," 223.

3 Jon Kertzer, "Destiny into Chance," *Studies in Canadian Literature*, 24:2 (1999): 1-34.

4 See Misao Dean, *A Different Point of View: Sara Jeannette Duncan* (Montreal: McGill-Queen's UP, 1991); and Kertzer, "Destiny into Chance."

in the novel (between Advena and Hugh, Dora and Hesketh, Christie and Dr. Drummond) take place between representatives of Canada and of Britain, empowering women to undertake active roles in the politics of Empire.

None of these early readings dealt satisfactorily with race, and recent postcolonial approaches to the novel have pointed this out.[1] As Carl Berger makes clear in his classic study, *The Sense of Power*, Imperialists argued for the existence of a separate "Anglo-Saxon Race" supposedly derived from a mixture of the ancient peoples of England and sharing the qualities of enterprise, thrift, energy, and democracy. Following from this assumption they argued that the white citizens of the Empire were a "natural" unity, and that the Imperial Federation movement was the political manifestation of a biological reality. Some Canadians went further than this, arguing that Canada's northern climate would promote the formation of a new race, a "northern people," and correspondingly discourage an admixture of (undesirable) immigrants from warmer climates like the Mediterranean, Africa, and Asia.[2] The overt racism of this discourse suggests the general overlap between the definition of Imperialism specific to late nineteenth-century Canada and the more common associations of the word with racism, oppression, economic exploitation, and genocide.

Canadian Imperialist discourse, as a form of Canadian nationalism, worked to justify the theft of Aboriginal lands by settler society and the cultural genocide of First Nations. It does this by presenting Canadians themselves as a colonised, powerless, indigenous group, and by largely failing to represent real indigenous peoples at all. Literature from this period is filled with images of white Canadians being moulded and changed by the landscape itself, images that aim to literally replace Aboriginal Peoples with a new, white "native" Canadian in opposition to a British imperial centre. In this way Canadian nationalism usurps

1   See Kertzer, "Destiny into Chance"; Gabrielle Collu, "Sara Jeannette Duncan: Portrait of a Colonizer/Colonized," *Textual Studies in Canada*, 5 (1994): 22-31; and Cecily Devereux, "Are we there yet? Reading the 'Post Colonial' and *The Imperialist* in Canada," in Laura Moss, ed., *Is Canada Postcolonial?* (Waterloo, ON: Wilfrid Laurier UP, 2003), for example.

2   See Carl Berger, "The True North Strong and Free," in Elspeth Cameron, ed., *Canadian Culture: An Introductory Reader* (Toronto: Canadian Scholars' Press, 1997), 83-102.

the land and the culture of First Nations peoples, and ignores or downplays its own role as the instrument of the oppression, economic exploitation, and death. Thus supporters of nineteenth-century Canadian Imperialism could propose the fictional Lorne Murchison, a white man of Scottish ancestry, as a representative Canadian, and see such a choice as unproblematic.

The Imperialist uses unmistakable strategies of "othering," referring to an eternal "Indian" to suggest that all "Indians" are alike and their "nature" is unchanging. The novel represents "the remaining red man of Moneida," according to the racist codes of the day, as dirty, untrustworthy, self-important, and frequently drunk. Most importantly, the inhabitants of "Moneida reservation" (based on the Six Nations Reserve near Brantford) become the chief impediments to Lorne's election, several testifying that they were intimidated into voting for him because he appeared at the polling station on election day endorsed by Squire Ormiston. Lorne's triumphant victory for what he thinks of as "the moral advantage" of Imperialism is called into question by accusations of self-interest.

That the inhabitants of the Reserve vote at all in *The Imperialist* is surprising. Aboriginal Peoples in Canada were deprived of the vote by the Canadian Parliament in 1898 and only regained that right in 1960. However, those who lived in "old Canada" (Ontario, Quebec and the Atlantic Provinces) were granted the right to vote by the Dominion Franchise Act of 1885 because Conservative Prime Minister John A. Macdonald believed that those who chose to vote would vote for him. This right was rescinded in 1898 when the Liberals came to power.[1] Duncan was aware that having her "Indians" vote in the Elgin election in 1903 was an anachronism, but, as she explained in a letter to John Willison, the editor of the Toronto *News*, "it is only a matter of a few years, and I was in the difficulty of either having to sacrifice the whole Imperial situation—as it is now—or my 'Indian interest' neither of which I could make up my mind to do. So I left it."[2]

The significance of Duncan's decision to build the crucial event in *The Imperialist*, Lorne's defeat at the polls, on what she admitted was a mistake, is worth teasing out. On the one hand, it

---

1   See Malcolm Montgomery, "The Six Nations Indians and the MacDonald Franchise," *Ontario History*, LVII: 1 (1965): 13-25.

2   Duncan to Willison, 24 February 1904.

shows Duncan's willingness to cater to what she called "the unappeasable flame of British curiosity about the North American Indian"[1] by refusing to sacrifice her "Indian interest" to historical accuracy. On the other hand, it demonstrates her desire to contradict the stereotype of "Indians" created by authors like James Fenimore Cooper, "paint, feathers, wampum and all," and represent First Nations as a part of the cultural fabric of Elgin, Ontario, rather than separate from it. The "Indian" that she imagines in *The Imperialist* "had taken on the signs of civilization at the level which he occupied," fitting in seamlessly among the crowd of farmers on market day, indistinguishable from his fellows "unless you looked twice." If you do look twice, Duncan writes, what appears is a figure unmistakably inferior, described in the language of horse-breeding as "high shouldered and lank of leg." The same, but different; a farmer, but also the "dying fragment of his race" implicated in the growth and development of the nation, but an impediment to it.

In *The Imperialist* the actual intimacy between the colonisers and colonised, the white settler society that Lorne represents and the First Nations of the Moneida Reserve, works to undo the illusion of a homogenous nation. As Edward Said has argued,[2] classic realist novels that represent life in places like New York and London can seem to bracket the experiences of colonial oppression that make metropolitan life possible, but local colour novels set in places like Elgin, Ontario, necessarily take as their subject the ways that imperial power saturates the relations of everyday life.[3] The "Indians" in the novel cannot be fully excluded, even though the logic of their displacement by white settler culture requires it. As Cecily Devereux argues, *The Imperialist* "identifies itself as a novel of colonial displacement and imperialism when it thus indicates what is overwritten by Lorne's story."[4] Devereux makes an important point when she situates her reading of *The Imperialist* within a consideration of the meanings of the critical category of the "postcolonial." *The Imperialist* can be called a postcolonial novel in the strict sense that it represents Canada after

---

1   See Appendix A.1.
2   Edward Said, *Culture and Imperialism* (New York: Knopf, 1993).
3   For background to this argument, see for example, Willmott, *Unreal Country*, 44-46; and Anna Johnston and Alan Lawson, "Settler Colonies," in Schwartz and Ray, eds., *A Companion to Postcolonial Studies* (Malden, MA: Blackwell, 2000), 360-76.
4   Devereux, "Are we there yet?," 187.

Confederation (as Willmott suggests); but the term implies somehow that colonialism has been left behind, and the representation of race in the novel demonstrates clearly that this is not the case. Instead, a contemporary consideration of *The Imperialist* from a postcolonial perspective should confirm the way that "the post in postcolonial ... designates such lingering persistences of the kinds of attitudes that made colonialism possible and that keep Canada an inequitable society today."[1]

French Canada was an ambiguous element in this discourse; while many Imperialists sought to include, or at least account for the Quebecois in their definition of the nation, their insistence on the essential Britishness of Canada was largely exclusive of French Canada, and not surprisingly Imperialism gained few francophone adherents. The antipathy between French and English Canada became even more evident after the 1885 Riel Rebellion, when jingoistic Ontario Protestants celebrated the triumph of "British" Canada over the French-speaking Metis, and the execution of their leader, Louis Riel. Duncan herself suggests the way the Imperialists discounted the views of the Quebecois when she characterises "Johnny François" as the second horse in a tandem hitch in *The Imperialist*. She described Liberal Prime Minister Wilfrid Laurier in a letter to John Willison as "a nice thing" though "a politician and a Frenchman"[2] suggesting she shared an ambivalence toward Canadian francophones that was typical of English-Canadians in this period.

While contemporary readers may find the racial politics of *The Imperialist* distasteful, this is in itself a powerful reason to keep reading the novel, for it demonstrates with clarity the way that "settler colonies" are places where power relationships are negotiated, and racial and cultural identity meets its Other. This edition encourages Canadian readers to rethink settler nationalism, not so much as a movement to be celebrated and certainly not one to be recovered, but as a moment of remembering and forgetting that both reveals and distorts Canada's position in global empire. This kind of reading is unlikely to produce the sources of pleasure that readers in Britain, the US, and Canada enjoyed when *The Imperialist* was first published in 1904: the "humorous eye for provincial marks," and "pleasing fashion of comment on

---

1 Diana Brydon, "Canada and Postcolonialism: Questions, Inventories, and Futures," in Moss, ed., *Is Canada Postcolonial?*, 55-56.

2 Duncan to Willison, 20 December [1903].

the side," as the reviewer for the *New York Times* put it.[1] These can be recovered through attention to the language itself: the complex and elegant sentence, the ironic and sympathetic narration, the detail of physical description and social analysis demonstrate why this novel has been celebrated as an important achievement in development of the Canadian novel as a genre. In addition, *The Imperialist* addresses important themes of Edwardian English literature: the position of women, the role and nature of the British Empire in the twentieth century, "efficiency" in governmental administration, and social welfare. These preoccupations suggest the way *The Imperialist* engages readers on many levels—aesthetic, historical, and political—and provides an enjoyable and a challenging read.

---

1   See Appendix C.1.

Sara Jeannette Duncan: A Brief Chronology

December 22, 1861
>   Sarah Janet Duncan born in Brantford (Ontario), the
>   eldest daughter of Charles Duncan (b. Cupar, Scotland),
>   owner of a successful dry goods store, and Jane (Bell)
>   Duncan (b. Shediac, NB), who would have nine more
>   children.

May 18, 1862
>   Christened in Zion Presbyterian Church in Brantford.

1879   After attending Central School and Brantford Presbyter-
>   ian Ladies' College, graduates from Brantford Collegiate
>   Institute. Earns her third-class teaching certificate at
>   Brant County Model school.

February 1880
>   Her first publication appears: a poem entitled "My
>   Prayer," under the initials "S.D." in *The Globe* (Toronto).

1880-1882
>   Teaches school in the Brantford area; registers at the
>   Toronto Normal School in the Spring term of 1882 to
>   obtain her second-class teaching certificate.

June 1881
>   Her first article, "Diogenes on Bric-a-Brac" appears in
>   *Rose-Belford's Canadian Monthly and National Review*. A
>   number of articles and poems appear in Canadian publi-
>   cations over the next few years.

Fall 1884
>   Decides to attend the New Orleans Cotton Centennial
>   and approaches *The Globe* (Toronto) and the *Advertiser*
>   (London, ON) to take freelance articles about her trip.

December 1884-March 1885
>   Publishes articles on the American South in Canadian
>   and US newspapers under the pen-name "Garth"; travels
>   to Florida in the company of Joaquin Miller, and returns
>   to Brantford in April.

May-September 1885

Writes a regular column, "Other People and I," published in *The Globe* under the pseudonym "Garth Grafton" and republished in the *Washington Post*. At the end of the summer moves to Washington to join the staff of the *Post* as an editorial writer and subsequently manager of the "Current Literature" department.

February 1886

Begins to contribute columns under her own name to *The Week*, an important literary and political journal edited by Toronto intellectual Goldwin Smith. Meets US realist novelist William Dean Howells and attends a US suffrage convention in March.

June 1886

Begins writing a column called "Woman's World" for the Toronto *Globe* under the byline Garth Grafton and by September is in Toronto, the first woman to work in the *Globe* newsroom.

1887-1888

Leaves the *Globe* to work for the *Montreal Star*, writing a column called "Bric-a-Brac," beginning 1 November 1887. Covers the opening of Parliament in Ottawa for the *Star* on 29 February 1888, and remains in Ottawa as a parliamentary correspondent. Invited to Government House, where she meets the Governor-General Lord Lansdowne.

September 1888

Conceives the plan of travelling around the world "without a chaperone," in order to provide material for her first book. In company with fellow *Star* journalist, Lily Lewis, departs by CPR, travelling west, and visits Japan, Ceylon, India, and Egypt. Contributes articles to the *Star* describing her adventures in Western Canada.

February 28, 1889

At a reception hosted by Lord Lansdowne, now Viceroy in India, she meets Everard Cotes, an assistant curator at the Calcutta Museum. In March, he proposes to her during a visit to the Taj Mahal at Agra.

1 May 1889

Arrives in London. Works on the manuscript of *A Social*

Departure, which is serialised in *The Ladies' Pictorial* in the fall.

1890 *A Social Departure* is published by Chatto and Windus in London and by D. Appleton in New York. Duncan returns to Canada and prepares for her wedding while working on the manuscripts of two new novels, *An American Girl in London* and *Two Girls on a Barge*. She returns to India via England, and marries Cotes in Calcutta on 6 December 1890.

1891 *An American Girl In London* is published by Chatto and Windus in March; *Two Girls on a Barge* appears in August under the pseudonym V. Cecil Cotes. Duncan and Cotes travel to Europe "on leave." They return to Calcutta in June.

1892-1894
  Duncan is at work on three books: *The Simple Adventures of a Memsahib* (1893), based on her early married life, a comic novel entitled *Vernon's Aunt* (1893), and *A Daughter of To-day* (1894), partly based on Lily Lewis's experiences as a freelance writer in Paris. Cotes resigns from his museum job in 1894 in hopes of obtaining permanent employment in London, but after a summer in England he is offered the editorship of the *Indian Daily News* and the couple return to Calcutta. Just before they leave, Duncan engages AP Watt and Son to be her literary agents.

1895 Duncan assists Cotes on the *Indian Daily News* by writing editorials, and begins work on *His Honor, and a Lady*. She travels to London to avoid the hot weather, and returns to Calcutta in the fall.

1896 *His Honor, and a Lady* published by Macmillan in London and Appleton in New York. Duncan begins work on *A Voyage of Consolation*, a sequel to the highly successful *An American Girl in London*. Wilfrid Laurier and the Liberals win the federal election in Canada; Duncan writes an editorial on "Imperial Sentiment in Canada" in the *Indian Daily News*.

1897 Cotes resigns his job at the *Indian Daily News* and becomes a government press correspondent in Simla.

1898 *A Voyage of Consolation* is published. Duncan again travels to England for the hot weather, and continues on to visit her family in Brantford where she gathers goldenrod seed to plant in her Simla garden. In the summer she takes hydropathic treatment in New York for her chronic lung problems.

1899   *The Path of a Star* published by Methuen in London, and, under the title *Hilda, a Story of Calcutta* by Frederick Stokes in New York.

1900   Duncan is diagnosed with tuberculosis, and is required to spend the summer sitting outside in her Simla garden as part of her treatment. Writes *The Crow's Nest* which is published by Dodd Mead in the US and by Methuen (under the title *On the Other Side of the Latch*) in 1901.

1901   Duncan begins work on *Those Delightful Americans*, and travels with her husband as part of the press party accompanying the new Viceroy, Lord Curzon, on a state trip to Burma.

1902   Publishes a number of articles and stories in American magazines, some based on her trip to Burma; *Those Delightful Americans* published. In September writes to John Willison in Toronto to ask him for research material on Imperial Federation. Laurier attends the Colonial Conference in London and agrees to adjust the Canadian tariff in favour of British goods in return for similar consideration.

1903   Rescinds her agreement with Watt, perhaps in a dispute over articles and stories placed in American magazines without reference to the firm. *The Pool in the Desert* is published by Methuen and by Appleton in New York. British Colonial Secretary Joseph Chamberlain gives speeches in favour of Imperial Preference and is forced to resign from the cabinet. *The Imperialist* is serialised in *The Queen* and *The Australasian* in the late fall. Duncan travels to London and to Brantford, where in November she sends revised proofs of *The Queen* chapters to Willison for serialisation in the *Toronto News*.

1904   *The Imperialist* appears in the *Toronto News*. Duncan takes advantage of further research carried out in Brantford to revise the novel again. *The Imperialist* appears in book form, published by Appleton in New York, Constable in

London, and Copp Clark in Toronto. The book is praised in Willison's *Toronto News* and in *Saturday Night*, but the *Globe* finds its political theme unsuitable for women readers, and British reviews are unfavorable. Duncan returns to Simla.

1905 Begins correspondence with Archibald MacMechan. Writes a play for the Simla Amateur Dramatic Society ("Browne with an E"). Makes up with A.P. Watt, and again signs a contract appointing him her agent. Asks Watt to take over negotiations from Jean Newton McIlwraith for the publication of *Set in Authority* by Doubleday.

1906 *Set in Authority* published by Constable, and in New York by Doubleday Page. Cotes travels to the Far East with a group of journalists (his articles on China and Korea appear in the Toronto *Globe* throughout 1906); Duncan moves to London and takes a flat in Kensington. Begins work on *Two in a Flat* based on her life in London.

1907 Cotes and Duncan separately return to India, where she begins "Cinderella of Canada," conceived of as a sequel to *The Imperialist*. Signs a three-book contract with Methuen, specifying "Cinderella," *The Burnt Offering*, and "Mary Pargeter" (*The Consort*) as the novels to be delivered.

1908 "Cinderella of Canada" is published in 1908 by Methuen in London and Macmillan in New York as *Cousin Cinderella*, a title chosen by a Macmillan's editor. Duncan spends the spring in London, working on *The Burnt Offering*, and returns to India after the hot weather. *Two in a Flat* is published by Hodder and Stoughton, using the pseudonym "Jane Wintergreen" to hide the identities of the characters.

1909 Duncan spends the spring in London. *The Burnt Offering* published by Methuen in the fall.

1910 Cotes hired as Managing Director of the Eastern News Agency, a position he holds until 1919.

1911-12
The Consort is completed by July 1911 and appears in 1912. Duncan and Cotes visit England in the spring of 1911 and continue on to "make a tour of Canada,"

including Prince Rupert, BC. She visits England alone in the spring of 1912, and when she returns to Simla brings Cotes's niece Nellie Masterman with her. E.M. Forster visits in Simla in November; the family moves to Delhi, the new capital, to be closer to Cotes's work.

1913   Forster visits in Delhi in March. Duncan spends much of the rest of the year in Simla, working on *His Royal Happiness*; she completes the purchase of four lots of land in Prince Rupert.

1914   *His Royal Happiness* is published in New York by Appleton. Duncan visits Brantford, and is there on 4 August when war is declared. She stays on, turning *His Royal Happiness* into a play.

1915   The stage version of *His Royal Happiness* produced at the Princess Theatre in Toronto. Duncan leaves for England where the novel version has just appeared. She continues on to Simla, but returns to England in the late fall.

1916-1919
   Duncan lives in a flat in Chelsea; writes another set of sketches by "Jane Wintergreen," about living in London during the war, and several plays. Cotes remains in India until 1919, when he sells the Indian News Agency and returns with Nellie to London.

September 1919
   Cotes and Duncan travel to Canada as part of the press entourage accompanying the Prince of Wales. They visit Brantford, and Duncan writes two articles about their visit to western Canada that appear in the Toronto *Globe*.

1920-22
   Duncan stays in London while Cotes spends seven months touring Australia with the Prince of Wales. Writes *Title Clear* and *The Gold Cure*; the former will be published in 1922, and the latter posthumously.

Spring 1922
   Duncan and Cotes buy a house in Ashstead, Surrey; they move in May. Duncan falls ill with pneumonia in June and dies on 22 July. She is buried in the churchyard at St. Giles's Anglican Church, Ashstead.

A Note on the Text

The Imperialist was published in five versions between October 1903 and April 1904. Previous scholars have identified its initial publication in the London ladies' periodical *The Queen* from 3 October to 26 December 1903. In the course of researching this volume a second serial version of the novel was discovered that appeared during the same time period from 3 October to 26 December 1903, in *The Australasian*, a weekly paper published in Melbourne, Australia. A partial comparison of these simultaneously published versions suggests that these texts may be identical, excepting accidentals (such as comma placement, paragraph breaks, etc). Duncan had been required by contract to supply the novel to *The Queen* the previous June; the time lag between submission of the text and its appearance in both *The Queen* and *The Australasian* would allow for communication with Melbourne. Her contract with *The Australasian* specifies simultaneous publication, a common arrangement usually required to protect copyright.

Duncan forwarded revised proofs of *The Queen* to Toronto, where the novel appeared in a second version in the *Toronto Daily News* from 28 November 1903 to 17 February 1904. Extensive changes are evident in the first book publication, a US edition that appeared with Duncan's regular US publisher, D. Appleton, in February 1904, and further revisions appear in a British edition published by Constable, probably in early April 1904. A Canadian edition published by Copp Clark, identical to the British except for the imprint, appeared in June 1904. This text was reprinted in the New Canadian Library edition of 1971, and provides the copy-text for this edition.

Two detailed comparisons of versions of *The Imperialist* have been published, and both support the choice of the Canadian edition as copy-text. The results of a comparison of four versions by Darlene Kelly were published in *Canadian Literature* in 1989.[1] Kelly suggests that successive revisions of the text corrected obvious errors, sharpened the political analysis and improved the characterisation of Lorne Murchison and his family. While the

---

1   Darlene Kelly, "Rewriting *The Imperialist*: Duncan's Revisions," *Canadian Literature*, 121 (Summer 1989): 26-38.

News version shows some minor changes (the court scene in chapters ten and eleven was revised to focus more completely on Lorne's triumph, for example), more extensive revisions followed Duncan's trip to Canada in the fall of 1903, during which she carried out additional research on her political theme and revised the presentation of characters modelled on family members. The US, and subsequently the British edition, reflect a more accurate and detailed knowledge of the Canadian perspective on Imperial Preference Trade, with details of the trade status of particular goods and services revised and augmented.[1] The London edition is the only version to contain a reference to the "policy urged by the colonial representatives at the last [Imperial] Conference."[2] It also contains revisions intended to make Wallingham "a more charismatic leader" and Lorne "his yet more ardent follower."[3] Changes to characterisation seem designed to elevate the class position of the Murchisons, with some of Mrs. Murchison's more colloquial judgements emended, and significantly, her practice of making soft soap every spring with her own hands delegated in later versions to a servant. Lorne becomes more gentlemanly and more poetically committed to the idealism that his political affiliation represents. The names of many of the minor characters are changed several times in the various versions, with little obvious rationale for the changes.

Kelly's analysis as well as the chronology of the five versions suggest that the British edition (and, therefore, the identical Canadian edition) incorporates the most recent revisions and is the authoritative text. This conclusion is supported by the textual appendix to Thomas Tausky's edition of the novel,[4] which compares the British edition to the *Queen* serialisation and the US edition. An unpublished comparison of the *News* serialisation with the British edition was carried out by John Roscoe in support of this project.

The text given here is that of the Canadian edition of the novel with historical spellings preserved and only obvious errors corrected.

---

1 Kelly, "Rewriting *The Imperialist*," 28.
2 Kelly, "Rewriting *The Imperialist*," 28.
3 Kelly, "Rewriting *The Imperialist*," 32.
4 *The Imperialist*, ed. Thomas Tausky (Ottawa: Tecumseh, 1996).

THE IMPERIALIST

BY

MRS. EVERARD COTES
(Sara Jeannette Duncan)

TORONTO
THE COPP CLARK COMPANY LTD
1904

ONE

It would have been idle to inquire into the antecedents, or even the circumstances, of old Mother Beggarlegs. She would never tell; the children, at all events, were convinced of that; and it was only the children, perhaps, who had the time and the inclination to speculate. Her occupation was clear; she presided like a venerable stooping hawk, over a stall in the covered part of the Elgin market-place, where she sold gingerbread horses and large round gingerbread cookies, and brown sticky squares of what was known in all circles in Elgin as taffy. She came, it was understood, with the dawn; with the night she vanished, spending the interval on a not improbable broomstick. Her gingerbread was better than anybody's; but there was no comfort in standing, first on one foot and then on the other, while you made up your mind—the horses were spirited, and you could eat them a leg at a time, but there was more in the cookies—she bent such a look on you, so fierce and intolerant of vacillation. She belonged to the group of odd characters, rarer now than they used to be, etched upon the vague consciousness of small towns as in a way mysterious and uncanny; some said that Mother Beggarlegs was connected with the aristocracy and some that she had been "let off" being hanged. The alternative was allowed full swing, but in any case it was clear that such persons contributed little to the common good, and, being reticent, were not entertaining. So you bought your gingerbread, concealing, as it were, your weapons, paying your copper coins with a neutral nervous eye, and made off to a safe distance, whence you turned to shout insultingly, if you were an untrounced young male of Elgin, "Old Mother Beggarlegs! Old Mother Beggarlegs!" And why "Beggarlegs" nobody in the world could tell you. It might have been a dateless waggery, or it might have been a corruption of some more dignified surname, but it was all she ever got. Serious, meticulous persons called her "Mrs." Beggarlegs, slightly lowering their voices and slurring it, however, it must be admitted. The name invested her with a graceless, anatomical interest, it penetrated her wizened black and derisively exposed her; her name went far indeed to make her dramatic. Lorne Murchison, when he was quite a little boy, was affected by this, and by the unfairness of the way it singled her out. Moved partly by the oppression of the feeling and partly by a desire for information, he asked her sociably one day, in the act of purchase, why the gilt was generally off her gingerbread.[1] He had been looking long, as a matter of fact, for gingerbread with the gilt on it, being accustomed to the phrase on the lips of his father in connection with small profits. Mother Beggarlegs, so unaccustomed to politeness that she could not instantly recognize it, answered him with an imprecation, at which he, no doubt, retreated, suddenly thrown on the defensive, hurling the usual taunt. One prefers to hope he didn't, with the invincible optimism one has for the behaviour of lovable people; but whether or not, his kind attempt at colloquy is the first indication I can find of that active sympathy with the disabilities of his fellow beings which stamped him later so intelligent a meliorist. Even in his boy's beginning he had a heart for the work; and Mother Beggarlegs, but for a hasty conclusion, might have made him a friend.

It is hard to invest Mother Beggarlegs with importance, but the date helps me—the date, I mean, of this chapter about Elgin; she was a person to be reckoned with on the twenty-fourth of May. I will say at once, for the reminder to persons living in England, that the twenty-fourth of May was the Queen's Birthday. Nobody in Elgin can possibly have forgotten it. The Elgin children had a rhyme about it—

The twenty-fourth of May
Is the Queen's Birthday;
If you don't give us a holiday,
We'll all run away.

But Elgin was in Canada. In Canada the twenty-fourth of May *was* the Queen's Birthday; and these were times and regions far removed from the prescription that the anniversary "should be observed" on any of those various outlying dates which, by now, must have produced in her immediate people such indecision as to the date upon which Her Majesty really did come into the world. That day, and that only, was the observed, the celebrated, a day with an essence in it, dawning more gloriously than other days and ending more regretfully, unless, indeed, it fell on a Sunday, when it was "kept" on the Monday, with a slightly clouded

---

1   The metaphorical expression, "the gilt is off the gingerbread" suggests that whatever is extra or attractive has been removed. According to the OED, the expression dates from the 1880s when it was common to decorate gingerbread with icing and gold leaf.

feeling that it wasn't exactly the same thing. Travelled persons, who had spent the anniversary there, were apt to come back with a poor opinion of its celebration in "the old country"—a pleasant relish to the more than ever appreciated advantages of the new, the advantages that came out so by contrast. More space such persons indicated, more enterprise they boasted, and even more loyalty they would flourish, all with an affectionate reminiscent smile at the little ways of a grandmother. A "Bank" holiday, indeed![1] Here it was a real holiday, that woke you with bells and cannon—who has forgotten the time the ancient piece of ordnance in "the Square" blew out all the windows in the Methodist church?—and went on with squibs and crackers till you didn't know where to step on the sidewalks, and ended up splendidly with rockets and fire-balloons and drunken Indians vociferous on their way to the lock-up. Such a day for the hotels, with teams hitched three abreast in front of their aromatic bar-rooms; such a day for the circus, with half the farmers of Fox County agape before the posters—with all their *chic* and shock they cannot produce such posters nowadays, nor are there any vacant lots to form attractive backgrounds—such a day for Mother Beggarlegs! The hotels, and the shops and stalls for eating and drinking, were the only places in which business was done; the public sentiment put universal shutters up, but the public appetite insisted upon excepting the means to carnival. An air of ceremonial festivity those fastened shutters gave; the sunny little town sat round them, important and significant, and nobody was ever known to forget that they were up, and go on a fool's errand. No doubt they had an impressiveness for the young countryfolk that strolled up and down Main Street in their honest best, turning into Snow's for ice-cream when a youth was disposed to treat. (Gallantry exacted ten-cent dishes, but for young ladies alone, or family parties, Mrs. Snow would bring five-cent quantities almost without asking, and for very small boys one dish and the requisite number of spoons.) There was discrimination, there was choice, in this matter of treating. A happy excitement accompanied it, which you could read in the way Corydon[2] clapped his soft felt hat on his head as he pocketed the change. To be treated—to ten-cent

---

1 In England, banks were closed on "Bank Holidays" but many other businesses stayed open; thus, from the point of view of Elgin, they were not "real" holidays.
2 A generic name for a male character in pastoral poetry.

dishes—three times in the course of the day by the same young man gave matter for private reflection and for public entertainment, expressed in the broad grins of less reckless people. I speak of a soft felt hat, but it might be more than that: it might be a dark green one, with a feather in it; and here was distinction, for such a hat indicated that its owner belonged to the Independent Order of Foresters,[1] who would leave their spring wheat for forty miles round to meet in Elgin and march in procession, wearing their hats, and dazzlingly scatter upon Main Street. They gave the day its touch of imagination, those green cocked hats; they were lyrical upon the highways; along the prosaic sidewalks by twos and threes they sang together. It is no great thing, a hat of any quality; but a small thing may ring dramatic on the right metal, and in the vivid idea of Lorne Murchison and his sister Advena a Robin Hood walked in every Independent Forester, especially in the procession. Which shows the risks you run if you, a person of honest livelihood and solicited vote, adopt any portion of a habit not familiar to you, and go marching about with a banner and a band. Two children may be standing at the first street corner, to whom your respectability and your property may at once become illusion and your outlawry the delightful fact.

A cheap trip brought the Order of Green Hats to Elgin; and there were cheap trips on this great day to persuade other persons to leave it. The Grand Trunk[2] had even then an idea of encouraging social combination for change of scene, and it was quite a common thing for the operatives of the Milburn Boiler Company to arrange to get themselves carried to the lakeside or "the Falls" at half a dollar a head. The "hands" got it up themselves, and it was a question in Elgin whether one might sink one's dignity and go as a hand for the sake of the fifty-cent opportunity, a question usually decided in the negative. The social distinctions of Elgin may not be easily appreciated by people accustomed to the rough and ready standards of a world at the other end of the Grand Trunk; but it will be clear at a glance that nobody whose occupa-

---

1 A non-profit "fraternal" society that offered sick benefits, disability, and death benefits to subscribers. It was promoted in Ontario in the 1880s by Peter Martin (Oronhyatekha), a physician born on the Six Nations reserve near Brantford.
2 The Grand Trunk Railway was founded in 1852, and by 1880 it joined Ontario towns like Stratford and Guelph with Toronto and Montreal and with US seaports.

tion prescribed a clean face could be expected to travel cheek by jowl, as a privilege, with persons who were habitually seen with smutty ones, barefaced smut, streaming out at the polite afternoon hour of six, jangling an empty dinner pail. So much we may decide, and leave it, reflecting as we go how simple and satisfactory, after all, are the prejudices which can hold up such obvious justification. There was recently to be pointed out in England the heir to a dukedom who loved stoking, and got his face smutty by preference. He would have been deplorably subversive of accepted conventions in Elgin; but, happily or otherwise, such persons and such places have at present little more than an imaginative acquaintance, vaguely cordial on the one side, vaguely critical on the other, and of no importance in the sum.

Polite society, to return to it, preferred the alternative of staying at home and mowing the lawn, or drinking raspberry vinegar[1] on its own beflagged verandah; looking forward in the afternoon to the lacrosse match. There was nearly always a lacrosse match on the Queen's Birthday, and it was the part of elegance to attend and encourage the home team, as well as that of small boys, with broken straw hats, who sneaked an entrance, and were more enthusiastic than anyone. It was "a quarter" to get in, so the spectators were naturally composed of persons who could afford the quarter, and persons like the young Flannigans and Finnigans, who absolutely couldn't, but who had to be there all the same. Lorne and Advena Murchison never had the quarter, so they witnessed few lacrosse matches, though they seldom failed to refresh themselves by a sight of the players after the game, when, crimson and perspiring, but still glorious in striped jerseys, their lacrosses and running shoes slung over one shoulder, these heroes left the field.

The Birthday I am thinking of, with Mrs. Murchison as a central figure in the kitchen, peeling potatoes for dinner, there was a lacrosse match of some importance, for the Fox County Championship and the Fox County Cup, as presented by the Member for the South Riding. Mrs. Murchison remains the central figure, nevertheless, with her family radiating from her, gathered to help or to hinder in one of those domestic crises which arose when the Murchisons were temporarily deprived of a "girl." Everybody was subject to them in Elgin, everybody had to acknowledge and face

1 A tart summer drink made by adding water to a syrup of raspberries, vinegar, and sugar.

them. Let a new mill be opened, and it didn't matter what you paid her or how comfortable you made her, off she would go, and you might think yourself lucky if she gave a week's warning. Hard times shut down the mills and brought her back again; but periods of prosperity were very apt to find the ladies of Elgin where I am compelled to introduce Mrs. Murchison—in the kitchen. "You'd better get up—the girl's gone," Lorne had stuck his head into his sister's room to announce, while yet the bells were ringing and the rifles of the local volunteers were spitting out the *feu de joie*.[1] "I've lit the fire an' swep' out the dining-room. You tell mother. Queen's Birthday, too—I guess Lobelia's about as mean as they're made!" And the Murchisons had descended to face the situation. Lorne had by then done his part, and gone out into the chromatic possibilities of the day; but the sense of injury he had communicated to Advena in her bed remained and expanded. Lobelia, it was felt, had scurvily manipulated the situation—her situation, it might have been put, if any Murchison had been in the temper for jesting. She had taken unjustifiable means to do a more unjustifiable thing, to secure for herself an improper and unlawful share of the day's excitements, transferring her work, by the force of circumstances, to the shoulders of other people, since, as Mrs. Murchison remarked, somebody had to do it. Nor had she, her mistress testified, the excuse of fearing unreasonable confinement. "I told her she might go when she had done her dishes after dinner," said Mrs. Murchison, "and then she had only to come back at six and get tea—what's getting tea? I advised her to finish her ironing yesterday, so as to be free of it to-day; and she said she would be very glad to. Now, I wonder if she *did* finish it!" and Mrs. Murchison put down her pan of potatoes with a thump to look in the family clothes-basket. "Not she! Five shirts and *all* the coloured things. I call it downright deceit!"

"I believe I know the reason she'll *say*," said Advena. "She objects to rag carpet[2] in her bedroom. She told me so."

"Rag carpet—upon my word!" Mrs. Murchison dropped her knife to exclaim. "It's what her betters have to do with! I've known the day when that very piece of rag carpet—sixty balls there were in it, and every one I sewed with my own fingers—was the best I had for my spare room, with a bit of ingrain in the mid-

---

1   A salute fired by guns.
2   Rag carpet was unfashionable in town homes by the first decade of the twentieth century, when machine-made carpet was widely available.

dle. Dear me!" she went on with a smile that lightened the whole situation, "how proud I was of that performance! She didn't tell *me* she objected to rag carpet!"

"No, Mother," Advena agreed, "she knew better."

They were all there, in the kitchen, supporting their mother, and it seems an opportunity to name them. Advena, the eldest, stood by the long kitchen table washing the breakfast cups in "soft" soap and hot water. The soft soap—Mrs. Murchison had a barrelful boiled every spring in the back yard, an old colonial economy she hated to resign—made a fascinating brown lather with iridescent bubbles. Advena poured cupfuls of it from on high to see the foam rise, till her mother told her for mercy's sake to get on with those dishes. She stood before a long low window, looking out into the garden, and the light, filtering through apple branches on her face, showed her strongly featured and intelligent for fourteen. Advena was named after one grandmother; when the next girl came Mrs. Murchison, to make an end of the matter, named it Abigail, after the other. She thought both names outlandish, and acted under protest, but hoped that now everybody would be satisfied. Lorne came after Advena, at the period of a *naïve* fashion of christening the young sons of Canada in the name of her Governor-General. It was a simple way of attesting a loyal spirit, but with Mrs. Murchison more particular motives operated. The Marquis of Lorne was not only the deputy of the throne, he was the son-in-law of a good woman,[1] of whom Mrs. Murchison thought more, and often said it, for being the woman she was than for being twenty times a Queen; and he had made a metrical translation of the Psalms, several of which were included in the revised psalter for the use of the Presbyterian Church in Canada, from which the whole of Knox Church sang to the praise of God every Sunday. These were circumstances that weighed with Mrs. Murchison, and she called her son after the Royal representative, feeling that she was doing well for him in a sense beyond the mere bestowal of a distinguished and a euphonious name, though that, as she would have willingly acknowledged, was "well enough in its place."

---

1 Lorne is named after Sir John Douglas Sutherland Campbell, Marquis of Lorne, who was Governor-General of Canada from 1878-83. The Marquis of Lorne was married to Princess Louise, Queen Victoria's fourth daughter, and so "son-in-law of a good woman," according to Mrs. Murchison.

We must take this matter of names seriously; the Murchisons always did. Indeed, from the arrival of a new baby until the important Sunday of the christening, nothing was discussed with such eager zest and such sustained interest as the name he should get—there was a fascinating list at the back of the dictionary— and to the last minute it was problematical. In Stella's case, Mrs. Murchison actually changed her mind on the way to the church; and Abby, who had sat through the sermon expecting Dorothy Maud, which she thought lovely, publicly cried with disappointment. Stella was the youngest, and Mrs. Murchison was thankful to have a girl at last whom she could name without regard to her own relations or anybody else's. I have skipped about a good deal, but I have only left out two, the boys who came between Abby and Stella. In their names the contemporary observer need not be too acute to discover both an avowal and to some extent an enforcement of Mr. Murchison's political views; neither an Alexander Mackenzie[1] nor an Oliver Mowat[2] could very well grow up into anything but a sound Liberal in that part of the world without feeling himself an unendurable paradox. To christen a baby like that was, in a manner, a challenge to public attention; the faint relaxation about the lips of Dr. Drummond—the best of Liberals himself, though he made a great show of keeping it out of the pulpit—recognized this, and the just perceptible stir of the congregation proved it. Sonorously he said it. "Oliver Mowat, I baptize thee in the Name of the Father—" The compliment should have all the impressiveness the rite could give it, while the Murchison brothers and sisters, a-row in the family pew, stood on one foot with excitement as to how Oliver Mowat would take the drops that defined him. The verdict was, on the way home, that he behaved splendidly. Alexander Mackenzie, the year before, had roared.

He was weeping now, at the age of seven, silently, but very copiously, behind the wood-pile. His father had finally cuffed him for importunity; and the world was no place for a just boy, who asked nothing but his rights. Only the wood-pile, friendly mossy logs unsplit, stood inconscient[3] and irresponsible for any share in

---

1 Alexander Mackenzie (1822-92), Canada's second Prime Minister (1873-78) and the first Liberal Prime Minister.
2 Oliver Mowat (1820-94), Liberal premier of Ontario from 1872 to 1896.
3 Unconscious.

his black circumstances; and his tears fell among the lichens of the stump he was bowed on till, observing them, he began to wonder whether he could cry enough to make a pond there, and was presently disappointed to find the source exhausted. The Murchisons were all imaginative.

The others, Oliver and Abby and Stella, still "tormented." Poor Alec's rights—to a present of pocket-money on the Queen's Birthday—were common ones, and almost statutory. How their father, sitting comfortably with his pipe in the flickering May shadows under the golden pippin,[1] reading the Toronto paper, could evade his liability in the matter was unfathomable to the Murchisons; it was certainly illiberal; they had a feeling that it was illegal. A little teasing was generally necessary, but the resistance to-day had begun to look ominous, and Alec, as we know, too temerarious,[2] had retired in disorder to the wood-pile.

Oliver was wiping Advena's dishes. He exercised himself ostentatiously upon a plate, standing in the door to be within earshot of his father.

"Eph Wheeler," he informed his family, "Eph Wheeler, he's got twenty-five cents, an' a English sixpence, an' a Yankee nickel. An' Mr. Wheeler's only a common working man, a lot poorer'n we are."

Mr. Murchison removed his pipe from his lips, in order, apparently, to follow unimpeded the trend of the *Dominion's* leading article. Oliver eyed him anxiously. "Do, father," he continued in logical sequence. "Aw, do."

"Make him, mother," said Abby indignantly. "It's the Queen's *Birth*day!"

"Time enough when the butter bill's paid," said Mrs. Murchison.

"Oh, the *butter* bill! Say, Father, aren't you going to?"

"What?" asked John Murchison, and again took out his pipe, as if this were the first he had heard of the matter.

"Give us our fifteen cents each to celebrate with. You can't do it under that," Oliver added firmly. "Crackers are eight cents a packet this year, the small size."

"Nonsense," said Mr. Murchison. The reply was definite and final, and its ambiguity was merely due to the fact that their father

---

1 A popular variety of apple tree, originally from England, with yellow fruit.
2 Characterized by temerity: heedless, rash.

disliked giving a plump refusal. "Nonsense" was easier to say, if not to hear, than "No." Oliver considered for a moment, drew Abby to colloquy by the pump, and sought his brother behind the wood-pile. Then he returned to the charge.

"Look here, father," he said, "*cash down*, we'll take ten."

John Murchison was a man of few words, but they were usually impregnated with meaning, especially in anger. "No more of this," he said. "Celebrate fiddlesticks! Go and make yourselves of some use. You'll get nothing from me, for I haven't got it." So saying, he went through the kitchen with a step that forbade him to be followed. His eldest son, arriving over the back yard fence in a state of heat, was just in time to hear him. Lorne's apprehension of the situation was instant, and his face fell, but the depression plainly covered such splendid spirits that his brother asked resentfully, "Well, what's the matter with *you?*"

"Matter? Oh, not much. I'm going to see the Cayugas beat the Wanderers, that's all; an' Abe Mackinnon's mother said he could ask me to come back to tea with them. Can I, Mother?"

"There's no objection that I know of," said Mrs. Murchison, shaking her apron free of stray potato-parings, "but you won't get money for the lacrosse match or anything else from your father to-day, *I* can assure you. They didn't do five dollars' worth of business at the store all day yesterday, and he's as cross as two sticks."

"Oh, that's all right." Lorne jingled his pocket and Oliver took a fascinated step toward him. "I made thirty cents this morning, delivering papers for Fisher. His boy's sick. I did the North Ward—took me over'n hour. Guess I can go all right, can't I?"

"Why, yes, I suppose you can," said his mother. The others were dumb. Oliver hunched his shoulders and kicked at the nearest thing that had paint on it. Abby clung to the pump handle and sobbed aloud. Lorne looked gloomily about him and went out. Making once more for the back fence, he encountered Alexander in the recognized family retreat. "Oh, my goodness!" he said, and stopped. In a very few minutes he was back in the kitchen, followed sheepishly by Alexander, whose grimy face expressed the hope that beat behind his little waistcoat.

"Say, you kids," he announced, "Alec's got four cents, an' he says he'll join up. This family's going to celebrate all right. Come on down town."

No one could say that the Murchisons were demonstrative. They said nothing, but they got their hats. Mrs. Murchison looked up from her occupation.

"Alec," she said, "out of this house you don't go till you've washed your face. Lorne, come here," she added in a lower voice, producing a bunch of keys. "If you look in the right-hand corner of the top small drawer in my bureau you'll find about twenty cents. Say nothing about it, and mind you don't meddle with anything else. I guess the Queen isn't going to owe it all to you."

TWO

"We've seen changes, Mr. Murchison. Aye. We've seen changes."

Dr. Drummond[1] and Mr. Murchison stood together in the store door, over which the sign, "John Murchison: Hardware" had explained thirty years of varying commercial fortune. They had pretty well begun life together in Elgin. John Murchison was one of those who had listened to Mr. Drummond's trial sermon, and had given his vote to "call" him to the charge. Since then there had been few Sundays when, morning and evening, Mr. Murchison had not been in his place at the top of his pew, where his dignified and intelligent head appeared with the isolated significance of a strong individuality. People looked twice at John Murchison in a crowd; so did his own children at home. Hearing some discussion of the selection of a Premier, Alec, looking earnestly at him once said, "Why don't they tell Father to be it?" The young minister looked twice at him that morning of the trial sermon, and asked afterward who he was. A Scotchman, Mr. Drummond was told, not very long from the old country, who had bought the Playfair business on Main Street, and settled in the "Plummer Place," which already had a quarter of a century's standing in the annals of the town. The Playfair business was a respectable business to buy; the Plummer Place, though it stood in an unfashionable outskirt, was a respectable place to settle in; and the minister, in casting his lot in Elgin, envisaged John Murchison as part of it, thought of him confidently as a "dependance," saw him among the future elders and office-bearers of the congregation, a man who would be punctual with his pew-rent, sage in his judgments, and whose views upon church attendance would be extended to his family.

So the two came, contemporaries, to add their labour and their

---

1 Dr. Drummond is based on a real person, Rev. William Cochrane, who was minister of Zion Presbyterian Church in Brantford.

lives to the building of this little outpost of Empire. It was the frankest transfer, without thought of return; they were there to spend and be spent within the circumference of the spot they had chosen, with no ambition beyond. In the course of nature, even their bones and their memories would enter into the fabric. The new country filled their eyes; the new town was their opportunity, its destiny their fate. They were altogether occupied with its affairs, and the affairs of the growing Dominion,[1] yet obscure in the heart of each of them ran the undercurrent of the old allegiance. They had gone the length of their tether, but the tether was always there. Thus, before a congregation that always stood in the early days, had the minister every Sunday morning for thirty years besought the Almighty, with ardour and humility, on behalf of the Royal Family. It came in the long prayer, about the middle. Not in the perfunctory words of a ritual, but in the language of his choice, which varied according to what he believed to be the spiritual needs of the reigning House, and was at one period, touching certain of its members, though respectful, extremely candid. The General Assembly of the Church of Scotland, "now in session," also—was it ever forgotten once? And even the Prime Minister, "and those who sit in council with him," with just a hint of extra commendation if it happened to be Mr. Gladstone.[2] The minister of Knox Church, Elgin, Ontario, Canada, kept his eye on them all. Remote as he was, and concerned with affairs of which they could know little, his sphere of duty could never revolve too far westward to embrace them, nor could his influence, under any circumstances, cease to be at their disposal. It was noted by some that after Mr. Drummond had got his "D.D."[3] from an American University he also prayed occasionally for the President of the neighbouring Republic; but this was rebutted by others, who pointed out that it happened only on the occurrence of assassinations,[4] and held it reasonable enough. The

---

1 Nation of Canada. The British North America Act adopted the term "Dominion" to indicate that while Canada was self-governing, it was also still in a subordinate relationship to England.
2 William Gladstone (1809-98) served four terms as British Prime Minister between 1868 and 1894; he was a publicly committed Christian and a Liberal.
3 "Doctor of Divinity."
4 By the time Duncan wrote *The Imperialist*, there had been three presidential assassinations during her lifetime: Abraham Lincoln (1865), James Garfield (1881), and William McKinley (1901).

cavillers mostly belonged to the congregation of St. Andrew's, "Established"—a glum, old-fashioned lot indeed, who now and then dropped in of a Sunday evening to hear Mr. Drummond preach. (There wasn't much to be said for the preaching at St. Andrew's.) The Established folk went on calling the minister of Knox Church "Mr." Drummond long after he was "Doctor" to his own congregation, on account of what they chose to consider the dubious source of the dignity; but the Knox Church people had their own theory to explain this hypercriticism, and would promptly turn the conversation to the merits of the sermon.

Twenty-five years it was, in point, this Monday morning when the Doctor—not being Established we need not hesitate, besides by this time nobody did—stood with Mr. Murchison in the store door and talked about having seen changes. He had preached his anniversary sermon the night before to a full church, when, laying his hand upon his people's heart, he had himself to repress tears. He was aware of another strand completed in their mutual bond; the sermon had been a moral, an emotional, and an oratorical success; and in the expansion of the following morning Dr. Drummond had remembered that he had promised his housekeeper a new gas cooking-range, and that it was high time he should drop into Murchison's to inquire about it. Mrs. Forsyth had mentioned at breakfast that they had ranges with exactly the improvement she wanted at Thompson's, but the minister was deaf to the hint. Thompson was a Congregationalist, and, improvement or no improvement, it wasn't likely that Dr. Drummond was going "outside the congregation" for anything he required. It would have been on a par with a wandering tendency in his flock, upon which he systematically frowned. He was as great an autocrat in this as the rector of any country parish in England undermined by Dissent; but his sense of obligation worked unfailingly both ways.

John Murchison had not said much about the sermon; it wasn't his way, and Dr. Drummond knew it. "You gave us a good sermon last night, Doctor;" not much more than that, and "I noticed the Milburns there; we don't often get Episcopalians;"[1] and again, "The Wilcoxes"—Thomas Wilcox, wholesale grocer, was the chief prop of St. Andrew's—"were sitting just in front of us. We overtook them going home, and Wilcox explained how

---

1 Duncan uses the terms Episcopalian, Anglican, and Church of England interchangeably.

much they liked the music. 'Glad to see you,' I said. 'Glad to see you for any reason,'" Mr. Murchison's eye twinkled. "But they had a great deal to say about 'the music.'" It was not an effusive form of felicitation; the minister would have liked it less if it had been, felt less justified, perhaps, in remembering about the range on that particular morning. As it was, he was able to take it with perfect dignity and good humour, and to enjoy the point against the Wilcoxes with that laugh of his that did everybody good to hear; so hearty it was, so rich in the grain of the voice, so full of the zest and flavour of the joke. The range had been selected, and their talk of changes had begun with it, Mr. Murchison pointing out the new idea in the boiler, and Dr. Drummond remembering his first kitchen stove that burned wood and stood on its four legs, with nothing behind but the stove pipe, and if you wanted a boiler you took off the front lids and put it on, and how remarkable even that had seemed to his eyes, fresh from the conservative kitchen notions of the old country. He had come, unhappily, a widower to the domestic improvements on the other side of the Atlantic. "Often I used to think," he said to Mr. Murchison, "if my poor wife could have seen that stove how delighted she would have been! But I doubt this would have been too much for her altogether!"

"That stove!" answered Mr. Murchison. "Well I remember it. I sold it myself to your predecessor, Mr. Wishart, for thirty dollars—the last purchase he ever made, poor man. It was great business for me—I had only two others in the store like it. One of them old Milburn bought—the father of this man, d'ye mind him?—the other stayed by me a matter of seven years. I carried a light stock in those days."

It was no longer a light stock. The two men involuntarily glanced round them for the satisfaction of the contrast Murchison evoked, though neither of them, from motives of vague delicacy, felt inclined to dwell upon it. John Murchison had the shyness of an artist in his commercial success, and the minister possibly felt that his relation toward the prosperity of a member had in some degree the embarrassment of a tax-gatherer's. The stock was indeed heavy now. You had to go upstairs to see the ranges, where they stood in rows, and every one of them bore somewhere upon it, in raised black letters, John Murchison's name. Through the windows came the iterating ring on the iron from the foundry in Chestnut Street which fed the shop, with an overflow that found its way from one end of the country to the other. Finicking visitors to Elgin found this wearing, but to John Murchison it was the music that honours the conqueror of circumstances. The ground floor was given up to the small wares of the business, chiefly imported; two or three young men, steady and knowledgeable-looking, moved about in their shirt sleeves among shelves and packing cases. One of them was our friend Alec; our other friend Oliver looked after the books at the foundry. Their father did everything deliberately; but presently, in his own good time, his commercial letter paper would be headed, with regard to these two, "John Murchison and Sons." It had long announced that the business was "Wholesale and Retail."

Dr. Drummond and Mr. Murchison, considering the changes in Elgin from the store door, did it at their leisure, the merchant with his thumbs thrust comfortably in the armholes of his waistcoat, the minister, with that familiar trick of his, balancing on one foot and suddenly throwing his slight weight forward on the other. "A bundle of nerves" people called the Doctor: to stand still would have been a penance to him; even as he swayed backward and forward in talking his hand must be busy at the seals on his watch chain and his shrewd glance travelling over a dozen things you would never dream so clever a man would take notice of. It was a prospect of moderate commercial activity they looked out upon, a street of mellow shop-fronts, on both sides, of varying height and importance, wearing that air of marking a period, a definite stop in growth, that so often co-exists with quite a reasonable degree of activity and independence in colonial towns. One could almost say, standing there in the door at Murchison's, where the line of legitimate enterprise had been over-passed and where its intention had been none too sanguine—on the one hand in the faded and pretentious red brick building with the false third story, occupied by Cleary, which must have been let at a loss to dry-goods or anything else; on the other hand in the solid "Gregory block," opposite the market, where rents were as certain as the dividends of the Bank of British North America.

Main Street expressed the idea that, for the purpose of growing and doing business, it had always found the days long enough. Drays passed through it to the Grand Trunk station, but they passed one at a time; a certain number of people went up and down about their affairs, but they were never in a hurry; a street car jogged by every ten minutes or so, but nobody ran after it. There was a decent procedure; and it was felt that Bofield—he was dry-goods, too—in putting in an elevator was just a little

unnecessarily in advance of the times. Bofield had only two stories, like everybody else, and a very easy staircase, up which people often declared they preferred to walk rather than wait in the
elevator for a young man to finish serving and work it. These, of
course, were the sophisticated people of Elgin; country folk, on a
market day, would wait a quarter of an hour for the young man,
and think nothing of it; and I imagine Bofield found his account
in the elevator, though he did complain sometimes that such persons went up and down on frivolous pretexts or to amuse the
baby. As a matter of fact, Elgin had begun as the centre of "trading" for the farmers of Fox County, and had soon over-supplied
that limit in demand; so that when other interests added themselves to the activity of the town there was still plenty of room for
the business they brought. Main Street was really, therefore, not
a fair index; nobody in Elgin would have admitted it. Its appearance and demeanour would never have suggested that it was now
the chief artery of a thriving manufacturing town, with a collegiate institute, eleven churches, two newspapers, and an asylum
for the deaf and dumb, to say nothing of a fire department unsur-
passed for organization and achievement in the Province of
Ontario. Only at twelve noon it might be partly realized, when the
prolonged "toots" of seven factory whistles at once let off, so to
speak, the hour. Elgin liked the demonstration; it was held to be
cheerful and unmistakable, an indication of "go-ahead" proclivi-
ties which spoke for itself. It occurred while yet Dr. Drummond
and Mr. Murchison stood together in the store door.

"I must be getting on," said the minister, looking at his watch.
"And what news have you of Lorne?"

"Well, he seems to have got through all right."

"What—you've heard already, then?"

"He telegraphed from Toronto on Saturday night." Mr.
Murchison stroked his chin, the better to retain his satisfaction.
"Waste of money—the post would have brought it this morning—
but it pleased his mother. Yes, he's through his Law Schools
examination, and at the top, too, as far as I can make out."

"Dear me, and you never mentioned it!" Dr. Drummond
spoke with the resigned impatience of a familiar grievance. It was
certainly a trying characteristic of John Murchison that he never
cared about communicating anything that might seem to ask for
congratulation. "Well, well! I'm very glad to hear it."

"It slipped my mind," said Mr. Murchison. "Yes, he's full-
fledged 'barrister and solicitor' now; he can plead your case or

draw you up a deed with the best of them.[1] Lorne's made a fair record, so far. We've no reason to be ashamed of him."

"That you have not." Personal sentiments between these two Scotchmen were rather indicated than indulged. "He's going in with Fulke and Warner, I suppose—you've got that fixed up?"

"Pretty well. Old man Warner was in this morning to talk it over. He says they look to Lorne to bring them in touch with the new generation. It's a pity he lost that son of his."

"Oh, a great pity. But since they had to go outside the firm they couldn't have done better; they couldn't have done better. I hope Lorne will bring them a bit of Knox Church business too; there's no reason why Bob Mackintosh should have it all. They'll be glad to see him back at the Hampden Debating Society. He's a great light there, is Lorne; and the Young Liberals, I hear, are wanting him for chairman this year."

"There's some talk of it. But time enough—time enough for that! He'll do first-rate if he gets the law to practise, let alone the making of it."

"Maybe so; he's young yet. Well, good-morning to you. I'll just step over the way to the *Express* office and get a proof out of them of that sermon of mine. I noticed their reporter fellow —what's his name?—Rawlins with his pencil out last night, and I've no faith in Rawlins."

"Better cast an eye over it," responded Mr. Murchison, cordially, and stood for a moment or two longer in the door watching the crisp, significant little figure of the minister as he stepped briskly over the crossing to the newspaper office. There Dr. Drummond sat down, before he explained his errand, and wrote a paragraph.

"We are pleased to learn," it ran, "that Mr. Lorne Murchison, eldest son of Mr. John Murchison, of this town, has passed at the capital of the Province his final examination in Law, distinguishing himself by coming out at the top of the list. It will be remembered that Mr. Murchison, upon entering the Law Schools, also carried off a valuable scholarship. We are glad to be able to announce that Mr. Murchison, junior, will embark upon his pro-

---

1 In Canada, lawyers are qualified as both "barristers" who argue cases in court and "solicitors" who prepare wills or deal with tax, business, and real estate law, although in practice Canadian lawyers tend to specialise in one or the other.

fession in his native town, where he will enter the well-known firm of Fulke and Warner."

The editor, Mr. Horace Williams, had gone to dinner, and Rawlins was out, so Dr. Drummond had to leave it with the press foreman. Mr. Williams read it appreciatively on his return, and sent it down with the following addition—

"This is doing it as well as it can be done. Elgin congratulates Mr. L. Murchison upon having produced these results, and herself upon having produced Mr. L. Murchison."

THREE

From the day she stepped into it Mrs. Murchison knew that the Plummer Place[1] was going to be the bane of her existence. This may have been partly because Mr. Murchison had bought it, since a circumstance welded like that into one's life is very apt to assume the character of a bane, unless one's temperament leads one to philosophy, which Mrs. Murchison's didn't. But there were other reasons more difficult to traverse: it was plainly true that the place did require a tremendous amount of "looking after," as such things were measured in Elgin, far more looking after than the Murchisons could afford to give it. They could never have afforded, in the beginning, to possess it, had it not been sold, under mortgage, at a dramatic sacrifice. The house was a dignified old affair, built of wood and painted white, with wide green verandahs compassing the four sides of it, as they often did in days when the builder had only to turn his hand to the forest. It stood on the very edge of the town; wheatfields in the summer billowed up to its fences, and cornstacks in the autumn camped around it like a besieging army. The plank sidewalk finished there; after that you took the road, or, if you were so inclined, the river, into which you could throw a stone from the orchard of the Plummer Place. The house stood roomily and shadily in ornamental grounds, with a lawn in front of it and a shrubbery at each side, an orchard behind, and a vegetable garden, the whole intersected by winding gravel walks, of which Mrs. Murchison was wont to say that a man might do nothing but weed them and have his hands full. In the middle of the lawn was a fountain, an empty

---

1   The "Plummer Place" is based on the Duncan family home at 94 West Street in Brantford.

basin with a plaster Triton,[1] most difficult to keep looking respectable and pathetic in his frayed air of exile from some garden of Italy sloping to the sea. There was also a barn with stabling, a loft, and big carriage doors opening on a lane to the street. The originating Plummer, Mrs. Murchison often said, must have been a person of large ideas, and she hoped he had the money to live up to them. The Murchisons at one time kept a cow in the barn, till a succession of "girls" left on account of the milking, and the lane was useful as an approach to the back yard by the teams that brought the cordwood in the winter. It was trying enough for a person with the instinct of order to find herself surrounded by out-of-door circumstances which she simply could not control, but Mrs. Murchison often declared that she could put up with the grounds if it had stopped there. It did not stop there. Though I was compelled to introduce Mrs. Murchison in the kitchen, she had a drawing-room in which she might have received the Lieutenant Governor, with French windows and a cut-glass chandelier, and a library with an Italian marble mantelpiece. She had an ice-house and a wine cellar, and a string of bells[2] in the kitchen that connected with every room in the house; it was a negligible misfortune that not one of them was in order. She had far too much, as she declared, for any one pair of hands and a growing family, and if the ceiling was not dropping in the drawing-room, the cornice was cracked in the library, or the gas was leaking in the dining-room, or the verandah wanted re-flooring if any one coming to the house was not to put his foot through it; and as to the barn, if it was dropping to pieces it would just have to drop. The barn was definitely outside the radius of possible amelioration—it passed gradually, visibly, into decrepitude, and Mrs. Murchison often wished she could afford to pull it down.

It may be realized that in spite of its air of being impossible to "overtake"—I must, in this connection, continue to quote its mistress—there was an attractiveness about the dwelling of the Murchisons, the attractiveness of the large ideas upon which it had been built and designed, no doubt by one of those gentlefolk of reduced income who wander out to the colonies with a nebulous view to economy and occupation, to perish of the readjustment. The case of such persons, when they arrive, is at once felt

---

1 A sea-god found in Greek mythology.
2 These would have been intended to summon servants.

to be pathetic; there is a tacit local understanding that they have made a mistake. They may be entitled to respect, but nothing can save them from the isolation of their difference and their misapprehension. It was like that with the house. The house was admired—without enthusiasm—but it was not copied. It was felt to be outside the general need, misjudged, adventitious; and it wore its superiority in the popular view like a folly. It was in Elgin, but not of it; it represented a different tradition; and Elgin made the same allowance for its bedroom bells and its old-fashioned dignities as was conceded to its original master's habit of a six o'clock dinner, with wine.[1]

The architectural expression of the town was on a different scale, beginning with "frame," rising through the semi-detached, culminating expensively in Mansard roofs, cupolas and modern conveniences, and blossoming, in extreme instances, into Moorish fretwork and silk *portières*[2] for interior decoration. The Murchison house gained by force of contrast: one felt, stepping into it, under influences of less expediency and more dignity, wider scope and more leisured intention; its shabby spaces had a redundancy the pleasanter and its yellow plaster cornices a charm the greater for the numerous close-set examples of contemporary taste in red brick which made, surrounded by geranium beds, so creditable an appearance in the West Ward. John Murchison in taking possession of the house had felt in it these satisfactions, had been definitely penetrated and soothed by them, the more perhaps because he brought to them a capacity for feeling the worthier things of life which circumstances had not previously developed. He seized the place with a sense of opportunity leaping sharp and conscious out of early years in the grey "wynds"[3] of a northern Scottish town; and its personality sustained him, very privately but none the less effectively, through the worry and expense of it for years. He would take his pipe and walk silently for long together about the untidy shrubberies in the evening for

---

1 A formal dinner at six o'clock would have been the custom for the upper classes at the beginning of Victoria's reign. The dinner hour in English urban areas became later and later as the century went on, while in rural and farming families mid-day "dinner" was still common. Drinking wine with meals was unusual in turn-of-the-century Ontario, and associated with the rich, with "foreigners," and with non-Protestants.
2 A curtain hung across a doorway, in this case for decoration.
3 A narrow street or laneway.

the acute pleasure of seeing the big horse-chestnuts in flower; and he never opened the hall door without a feeling of gratification in its weight as it swung under his hand. In so far as he could, he supplemented the idiosyncrasies he found. The drawing-room walls, though mostly bare in their old-fashioned French paper—lavender and gilt, a grape-vine pattern—held a few good engravings; the library was reduced to contain a single bookcase, but it was filled with English classics. John Murchison had been made a careful man, not by nature, by the discipline of circumstances; but he would buy books. He bought them between long periods of abstinence, during which he would scout the expenditure of an unnecessary dollar, coming home with a parcel under his arm for which he vouchsafed no explanation, and which would disclose itself to be Lockhart, or Sterne, or Borrow, or Defoe.[1] Mrs. Murchison kept a discouraging eye upon such purchases; and when her husband brought home Chambers' *Dictionary of English Literature*, after shortly and definitely repulsing her demand that he should get himself a new winter overcoat, she declared that it was beyond all endurance. Mrs. Murchison was surrounded, indeed, by more of "that sort of thing" than she could find use or excuse for; since, though books made but a sporadic appearance, current literature, daily, weekly, and monthly, was perpetually under her feet. The Toronto paper came as a matter of course, as the London daily takes its morning flight into the provinces, the local organ as simply indispensable, the *Westminster*[2] as the corollary of church membership and for Sunday reading. These were constant, but there were also mutables—*Once a Week*, *Good Words for the Young*, *Blackwood's* and the *Cornhill*,[3] they used to be; years of back numbers Mrs. Murchison had packed away in the attic, where Advena on rainy days came into the inheritance of them, and made an early acquaintance of fiction in *Ready Money Mortiboy* and *Verner's Pride*, while Lorne, flat on his stomach beside

---

1 John Gibson Lockhart (1794-1854) biographer of Sir Walter Scott; Laurence Sterne (1713-68), author of *Tristram Shandy*; George Borrow (1803-81), author of *Lavengro*; Daniel Defoe (1661?-1731), author of *Moll Flanders*, *Robinson Crusoe*, and other works.
2 A weekly paper published by the Presbyterian Church in Canada, 1896-1916.
3 The Toronto *Daily News* version of the novel substituted the New York journal *Appleton's* for the British *Blackwood's* and the *Cornhill*.

her, had glorious hours on *The Back of the North Wind.*[1] Their father considered such publications and their successors essential, like tobacco and tea. He was also an easy prey to the subscription agent, for works published in parts and paid for in instalments, a custom which Mrs. Murchison regarded with abhorrence. So much so that when John put his name down for *Masterpieces of the World's Art,* which was to cost twenty dollars by the time it was complete, he thought it advisable to let the numbers accumulate at the store.

Whatever the place represented to their parents, it was pure joy to the young Murchisons. It offered a margin and a mystery to life. They saw it far larger than it was; they invested it, arguing purely by its difference from other habitations, with a romantic past. "I guess when the Prince of Wales came to Elgin, mother, he stayed here,"[2] Lorne remarked, as a little boy. Secretly he and Advena took up boards in more than one unused room, and rapped on more than one thick wall to find a hollow chamber; the house revealed so much that was interesting, it was apparent to the meanest understanding that it must hide even more. It was never half lighted, and there was a passage in which fear dwelt— wild were the gallopades from attic to cellar in the early nightfall, when every young Murchison tore after every other, possessed, like cats, by a demoniac ecstasy of the gloaming. And the garden, with the autumn moon coming over the apple trees and the neglected asparagus thick for ambush, and a casual untrimmed boy or two with the delicious recommendation of being utterly without credentials, to join in the rout and be trusted to make for the back fence without further hint at the voice of Mrs. Murchison—these were joys of the very fibre, things to push ideas and envisage life with an attraction that made it worth while to grow up.

And they had all achieved it—all six. They had grown up sturdily, emerging into sobriety and decorum by much the same degrees as the old house, under John Murchison's improving fortunes, grew cared for and presentable. The new roof went on, slate replacing shingles, the year Abby put her hair up; the bath-

---

1   *Ready-Money Mortiboy, a Matter-of-Fact Story* (1887) by Sir Walter Besant; *Verner's Pride* (1895) by Ellen (Price) Wood; *At the Back of the North Wind* (1871) by George MacDonald.
2   The Prince of Wales, later Edward VII, visited Brantford in 1860.

room[1] was contemporary with Oliver's leaving school; the electric light was actually turned on for the first time[2] in honour of Lorne's return from Toronto, a barrister and solicitor; several rooms had been done up for Abby's wedding. Abby had married, early and satisfactorily, Dr. Harry Johnson, who had placidly settled down to await the gradual succession of his father's practice; "Dr. Harry and Dr. Henry" they were called. Dr. Harry lived next door to Dr. Henry, and had a good deal of the old man's popular manner. It was an unacknowledged partnership, which often provided two opinions for the same price; the town prophesied well of it. That left only five at home, but they always had Abby over in the West Ward, where Abby's housekeeping made an interest and Abby's baby a point of pilgrimage. These considerations almost consoled Mrs. Murchison, declaring, as she did, that all of them might have gone but Abby, who alone knew how to be "any comfort or any dependence" in the house; who could be left with a day's preserving; and I tell you that to be left by Mrs. Murchison with a day's preserving, be it cherries or strawberries, damsons or pears, was a mark of confidence not easy to obtain. Advena never had it; Advena, indeed, might have married and removed no prop of the family economy. Mrs. Murchison would have been "sorry for the man"—she maintained a candour toward and about those belonging to her that permitted no illusions—but she would have stood cheerfully out of the way on her own account. When you have seen your daughter reach and pass the age of twenty-five without having learned properly to make her own bed, you know, without being told, that she will never be fit for the management of a house—don't you? Very well then. And for ever and for ever, no matter what there was to do, with a book in her hand—Mrs. Murchison would put an emphasis on the "book" which scarcely concealed a contempt for such absorption. And if, at the end of your patience, you told her for any sake

---

1 Between 1874 and 1914 Canadian cities and larger towns built water and sanitary sewers, enabling the installation of indoor bathrooms. However, by 1941, only slightly more than half of all households in the nation had an indoor flush toilet.

2 In 1903, Brantford voted on a by-law to construct a municipal Hydro-electric system; this debate was ongoing when Duncan visited Brantford in 1903. However, the by-law was defeated and not reintroduced until 1912. ("Development of Hydro in the City of Branford," *Brantford Expositor*, 1 July 1927: 463.)

to put it down and attend to matters, obeying in a kind of dream that generally drove you to take the thing out of her hands and do it yourself, rather than jump out of your skin watching her.

Sincerely Mrs. Murchison would have been sorry for the man if he had arrived, but he had not arrived. Advena justified her existence by taking the university course for women at Toronto, and afterward teaching the English branches to the junior forms in the Collegiate Institute, which placed her arbitrarily outside the sphere of domestic criticism. Mrs. Murchison was thankful to have her there—outside—where little more could reasonably be expected of her than that she should be down in time for breakfast. It is so irritating to be justified in expecting more than seems likely to come. Mrs. Murchison's ideas circulated strictly in the orbit of equity and reason; she expected nothing from anybody that she did not expect from herself; indeed, she would spare others in far larger proportion. But the sense of obligation which led her to offer herself up to the last volt of her energy made her miserable when she considered that she was not fairly done by in return. Pressed down and running over were the services she offered to the general good, and it was on the ground of the merest justice that she required from her daughters "some sort of interest" in domestic affairs. From her eldest she got no sort of interest, and it was like the removal of a grievance from the hearth when Advena took up employment which ranged her definitely beyond the necessity of being of any earthly use in the house. Advena's occupation to some extent absorbed her shortcomings, which was much better than having to attribute them to her being naturally "through-other,"[1] or naturally clever, according to the bias of the moment. Mrs. Murchison no longer excused or complained of her daughter; but she still pitied the man.

"The boys," of course, were too young to think of matrimony. They were still the boys, the Murchison boys; they would be the boys at forty if they remained under their father's roof. In the mother country, men in short jackets and round collars emerge from the preparatory schools; in the daughter lands boys in tail coats conduct serious affairs. Alec and Oliver, in the business, were frivolous enough as to the feminine interest. For all Dr. Drummond's expressed and widely-known views upon the subject, it was a common thing for one or both of these young men

---

1 Disorderly, reckless, wild.

to stray from the family pew on Sunday evenings to the services of other communions, thereafter to walk home in the dusk under the maples with some attractive young person, and be sedately invited to finish the evening on her father's verandah. Neither of them was guiltless of silk ties knitted or handkerchiefs initialled by certain fingers; without repeating scandal, one might say by various fingers. For while the ultimate import of these matters was not denied in Elgin, there was a general feeling against giving too much meaning to them, probably originating in a reluctance among heads of families to add to their responsibilities. These early spring indications were belittled and laughed at; so much so that the young people themselves hardly took them seriously, but regarded them as a form of amusement almost conventional. Nothing would have surprised or embarrassed them more than to learn that their predilections had an imperative corollary, that anything should, of necessity, "come of it." Something, of course, occasionally did come of it; and, usually after years of "attention," a young man of Elgin found himself mated to a young woman, but never under circumstances that could be called precipitate or rash. The cautious blood and far sight of the early settlers, who had much to reckon with, were still preponderant social characteristics of the town they cleared the site for. Meanwhile, however, flowers were gathered, and all sorts of evanescent idylls came and went in the relations of young men and maidens. Alec and Oliver Murchison were already in the full tide of them.

From this point of view they did not know what to make of Lorne. It was not as if their brother were in any way ill calculated to attract that interest which gave to youthful existence in Elgin almost the only flavour that it had. Looks are looks, and Lorne had plenty of them; taller by an inch than Alec, broader by two than Oliver, with a fine square head and blue eyes in it, and features which conveyed purpose and humour, lighted by a certain simplicity of soul that pleased even when it was not understood. "Open," people said he was, and "frank"—so he was, frank and open, with horizons and intentions; you could see them in his face. Perhaps it was more conscious of them than he was. Ambition, definitely shining goals, adorn the perspectives of young men in new countries less often than is commonly supposed. Lorne meant to be a good lawyer, squarely proposed to himself that the country should hold no better, and as to more selective usefulness, he hoped to do a little stumping for the right side when Frank Jennings ran for the Ontario House in the fall. It wouldn't be his first electioneering: from the day he became chairman of the Young Liberals the party had an eye on him, and when occasion arose, winter or summer, by bobsleigh or buggy, weatherbeaten local bosses would convey him to country schoolhouses for miles about to keep a district sound on railway policy, or education, or tariff reform. He came home smiling with the triumphs of these occasions, and offered them, with the slow, good-humoured, capable drawl that inspired such confidence in him, to his family at breakfast, who said "Great!" or "Good for you, Lorne!" John Murchison oftenest said nothing, but would glance significantly at his wife, frowning and pursing his lips when she, who had most spirit of them all, would exclaim, "You'll be Premier yet, Lorne!" It was no part of the Murchison policy to draw against future balances: they might believe everything, they would express nothing; and I doubt whether Lorne himself had any map of the country he meant to travel over in that vague future, already defining in local approbation, and law business coming freely in with a special eye on the junior partner. But the tract was there, sub-conscious, plain in the wider glance, the alerter manner, plain even in the grasp and stride which marked him in a crowd; plain, too, in the preoccupation with other issues, were it only turning over a leader in the morning's *Dominion*, that carried him along indifferent to the allurements I have described. The family had a bond of union in their respect for Lorne, and this absence of nugatory inclinations in him was among its elements. Even Stella, who, being just fourteen, was the natural mouthpiece of family sentiment, would declare that Lorne had something better to do than go hanging about after girls, and for her part she thought all the more of him for it.

FOUR

"I am requested to announce," said Dr. Drummond after the singing of the last hymn, "the death, yesterday morning, of James Archibald Ramsay, for fifteen years an adherent and for twenty-five years a member of this church. The funeral will take place from the residence of the deceased, on Court House Street, tomorrow afternoon at four o'clock. Friends and acquaintances are respectfully—invited—to attend."

The minister's voice changed with the character of its affairs. Still vibrating with the delivery of his sermon, it was now charged with the official business of the interment. In its inflections it expressed both elegy and eulogy; and in the brief pause before and after "invited" and the fall of "attend" there was the last word of comment upon the mortal term. A crispation of interest passed over the congregation; every chin was raised. Dr. Drummond's voice had a wonderful claiming power, but he often said he wished his congregation would pay as undivided attention to the sermon as they did to the announcements.

"The usual weekly prayer meeting will be held in the basement of the church on Wednesday evening." Then almost in a tone of colloquy, and with just a hint of satire about his long upper lip—

"I should be glad to see a better attendance of the young people at these gatherings. Time was when the prayer meeting counted among our young men and women as an occasion not to be lightly passed over. In these days it would seem that there is too much business to be done, or too much pleasure to be enjoyed, for the oncoming generation to remember their weekly engagement with the Lord. This is not as it should be; and I rely upon the fathers and mothers of this congregation, who brought these children in their arms to the baptismal font, there to be admitted to the good hopes and great privileges of the Church of God—I rely upon them to see that there shall be no departure from the good old rule, and that time is found for the weekly prayer meeting."

Mrs. Murchison nudged Stella, who returned the attention, looking elaborately uninterested, with her foot. Alec and Oliver smiled consciously; their father, with an expression of severe gravity, backed up the minister, who, after an instant's pause, continued—

"On Tuesday afternoon next, God willing, I shall visit the following families in the East Ward—Mr. Peterson, Mr. Macormack, Mrs. Samuel Smith, and Mr. John Flint. On Thursday afternoon in the South Ward, Mrs. Reid, Mr. P.C. Cameron, and Mr. Murchison. We will close by singing the Third Doxology:[1]

Blessed, blessed be Jehovah,
Israel's God to all eternity—

---

1 A doxology is a short expression of praise to the Christian God, in a metrical form.

The congregation trooped out; the Murchisons walked home in a clan, Mr. and Mrs. Murchison, with Stella skirting the edge of the side-walk beside them, the two young men behind. Abby, when she married Harry, had "gone over" to the Church of England. The wife must worship with the husband; even Dr. Drummond recognised the necessity, though he professed small opinion of the sway of the spouse who, with Presbyterian traditions behind her, could not achieve union the other way about; and Abby's sanctioned defection was a matter of rather shamefaced reference by her family. Advena and Lorne had fallen into the degenerate modern habit of preferring the evening service.

"So we're to have the Doctor on Thursday," said Mrs. Murchison, plainly not displeased. "Well, I hope the dining-room carpet will be down."

"I expect he'll be wanting his tea," replied Mr. Murchison. "He's got you in the right place on the list for that, mother—as usual."

"I'd just like to see him go anywhere else for his tea the day he was coming to our house," declared Stella. "But he *generally* has too much sense."

"You boys," said Mrs. Murchison, turning back to her sons, "will see that you're on hand that evening. And I hope the doctor will rub it in about the prayer meeting." Mrs. Murchison chuckled. "I saw it went home to both of you, and well it might. Yes; I think I may as well expect him to tea. He enjoys my scalloped oysters, if I do say it myself."

"We'll get Abby over," said Mr. Murchison. "That'll please the Doctor."

"I must say," remarked Stella, "he seems to think a lot more of Abby now that she's Mrs. Episcopal Johnson."

"Yes, Abby and Harry must come," said Mrs. Murchison, "and I was thinking of inviting Mr. and Mrs. Horace Williams. We've been there till I'm ashamed to look them in the face. And I've pretty well decided," she added autocratically, "to have chicken salad. So if Dr. Drummond has made up his mouth for scalloped oysters he'll be disappointed."

"Mother," announced Stella, "I'm perfectly certain you'll have both."

"I'll consider it," replied her mother. "Meanwhile we would be better employed in thinking of what we have been hearing. That's the third sermon from the Book of Job in six weeks. I must say, with the whole of the two Testaments to select from, I don't see why the Doctor should be so taken up with Job."

Stella was vindicated; Mrs. Murchison did have both. The chicken salad gleamed at one end of the table and the scalloped oysters smoked delicious at the other. Lorne had charge of the cold tongue and Advena was entrusted with the pickled pears. The rest of the family were expected to think about the tea biscuits and the cake, for Lobelia had never yet had a successor that was any hand with company. Mrs. Murchison had enough to do to pour out the tea. It was a table to do anybody credit, with its glossy damask and the old-fashioned silver and best china that Mrs. Murchison had brought as a bride to her housekeeping—for, thank goodness, her mother had known what was what in such matters—a generous attractive table that you took some satisfaction in looking at. Mrs. Murchison came of a family of noted housekeepers; where she got her charm I don't know. Six o'clock tea, and that the last meal in the day, was the rule in Elgin, and a good enough rule for Mrs. Murchison, who had no patience with the innovation of a late dinner recently adopted by some people who could keep neither their servants nor their digestions in consequence.[1] It had been a crisp October day; as Mr. Murchison remarked, the fall evenings were beginning to draw in early; everybody was glad of the fire in the grate and the closed curtains. Dr. Drummond had come about five, and the inquiries and comments upon family matters that the occasion made incumbent had been briskly exchanged, with just the word that marked the pastoral visit and the practical interest that relieved it. And he had thought, on the whole, that he might manage to stay to tea, at which Mrs. Murchison's eyes twinkled as she said affectionately—

"Now, Doctor, you know we could never let you off."

Then Abby had arrived and her husband, and finally Mr. and Mrs. Williams, just a trifle late for etiquette, but well knowing that it mustn't be enough to spoil the biscuits. Dr. Drummond, in the place of honour, had asked the blessing, and that brief reminder of the semi-official character of the occasion having been delivered, was in the best of humours. The Murchisons were not far wrong in the happy divination that he liked coming to their house. Its atmosphere appealed to him; he expanded in its

---

1 Like many modest middle-class families in Ontario at the time, the Murchisons have a substantial "high tea" as the last meal of the day. The Victorian practice of an early tea (5 pm) and late supper (7:30 pm or later), customary among the well-to-do in the new residential suburbs of English towns and cities, is criticised in the novel as pretentious and impractical in Elgin.

humour, its irregularity, its sense of temperament. They were doubtful allurements, from the point of view of a minister of the Gospel, but it would not occur to Dr. Drummond to analyse them. So far as he was aware, John Murchison was just a decent, prosperous Christian man, on whose word and will you might depend, and Mrs. Murchison a stirring, independent little woman, who could be very good company when she felt inclined. As to their sons and daughters, in so far as they were a credit, he was as proud of them as their parents could possibly be, regarding himself as in a much higher degree responsible for the formation of their characters and the promise of their talents. And indeed, since every one of them had "sat under" Dr. Drummond from the day he or she was capable of sitting under anybody, Mr. and Mrs. Murchison would have been the last to dispute this. It was not one of those houses where a pastor could always be sure of leaving some spiritual benefit behind; but then he came away himself with a pleasant sense of nervous stimulus which was apt to take his mind off the matter. It is not given to all of us to receive or to extend the communion of the saints; Mr. and Mrs. Murchison were indubitably of the elect, but he was singularly close-mouthed about it, and she had an extraordinary way of seeing the humorous side—altogether it was paralysing, and the conversation would wonderfully soon slip round to some robust secular subject, public or domestic. I have mentioned Dr. Drummond's long upper lip; all sorts of racial virtues resided there, but his mouth was also wide and much frequented by a critical, humorous, philosophical smile which revealed a view of life at once kindly and trenchant. His shrewd grey eyes were encased in wrinkles, and when he laughed his hearty laugh they almost disappeared in a merry line. He had a fund of Scotch stories, and one or two he was very fond of, at the expense of the Methodists, that were known up and down the Dominion, and nobody enjoyed them more than he did himself. He had once worn his hair in a high curl on his scholarly forehead, and a silvering tuft remained brushed upright; he took the old-fashioned precaution of putting cotton wool in his ears, which gave him more than ever the look of something highly-concentrated and conserved but in no way detracted from his dignity. St. Andrew's folk accused him of vanity because of the diamond he wore on his little finger. He was by no means handsome, but he was intensely individual; perhaps he had vanity; his people would have forgiven him worse things. And at Mrs. Murchison's tea party he was certainly, as John Murchison afterwards said, "in fine feather."

An absorbing topic held them, a local topic, a topic involving loss and crime and reprisals. The Federal Bank had sustained a robbery of five thousand dollars, and in the course of a few days had placed their cashier under arrest for suspected complicity. Their cashier was Walter Ormiston, the only son of old Squire Ormiston, of Moneida Reservation,[1] ten miles out of Elgin, who had administered the affairs of the Indians there for more years than the Federal Bank had existed. Mr. Williams brought the latest news, as was to be expected; news flowed in rivulets to Mr. Williams all day long; he paid for it, dealt in it, could spread or suppress it.

"They've admitted the bail," Mr. Williams announced, with an air of self-surveillance. Rawlins had brought the intelligence in too late for the current issue, and Mr. Williams was divided between his human desire to communicate and his journalistic sense that the item would be the main feature of the next afternoon's *Express*.

"I'm glad of that. I'm glad of that," repeated Dr. Drummond. "Thank you, Mrs. Murchison, I'll send my cup. And did you learn, Williams, for what amount?"

Mr. Williams ran his hand through his hair in the effort to remember, and decided that he might as well let it all go. The *Mercury* couldn't fail to get it by to-morrow anyhow.

"Three thousand," he said; "Milburn and Dr. Henry Johnson."

"I thought Father was bound to be in it," remarked Dr. Harry.

"Half and half?" asked John Murchison.

"No," contributed Mrs. Williams. "Mr. Milburn two and Dr. Henry one. Mr. Milburn is Walter's uncle, you know."

Mr. Williams fastened an outraged glance on his wife, who looked another way. Whatever he thought proper to do, it was absolutely understood that she was to reveal nothing of what "came in," and was even carefully to conserve anything she heard outside with a view to bringing it in. Mrs. Williams was too prone to indiscretion in the matter of letting news slip prematurely; and as to its capture, her husband would often confess, with private humour, that Minnie wasn't much of a mouser.

---

1 Probably based on the Six Nations Reserve located near Brantford on the south side of the Grand River. "Moneida" is an invented name: the Six Nations of the Iroquois Confederacy are the Mohawks, Oneidas, Onondagas, Cayugas, Senecas, and Tuscaroras.

"Well, that's something to be thankful for," said Mrs. Murchison. "I lay awake for two hours last night thinking of that boy in jail, and his poor old father, seventy-nine years of age, and such a fine old man, so thoroughly respected."

"I don't know the young fellow," said Dr. Drummond, "but they say he's of good character, not over-solid, but bears a clean reputation. They're all Tories together, of course, the Ormistons."

"It's an old U.E. Loyalist family,"[1] remarked Advena. "Mr. Ormiston has one or two rather interesting Revolutionary trophies at his house out there."

"None the worse for that. None the worse for that," said Dr. Drummond.

"Old Ormiston's father," contributed the editor of the *Express*, "had a Crown grant of the whole of Moneida Reservation at one time. Government actually bought it back from him to settle the Indians there. He was a well-known Family Compact man, and fought tooth and nail for the Clergy Reserves in 'fifty."[2]

"Well, well," said Dr. Drummond, with a twinkle. "We'll hope young Ormiston is innocent, nevertheless."

"Nasty business for the Federal Bank if he is," Mr. Williams went on. "They're a pretty unpopular bunch as it is."

"Of course he's innocent," contributed Stella, with indignant eyes; "and when they prove it, what can he do to the bank for taking him up? That's what I want to know."

Her elders smiled indulgently. "A lot you know about it, kiddie," said Oliver. It was the only remark he made during the meal. Alec passed the butter assiduously, but said nothing at all. Adolescence was inarticulate in Elgin on occasions of ceremony.

"I hear they've piled up some big evidence," said Mr. Williams. "Young Ormiston's been fool enough to do some race-betting lately. Minnie, I wish you'd get Mrs. Murchison to show you how

---

1   United Empire Loyalist, a designation claimed by Ontarians whose ancestors fled the United States during their revolutionary war.

2   The original elite of Upper Canada (known by the nickname the "Family Compact") favored the establishment of the Anglican Church in Ontario and reserved one seventh of the Crown lands to support it, a system which was discontinued in 1854 after much agitation by the non-Anglican majority. "Old Ormiston's father" was associated with this conservative and colonialist group, and fought against the abolishment of "Clergy Reserves."

to pickle pears. Of course," he added, "they're keeping it up their sleeve."

"It's a hard place to keep evidence," said Lorne Murchison at last, with a smile which seemed to throw light on the matter. They had all been waiting, more or less consciously, for what Lorne would have to say.

"Lorne, you've got it!" divined his mother instantly.

"Got what, Mother?"

"The case! I've suspected it from the minute the subject was mentioned! That case came in to-day!"

"And you sitting there like a bump on a log, and never telling us!" exclaimed Stella, with reproach.

"Stella, you have a great deal too much to say," replied her brother. "Suppose you try sitting like a bump on a log. We won't complain. Yes, the Squire seems to have made up his mind about the defence, and my seniors haven't done much else to-day."

"Rawlins saw him hitched up in front of your place for about two hours this morning," said Mr. Williams. "I told him I thought that was good enough, but we didn't say anything, Rawlins having heard it was to be Flynn from Toronto. And I hadn't forgotten the Grand Trunk case we put down to you last week without exactly askin'. Your old man was as mad as a hornet —wanted to stop his subscription; Rawlins had no end of a time to get round him. Little things like that will creep in when you've got to trust to one man to run the whole local show. But I didn't want the *Mercury* to have another horse on us."

"Do you think you'll get a look in, Lorne?" asked Dr. Harry.

"Oh, not a chance of it. The old man's as keen as a razor on the case, and you'd think Warner never had one before! If I get a bit of grubbing to do, under supervision, they'll consider I ought to be pleased." It was the sunniest possible tone of grumbling; it enlisted your sympathy by its very acknowledgement that it had not a leg to stand on.

"They're pretty wild about it out Moneida way," said Dr. Harry. "My father says the township would put down the bail three times over."

"They swear by the Squire out there," said Mr. Horace Williams, liberally applying his napkin to his moustache. "He treated some of them more than square when the fall wheat failed three years running, about ten years back; do you remember, Mr. Murchison? Lent them money at about half the bank rate, and wasn't in an awful sweat about getting it in at that either."

"And wasn't there something about his rebuilding the school-house at his own expense not so long ago?" asked Dr. Drummond.

"Just what he did. I wanted to send Rawlins out and make a story of it—we'd have given it a column, with full heads; but the old man didn't like it. It's hard to know what some people will like. But it was my own foolishness for asking. A thing like that is public property."

"There's a good deal of feeling," said Lorne. "So much that I understand the bank is moving for change of venue."

"I hope they won't get it," said Dr. Drummond sharply. "A strong local feeling is valuable evidence in a case like this. I don't half approve this notion that a community can't manage its own justice when it happens to take an interest in the case. I've no more acquaintance with the Squire than 'How d'ye do?' and I don't know his son from Adam; but I'd serve on the jury to-morrow if the Crown asked it, and there's many more like me."

Mr. Williams, who had made a brief note on his shirt cuff, restored his pencil to his waistcoat pocket. "I shall oppose a change of venue," said he.

FIVE

It was confidently expected by the Murchison family that when Stella was old enough she would be a good deal in society. Stella, without doubt, was well equipped for society; she had exactly those qualities which appealed to it in Elgin, among which I will mention two—the quality of being able to suggest that she was quite as good as anybody without saying so, and the even more important quality of not being any better. Other things being equal—those common worldly standards that prevailed in Elgin as well as anywhere else in their degree—other things being equal, this second simple quality was perhaps the most important of all. Mr. and Mrs. Murchison made no claim and small attempt upon society. One doubts whether, with children coming fast and hard times long at the door, they gave the subject much consideration; but if they did, it is highly unlikely to have occurred to them that they were too good for their environment. Yet in a manner they were. It was a matter of quality, of spiritual and mental fabric; they were hardly aware that they had it, but it marked them with a difference, and a difference is the one thing a small community, accustomed comfortably to scan its own intelligible averages, will not tolerate. The unusual may take on an exaggeration of these; an excess of money, an excess of piety, is understood; but idiosyncrasy susceptible to no common translation is regarded with the hostility earned by the white crow, modified, among law-abiding humans, into tacit repudiation. It is a sound enough social principle to distrust that which is not understood, like the strain of temperament inarticulate but vaguely manifest in the Murchisons. Such a strain may any day produce an eccentric or a genius, emancipated from the common interests, possibly inimical to the general good; and when, later on, your genius takes flight or your eccentric sells all that he has and gives it to the poor, his fellow townsmen exchange shrewd nods before the vindicating fact.

Nobody knew it at all in Elgin, but this was the Murchisons' case. They had produced nothing abnormal, but they had to prove that they weren't going to, and Stella was the last and most convincing demonstration. Advena, bookish and unconventional, was regarded with dubiety. She was out of the type; she had queer satisfactions and enthusiasms. Once as a little girl she had taken a papoose from a drunken squaw and brought it home for her mother to adopt. Mrs. Murchison's reception of the suggested duty may be imagined, also the comments of acquaintances—a trick like that! The inevitable hour arrived when she should be instructed on the piano, and the second time the music teacher came her pupil was discovered on the roof of the house, with the ladder drawn up after her. She did not wish to learn the piano, and from that point of vantage informed her family that it was a waste of money. She would hide in the hayloft with a novel; she would be off by herself in a canoe at six o'clock in the morning; she would go for walks in the rain of windy October twilights and be met kicking the wet leaves along in front of her "in a dream." No one could dream with impunity in Elgin, except in bed. Mothers of daughters sympathized in good set terms with Mrs. Murchison. "If that girl were mine—" they would say, and leave you with a stimulated notion of the value of corporal punishment. When she took to passing examinations and teaching, Elgin considered that her parents ought to be thankful in the probability that she had escaped some dramatic end. But her occupation further removed her from intercourse with the town's more exclusive circles: she had taken a definite line, and she pursued it, preoccupied. If she was a brand snatched from the burning, she sent up a little curl of reflection in a safe place, where she was not further interrupted.

Abby, inheriting all these prejudices, had nevertheless not done so badly; she had taken no time at all to establish herself; she had almost immediately married. In the social estimates of Elgin the Johnsons were "nice people," Dr. Henry was a fine old figure in the town, and Abby's chances were good enough. At all events, when she opened her doors as a bride, receiving for three afternoons in her wedding dress, everybody had "called." It was very distinctly understood, of course, that this was a civility that need not lead to anything whatever, a kind of bowing recognition, to be formally returned and quite possibly to end there. With Abby, in a good many cases, it hadn't ended there; she was doing very well, and as she often said with private satisfaction, if she went out anywhere she was just as likely as not to meet her brothers. Elgin society, shaping itself, I suppose, to ultimate increase and prosperity, had this peculiarity, that the females of a family, in general acceptance, were apt to lag far behind the males. Alec and Oliver enjoyed a good deal of popularity, and it was Stella's boast that if Lorne didn't go out much it needn't be supposed he wasn't asked. It was an accepted state of things in Elgin that young men might be invited without their sisters, implying an imperturbability greater than London's, since London may not be aware of the existence of sisters, while Elgin knew all sorts of more interesting things about them. The young men were more desirable than the young women; they forged ahead, carrying the family fortunes, and the "nicest" of them were the young men in the banks. Others might be more substantial, but there was an allure about a young man in a bank as difficult to define as to resist. To say of a certain party-giver that she had "about every bank clerk in town" was to announce the success of her entertainment in ultimate terms. These things are not always penetrable, but no doubt his gentlemanly form of labour and its abridgement in the afternoons, when other young men toiled on till the stroke of six, had something to do with this apotheosis of the bank clerk, as well as his invariable taste in tailoring, and the fact that some local family influence was probably represented in his appointment. Privilege has always its last little stronghold, and it still operates to admiration on the office stools of minor finance in towns like Elgin. At all events, the sprouting tellers and cashiers held unquestioned sway—young doctors and lawyers simply didn't think of competing; and since this sort of thing carries its own penalty, the designation which they shared with so many distinguished persons in history became a byword on the lips of envious persons and small boys, by which they wished to express effeminacy and the substantive of the "stuck-up." "D'ye take me fur a bank clurk?" was a form of repudiation among corner loafers as forcible as it was unjustifiable.

I seem to have embarked, by way of getting to the Milburns' party—there is a party at the Milburns and some of us are going—upon an analysis of social principles in Elgin, an adventure of difficulty, as I have once or twice hinted, but one from which I cannot well extricate myself without at least leaving a clue or two more for the use of the curious. No doubt these rules had their nucleus in the half-dozen families, among whom we may count the shadowy Plummers, who took upon themselves for Fox County, by the King's pleasure, the administration of justice, the practice of medicine and of the law, and the performance of the charges of the Church of England a long time ago. Such persons would bring their lines of demarcation with them, and in their new *milieu* of backwoods settlers and small traders would find no difficulty in drawing them again. But it was a very long time ago. The little knot of gentry-folk soon found the limitations of their new conditions; years went by in decades, aggrandizing none of them. They took, perforce, to the ways of the country, and soon nobody kept a groom but the doctor, and nobody dined late but the Judge. There came a time when the Sheriff's whist club and the Archdeacon's port became a tradition to the oldest inhabitant. Trade flourished, education improved, politics changed. Her Majesty removed her troops—the Dominion wouldn't pay, a poor-spirited business—and a bulwark went with the regiment. The original dignified group broke, dissolved, scattered. Prosperous traders foreclosed them, the spirit of the times defeated them, young Liberals succeeded them in office. Their grandsons married the daughters of well-to-do persons who came from the north of Ireland, the east of Scotland, and the Lord knows where. It was a sorry tale of disintegration with a cheerful sequel of rebuilding, leading to a little unavoidable confusion as the edifice went up. Any process of blending implies confusion to begin with; we are here at the making of a nation.

This large consideration must dispose of small anomalies, such as the acceptance, without cant, of certain forms of the shop, euphemized as the store,[1] but containing the same old vertebral counter. Not all forms. Dry goods were held in respect and chemists in comparative esteem; house furnishings and hardware made an appreciable claim, and quite a leading family was occupied with seed grains. Groceries, on the other hand, were harder to swallow, possibly on account of the apron, though the grocer's apron, being of linen, had several degrees more consideration than the shoemaker's, which was of leather; smaller trades made smaller pretensions; Mrs. Milburn could tell you where to draw the line. They were all hard-working folk together, but they had their little prejudices; the dentist was known as "Doc," but he was not considered quite on a medical level; it was doubtful whether you bowed to the piano-tuner, and quite a curious and unreasonable contempt was bound up in the word "veterinary." Anything "wholesale" or manufacturing stood, of course, on its own feet; there was nothing ridiculous in molasses, nothing objectionable in a tannery, nothing amusing in soap. Such airs and graces were far from Elgin, too fundamentally occupied with the amount of capital invested, and too profoundly aware how hard it was to come by. The valuable part of it all was a certain bright freedom, and this was of the essence. Trade was a decent communal way of making a living, rooted in independence and the general need; it had none of the meaner aspects. Your bow was negligible to the piano-tuner, and everything veterinary held up its head. And all this again qualified, as everywhere, by the presence or absence of the social faculty, that magnetic capacity for coming, as Mrs. Murchison would say, "to the fore," which makes little of disadvantages that might seem insuperable, and, in default, renders null and void the most unquestionable claims. Any one would think of the Delarues. Mr. Delarue had in the dim past married his milliner, yet the Delarues were now very much indeed to the fore. And, on the other hand, the Leverets of the saw mills, rich and benevolent; the Leverets were not in society simply, if you analysed it, because they did not appear to expect to be in it. Certainly it was well not to be too modest; assuredly, as Mrs. Murchison said, you put your own ticket on, though that dear soul never marked herself in very plain figures; not knowing, perhaps, for one thing, quite how much she was worth. On the other hand, "Scarce of company, welcome trumpery," Mrs. Murchison always

---

1   "Shop" is British usage; "store" is Canadian.

emphatically declared to be no part of her social philosophy. The upshot was that the Murchisons were confined to a few old friends and looked, as we know, half humorously, half ironically, for more brilliant excursions, to Stella and "the boys."

It was only, however, the pleasure of Mr. Lorne Murchison's company that was requested at the Milburns' dance. Almost alone among those who had slipped into wider and more promiscuous circles with the widening of the stream, the Milburns had made something like an effort to hold out. The resisting power was not thought to reside in Mr. Milburn, who was personally aware of no special ground for it, but in Mrs. Milburn and her sister, Miss Filkin, who seemed to have inherited the strongest ideas, in the phrase of the place, about keeping themselves *to* themselves. A strain of this kind is sometimes constant, even so far from the fountain head, with its pleasing proof that such views were once the most general and the most sacred defence of middle-class firesides, and that Thackeray had, after all, a good deal to excuse him. Crossing the Atlantic they doubtless suffered some dilution; but all that was possible to conserve them under very adverse conditions Mrs. Milburn and Miss Filkin made it their duty to do. Nor were these ideas opposed, contested, or much traversed in Elgin. It was recognized that there was "something about" Mrs. Milburn and her sister—vaguely felt that you did not come upon that thinness of nostril, and slope of shoulder, and set of elbow at every corner. They must have got it somewhere. A Filkin tradition prevailed, said to have originated in Nova Scotia: the Filkins never had been accessible, but if they wanted to keep to themselves, let them. In this respect Dora Milburn, the only child, was said to be her mother's own daughter. The shoulders, at all events, testified to it; and the young lady had been taught to speak, like Mrs. Milburn, with what was known as an "English accent." The accent in general use in Elgin was borrowed—let us hope temporarily—from the other side of the line. It suffered local modifications and exaggerations, but it was clearly an American product. The English accent was thought affected, especially the broad "a." The time may come when Elgin will be at considerable pains to teach itself the broad "a," but that is in the embroidery of the future, and in no way modifies the criticism of Dora Milburn.

Lorne Murchison, however, was invited to the dance. The invitation reached him through the post: coming home from office early on Saturday he produced it from his pocket. Mrs. Murchison and Abby sat on the verandah enjoying the Indian summer afternoon; the horse-chestnuts dropped crashing among the fallen leaves, the roadside maples blazed, the quiet streets ran into smoky purple, and one belated robin hopped about the lawn. Mrs. Murchison had just remarked that she didn't know why, at this time of year, you always felt as if you were waiting for something.

"Well, I hope you feel honoured," remarked Abby. Not one of them would have thought that Lorne should feel especially honoured; but the insincerity was so obvious that it didn't matter. Mrs. Murchison, cocking her head to read the card, tried hard not to look pleased.

"'Mrs. Milburn. At Home,'" she read. "'Dancing.' Well, she might *be* at home dancing, for all me! Why couldn't she just write you a little friendly note, or let Dora do it? It's that Ormiston case," she went on shrewdly. "They know you're taking a lot of trouble about it. And the least they could do, too."

Lorne sat down on the edge of the verandah with his hands in his trousers pockets, and stuck his long legs out in front of him. "Oh, I don't know," he said. "They have the name of being nifty, but I haven't got anything against the Milburns."

"Name!" ejaculated Mrs. Murchison. "How long ago was it the Episcopalians began that sewing circle business for the destitute clergy of Saskatchewan?"

"Mother!" put in Abby, with deprecation.

"Well, I won't be certain about the clergy, but I tell you it had to do with Saskatchewan, for that I remember! And anyhow, the first meeting was held at the Milburns'—members lent their drawing-rooms. Well, Mrs. Leveret and Mrs. Delarue went to the meeting—they were very thick just then, the Leverets and the Delarues. They were so pleased to be going that they got there about five minutes too soon, and they were the first to come. Well, they rang the bell and in they went. The girl showed them into the front drawing-room and asked them to sit down. And there in the back drawing-room sat Mrs. Milburn and Miss Filkin, *and never spoke to them!* Their own denomination, mind you, too! And there they might have been sitting still if Mrs. Leveret hadn't had the spirit to get up and march out. No, thank you. No Milburns for me."

Lorne watched his mother with twinkling eyes till she finished.

"Well, mother, after that, if it was going to be a sewing circle I think I'd send an excuse," he said, "but maybe they won't be so mean at a dance."

SIX

Octavius Milburn would not, I think, have objected to being considered, with relation to his own line in life, a representative man.[1] He would have been wary to claim it, but if the stranger had arrived unaided at this view of him, he would have been inclined to think well of the stranger's power of induction. That is what he was—a man of averages, balances, the safe level, no more disposed to an extravagant opinion than to wear one side whisker longer than the other. You would take him any day, especially on Sunday in a silk hat, for the correct medium: by his careful walk with the spring in it, his shrewd glance with the caution in it, his look of being prepared to account for himself, categorically, from head to foot. He was fond of explaining, in connection with an offer once made him to embark his capital in Chicago, that he preferred a fair living under his own flag to a fortune under the Stars and Stripes. There we have the turn of his mind, convertible into the language of book-keeping, a balance struck, with a profit on the side of the flag, the patriotic equivalent in good sound terms of dollars and cents. With this position understood, he was prepared to take you up on any point of comparison between the status and privileges of a subject and a citizen—the political *morale* of a monarchy and a republic—the advantage of life on this and the other side of the line. There was nothing he liked better to expatiate upon, with that valuable proof of his own sincerity always at hand for reference and illustration. His ideal was life in a practical, go-ahead, self-governing colony, far enough from England actually to be disabused of her inherited anachronisms and make your own tariff, near enough politically to keep your securities up by virtue of her protection. He was extremely satisfied with his own country; one saw in his talk the phenomenon of patriotism in double bloom, flower within flower. I have mentioned his side whiskers: he preserved that facial decoration of the Prince Consort;[2] and the large steel engraving that represents Queen Victoria in a flowing habit and the Prince in a double-breasted frock coat and a stock, on horseback, hung over the

---

1 A reference to the term "representative man" as used by Matthew Arnold (1833-88) in *Culture and Anarchy* (1869), for a man who illustrates in his person both the virtues and the defects of his class.
2 Prince Albert, husband of Queen Victoria, wore long sidewhiskers (sideburns). He died in 1861, so this style would be old-fashioned in 1904.

mantelpiece in his drawing-room. If the outer patriotism was a little vague, the inner had vigour enough. Canada was a great place. Mr. Milburn had been born in the country, and had never "gone over" to England; Canada was good enough for him. He was born, one might say, in the manufacturing interest, and inherited the complacent and Conservative political views of a tenderly-nourished industry.[1] Mr. Milburn was of those who were building up the country; with sufficient protection he was prepared to go on doing it long and loyally; meanwhile he admired the structure from all points of view. As President of the Elgin Chamber of Commerce, he was enabled once a year to produce no end of gratifying figures; he was fond of wearing on such occasions the national emblem in a little enamelled maple leaf; and his portrait and biography occupied a full page in a sumptuous work entitled *Canadians of To-Day*, sold by subscription, wherein he was described as the "Father of the Elgin Boiler."

Mr. and Mrs. Milburn were in the drawing-room to receive their young guests, a circumstance which alone imparted a distinction to the entertainment. At such parties the appearance of the heads of the house was by no means invariable; frequently they went to bed. The simple explanation was that the young people could stand late hours and be none the worse next day; their elders had to be more careful if they wanted to get down to business. Moreover, as in all new societies, between the older and the younger generation there was a great gulf fixed, across which intercourse was difficult. The sons and daughters, born to different circumstances, evolved their own conventions, the old people used the ways and manners of narrower days; one paralysed the other. It might be gathered from the slight tone of patronage in the address of youth to age that the advantage lay with the former; but polite conversation, at best, was sustained with discomfort. Such considerations, however, were far from operating with the Milburns. Mrs. Milburn would have said that they were characteristic of quite a different class of people; and so they were.

No one would have supposed, from the way in which the family disposed itself in the drawing-room, that Miss Filkin had only just finished making the claret-cup, or that Dora had been cutting

---

1   Mr. Milburn's manufacturing business is "nourished" by the Conservative Party policy of high tariffs on imported manufactured goods (instituted by John A. Macdonald as part of the National Policy, or NP, in 1879).

sandwiches till the last minute, or that Mrs. Milburn had been obliged to have a distinct understanding with the maid—Mrs. Milburn's servants were all "maids," even the charwoman, who had buried three husbands—on the subject of wearing a cap when she answered the door. Mrs. Milburn sat on a chair she had worked herself, occupied with something in the new stitch, Dora performed lightly at the piano, Miss Filkin dipped into *Selections from the Poets of the Century*, placed as remotely as possible from the others; Mr. Milburn, with his legs crossed, turned and folded a Toronto evening paper. Mrs. Milburn had somewhat objected to the evening paper in the drawing-room. "Won't you look at a magazine, Octavius?" she said; but Mr. Milburn advanced the argument that it removed "any appearance of stiffness," and prevailed. It was impossible to imagine a group more disengaged from the absurd fuss that precedes a party among some classes of people; indeed, when Mr. Lorne Murchison arrived—like the unfortunate Mrs. Leveret and Mrs. Delarue, he was the first—they looked almost surprised to see him.

Lorne told his mother afterwards that he thought, in that embarrassing circumstance, of Mrs. Leveret and Mrs. Delarue, and they laughed consumedly together over his discomfiture; but what he felt at the moment was not the humour of the situation. To be the very first and solitary arrival is nowhere esteemed the happiest fortune, but in Elgin a kind of ridiculous humiliation attached to it, a greed for the entertainment, a painful unsophistication. A young man of Elgin would walk up and down in the snow for a quarter of an hour with the thermometer at zero to escape the ignominy of it; Lorne Murchison would have so walked. Our young man was potentially capable of not minding, by next morning he didn't mind; but immediately he was fast tied in the cobwebs of the common prescription, and he made his way to each of the points of the compass of the Milburns' drawing-room to shake hands, burning to the ears. Before he subsided into a chair near Mr. Milburn he grasped the collar of his dress coat on each side and drew it forward, a trick he had with his gown in court, a nervous and mechanical action. Dora, who continued to play, watched him over the piano with an amusement not untinged with malice. She was a tall fair girl, with several kinds of cleverness. She did her hair quite beautifully, and she had a remarkable, effective, useful reticence. Her father declared that Dora took in a great deal more than she ever gave out—an accomplishment, in Mr. Milburn's eyes, on the soundest basis.

She looked remarkably pretty and had remarkably good style, and as she proceeded with her mazurka she was thinking, "He has never been asked here before: how perfectly silly he must feel coming so early!" Presently as Lorne grew absorbed in talk and forgot his unhappy chance, she further reflected, "I don't think I've ever seen him till now in evening dress; it does make him a good figure." This went on behind a faultless coiffure and an expression almost classical in its detachment; but if Miss Milburn could have thought on a level with her looks, I, for one, would hesitate to take any liberty with her meditations.

However, the bell began to ring with the briefest intermissions, the maid in the cap to make constant journeys. She opened the door with a welcoming smile, having practically no deportment to go with the cap; human nature does not freeze readily anywhere. Dora had to leave the piano; Miss Filkin decided that when fifteen had come she would change her chair. Fifteen soon came, the young ladies mostly in light silks or muslins cut square, not low, in the neck, with half sleeves.[1] This moderation was prescribed in Elgin, where evening dress was more a matter of material than of cut, a thing in itself symbolical if it were desirable to consider social evolution here. For middle-aged ladies high necks and long sleeves were usual; and Mrs. Milburn might almost have been expected to appear thus, in a nicely-made black *broché*,[2] perhaps. It was recognized as like Mrs. Milburn, in keeping with her unbending ideas, to wear a dress cut as square as any young lady's, with just a little lace let in, of a lavender stripe. The young men were nearly all in the tailor's convention for their sex the world over, with here and there a short coat that also went to church; but there were some departures from orthodoxy in the matter of collars and ties, and where white bows were achieved, I fear none of the wearers would have dreamed of defending them from the charge of being ready-made.

It was a clear, cold January night, and everybody, as usual, walked to the party; the snow creaked and ground underfoot, one could hear the arriving steps in the drawing-room. They stamped and scraped to get rid of it in the porch, and hurried through the hall, muffled figures in overshoes, to emerge from an upstairs bedroom radiant, putting a last touch to hair or button hole,

---

1 In contrast to the fashion in London, where young ladies might appear at evening parties in low-cut gowns with no sleeves.
2 A material woven with a pattern on the surface.

smelling of the fresh winter air. Such gatherings usually consisted entirely of bachelors and maidens, with one or two exceptions
so recently yoked together that they had not yet changed the
plane of existence; married people, by general consent, left these
amusements to the unculled. They had, as I have hinted, more
serious pre-occupations, "something else to do"; nobody thought
of inviting them. Nobody, that is, but Mrs. Milburn and a few
others of her way of thinking, who saw more elegance and more
propriety in a mixture. On this occasion she had asked her own
clergyman, the pleasant-faced rector of St. Stephen's, and Mrs.
Emmett, who wore that pathetic expression of fragile wives and
mothers who have also a congregation at their skirts. Walter Winter was there, too. Mr. Winter had the distinction of having contested South Fox in the Conservative interest three times unsuc-
cessfully. Undeterred, he went on contesting things: invariably
beaten, he invariably came up smiling and ready to try again. His
imperturbability was a valuable asset; he never lost heart or
dreamed of retiring from the arena, nor did he ever cease to
impress his party as being their most useful and acceptable representative. His business history was chequered and his exact
financial equivalent uncertain, but he had tremendously the air of
a man of affairs; as the phrase went, he was full of politics, the
plain repository of deep things. He had a shrewd eye, a double
chin, and a bluff, crisp, jovial manner of talking as he lay back in
an arm-chair with his legs crossed and played with his watch
chain, an important way of nodding assent, a weighty shake of
denial. Voting on purely party lines, the town had lately rewarded
his invincible expectation by electing him Mayor, and then provided itself with unlimited entertainment by putting in a Liberal
majority on his council, the reports of the weekly sittings being
constantly considered as good as a cake-walk. South Fox, as people said, was not a healthy locality for Conservatives. Yet Walter
Winter wore a look of remarkable hardiness. He had also tremendously the air of a dark horse, the result both of natural selection
and careful cultivation. Even his political enemies took it kindly
when he "got in" for Mayor, and offered him amused congratulations. He made a personal claim on their cordiality, which was
not the least of his political resources. Nature had fitted him to
public uses; the impression overflowed the ranks of his own supporters and softened asperity among his opponents. Illustration
lies, at this moment, close to us. They had not been in the same
room a quarter of an hour before he was in deep and affectionate

converse with Lorne Murchison, whose party we know, and whose political weight was increasing, as this influence often does, with a rapidity out of proportion with his professional and general significance.

"It's a pity now," said Mr. Winter, with genial interest, "you can't get that Ormiston defence into your own hands. Very useful thing for you."

The younger man shifted a little uncomfortably in his seat. It is one thing to entertain a private vision and another to see it materialized on other lips.

"Oh, I'd like it well enough," he said, "but it's out of the question, of course. I'm too small potatoes."

"There's a lot of feeling for old Ormiston. Folks out there on the Reserve[1] don't know how to show it enough."

"They've shown it a great deal too much. We don't want to win on 'feeling,' or have it said either. And we were as near as possible having to take the case to the Hamilton Assizes."

"I guess you were—I guess you were." Mr. Winter's suddenly increased gravity expressed his appreciation of the danger. "I saw Lister of the Bank the day they heard from Toronto—rule refused. Never saw a man more put out. Seems they considered the thing as good as settled. General opinion was it would go to Hamilton, sure. Well, I don't know how you pulled it off, but it was a smart piece of work, sir."[2]

Lorne encountered Mr. Winter's frank smile with an expression of crude and rather stolid discomfort. It had a base of indignation, corrected by a concession to the common idea that most events, with an issue pendent, were the result of a smart piece of work: a kind of awkward shrug was in it. He had no desire to be unpleasant to Walter Winter—on the contrary. Nevertheless, an uncompromising line came on each side of his mouth with his reply.

"As far as I know," he said, "the application was dismissed on its demerits."

"Of course it was," said Mr. Winter good-humouredly. "You don't need to tell me that. Well, now, this looks like dancing. Miss

---

1 In Canada, lands legally defined as "reserved for Indians" are called "reserves," in contrast to the US term, "reservation."
2 Mr. Winter is suggesting that Lorne's firm did something "smart" or unethical in order to prevent young Ormiston's trial from being moved to Hamilton.

Filkin, I see, is going to oblige on the piano. Now I wonder whether I'm going to get Miss Dora to give me a waltz or not."

Chairs and tables were in effect being pushed back, and folding doors opened which disclosed another room prepared for this relaxation. Miss Filkin began to oblige vigorously on the piano, Miss Dora granted Mr. Winter's request, which he made with elaborate humour as an impudent old bachelor whom "the boys" would presently take outside and kill. Lorne watched him make it, envying him his assurance; and Miss Milburn was aware that he watched and aware that he envied. The room filled with gaiety and movement: Mr. Milburn, sidling dramatically along the wall to escape the rotatory couples, admonished Mr. Murchison to get a partner. He withdrew himself from the observation of Miss Dora and Mr. Winter, and approached a young lady on a sofa, who said "With very great pleasure." When the dance was over he re-established the young lady on the sofa, and fanned her with energy. Looking across the room, he saw that Walter Winter, seated beside Dora, was fanning himself. He thought it disgusting and, for some reason which he did not pause to explore, exactly like Winter. He had met Miss Milburn once or twice before without seeing her in any special way: here, at home, the centre of the little conventions that at once protected and revealed her, conventions bound up in the impressive figures of her mother and her aunt, she had a new interest, and all the attraction of that which is not easily come by. It is also possible that although Lorne had met her before, she had not met him; she was meeting him now for the first time, as she sat directly opposite and talked very gracefully to Walter Winter. Addressing Walter Winter, Lorne was the object of her pretty remarks. While Mr. Winter had her superficial attention, he was the bland medium which handed her on. Her consciousness was fixed on young Mr. Murchison, quite occupied with him: she could not imagine why they had not asked him long ago; he wasn't exactly "swell," but you could see he was somebody. So already she figured the potential distinction in the set of his shoulders and the carriage of his head. It might have been translated in simple terms of integrity and force by any one who looked for those things. Miss Milburn was incapable of such detail, but she saw truly enough in the mass.

Lorne, on the opposite sofa, looked at her across all the town's traditions of Milburn exclusiveness. Oddly enough, at this moment, when he might have considered that he had overcome them, they seemed to gather force, exactly in his line of vision. He had never before been so near Dora Milburn, and he had never before perceived her so remote. He had a sense of her distance beyond those few yards of carpet quite incompatible with the fact. It weighed upon him, but until she sent him a sudden unexpected smile he did not know how heavily. It was a dissipating smile; nothing remained before it. Lorne carefully restored his partner's fan, bowed before her, and went straight across the room.

SEVEN

It is determined with something like humour that communities very young should occupy themselves almost altogether with matters of grave and serious import. The vision of life at that period is no doubt unimpeded and clear; its conditions offer themselves with a certain nakedness and force, both as to this world and to that which is to come. The town of Elgin thus knew two controlling interests—the interest of politics and the interest of religion. Both are terms we must nevertheless circumscribe. Politics wore a complexion strictly local, provincial, or Dominion. The last step of France in Siam, the disputed influence of Germany in the Persian Gulf, the struggle of the Powers in China were not matters greatly talked over in Elgin; the theatre of European diplomacy had no absorbed spectators here. Nor can I claim that interest in the affairs of Great Britain was in any way extravagant.

A sentiment of affection for the reigning house certainly prevailed. It was arbitrary, rococo, unrelated to current conditions as a tradition sung down in a ballad, an anachronism of the heart, cherished through long rude lifetimes for the beauty and poetry of it—when you consider, beauty and poetry can be thought of in this. Here was no Court aiding the transmutation of the middle class, no King spending money; here were no picturesque contacts of Royalty and the people, no pageantry, no blazonry of the past, nothing to lift the heart but an occasional telegram from the monarch expressing, upon an event of public importance, a suitable emotion. Yet the common love for the throne amounted to a half-ashamed enthusiasm that burned with something like a sacred flame, and was among the things not ordinarily alluded to, because of the shyness that attaches to all feeling that cannot be justified in plain terms. A sentiment of affection for the reigning house certainly prevailed; but it was a thing by itself. The fall of a

British Government would hardly fail to excite comment, and the retirement of a Prime Minister would induce both the *Mercury* and the *Express* to publish a biographical sketch of him, considerably shorter than the leader embodying the editor's views as to who should get the electric light contract. But the Government might become the sole employer of labour in those islands, Church and school might part company for ever, landlords might be deprived of all but compassionate allowances, and, except for the degree of extravagance involved in these propositions, they would hardly be current in Elgin. The complications of England's foreign policy were less significant still. It was recognized dimly that England had a foreign policy, more or less had to have it, as they would have said in Elgin; it was part of the huge unnecessary scheme of things for which she was responsible—unnecessary from Elgin's point of view as a father's financial obligations might be to a child he had parted with at birth. It all lay outside the facts of life, far beyond the actual horizon, like the affairs of a distant relation from whom one has nothing to hope, not even personal contact, and of whose wealth and greatness one does not boast much, because of the irony involved. Information upon all these matters was duly put before Elgin every morning in the telegrams of the Toronto papers; the information came, until the other day, over cables to New York and was disseminated by American news agencies. It was, therefore, not devoid of bias; but if this was perceived it was by no means thought a matter for protesting measures, especially as they would be bound to involve expense. The injury was too vague, too remote, to be more than sturdily discounted by a mental attitude. Belief in England was in the blood, it would not yield to the temporary distortion of facts in the newspapers—at all events, it would not yield with a rush. Whether there was any chance of insidious sapping was precisely what the country was too indifferent to discover. Indifferent, apathetic, self-centred—until whenever, down the wind, across the Atlantic, came the faint far music of the call to arms. Then the old dog of war that has his kennel in every man rose and shook himself, and presently there would be a baying! The sense of kinship, lying too deep for the touch of ordinary circumstance, quickened to that; and in a moment "we" were fighting, "we" had lost or won.

Apart, however, from the extraordinary, the politics of Elgin's daily absorption were those of the town, the Province, the Dominion. Centres of small circumference yield a quick swing; the concern of the average intelligent Englishman as to the consolidation of his country's interests in the Yangtse Valley would be a languid manifestation beside that of an Elgin elector in the chances of an appropriation for a new court house. The single mind is the most fervid: Elgin had few distractions from the question of the court house or the branch line to Clayfield. The arts conspired to be absent;[1] letters resided at the nearest university city; science was imported as required, in practical improvements. There was nothing, indeed, to interfere with Elgin's attention to the immediate, the vital, the municipal: one might almost read this concentration of interest in the white dust of the rambling streets, and the shutters closed against it. Like other movements of the single mind, it had something of the ferocious, of the inflexible, of the unintelligent; but it proudly wore the character of the go-ahead, and, as Walter Winter would have pointed out to you, it had granted eleven bonuses to "capture" sound commercial concerns in six years.

In wholesome fear of mistake, one would hesitate to put church matters either before or after politics among the preoccupations of Elgin. It would be safer and more indisputable to say that nothing compared with religion but politics, and nothing compared with politics but religion. In offering this proposition also we must think of our dimensions. There is a religious fervour in Oxford, in Mecca, in Benares, and the sign for these ideas is the same; we have to apply ourselves to the interpretation. In Elgin religious fervour was not beautiful, or dramatic, or self-immolating; it was reasonable. You were perhaps your own first creditor; after that your debt was to your Maker. You discharged this obligation in a spirit of sturdy equity: if the children didn't go to Sunday school you knew the reason why. The habit of church attendance was not only a basis of respectability, but practically the only one: a person who was "never known to put his head inside a church door" could not be more severely reprobated, by Mrs. Murchison at all events. It was the normal thing, the thing which formed the backbone of life, sustaining to the serious, impressive to the light, indispensable to the rest, and the thing that was more than any of these, which you can only know when you stand in the churches among the congregations. Within its prescribed limitations it was for many the intellectual exercise, for

---

1   In an article published in *The Week*, Duncan complained "We are still an eminently unliterary people.... The Province of Ontario is one great camp of the Philistines" (30 September 1886).

more the emotional lift, and for all the unfailing distraction of the week. The repressed magnetic excitement in gatherings of familiar faces, fellow beings bound by the same convention to the same kind of behaviour, is precious in communities where the human interest is still thin and sparse. It is valuable in itself, and it produces an occasional detached sensation. There was the case, in Dr. Drummond's church, of placid-faced, saintly old Sandy MacQuhot, the epileptic. It used to be a common regret with Lorne Murchison that as sure as he was allowed to stay away from church Sandy would have a fit. That was his little boy's honesty; the elders enjoyed the fit and deprecated the disturbance.

There was a simple and definite family feeling within communions. "They come to our church" was the argument of first force whether for calling or for charity. It was impossible to feel toward a Congregationalist or an Episcopalian as you felt toward one who sang the same hymns and sat under the same admonition week by week, year in and year out, as yourself. "Wesleyans, are they?" a lady of Knox Church would remark of the newly arrived, in whom her interest was suggested. "Then let the Wesleyans look after them." A pew-holder had a distinct status; an "adherent" enjoyed friendly consideration, especially if he adhered faithfully; and stray attendants from other congregations were treated with punctilious hospitality, places being found for them in the Old Testament, as if they could hardly be expected to discover such things for themselves. The religious interest had also the strongest domestic character in quite another sense from that of the family prayers which Dr. Drummond was always enjoining. "Set your own house in order and then your own church" was a wordless working precept in Elgin. Threadbare carpet in the aisles was almost as personal a reproach as a hole under the dining-room table; and self-respect was barely possible to a congregation that sat in faded pews. The minister's gown even was the subject of scrutiny as the years went on. It was an expensive thing to buy, but an oyster supper would do it and leave something over for the organ. Which brings us to the very core and centre of these activities, their pivot, their focus, and, in a human sense, their inspiration—the minister himself.

The minister was curiously special among a people so general; he was in a manner raised in life on week-days as he was in the pulpit on Sundays. He had what one might call prestige; some form of authority still survived in his person, to which the spiritual democracy he presided over gave a humorous, voluntary

assent. He was supposed to be a person of undetermined leisure
—what was writing two sermons a week to earn your living by?—
and he was probably the more reverend, or the more revered,
from the fact that he was in the house all day. A particular importance attached to everything he said and did; he was a person
whose life answered different springs, and was sustained on quite
another principle than that of supply and demand. The province
of public criticism was his; but his people made up for the meek-
ness with which they sat under it by a generous use of the corre-
sponding privilege in private. Comments upon the minister par-
took of hardiness; it was as if the members were determined to
live up to the fact that the office-bearers could reduce his salary
if they liked. Needless to say, they never did like. Congregations
stood loyally by their pastors, and discussion was strictly intra-
mural. If the Methodists handed theirs on at the end of three
years with a breath of relief, they exhaled it among themselves;
after all, for them it was a matter of luck. The Presbyterians, as in
the case of old Mr. Jamieson of St. Andrew's, held on till death,
pulling a long upper lip: election was not a thing to be trifled with
in heaven or upon earth.

It will be imagined whether Dr. Drummond did not see in
these conditions his natural and wholesome element, whether he
did not fit exactly in. The God he loved to worship as Jehovah had
made him a beneficent despot, and given him, as it were, a commission. If the temporal power had charged him to rule an eastern province, he would have brought much the same qualities to
the task. Knox Church, Elgin, was his dominion, its moral and
material affairs his jealous interest, and its legitimate expansion
his chief pride. In "anniversary" sermons, which he always
announced the Sunday before, he seldom refrained from con-
trasting the number on the roll of church membership then and
now, with the particular increase in the year just closed. If the
increase was satisfactory, he made little comment beyond the
duty of thanksgiving—figures spoke for themselves. If it was otherwise Dr. Drummond's displeasure was not a thing he would
conceal. He would wing it eloquently on the shaft of his grief that
the harvest had been so light; but he would more than hint the
possibility that the labourers had been few. Most important
among his statistics was the number of young communicants.
Wanderers from other folds he admitted, with a not wholly satisfied eye upon their early theological training, and to persons duly
accredited from Presbyterian churches elsewhere he gave the

right hand of fellowship; but the young people of his own congregation were his chief concern always, and if a gratifying number of these had failed to "come forward" during the year, the responsibility must lie somewhere. Dr. Drummond was willing to take his own share; "the ministrations of this pulpit" would be more than suspected of having come short, and the admission would enable him to tax the rest upon parents and Bible-class teachers with searching effect. The congregation would go gloomily home to dinner, and old Sandy MacQuhot would remark to his wife, "It's hard to say why will the Doctor get himself in sic a state aboot mere numbers. We're told 'where two or three are gathered together.'[1] But the Doctor's all for a grand congregation."

Knox Church, under such auspices, could hardly fail to enlarge her borders; but Elgin enlarged hers faster. Almost before you knew where you were there spread out the district of East Elgin, all stacks of tall chimneys and rows of little houses. East Elgin was not an attractive locality; it suffered from inundation sometimes, when the river was in spring flood; it gave unresentful room to a tannery. It was the home of dubious practices at the polls, and the invariable hunting ground for domestic servants. Nevertheless, in the view of Knox Church, it could not bear a character wholly degraded; too many Presbyterians, Scotch foremen and others, had their respectable residence there. For these it was a far cry to Dr. Drummond in bad weather, and there began to be talk of hiring the East Elgin schoolhouse for Sunday exercises if suitable persons could be got to come over from Knox Church and lead them. I do not know who was found to broach the matter to Dr. Drummond; report says his relative and housekeeper, Mrs. Forsyth, who perhaps might do it under circumstances of strategical advantage. Mrs. Forsyth, or whoever it was, had her reply in the hidden terms of an equation—was it any farther for the people of East Elgin to walk to hear him preach than for him to walk to minister to the people of East Elgin, which he did quite once a week, and if so, how much? Mrs. Forsyth, or whoever it was, might eliminate the unknown quantity. It cannot be said that Dr. Drummond discouraged the project; he simply did not mention it, and as it was known to have been communicated to him, this represented effectively the policy of the closed

---

1 A quote from the Bible, Matthew 18:20.

door. He found himself even oftener in East Elgin, walking about on his pastoral errands with a fierce briskness of aspect and a sharp inquiring eye, before which one might say the proposition slunk away. Meanwhile, the Methodists, who, it seemed, could tolerate decentralization, or anything short of round dances, opened a chapel with a cheerful sociable, and popularized the practice of backsliding among those for whom the position was theologically impossible. Good Presbyterians in East Elgin began to turn into makeshift Methodists. The Doctor missed certain occupants of the gallery seats and felt the logic of circumstances. Here we must all yield, and the minister concealed his discomfiture in a masterly initiative. The matter came up again at a meeting of the church managers, brought up by Dr. Drummond, who had the satisfaction of hearing that a thing put into the Doctor's hands was already half done. In a very few weeks it was entirely done. The use of the school-house was granted, through Dr. Drummond's influence with the Board, free of charge; and to understand the triumph of this it should be taken into account that three of the trustees were Wesleyans. Services were held regularly, certain of Dr. Drummond's elders officiating; and the conventicle in the school-house speedily became known as Knox Church Mission. It grew and prospered. The first night "I to the hills will lift mine eyes"[1] went up from East Elgin on the uplifting tune that belongs to it, the strayed came flocking back.

This kind never go forth again; once they re-find the ark of the covenant[2] there they abide. In the course of time it became a question of a better one, and money was raised locally to build it. Dr. Drummond pronounced the first benediction in Knox Mission Church, and waited, well knowing human nature in its Presbyterian aspect, for the next development. It came, and not later than he anticipated, in the form of a prayer to Knox Church for help to obtain the services of a regularly ordained minister. Dr. Drummond had his guns ready: he opposed the application; where a regularly ordained minister was already at the disposal of those who chose to walk a mile and a half to hear him, the luxury of more locally consecrated services should be at the charge of the locality. He himself was willing to spend and be spent in the

---

1 A sung version of the Biblical Psalm 121, much beloved in Protestant churches.
2 In the Bible, Exodus 25, the ark is a container for the written covenant between humanity and God; metaphorically, the church.

spiritual interests of East Elgin; that was abundantly proven; what he could not comfortably tolerate was the deviation of congregational funds, the very blood of the body of belief, into other than legitimate channels. He fought for his view with all his tactician's resources, putting up one office-bearer after another to endorse it, but the matter was decided at the general yearly meeting of the congregation; and the occasion showed Knox Church in singular sympathy with its struggling offspring. Dr. Drummond, for the first time in his ministry, was defeated by his people. It was less a defeat than a defence, an unexpected rally round the corporate right to direct corporate activities; and the congregation was so anxious to wound the minister's feelings as little as possible that the grant in aid of the East Elgin Mission was embodied in a motion to increase Dr. Drummond's salary by two hundred and fifty dollars a year. The Doctor, with a wry joke, swallowed his gilded pill, but no coating could dissimulate its bitterness, and his chagrin was plain for long. The issue with which we are immediately concerned is that three months later Knox Church Mission called to minister to it the Reverend Hugh Finlay, a young man from Dumfriesshire and not long out. Dr. Drummond had known beforehand what their choice would be. He had brought Mr. Finlay to occupy Knox Church pulpit during his last July and August vacation, and Mrs. Forsyth had reported that such midsummer congregations she had simply never worshipped with. Mrs. Forsyth was an excellent hand at pressed tongue and a wonder at knitted counterpanes, but she had not acquired tact and never would.

EIGHT

The suggestion that the Reverend Hugh Finlay preached from the pulpit of Knox Church "better sermons" than its permanent occupant, would have been justly considered absurd, and nobody pronounced it. The church was full, as Mrs. Forsyth observed, on these occasions; but there were many other ways of accounting for that. The Murchisons, as a family, would have been the last to make such an admission. The regular attendance might have been, as much as anything, out of deference to the wishes of the Doctor himself, who invariably and sternly hoped, in his last sermon, that no stranger occupying his place would have to preach to empty pews. He was thinking, of course, of old Mr. Jamieson, with whom he occasionally exchanged, and whose effect on the attendance had not failed to reach him. With regard to Mr. Jamieson he was compelled, in the end, to resort to tactics: he omitted to announce the Sunday before that his venerable neighbour would preach, and the congregation, outwitted, had no resource but to sustain the beard-wagging old gentleman through seventhly to the finish. There came a time when the dear human Doctor also omitted to announce that Mr. Finlay would preach, but for other reasons. Meanwhile, as Mrs. Forsyth said, he had no difficulty in conjuring a vacation congregation for his young substitute. They came trooping, old and young. Mr. and Mrs. Murchison would survey their creditable family rank with a secret compunction, remembering its invariable gaps at other times, and then resolutely turn to the praise of God with the reflection that one means to righteousness was as blessed as another. They themselves never missed a Sunday, and as seldom failed to remark on the way back that it was all very interesting, but Mr. Finlay couldn't drive it home like the Doctor. There were times, sparse and special occasions, when the Doctor himself made one of the congregation. Then he would lean back luxuriously in the corner of his own pew, his wiry little form half lost in the upholstery, his arms folded, his knees crossed, his face all humorous indulgence; yes, humorous. At the announcement of the text a twinkle would lodge in the shrewd grey eyes and a smile but half suppressed would settle about the corners of the flexible mouth: he knew what the young fellow there would be at. And as the young fellow proceeded, his points would be weighed to the accompaniment of the Doctor's pendent foot, which moved perpetually, judiciously; while the smile sometimes deepened, sometimes lapsed, since there were moments when any young fellow had to be taken seriously. It was an attitude which only the Doctor was privileged to adopt thus outwardly; but in private it was imitated all up and down the aisles, where responsible heads of families sat considering the quality of the manna that was offered them. When it fell from the lips of Mr. Finlay the verdict was, upon the whole, very favourable, as long as there was no question of comparison with the Doctor.

There could be, indeed, very little question of such comparison. There was a generation between them and a school, and to that you had to add every set and cast of mind and body that can make men different. Dr. Drummond, in faith and practice, moved with precision along formal and implicit lines; his orbit was established, and his operation within it as unquestionable as the simplest exhibit of nature. He took in a wonderful degree the stamp of the teaching of his adolescent period; not a line was missing nor a precept; nor was the mould defaced by a single wavering tendency of later date. Religious doctrine was to him a thing for ever accomplished, to be accepted or rejected as a whole. He taught eternal punishment and retribution, reconciling both with Divine love and mercy; he liked to defeat the infidel with the crashing question, "Who then was the architect of the Universe?" The celebrated among such persons he pursued to their death-beds; Voltaire[1] and Rousseau[2] owed their reputation, with many persons in Knox Church, to their last moments and to Dr. Drummond. He had a triumphant invective which drew the mind from chasms in logic, and a tender sense of poetic beauty which drew it, when he quoted great lines, from everything else. He loved the euphony of the Old Testament; his sonorous delivery would lift a chapter from Isaiah to the height of ritual, and every Psalm he read was a Magnificat[3] whether he would or no. The warrior in him was happy among the Princes of Issachar;[4] and the parallels he would find for modern events in the annals of Judah and of Israel[5] were astounding. Yet he kept a sharp eye upon the daily paper, and his reference to current events would often give his listeners an audacious sense of up-to-dateness which might have been easily discounted by the argument they illustrated. The survivors of a convulsion of nature, for instance, might have learned from his lips the cause and kind of their disaster traced back forcibly to local acquiescence in iniquity, and drawn unflinchingly from the text, "Vengeance is mine; I will repay, saith the Lord."[6] The militant history of his Church was a passion with him; if ever he had to countenance canonization he

---

1   Pen name of Francois Marie Arouet (1694-1778), French writer and philosopher, who argued against traditional religious beliefs and lived openly with a woman to whom he was not married.
2   Jean-Jacques Rousseau (1712-78), French writer and philosopher, whose ideas about political and personal liberty inspired the French Revolutionaries.
3   The hymn of praise spoken by Mary, the mother of Jesus, found in the Bible at Luke 1:46-55, regarded as one of the most beautiful religious poems in Christianity and often set to music.
4   See Judges 5 in the Bible.
5   I.e., the Old Testament of the Bible.
6   See Romans 12:19 in the Bible.

would have led off with Jenny Geddes.[1] "A tremendous Presbyterian" they called him in the town. To hear him give out a single
psalm, and sing it with his people, would convince anybody of
that. There was a choir, of course, but to the front pews, at all
events, Dr. Drummond's leading was more important than the
choir's. It was a note of dauntless vigour, and it was plain by the
regular forward jerk of his surpliced shoulder that his foot was
keeping time:

> Where the assemblies of the just
> And congregations are.[2]

You could not help admiring, and you could not help respect-
ing; you were compelled by his natural force and his unqualified
conviction, his tireless energy and his sterling sort.

It is possible to understand, however, that after sitting for
twenty-five years under direction so unfailing and so uncompromising, the congregation of Knox Church might turn with a
moderate curiosity to the spiritual indications of the Reverend
Hugh Finlay. He was a passionate romantic, and his body had
shot up into a fitting temple for such an inhabitant as his soul. He
was a great long fellow, with a shock of black hair and deep
dreams in his eyes; his head was what people called a type, a type
I suppose of the simple motive and the noble intention, the
detached point of view and the somewhat indifferent attitude to
material things, as it may be humanly featured anywhere. His face
bore a confusion of ideals; he had the brow of a Covenanter and
the mouth of Adonais,[3] the flame of religious ardour in his eyes
and the composure of perceived philosophy on his lips. He was
fettered by an impenetrable shyness; it was in the pulpit alone
that he could expand, and then only upon written lines, with

---

1 In 1637 Jenny Geddes (1600-60) hurled a stool at St. Giles Church in
  Edinburgh to protest the introduction of an English prayer book. She is
  a hero to Dr. Drummond because she epitomizes the struggle of the
  Presbyterian Church to remain independent of English authority and
  true to its spiritual beliefs.
2 Two lines from Psalm 111 in the Scottish Metrical Psalter of 1650 (used
  in the Presbyterian Church).
3 A Covenanter was a defender of the independence of Scotland and the
  Presbyterian Church against England during the wars of the seventeenth
  century; Adonais is the title character in a poem by Percy Bysshe Shelley.

hardly a gesture, and the most perfunctory glances, at conscientious intervals, towards his hearers. A poor creature, indeed, in this respect, Dr. Drummond thought him—Dr. Drummond, who wore an untrammeled surplice which filled like an agitated sail in his quick tacks from right to left. "The man loses half his points," said Dr. Drummond. I doubt whether he did, people followed so closely, though Sandy MacQuhot was of the general opinion when he said that it would do nobody any harm if Mr. Finlay would lift his head oftener from the book.

Advena Murchison thought him the probable antitype of an Oxford don.[1] She had never seen an Oxford don, but Mr. Finlay wore the characteristics these schoolmen were dressed in by novelists; and Advena noted with delight the ingenuity of fate in casting such a person into the pulpit of the Presbyterian Church in a young country. She had her perception of comedy in life; till Finlay came she had found nothing so interesting. With his arrival, however, other preoccupations fell into their proper places.

Finlay, indeed, it may be confessed at once, he, and not his message, was her engrossment from the beginning. The message she took with reverent gentleness; but her passionate interest was for the nature upon which it travelled, and never for the briefest instant did she confuse these emotions. Those who write, we are told, transcribe themselves in spite of themselves; it is more true of those who preach, for they are also candid by profession, and when they are not there is the eye and the voice to help to betray them. Hugh Finlay, in the pulpit, made himself manifest in all the things that matter to Advena Murchison in the pew; and from the pew to the pulpit her love went back with certainty, clear in its authority and worshipping the ground of its justification. When she bowed her head it was he whom she heard in the language of his invocations; his doctrine rode, for her, on a spirit of wide and sweet philosophy; in his contemplation of the Deity she saw the man. He had those lips at once mobile, governed and patient, upon which genius chooses oftenest to rest. As to this, Advena's convictions were so private as to be hidden from herself; she never admitted that she thought Finlay had it, and in the supreme difficulty of proving anything else we may wisely accept her view. But he had something, the subtle Celt; he had horizons, lifted

---

1   A head, fellow, or tutor appointed at one of the colleges of Oxford University in England.

lines beyond the common vision, and an eye rapt and a heart intrepid; and though for a long time he was unconscious of it, he must have adventured there with a happier confidence because of her companionship.

From the first Advena knew no faltering or fluttering, none of the baser nervous betrayals. It was all one great delight to her, her discovery and her knowledge and her love of him. It came to her almost in a logical development; it found her grave, calm, and receptive. She had even a private formula of gratitude that the thing which happened to everybody, and happened to so many people irrelevantly, should arrive with her in such a glorious, defensible, demonstrable sequence. Toward him it gave her a kind of glad secret advantage; he was loved and he was unaware. She watched his academic awkwardness in church with the inward tender smile of the eternal habile feminine, and when they met she could have laughed and wept over his straitened sentences and his difficult manner, knowing how little significant they were. With his eyes upon her and his words offered to her intelligence, she found herself treating his shy formality as the convention it was, a kind of make-believe which she would politely and kindly play up to until he should happily forget it and they could enter upon simpler relations. She had to play up to it for a long time, but her love made her wonderfully clever and patient; and of course the day came when she had her reward. Knowing him as she did, she remembered the day and the difference it made.

It was toward the end of an afternoon in early April; the discoloured snow still lay huddled in the bleaker fence corners. Wide puddles stood along the roadsides, reflecting the twigs and branches of the naked maples; last year's leaves were thick and wet underfoot, and a soft damp wind was blowing. Advena was on her way home and Finlay overtook her. He passed her at first, with a hurried silent lifting of his hat; then perhaps the deserted street gave a suggestion of unfriendliness to his act, or some freshness in her voice stayed him. At all events, he waited and joined her, with a word or two about their going in the same direction; and they walked along together. He offered her his companionship, but he had nothing to say; the silence in which they pursued their way was no doubt to him just the embarrassing condition he usually had to contend with. To her it seemed pregnant, auspicious; it drew something from the low grey lights of the wet spring afternoon and the unbound heart-lifting wind; she had a passionate prevision that the steps they took together would lead somehow to freedom. They went on in that strange bound way, and the day drew away from them till they turned a sudden corner, when it lay all along the yellow sky across the river, behind a fringe of winter woods, stayed in the moment of its retreat on the edge of the unvexed landscape. They stopped involuntarily to look, and she saw a smile come up from some depth in him.

"Ah, well," he said, as if to himself, "it's something to be in a country where the sun still goes down with a thought of the primeval."

"I think I prefer the sophistication of chimney-pots," she replied. "I've always longed to see a sunset in London, with the fog breaking over Westminster."

"Then you don't care about them for themselves, sunsets?" he asked, with the simplest absence of mind.

> I never yet could see the sun go down,
>   But I was angry in my heart,[1]

she said, and this time he looked at her.

"How does it go on?" he said.

"Oh, I don't know. Only those two lines stay with me. I feel it that way, too. It's the seal upon an act of violence, isn't it, a sunset? Something taken from us against our will. It's a hateful reminder, in the midst of our delightful volitions, of how arbitrary every condition of life is."

"The conditions of business are always arbitrary. Life is a business—we have to work at ourselves till it is over. So much cut off and ended it is," he said, glancing at the sky again. "If space is the area of life and time is its opportunity, there goes a measure of opportunity."

"I wonder," said Advena, "where it goes?"

"Into the void behind time?" he suggested, smiling straight at her.

"Into the texture of the future," she answered, smiling back.

"We might bring it to bear very intelligently on the future, at any rate," he returned. "The world is wrapped in destiny, and but revolves to roll it out."

---

1 From the poem, "The Two Highwaymen," by Wilfrid Scawen Blunt (1840-1922). The metaphorical highwaymen of the poem are Time and Death.

"I don't remember that," she said curiously.

"No, you couldn't," he laughed outright. "I haven't thought it good enough to publish."

"And it isn't the sort of thing," she ventured gaily, "you could put in a sermon."

"No, it isn't." They came to a corner of the street which led to Mr. Finlay's boarding-house. It stretched narrowly to the north and there was a good deal more snow on each side of it. They lingered together for a moment talking, seizing the new joy in it, which was simply the joy of his sudden liberation with her, consciously pushing away the moment of parting; and Finlay's eyes rested once again on the evening sky beyond the river.

"I believe you are right, and I am a moralizer," he said. "There *is* pain over there. One thinks a sunset beautiful and impressive, but one doesn't look at it long."

Then they separated, and he took the road to the north, which was still snowbound, while she went on into the chilly yellow west, with the odd sweet illusion that a summer day was dawning.

NINE

The office of Messrs. Fulke, Warner, & Murchison was in Market Street, exactly over Scott's drug store. Scott, with his globular blue and red and green vessels in the window and his soda-water fountain inside, was on the ground floor; the passage leading upstairs separated him from Mickie, boots and shoes; and beyond Mickie, Elgin's leading tobacconist shared his place of business with a barber. The last two contributed most to the gaiety of Market Street: the barber with the ribanded pole, which stuck out at an angle; the tobacconist with a nobly-featured squaw in chocolate effigy,[1] who held her draperies under her chin with one hand and outstretched a packet of cigars with the other.

The passage staircase between Scott's and Mickie's had a hardened look, and bore witness to the habit of expectoration; ladies, going up to Dr. Simmons, held their skirts up and the corners of their mouths down. Dr. Simmons was the dentist: you turned to the right. The passage itself turned to the left, and after

---

1 Wooden "cigar store Indian" placed outside the door of a tobacco shop as a form of advertising.

passing two doors bearing the law firm's designation in black letters on ground glass, it conducted you with abruptness to the office of a bicycle agent, and left you there. For greater emphasis the name of the firm of Messrs. Fulke, Warner, & Murchison was painted on the windows also; it could be seen from any part of the market square, which lay, with the town hall in the middle, immediately below. During four days in the week the market square was empty. Odds and ends of straw and paper blew about it; an occasional pedestrian crossed it diagonally for the short cut to the post-office; the town hall rose in the middle, and defied you to take your mind off the ugliness of municipal institutions. On the other days it was a scene of activity. Farmers' wagons, with the shafts turned in, were ranged round three sides of it; on a big day they would form into parallel lanes and cut the square into sections as well. The produce of all Fox County filled the wagons, varying agreeably as the year went round. Bags of potatoes leaned against the side-walk, apples brimmed in bushel measures, ducks dropped their twisted necks over the cart wheels; the town hall, in this play of colour, stood redeemed. The produce was mostly left to the women to sell. On the fourth side of the square loads of hay and cordwood demanded the master mind, but small matters of fruit, vegetables, and poultry submitted to feminine judgment. The men "unhitched," and went away on their own business; it was the wives you accosted, as they sat in the middle, with their knees drawn up and their skirts tucked close, vigilant in rusty bonnets, if you wished to buy. Among them circulated the housewives of Elgin, pricing and comparing and acquiring; you could see it all from Dr. Simmons' window, sitting in his chair that screwed up and down. There was a little difficulty always about getting things home; only very ordinary people carried their own marketing. Trifling articles, like eggs or radishes, might be smuggled into a brown wicker basket with covers, but it did not consort with elegance to "trapse"[1] home with anything that looked inconvenient or had legs sticking out of it. So that arrangements of mutual obligation had to be made: the good woman from whom Mrs. Jones had bought her tomatoes would take charge of the spring chickens Mrs. Jones had bought from another good woman just as soon as not, and deliver them at Mrs.

---

1   Also spelled traipse, meaning to walk about in an untidy way; a word suggesting disapproval.

Jones's residence, as under any circumstances she was "going round that way."

It was a scene of activity but not of excitement, or in any sense of joy. The matter was of too hard an importance; it made too much difference on both sides whether potatoes were twelve or fifteen cents a peck. The dealers were laconic and the buyers anxious; country neighbours exchanged the time of day, but under the pressure of affairs. Now and then a lady of Elgin stopped to gossip with another; the countrywomen looked on, curious, grim, and a little contemptuous of so much demonstration and so many words. Life on an Elgin market day was a serious presentment even when the sun shone, and at times when it rained or snowed the aesthetic seemed a wholly unjustifiable point of view. It was not misery, it was even a difficult kind of prosperity, but the margin was small and the struggle plain. Plain, too, it was that here was no enterprise of yesterday, no fresh broken ground of dramatic promise, but a narrow inheritance of the opportunity to live which generations had grasped before. There were bones in the village graveyards of Fox County to father all these sharp features; Elgin market square, indeed, was the biography of Fox County, and, in little, the history of the whole Province. The heart of it was there, the enduring heart of the new country already old in acquiescence. It was the deep root of the race in the land, twisted and unlovely, but holding the promise of all. Something like that Lorne Murchison felt about it as he stood for a moment in the passage I have mentioned and looked across the road. The spectacle never failed to cheer him; he was uniformly in gayer spirits, better satisfied with life and more consciously equal to what he had to do, on days when the square was full than on days when it was empty. This morning he had an elation of his own; it touched everything with more vivid reality. The familiar picture stirred a joy in him in tune with his private happiness; its under-note came to him with a pang as keen. The sense of kinship surged in his heart; these were his people, this his lot as well as theirs. For the first time he saw it in detachment. Till now he had regarded it with the friendly eyes of a participator who looked no further. To-day he did look further: the whole world invited his eyes, offering him a great piece of luck to look through. The opportunity was in his hand, which, if he could seize and hold, would lift and carry him on. He was as much aware of its potential significance as any one could be, and what leapt in his veins till he could have laughed aloud was the splendid conviction of resource. Already in the door of the passage he had achieved, and from that point he looked at the scene before him with an impulse of loyalty and devotion. A tenderness seized him for the farmers of Fox County, a throb of enthusiasm for the idea they represented, which had become for him suddenly moving and pictorial. At that moment his country came subjectively into his possession; great and helpless it came into his inheritance as it comes into the inheritance of every man who can take it, by deed of imagination and energy and love. He held this microcosm of it, as one might say, in his hand and looked at it ardently; then he took his way across the road.

A tall thickly-built young fellow detached himself from a group, smiling broadly at the sight of Murchison, and started to meet him.

"Hello, Lorne," he said. He had smiled all the way, anticipating the encounter. He was obviously in clothes which he did not put on every day, but the seriousness of this was counteracted by his hard felt hat, which he wore at an angle that disregarded convention.

"Hello, Elmore! You back?"

"That's about it."

"You don't say! Back to stay?"

"Far's I can see. Young Alf's made up his mind to learn the dentist business, and the old folks are backin' him; so I don't see but I've got to stop on and run the show. Father's gettin' up in years now."

"Why, yes. I suppose he must be. It's a good while since you went West. Well, what sort of a country have they got out Swan River way? Booming right along?"

"Boom nothing. I don't mean to say there's anything the matter with the country; there ain't; but you've got to get up just as early in the mornings out there as y'do anywhere, far's I noticed. An' it's a lonesome life. Now I *am* back I don't know but little old Ontario's good enough for me. 'N I hear you've taken up the law, Lorne. Y'always had a partiality for it, d'y' remember, up there to the Collegiate? I used to think it'd be fine to travel with samples,[1] those days. But you were dead gone on the law. 'N by all reports it pans out pretty well, don't it?"

The young men had taken their way among the shifting crowd

---

1 Be a sales representative.

together. Lorne Murchison, although there was something too large about him for the town's essential stamp, made by contrast as he threaded the desultory groups of country people, a type of the conventional and the formed; his companion glanced at him now and then with admiration. The values of carriage and of clothes are relative: in Fifth Avenue Lorne would have looked countrified, in Piccadilly colonial. Districts are imaginable, perhaps not in this world, where the frequenters of even those fashionable thoroughfares would attract glances of curiosity by their failure to achieve the common standard in such things. Lorne Murchison, to dismiss the matter, was well up to the standard of Elgin, though he wore his straw hat quite on the back of his head and buried both hands in his trouser pockets. His eye was full of pleasant easy familiarity with the things he saw, and ready to see larger things; it had that beam of active inquiry, curious but never amazed, that marks the man likely to expand his horizons. Meanwhile he was on capital terms with his little world, which seemed to take pleasure in hailing him by his Christian name; even morose Jim Webster, who had failed three times in groceries, said "Morning, Lorne," with a look of toleration. He moved alertly, the poise of his head was sanguine; the sun shone on him, the timidest soul came nearer to him. He and Elmore Crow, who walked beside him, had gone through the lower forms of the Elgin Collegiate Institute together, that really "public" kind of school[1] which has so much to do with reassorting the classes of a new country. The Collegiate Institute took in raw material and turned out teachers, more teachers than anything. The teachers taught, chiefly in rural districts where they could save money, and with the money they saved changed themselves into doctors, Fellows of the University, mining engineers. The Collegiate Institute was a potential melting-pot: you went in as your simple opportunities had made you; how you shaped coming out depended upon what was hidden in the core of you. You could not in any case be the same as your father before you; education in a new country is too powerful a stimulant for that, working upon material too plastic and too hypothetical; it is not yet a normal force, with an operation to be reckoned on with confidence. It is indeed the touchstone for character in a new people, for character acquired as

---

1 Publicly funded and open to all, as opposed to the British "public school," which was privately funded and exclusive. Duncan graduated from the Brantford Collegiate Institute in 1879.

apart from that inherited; it sometimes reveals surprises. Neither Lorne Murchison nor Elmore Crow illustrate this point very nearly. Lorne would have gone into the law in any case, since his father was able to send him, and Elmore would inevitably have gone back to the crops since he was early defeated by any other possibility. Nevertheless, as they walk together in my mind along the Elgin market square, the Elgin Collegiate Institute rises infallibly behind them, a directing influence and a responsible parent. Lorne was telling his great news.

"You don't say!" remarked Elmore in response to it. "Lumbago is it? Pa's subject to that too; gets an attack most springs. Mr. Fulke'll have to lay right up—it's the only thing."

"I'm afraid he will. And Warner never appeared in court in his life."

"What d'ye keep Warner for, then?"

"Oh, he does the conveyancing.[1] He's a good conveyancer, but he isn't any pleader and doesn't pretend to be. And it's too late to transfer the case; nobody could get to the bottom of it as we have in the time. So it falls on me."

"Caesar, his ghost! How d'ye feel about it, Lorne? I'd be scared green. Y'don't *talk* nervous. Now I bet you get there with both feet."

"I hope to get there," the young lawyer answered; and as he spoke a concentration came into his face which drove the elation and everything else that was boyish out of it. "It's bigger business than I could have expected for another five years. I'm sorry for the old man, though—*he's* nervous, if you like. They can hardly keep him in bed. Isn't that somebody beckoning to you?"

Elmore looked everywhere except in the right direction among the carts. If you had been "to the Collegiate," relatives among the carts selling squashes were embarrassing.

"There," his companion indicated.

"It's mother," replied Mr. Crow, with elaborate unconcern; "but I don't suppose she's in anything of a hurry. I'll just go along with you far's the post-office." He kept his glance carefully from the spot at which he was signalled, and a hint of copper colour crawled up the back of his neck.

"Oh, but she is. Come along, Elmore; I can go that way."

"It'll be longer for you."

---

1   The branch of law that deals with land titles and real estate.

"Not a bit." Lorne cast a shrewd glance at his companion. "And as we're passing you might just introduce me to your mother, see?"

"She won't expect it, Lorne."

"That's all right, my son. She won't refuse to meet a friend of yours." He led the way as he spoke to the point of vantage occupied by Mrs. Crow, followed, with plain reluctance, by her son. She was a frail-looking old woman, with a knitted shawl pinned tightly across her chest, and her bonnet, in the course of commercial activity, pushed so far back as to be almost falling off.

"You might smarten yourself with that change, Elmore," she addressed him, ignoring his companion. "There's folks coming back for it. Two-dollar bill, wa'n't it? Fifty cents—seventy-five—dollar'n a half. That's a Yankee dime, an' you kin march straight back with it. They don't pass but for nine cents, as you're old enough to know. Keep twenty-five cents for your dinner— you'll get most for the money at the Barker House—an' bring me back another quarter. Better go an' get your victuals now—it's gone twelve—while they're hot."

Elmore took his instructions without visible demur; and then, as Lorne had not seen fit to detach himself, performed the ceremony of introduction. As he performed it he drew one foot back and bowed himself, which seemed obscurely to facilitate it. The suspicion faded out of Mrs. Crow's tired old sharp eyes under the formula, and she said she was pleased to make our friend's acquaintance.

"Mr. Murchison's changed some since the old days at the Collegiate," Elmore explained, "but he ain't any different under his coat. He's practisin' the law."

"Lawyers," Mrs. Crow observed, "are folks I like to keep away from."

"Quite right, too," responded Lorne, unabashed. "And so you've got my friend here back on the farm, Mrs. Crow?"

"Well, yes, he's back on the farm, an' when he's wore out his Winnipeg clothes and his big ideas, we're lookin' to make him some use." Mrs. Crow's intention, though barbed, was humorous, and her son grinned broadly.

"There's more money in the law," he remarked, "once you get a start. Here's Mr. Murchison goin' to run the Ormiston case; his old man's down sick, an' I guess it depends on Lorne now whether Ormiston gets off or goes to penitentiary."

Mrs. Crow's face tied itself up into criticism as she looked our young man up and down. "Depends upon you, does it?" she commented. "Well, all I've got to say is it's a mighty young dependence. Coming on next week, ain't it? You won't be much older by then. Yes'm," she turned to business, "I don't say but what it's high for rhubarb, but there ain't another bunch in the market, and won't be for a week yet."

Under cover of this discussion Lorne bade the Crows good morning, retreating in the rear of the lady who found the rhubarb high. Mrs. Crow's drop of acid combined with his saving sense of the humour of it to adjust all his courage and his confidence, and with a braver face than ever he involuntarily hastened his steps to keep pace with his happy chance.

TEN

In the wide stretches of a new country there is nothing to bound a local excitement, or to impede its transmission at full value. Elgin was a manufacturing town in southern Ontario, but they would have known every development of the Federal Bank case at the North Pole if there had been anybody there to learn. In Halifax they did know it, and in Vancouver, B.C., while every hundred miles nearer it warmed as a topic in proportion. In Montreal the papers gave it headlines; from Toronto they sent special reporters. Of course, it was most of all the opportunity of Mr. Horace Williams, of the *Elgin Express*, and of Rawlins, who held all the cards in their hands, and played them, it must be said, admirably, reducing the *Mercury* to all sorts of futile expedients to score, which the *Express* would invariably explode with a guffaw of contradiction the following day. It was to the *Express* that the Toronto reporters came for details and local colour; and Mr. Williams gave them just as much as he thought they ought to have and no more. It was the *Express* that managed, while elaborately abstaining from improper comment upon a matter *sub judice*,[1] to feed and support the general conviction of young Ormiston's innocence, and thereby win for itself, though a "Grit"[2] paper, wide reading in that hotbed of Toryism, Moneida Reservation, while the Conservative *Mercury*, with its reckless

---

1 Before the courts and not yet resolved.
2 Associated with the Liberal party.

sympathy for an old party name, made itself criminally liable by reviewing cases of hard dealing by the bank among the farmers, and only escaped prosecution by the amplest retraction and the most contrite apology. As Mr. Williams remarked, there was no use in dwelling on the unpopularity of the bank, *that* didn't need pointing out; folks down Moneida way could put any newspaper wise on the number of mortgages foreclosed and the rate for secondary loans exacted by the bank in those parts. That consideration, no doubt, human nature being what it is, contributed the active principle to the feeling so widely aroused by the case. We are not very readily the prey to emotions of faith in our fellows, especially, perhaps, if we live under conditions somewhat hard and narrow; the greater animosity behind is, at all events, valuable to give force and relief and staying power to a sentiment of generous conviction. But however we may depreciate its origin, the conviction was there, widespread in the townships; young Ormiston would "get clear"; the case for the defence might be heard over every bushel of oats in Elgin market-place.

In Elgin itself opinion was more reserved. There was a general view that these bank clerks were fast fellows, and a tendency to contrast the habits and the pay of such dashing young men; an exercise which ended in a not unnatural query.[1] As to the irritating caste feeling maintained among them, young Ormiston perhaps gave himself as few airs as any. He was generally conceded indeed by the judging sex[2] to be "nice to everybody"; but was not that exactly the nature for which temptations were most easily spread? The town, moreover, had a sapience of its own. Was it likely that the bank would bring a case so publicly involving its character and management without knowing pretty well what it was about? The town would not be committed beyond the circle of young Ormiston's intimate friends, which was naturally small if you compared it with the public; the town wasn't going to be surprised at anything that might be proved. On the other hand, the town was much more vividly touched than the country by the accident which had made Lorne Murchison practically sole counsel for the defence, announced as it was by the *Express* with every appreciation of its dramatic value. Among what the *Express* called "the farming community" this, in so far

---

1 That is, how do bank clerks afford to live the way they do?
2 Women, who are represented in the novel as judges of proper social behaviour.

as it had penetrated, was regarded as a simple misfortune, a dull blow to expectancy, which expectancy had some work to survive. Elgin, with its finer palate for sensation, saw in it heightened chances, both for Lorne and for the case; and if any ratepayer within its limits had remained indifferent to the suit, the fact that one side of it had been confided to so young and so "smart" a fellow townsman would have been bound to draw him into the circle of speculation. Youth in a young country is a symbol wearing all its value. It stands not only for what it is. The trick of augury invests it, at a glance, with the sum of its possibilities, the augurs all sincere, confident, and exulting. They have been justified so often; they know, in their wide fair fields of opportunity, just what qualities will produce what results. There is thus a complacence among adolescent peoples which is vaguely irritating to their elders; but the greybeards need not be over-captious;[1] it is only a question of time, pathetically short-lived in the history of the race. Sanguine persons in Elgin were freely disposed to "bet on" Lorne Murchison, and there were none so despondent as to take the view that he would not come out of it, somehow, with an added personal significance. To make a spoon is a laudable achievement, but it may be no mean business to spoil a horn.[2]

As the *Express* put it, there was as little standing room for ladies and gentlemen in the courthouse the first day of the Spring Assizes as there was for horses in the Court House Square. The County Crown Attorney was unusually, oddly, reinforced by Cruickshank, of Toronto—the great Cruickshank, K.C., probably the most distinguished criminal lawyer in the Province. There were those who considered that Cruickshank should not have been brought down, that it argued undue influence on the part of the bank, and his retainer was a fierce fan to the feeling in Moneida; but there is no doubt that his appearance added all that was possible to the universal interest in the case. Henry Cruickshank was an able man, and, what was rarer, a fastidious politician. He had held office in the Dominion Cabinet, and had resigned it because of a difference with his colleagues in the application of a principle; they called him, after a British politician of lofty but

---

1 Disposed to find fault.
2 An expression signifying that while it would be good for Lorne to win his case (to make a spoon), he might also benefit by losing in a particularly spectacular or notable way (spoil a horn).

abortive views, the Canadian Renfaire.[1] He had that independence of personality, that intellectual candour, and that touch of magnetism which combine to make a man interesting in his public relations. Cruickshank's name alone would have filled the courthouse, and people would have gone away quoting him.

From the first word of the case for the prosecution there was that in the leading counsel's manner—a gravity, a kindness, an inclination to neglect the commoner methods of scoring—that suggested, with the sudden chill of unexpectedly bad news, a foregone conclusion. The reality of his feeling reference to the painful position of the defendant's father, the sincerity of his regret, on behalf of the bank, for the deplorable exigency under which proceedings had been instituted, spread a kind of blankness through the court; men frowned thoughtfully, and one or two ladies shed furtive tears. Even the counsel for the defence, it was afterward remembered, looked grave, sympathetic, and concerned, in response to the brief but significant and moving sentences with which his eminent opponent opened the case. It is not my duty to report the trial for any newspaper; I will therefore spare myself more than the most general references; but the facts undoubtedly were that a safe in the strong room of the bank had been opened between certain hours on a certain night and its contents abstracted; that young Ormiston, cashier of the bank, was sleeping, or supposed to be sleeping, upon the premises at this time, during the illness of the junior whose usual duty it was; and that the Crown was in possession of certain evidence which would be brought forward to prove collusion with the burglary on the part of the defendant, collusion to cover deficits for which he could be held responsible. In a strain almost apologetic, Mr. Cruickshank explained to the jury the circumstances which led the directors to the suspicion which they now believed only too regrettably well founded. These consisted in the fact that the young man was known to be living beyond his means, and so to be constantly visited by the temptation to such a crime; the special facilities which he controlled for its commission, and, in particular, the ease and confidence with which the actual operation had been carried out, arguing no fear of detection on the part of the burglars, no danger of interference from one who should have

---

1   This name seems to be invented. The phrase in the serial version of the novel is "the Canadian Rosebery," a reference to British Prime Minister Lord Rosebery. See Darlene Kelly, "Rewriting *The Imperialist*: Duncan's Revisions," *Canadian Literature*, 121 (Summer 1989): 36 n.5.

stood ready to defend with his life the property in his charge, but who would shortly be seen to have been toward it, first, a plunderer in his own person, and afterward the accomplice of plunderers to conceal his guilt. Examination showed the safe to have been opened with the dexterity that demands both time and coolness; and the ash from a pipe knocked out against the wall at the side of the passage offered ironical testimony to the comfort in which the business had been done.

The lawyer gave these considerations their full weight, and it was in dramatic contrast with the last of them that he produced the first significant fragment of evidence against Ormiston. There had been after all some hurry of departure. It was shown by a sheet of paper bearing the mark of a dirty thumb and a hasty bootheel, bearing also the combination formula for opening the safe.

The public was familiar with that piece of evidence, it had gone through every kind of mill of opinion; it made no special sensation. The evidence of the caretaker who found the formula and of the witnesses who established it to be in young Ormiston's handwriting, produced little interest. Mr. Cruickshank in elaborating his theory as to why, with the formula in their hands, the depredators still found it necessary to pick the lock, offered nothing to speculations already current—the duplicate key with which they had doubtless been enabled to supply themselves was a clumsy copy and had failed them; that conclusion had been drawn commonly enough. The next scrap of paper produced by the prosecution was another matter. It was the mere torn end of a greasy sheet; upon it was written "Not less than 3,000 net," and it had been found in the turning out of Ormiston's dressing-table. It might have been anything—a number of people pursed their lips contemptuously—or it might have been, without doubt, the fragment of a disreputable transaction that the prosecuting counsel endeavoured to show it. Here, no doubt, was one of the pieces of evidence the prosecution was understood to have up its sleeve, and that portion of the prosecuting counsel's garment was watched with feverish interest for further disclosures. They came rapidly enough, but we must hurry them even more. The name of Miss Florence Belton, when it rose to the surface of the evidence, riveted every eye and ear. Miss Belton was one of those ambiguous ladies who sometimes drift out from the metropolitan vortex and circle restfully in backwaters for varying periods, appearing and disappearing irrelevantly. They dress beautifully; they are known to "paint" and thought to dye their hair. They establish no relations, being much too preoccupied, making exceptions only, as a rule, in favour of one or two young men, to whom they extend amenities based—it is the common talk—upon late hours and whisky-and-soda. They seem superior to the little prevailing conventions; they excite an unlawful interest; though nobody knows them black, nobody imagines them white; and when they appear upon Main Street in search of shoelaces or elastic, heads are turned and nods, possibly nudges, exchanged. Miss Belton had come from New York to the Barker House, Elgin, and young Ormiston's intimacy with her was one of the things that counted against him in the general view. It was to so count more seriously in the particular instance. Witnesses were called to prove that he had spent the evening of the burglary with Miss Belton at her hotel, that he had remained with her until one o'clock, that he was in the habit of spending his evenings with Miss Belton.

Rawlins of the *Express* did not overdo the sensation which was caused in the court-room when the name of this lady herself was called to summon her to the witness-box. It was indeed the despair of his whole career. He thought despondingly ever after of the thrill, to which he himself was not superior, and which, if he had only been able to handle it adequately, might have led him straight up the ladder to a night editorship. Miss Belton appeared from some unsuspected seat near the door, throwing back a heavy veil, and walking as austerely as she could, considering the colour of her hair. She took her place without emotion, and there she corroborated the evidence of the servants of the hotel. To the grave questions of the prosecution she fluently replied that the distraction of these evenings had been cards—cards played, certainly, for money, and that she, certainly, had won very considerable sums from the defendant from time to time. In Elgin the very mention of cards played for money will cause a hush of something deeper than disapproval; there was silence in the court at this. In producing several banknotes for Miss Belton's identification Mr. Cruickshank seemed to profit by the silence. Miss Belton identified them without hesitation, as she might easily, since they had been traced to her possession. Asked to account for them, she stated, without winking, that they had been paid to her by Mr. Walter Ormiston at various times during the fortnight preceding the burglary, in satisfaction of debts at cards. She, Miss Belton, had left Elgin for Chicago the day after the burglary. Mr. Ormiston knew that she was going. He had paid her the four fifty-dollar notes actually traced, the night before she left, and said, "You won't need to break these here, will you?" He seemed anxious that she should not, but it was the merest accident that she hadn't. In all, she had received from Mr. Ormiston four hundred and fifty dollars. No, she had no suspicion that the young man might not be in a position to make such payments. She understood that Mr. Ormiston's family was wealthy, and never thought twice about it.

She spoke with a hard dignity, the lady, and a great effect of doing business, a kind of assertion of the legitimate. The farmers of Fox County told each other in chapfallen appreciation that she was about as level-headed as they make them. Lawyer Cruickshank, as they called him, brought forth from her detail after detail, and every detail fitted damningly with the last. The effect upon young Ormiston was so painful that many looked another way. His jaw was set and his features contorted to hold himself from the disgrace of tears. He was generally acknowledged to be overwhelmed by the unexpected demonstration of his guilt, but distress was so plain in him that there was not a soul in the place that was not sorry for him. In one or two resolute faces hope still glimmered, but it hardly survived the cross-examination of the Crown's chief witness by the counsel for the defence, which, as far as it went, had a perfunctory air and contributed little to the evidence before the Court. It did not go all the way, however. The case having opened late, the defence was reserved till the following day, when proceedings would be resumed with the further cross-examination of Miss Belton.

As the defendant's counsel went down the courthouse steps Rawlins came up to him to take note of his demeanour and anything else that might be going.

"Pretty stiff row to hoe you've got there, Lorne," he said.

"Pretty stiff," responded Lorne.

ELEVEN

Imagination, one gathers, is a quality dispensed with of necessity in the practice of most professions, being that of which nature is, for some reason, most niggardly. There is no such thing as passing in imagination for any department of public usefulness, even the government of Oriental races; the list of the known qualified would be exhausted, perhaps, in getting the papers set.[1] Yet nei-

---

1 In nineteenth-century England, access to jobs in the public service was restricted to those who could pass a set of examinations; Duncan would have known civil servants in India who had written such exams as a condition of their employment. Here the narrator imagines an exam in "imagination."

ther poet nor philosopher enjoys it in monopoly; the chemist may have it, and the inventor must; it has been proved the mainspring of the mathematician, and I have hinted it the property of at least two of the Murchisons. Lorne was indebted to it certainly for his constructive view of his client's situation, the view which came to him and stayed with him like a chapter in a novel, from the hour in which Ormiston had reluctantly accounted for himself upon the night of the burglary. It was a brilliant view, that perceived the young clerk the victim of the conspiracy he was charged with furthering; its justification lay back, dimly, among the intuitions about human nature which are part of the attribute I have quoted. I may shortly say that it was justified; another day's attendance at the Elgin Courthouse shall not be compulsory here, whatever it may have been there. Young Ormiston's commercial probity is really no special concern of ours; the thing which does matter, and considerably, is the special quality which Lorne Murchison brought to the task of its vindication, the quality that made new and striking appeal, through every channel of the great occasion, to those who heard him. It was that which reinforced and comforted every friend Ormiston had in the court-room, before Lorne proceeded either to deal with the evidence of the other side, or to produce any jot or tittle of his own; and it was that which affected his distinguished opponent to the special interest which afterwards showed itself so pleasantly superior to the sting of defeat. The fact that the defence was quite as extraordinarily indebted to circumstantial evidence as the prosecution in no way detracted from the character of Lorne's personal triumph; rather, indeed, in the popular view and Rawlins', enhanced it. There was in it the primitive joy of seeing a ruffian knocked down with his own illegitimate weapons, from the moment the dropped formula was proved to be an old superseded one, and unexpected indication was produced that Ormiston's room, as well as the bank vault, had been entered the night of the robbery, to the more glorious excitement of establishing Miss Belton's connection—not to be quoted—with a cracksman[1] at that moment being diligently inquired for by the New York police with reference to a dramatically bigger matter. You saw the plot at once as he constructed it; the pipe ash became explicable in the seduction of Miss Belton's charms. The cunning net

---

1 A housebreaker, a burglar.

unwove itself, delicately and deliberately, to tangle round the lady. There was in it that superiority in the art of legerdemain,[1] of mere calm, astonishing manipulation, so applauded in regions where romance has not yet been quite trampled down by reason. Lorne scored; he scored in face of probability, expectation, fact; it was the very climax and coruscation[2] of score. He scored not only by the cards he held but by the beautiful way he played them, if one may say so. His nature came into this, his gravity and gentleness, his sympathy, his young angry irony. To mention just one thing, there was the way he held Miss Belton up, after the exposure of her arts, as the lady for whom his client had so chivalric a regard that he had for some time refused to state his whereabouts at the hour the bank was entered in the fear of compromising her. For this, no doubt, his client could have strangled him, but it operated, of course, to raise the poor fellow in the estimation of everybody, with the possible exception of his employers. When, after the unmistakable summing-up, the foreman returned in a quarter of an hour with the verdict of "Not guilty," people noticed that the young man walked out of court behind his father with as drooping a head as if he had gone under sentence; so much so that by common consent he was allowed to slip quietly away. Miss Belton departed, followed by the detective, whose services were promptly transferred to the prosecution, and by a proportion of those who scented further entertainment in her perfumed, perjured wake. But the majority hung back, leaving their places slowly; it was Lorne the crowd wanted to shake hands with, to say just a word of congratulation to, Lorne's triumph that they desired to enhance by a hearty sentence, or at least an admiring glance. Walter Winter was among the most genial.

"Young man," he said, "what did I tell you? Didn't I tell you you ought to take this case?" Mr. Winter, with his chest thrust out, plumed and strutted in justifiable pride of prophecy. "Now, I'll tell you another thing: to-day's event will do more for you than it has for Ormiston. Mark my words!"

They were all of that opinion, all the fine foretellers of the profit Lorne should draw from his spirited and conspicuous success; they stood about in knots discussing it; to some extent it eclipsed the main interest and issue of the day, at that moment

---

1 Sleight of hand.
2 A glittering flash of light.

driving out, free and disconsolate, between the snake-fences of the South Riding to Moneida Reservation. The quick and friendly sense of opportunity was abroad on Lorne Murchison's behalf; friends and neighbours and Dr. Drummond, and people who hardly knew the fellow, exchanged wise words about what his chance would do for him. What it would immediately do was present to nobody so clearly, however, as to Mr. Henry Cruickshank, who decided that he would, after all, accept Dr. Drummond's invitation to spend the night with him, and find out the little he didn't know already about this young man.

That evening the Murchisons' doorbell rang twice. The first time it was to admit the Rev. Hugh Finlay, who had come to return *Sordello*,[1] which he had borrowed from Advena, and to find out whether she thought with him about the interpretation of certain passages, and if not—there was always the possibility—wherein their divergence lay. The second time the door opened to Dr. Drummond and Mr. Cruickshank; and the electric light had to be turned on in the drawing-room, since the library was already occupied by Mr. Finlay and Advena, Mr. and Mrs. Murchison never having got over their early habit of sitting in the dining-room after tea. Even then Mrs. Murchison had to put away her work-basket, and John Murchison to knock the ashes out of his pipe, looking at one another with surprised inquiry when Eliza informed them of their visitors. Luckily, Mr. Lorne was also in, and Eliza was sent to tell him, and Mr. Lorne came down the stairs two at a time to join the party in the drawing-room, which was presently supplied by Eliza with a dignified service of cake and wine. The hall divided that room from the library, and both doors were shut. We cannot hesitate about which to open; we have only, indeed, to follow the recognized tradition of Elgin, which would never have entered the library. No vivid conclusion should be drawn, no serious situation may even be indicated. It would simply have been considered, in Elgin, stupid to go into the library.

---

1 *Sordello* (1840): a book-length poem by Robert Browning (1812-89) about the problems encountered by men of genius living in a prosaic world. Discussion of Browning's literary works was a common activity in literary societies of the time.

"It isn't a case for the High Commissioner for Canada,"[1] Mr. Cruickshank was saying. "It's a case for direct representation of the interests concerned, and their view of the effect upon trade. That's the only voice to speak with if you want to get anything done. Conviction carries conviction. The High Commissioner is a very useful fellow to live in London and look after the ornamental, the sentimental, and immigration—nobody could do it better than Selkirk. And in England, of course, they like that kind of agency. It's the good old dignified way; but it won't do for everything. You don't find our friend Morgan[2] operating through the American equivalent of a High Commissioner."

"No, you don't," said John Murchison.

"He goes over there as a principal, and the British Government, if he wants to deal with it, is only another principal. That's the way our deputation will go. We're practically all shippers, though of course the matter of tenders[3] will come later. There is big business for them here, national business, and we propose to show it. The subsidy we want will come back to the country four times over in two years. Freights from Boston alone—"

"It's the patriotic, imperial argument you'll have to press, I doubt," said John Murchison. "They're not business people over there—the men in office are not. How should they be? the system draws them from the wrong class. They're gentlemen—noblemen, maybe—first, and they've no practical education. There's only one way of getting it, and that's to make your own living. How many of them have ever made tuppence? There's where the Americans beat them so badly—they've got the sixth sense, the business sense. No; you'll not find them responding greatly to what there is in it for trade—they'd like to well enough, but they just won't see it; and, by George! what a fine suspicion they'll have of ye! As to freights from Boston," he continued, as they all laughed, "I'm of opinion you'd better not mention them. What! steal the trade of a friendly Power! Tut, tut!"

It was a long speech for John Murchison, but they were all excited to a pitch beyond the usual. Henry Cruickshank had

---

1   Canada's official diplomatic representative in England.

2   J. Pierpont Morgan (1837-1913), US millionaire businessman, also involved in cross-Atlantic shipping.

3   Boats contracted from private owners to "tend" the large military vessels of the British navy by supplying provisions, facilitating communications, etc.

brought with him an event of extraordinary importance. It seemed to sit there with him, significant and propitious, in the middle of the sofa; they all looked at it in the pauses. Dr. Drummond, lost in an armchair, alternately contemplated it and remembered to assert himself part of it. As head of a deputation from the United Chambers of Commerce of Canada shortly to wait on the British Government to press for the encouragement of improved communications within the Empire, Cruickshank had been asked to select a secretary. The appointment, in view of the desirability, for political reasons, of giving the widest publicity to the hopes and motives of the deputation, was an important one. The action of the Canadian Government, in extending conditional promises of support, had to be justified to the Canadian taxpayer; and that shy and weary person whose shoulders uphold the greatness of Britain, had also to receive such conciliation and reassurance as it was possible to administer to him, by way of nerving the administrative arm over there to an act of enterprise. Mr. Cruickshank had had two or three young fellows, mostly newspaper men, in his mind's eye; but when Lorne came into his literal range of vision, the others had promptly been retired in our friend's favour. Young Mr. Murchison, he had concluded, was the man they wanted; and if his office could spare him, it would probably do young Mr. Murchison no harm in any sort of way to accompany the deputation to London and throw himself into the matter the deputation had at heart.

"But it's the Empire!" said Lorne, with a sort of shy fire, when Mr. Cruickshank enunciated this.

We need not, perhaps, dwell upon the significance of his agreement. It was then not long since the maple leaf had been stained brighter than ever, not without honour, to maintain the word that fell from him.[1] The three older men looked at him kindly; John Murchison, rubbing his chin as he considered the situation, slightly shook his head. One took it that in his view the Empire was not so readily envisaged.

"That has a strong bearing," Mr. Cruickshank assented.

"It's the whole case—it seems to me," repeated young Murchison.

"It should help to knit us up," said Dr. Drummond. "I'll put my name down on the first passenger list, if Knox Church will let

---

1 A reference to the Boer War (1899-1902) to which Canada contributed about 8000 troops on the side of the British.

me off. See that you have special rates," he added, with a twinkle, "for ministers and missionaries."

"And only ten days to get him ready in," said Mrs. Murchison. "It will take some seeing to, I assure you; and I don't know how it's to be done in the time. For once, Lorne, I'll have to order you ready-made shirts, and you'll just have to put up with it. Nothing else could possibly get back from the wash."

"I'll put up with it, mother."

They went into other details of Lorne's equipment while Mrs. Murchison's eye still wandered over the necessities of his wardrobe. They arranged the date on which he was to meet the members of the deputation in Montreal, and Mr. Cruickshank promised to send him all available documents, and such presentation of the project as had been made in the newspapers.

"You shall be put in immediate possession of the bones of the thing," he said, "but what really matters," he added, pleasantly, "I think you've got already."

It took, of course, some discussion, and it was quite ten o'clock before everything was gone into, and the prospect was clear to them all. As they emerged into the hall together, the door of the room opposite also opened, and the Rev. Hugh Finlay found himself added to their group. They all made the best of the unexpected encounter. It was rather an elaborate best, very polite and entirely grave, except in the instance of Dr. Drummond, who met his subaltern with a smile in which cordiality struggled in vain to overcome the delighted humour.

TWELVE

It was the talk of the town, the pride of the market-place, Lorne Murchison's having been selected to accompany what was known as the Cruickshank deputation to England. The general spirit of congratulation was corrected by a tendency to assert it another proof of sagacity on the chairman's part; Elgin wouldn't be too flattered; Lawyer Cruickshank couldn't have done better. You may be sure the *Express* was well ahead with it. "Honour to Our Young Fellow Townsman. A Well-Merited Compliment," and Rawlins was round promptly next morning to glean further particulars. He found only Mrs. Murchison, on a step-ladder tying up the clematis that climbed about the verandah, and she told him a little about clematis and a good deal about the inconvenience of having to abandon superintending the spring cleaning in order to get Lorne ready to go to the old country at such short notice, but nothing he could put in the paper. Lorne, sought at the office, was hardly more communicative. Mr. Williams himself dropped in there. He said the *Express* would now have a personal interest in the object of the deputation, and proposed to strike out a broad line, a broader line than ever.

"We've got into the way of taking it for granted," said Mr. Williams, "that the subsidy idea is a kind of mediaeval idea. Raise a big enough shout and you get things taken for granted in economics for a long while. Conditions keep changing, right along, all the time, and presently you've got to reconsider. There ain't any sort of ultimate truth in the finest economic position, my son; not any at all."

"We'll subsidize over here, right enough," said Lorne.

"That's the idea—that's the prevailing idea, just now. But lots of people think different— more than you'd imagine. I was talking to old man Milburn just now—he's dead against it. 'Government has no business,' he said, 'to apply the taxes in the interests of any company. It oughtn't to know how to spell "subsidy." If the trade was there it would get itself carried,' he said."

"Well, that surprises me," said Lorne.

"Surprised me, too. But I was on the spot with him; just thought of it in time. 'Well, now, Mr. Milburn,' I said, 'you've changed your mind. Thought that was a thing you Conservatives never did,' I said. 'We don't —I haven't,' he said. 'What d'ye mean?' 'Twenty-five years ago,' I said, 'when you were considering whether you'd start the Milburn Boiler Works here or in Hamilton, Hamilton offered you a free site, and Elgin offered you a free site and a dam for your water power. You took the biggest subsidy an' came here,' I said."

Lorne laughed: "What did he say to that?"

"Hadn't a word. 'I guess it's up to me,' he said. Then he turned round and came back. 'Hold on, Williams,' he said. 'You know so much already about my boiler works, it wouldn't be much trouble for you to write out an account of them from the beginning, would it? Working in the last quarter of a century of the town's progress, you know, and all that. Come round to the office tomorrow, and I'll give you some pointers.' And he fixed up a two-column ad. right away. He was afraid I'd round on him, I suppose, if I caught him saying anything more about the immorality of subsidies."

"He won't say anything more."

"Probably not. Milburn hasn't got much of a political con- science, but he's got a sense of what's silly. Well, now, I expect you want all the time there is."

Mr. Williams removed himself from the edge of the table, which was strewn with maps and bluebooks, printed official, and typewritten demi-official papers.

"Give 'em a notion of those Assiniboian wheat acres, my boy, and the ranch country we've got; tell 'em about the future of quick passage and cold storage. Get 'em a little ashamed to have made so many fortunes for Yankee beef combines; persuade 'em the cheapest market has a funny way of getting the dearest price in the end. Give it 'em, Lorne, hot and cold and fricasseed. The *Express* will back you up."

He slapped his young friend's shoulder, who seemed occupied with matters that prevented his at once feeling the value of this assurance. "Bye-bye," said Mr. Williams. "See you again before you start."

"Oh, of course!" Lorne replied. "I'll—I'll come round. By the way, Williams, Mr. Milburn didn't say anything—about me in connection with this business? Didn't mention, I suppose, what he thought about my going."

"Not a word, my boy! He was away up in abstract principles; he generally is. Bye-bye."

"It's gone to his head a little bit—only natural," Horace reflect- ed as he went down the stairs. "He's probably just feeding on what folks think of it. As if it mattered a pin's head what Octavius Milburn thinks or don't think!"

Lorne, however, left alone with his customs returns and his immigration reports, sat still, attaching a weight quite out of com- parison with a pin's head to Mr. Milburn's opinion. He turned it over and over, instead of the tabulated figures that were his busi- ness: he had to show himself his way to the conclusion that such a thing could not matter seriously in the end, since Milburn had- n't a dollar involved—it would be different if he were a share- holder in the Maple Line. He wished heartily, nevertheless, that he could demonstrate a special advantage to boiler-makers in competitive freights with New York. What did they import, con- found them! Pig-iron? Plates and rivets? Fortunately he was in a position to get at the facts, and he got at them with an interest of even greater intensity than he had shown to the whole question since ten that morning. Even now, the unprejudiced observer, turning up the literature connected with the Cruickshank deputation, may notice a stress laid upon the advantages to Canadian importers of ore in certain stages of manufacture which may strike him as slightly, very slightly, special. Of course there are a good many of them in the country. So that Mr. Horace Williams was justified to some extent in his kindly observation upon the excusable egotism of youth. Two or three letters, however, came in while Lorne was considering the relation of plates and rivets to the objects of his deputation. They were all congratulatory; one was from the chairman of the Liberal Association at its headquarters in Toronto. Lorne glanced at them and stowed them away in his pocket. He would read them when he got home, when it would be a pleasure to hand them over to his mother. She was making a collection of them.

He had a happy perception that same evening that Mr. Milburn's position was not, after all, finally and invincibly taken against the deputation and everything—everybody—concerned with it. He met that gentleman at his own garden gate. Octavius paused in his exit, to hold it open for young Murchison, thus even assisting the act of entry, a thing which thrilled Lorne sweetly enough when he had time to ponder its possible significance. Alas! the significance that lovers find! Lorne read a world in the behaviour of Dora's father in holding the gate open. He saw political principle put aside in his favour, and social position forgotten in kindness to him. He saw the gravest, sincerest appreciation of his recent success, which he took as humbly as a dog will take a bone; he read a fatherly thought at which his pulses bounded in an arrogance of triumph, and his heart rose to ask its trust. And Octavius Milburn had held the gate open because it was more convenient to hold it open than to leave it open. He had not a political view in the world that was calculated to affect his attitude toward a practical matter; and his opinion of Lorne was quite uncomplicated: he thought him a very likely young fellow. Milburn himself, in the Elgin way, preferred to see no great significance of this sort anywhere. Young people were young people; it was natural enough that they should like each other's society. They, the Milburns, were very glad to see Mr. Murchison, very glad indeed. It was frequent matter for veiled humorous reference at the table that he had been to call again, at which Dora would look very stiff and dignified, and have to be coaxed back into the conversation. As to anything serious, there was no hurry; plenty of time to think of that. Such matters dwelt under the horizon;

there was no need to scan them closely; and Mr. Milburn went his way, conscious of nothing more than a comfortable gratification that Dora, so far as the young men were concerned, seemed as popular as other girls.

Dora was not in the drawing room. Young ladies in Elgin had always to be summoned from somewhere. For all the Filkin instinct for the conservation of polite tradition, Dora was probably reading the Toronto society weekly—illustrated, with correspondents all over the Province—on the back verandah, and, but for the irruption of a visitor, would probably not have entered the formal apartment of the house at all that evening. Drawing-rooms in Elgin had their prescribed uses—to receive in, to practise in, and for the last sad entertainment of the dead, when the furniture was disarranged to accommodate the trestles, but the common business of life went out outside them, even among prosperous people, the survival, perhaps, of a habit based upon thrift. The shutters were opened when Lorne entered, to let in the spring twilight, and the servant pulled a chair into its proper relation with the room as she went out.

Mrs. Milburn and Miss Filkin both came in before Dora did. Lorne found their conversation enchanting, though it was mostly about the difficulty of keeping the lawn tidy; they had had so much rain. Mrs. Milburn assured him kindly that there was not such another lawn as his father's in Elgin. How Mr. Murchison managed to have it looking so nice always she could not think. Only yesterday she and Mr. Milburn had stopped to admire it as they passed.

"Spring is always a beautiful time in Elgin," she remarked. "There are so many pretty houses here, each standing in its own grounds. Nothing very grand, as I tell my friend, Miss Cham, from Buffalo, where the residences are, of course, on quite a different scale; but grandeur isn't everything, is it?"

"No, indeed," said Lorne.

"But you will be leaving for Great Britain very soon now, Mr. Murchison," said Miss Filkin. "Leaving Elgin and all its beauties! And I dare say you won't think of them once again till you get back!"

"I hope I shall not be so busy as that, Miss Filkin."

"Oh, no, I'm sure Mr. Murchison won't forget his native town altogether," said Mrs. Milburn, "though perhaps he won't like it so well after seeing dear old England!"

"I expect," said Lorne simply, "to like it better."

"Well, of course, we shall all be pleased if you say that, Mr. Murchison," Mrs. Milburn replied graciously. "We shall feel quite complimented. But I'm afraid you will find a great deal to criticize when you come back—that is, if you go at all into society over there. I always say there can be nothing like good English society."

"I want to attend a sitting of the House," Lorne said. "I hope I shall have time for that. I want to see those fellows handling their public business. I don't believe I shall find our men so far behind, for point of view and grasp and dispatch. Of course there's always Wallingham[1] to make a standard for us all. But they have't got so many Wallinghams."

"Wasn't it Wallingham, Louisa, that Mr. Milburn was saying at breakfast was such a dangerous man? So able, he said, but dangerous. Something to do with the tariff."

"Oh?" said Lorne, and he said no more, for at that moment Dora came in. She came in looking very straight and graceful and composed. Her personal note was carried out in her pretty clothes, which hung and "sat" upon her like the rhythm of verses; they could fall no other way. She had in every movement the definite accent of young ladyhood; she was very much aware of herself, of the situation, and of her value in it, a setting for herself she saw it, and saw it truly. No one, from the moment she entered the room, looked at anything else.

"Oh, Mr. Murchison," she said. "How do you do? Mother, do you mind if I open the window? It's quite warm out of doors—regular summer."

Lorne sprang to open the window, while Miss Filkin, murmuring that it had been a beautiful day, moved a little farther from it.

"Oh, please don't trouble, Mr. Murchison; thank you very much!" Miss Milburn continued, and subsided on a sofa. "Have you been playing tennis this week?"

Mr. Murchison said that he had been able to get down to the club only once.

"The courts aren't a bit in good order. They want about a week's rolling. The balls get up anywhere," said Dora.

---

1 Modeled on the British politician Joseph Chamberlain (1836-1914), a strong advocate of Imperial Federation. Chamberlain was Colonial Secretary in the Salisbury and Balfour governments from 1895 to 1903, when he resigned after giving speeches in favour of tariff preference for colonial goods that offended many of his cabinet colleagues.

"Lawn tennis," Mrs. Milburn asserted herself, "is a delightful exercise. I hope it will never go out of fashion; but that is what we used to say of croquet, and it has gone out and come in again."

Lorne listened to this with deference; there was a hint of patience in the regard Dora turned upon her mother. Mrs. Milburn continued to dilate upon lawn tennis, dealt lightly with badminton, and brought the conversation round with a graceful sweep to canoeing. Dora's attitude before she had done became slightly permissive, but Mrs. Milburn held on till she had accomplished her conception of conduct for the occasion; then she remembered a meeting in the schoolhouse.

"We are to have an address by an Indian bishop," she told them. "He is on his way to England by China and Japan, and is staying with our dear rector, Mr. Murchison. Such a treat I expect it will be."

"What I am dying to know," said Miss Filkin, in a sprightly way, "is whether he is black or white!"

Mrs. Milburn then left the room, and shortly afterward Miss Filkin thought she could not miss the bishop either, conveying the feeling that a bishop was a bishop, of whatever colour. She stayed three minutes longer than Mrs. Milburn, but she went. The Filkin tradition, though strong, could not hold out entirely against the unwritten laws, the silently claimed privileges, of youth in Elgin. It made its pretence and vanished.

Even as the door closed the two that were left looked at one another with a new significance. A simpler relation established itself between them and controlled all that surrounded them; the very twilight seemed conscious with it; the chairs and tables stood in attentive harmony.

"You know," said Dora, "I hate your going, Lorne!"

She did indeed seem moved, about the mouth, to discontent. There was some little injury in the way she swung her foot.

"I was hoping Mr. Fulke wouldn't get better in time; I was truly!"

The gratitude in young Murchison's eyes should have been dear to her. I don't know whether she saw it; but she must have been aware that she was saying what touched him, making her point.

"Oh, it's a good thing to go, Dora."

"A good thing for you! And the regatta coming off the first week in June, and a whole crowd coming from Toronto for it. There isn't another person in town I care to canoe with, Lorne, you know perfectly well!"

"I'm awfully sorry!" said Lorne. "I wish—"

"Oh, I'm *going*, I believe. Stephen Stuart has written from Toronto, and asked me to sail with him. I haven't told mother, but he's my second cousin, so I suppose she won't make a fuss."

The young man's face clouded; seeing which she relented. "Oh, of course, I'm glad you're going, really," she assured him. "And we'll all be proud to be acquainted with such a distinguished gentleman when you get back. Do you think you'll see the King? You might, you know, in London."

"I'll see him if he's visible," laughed Lorne. "That would be something to tell your mother, wouldn't it? But I'm afraid we won't be doing business with his Majesty."

"I expect you'll have the loveliest time you ever had in all your life. Do you think you'll be asked out much, Lorne?"

"I can't imagine who would ask me. We'll get off easy if the street boys don't shout: 'What price Canucks?' at us! But I'll see England, Dora; I'll feel England, eat and drink and sleep and live in England, for a little while. Isn't the very name great? I'll be a better man for going, till I die. We're all right out here, but we're young and thin and weedy. They didn't grow so fast in England, to begin with, and now they're rich with character and strong with conduct and hoary with ideals. I've been reading up the history of our political relations with England. It's astonishing what we've stuck to her through, but you can't help seeing why—it's for the moral advantage. Way down at the bottom, that's what it is. We have the sense to want all we can get of that sort of thing. They've developed the finest human product there is, the cleanest, the most disinterested, and we want to keep up the relationship—it's important. Their talk about the value of their protection doesn't take in the situation as it is now. Who would touch us if we were running our own show?"[1]

"I don't believe they are a bit better than we are," replied Miss Milburn. "I'm sure I haven't much opinion of the Englishmen that come out here. They don't think anything of getting into debt, and as often as not they drink, and they never know enough to—to come in out of the rain. But, Lorne—"

---

1   In 1904, Canada had no separate army and no formal citizenship; Canadians carried British passports, and British diplomats represented Canadian interests in foreign affairs. According to Lorne, the British consider this relationship of great value to Canada, but he argues that this attitude is outdated.

"Yes, but we're very apt to get the failures. The fellows their folks give five or six hundred pounds to and tell them they're not expected back till they're making a living. The best men find their level somewhere else, along recognized channels. Lord knows we don't want them—this country's for immigrants. We're manufacturing our own gentlemen quite fast enough for the demand."

"I should think we were! Why, Lorne, Canadians—nice Canadians—are just as gentlemanly as they can be! They'll compare with anybody. Perhaps Americans have got more style:" she weighed the matter; "but Canadians are much better form, I think. But, Lorne, how perfectly dear of you to send me those roses. I wore them, and nobody there had such beauties. All the girls wanted to know where I got them, but I only told Lily, just to make her feel a pig for not having asked you—my very greatest friend! She just about apologized—told me she wanted to ask about twenty more people, but her mother wouldn't let her. They've lost an uncle or something lately,[1] and if it hadn't been for Clara Sims staying with them they wouldn't have been giving anything."

"I'll try to survive not having been asked. But I'm glad you wore the roses, Dora."

"I dropped one, and Phil Carter wanted to keep it. He's so silly!"

"Did you—did you let him keep it?"

"Lorne Murchison! Do you think I'd let any man keep a rose I'd been wearing?"

He looked at her, suddenly emboldened.

"I don't know about roses, Dora, but pansies—those are awfully nice ones in your dress. I'm very fond of pansies; couldn't you spare me one? I wouldn't ask for a rose, but a pansy—"

His eyes were more ardent than what he found to say. Beneath them Dora grew delicately pink. The pansies drooped a little; she put her slender fingers under one, and lifted its petals.

"It's too faded for your buttonhole," she said.

---

1 By the middle of the nineteenth century, mourning custom in England prescribed black clothes for women for up to two years after the death of an immediate family member, and cancellation of all social engagements for a similar period. These customs were reinforced by the example of Queen Victoria, who wore mourning clothes for ten years following the death of her husband in 1861. By 1900, these customs were being relaxed somewhat.

"It needn't stay in my buttonhole. I know lots of other places!" he begged.

Dora considered the pansy again, then she pulled it slowly out, and the young man got up and went over to her, proffering the lapel of his coat.

"It spoils the bunch," she said prettily. "If I give you this you will have to give me something to take its place."

"I will," said Lorne.

"I know it will be something better," said Dora, and there was a little effort in her composure. "You send people such beautiful flowers, Lorne."

She rose beside him as she spoke, graceful and fair, to fasten it in; and it was his hand that shook.

"Then may I choose it?" said Lorne. "And will you wear it?"

"I suppose you may. Why are you—why do you—Oh, Lorne, stand still!"

"I'll give you, you sweet girl, my whole heart!" he said, in the vague tender knowledge that he offered her a garden, where she had but to walk, and smile, to bring about her unimaginable blooms.

THIRTEEN

They sat talking on the verandah in the close of the May evening, Mr. and Mrs. Murchison. The Plummer Place was the Murchison Place in the town's mouth now, and that was only fair; the Murchisons had overstamped the Plummers. It lay about them like a map of their lives: the big horse-chestnut stood again in flower to lighten the spring dusk for them, as it had done faithfully for thirty years. John was no longer in his shirt-sleeves; the growing authority of his family had long prescribed a black alpaca coat. He smoked his meerschaum[1] with the same old deliberation, however, holding it by the bowl as considerately as he held its original, which lasted him fifteen years. A great deal of John Murchison's character was there, in the way he held his pipe, his gentleness and patience, even the justice and repose and quiet strength of his nature. He smoked and read the paper, the unfail-

---

1 A pipe for smoking tobacco, with a bowl made from a material called meerschaum, and often carved.

ing double solace of his evenings. I should have said that it was Mrs. Murchison who talked. She had the advantage of a free mind, only subconsciously occupied with her white wool and agile needles; and John had frequently to choose between her observations and the politics of the day.

"You saw Lorne's letter this morning, father?"

John took his pipe out of his mouth. "Yes," he said.

"He seems tremendously taken up with Wallingham. It was all Wallingham, from one end to the other."

"It's not remarkable," said John Murchison, patiently.

"You'd think he had nothing else to write about. There was that reception at Lord What-you-may-call-him's, the Canadian Commissioner's, when the Prince and Princess of Wales came, and brought their family. I'd like to have heard something more about that than just that he was there. He might have noticed what the children had on. Now that Abby's family is coming about her I seem to have my hands as full of children's clothes as ever I had. Abby seems to think there's nothing like my old patterns; I'm sure I'm sick of the sight of them!"

Mr. Murchison refolded his newspaper, took his pipe once more from his mouth, and said nothing.

"John, put down that paper! I declare it's enough to drive anybody crazy! Now look at that boy walking across the lawn. He does it every night, delivering the *Express*, and you take no more notice! He's wearing a regular path!"

"Sonny," said Mr. Murchison, as the urchin approached, "you mustn't walk across the grass."

"Much good that will do!" remarked Mrs. Murchison. "I'd teach him to walk across the grass, if—if it were my business. Boy—isn't your name Willie Parker? Then it was your mother I promised the coat and the other things to, and you'll find them ready there, just inside the hall door. They'll make down very well for you, but you can tell her from me that she'd better double-seam them, for the stuff's apt to ravel. And attend to what Mr. Murchison says; go out by the gravel—what do you suppose it's there for?"

Mrs. Murchison readjusted her glasses, and turned another row of the tiny sock. "I must say it's a pleasure to have the lawn neat and green," she said, with a sigh. "Never did I expect to see the day it would be anything but chickweed and dandelions. We've a great deal to be thankful for, and all our children spared to us, too. John," she continued, casting a shrewd glance over her needles at nothing in particular; "do you suppose anything was settled between Lorne and Dora Milburn before he started?"

"He said nothing to me about it."

"Oh, well, very likely he wouldn't. Young people keep such a tremendous lot to themselves nowadays. But it's my belief they've come to an understanding."

"Dora might do worse," said John Murchison, judicially.

"I should think Dora might do worse! I don't know where she's going to do better! The most promising young man in Elgin, well brought up, well educated, well started in a profession! There's not a young fellow in this town to compare with Lorne, and perfectly well you know it, John. Might do worse! But that's you all over. Belittle your own belongings!"

Mr. Murchison smiled in amused tolerance. "They've always got you to blow their trumpet, mother," he replied.

"And more than me. You ought to hear Dr. Drummond about Lorne! He says that if the English Government starts that line of boats to Halifax the country will owe it to him, much more than to Cruickshank, or anybody else."

"Lorne's keeping his end up all right," remarked Stella, jumping off her bicycle in time to hear what her mother said. "It's great, that old Wallingham asking him to dinner. And haven't I just been spreading it!"

"Where have you been, Stella?" asked Mrs. Murchison.

"Oh, only over to the Milburns'. Dora asked me to come and show her the new flower-stitch for table-centres. Dora's suddenly taken to fancy work. She's started a lot—a lot too much!" Stella added gloomily.

"If Dora likes to do fancy work I don't see why anybody should want to stop her," remarked Mrs. Murchison, with a meaning glance at her husband.

"I suppose she thinks she's going to get Lorne," said Stella. Her resentment was only half serious, but the note was there.

"What put that into your head?" asked her mother.

"Oh, well, anybody can see that he's devoted to her, and has been for ages, and it isn't as if Lorne was one to *have* girl friends; she's absolutely the only thing he's ever looked at twice. She hasn't got a ring, that's true, but it would be just like her to want him to get it in England. And I know they correspond. She doesn't make any secret of it."

"Oh, I dare say! Other people have eyes in their head as well as you, Stella," said Mrs. Murchison, stooping for her ball. "But there's no need to take things for granted at such a rate. And, above all, you're not to go *talking*, remember!"

"Well, if you think Dora Milburn's good enough," returned Lorne's youngest sister in threatening accents, "it's more than I do, that's all. Hello, Miss Murchison!" she continued, as Advena appeared. "You're looking 'xtremely dinky-dink. Expecting his reverence?"

Advena made no further reply than a look of scornful amusement, which Stella, bicycling forth again, received in the back of her head.

"Father," said Mrs. Murchison, "if you had taken any share in the bringing up of this family, Stella ought to have her ears boxed this minute!"

"We'll have to box them," said Mr. Murchison, "when she comes back." Advena had retreated into the house. "Is she expecting his reverence?" asked her father with a twinkle.

"Don't ask me! I'm sure it's more than I can tell you. It's a mystery to me, that matter, altogether. I've known him come three evenings in a week and not again for a month of Sundays. And when he does come there they sit, talking about their books and their authors; you'd think the world had nothing else in it! I know, for I've heard them, hard at it, there in the library. Books and authors won't keep their house or look after their family for them, I can tell them that, if it does come to anything, which I hope it won't."

"Finlay's fine in the pulpit," said John Murchison cautiously.

"Oh, the man's well enough; it's him I'm sorry for. I don't call Advena fitted to be a wife, and last of all a minister's. Abby was a treasure for any man to get, and Stella won't turn out at all badly; she's taking hold very well for her age. But Advena simply hasn't got it in her, and that's all there is to say about it." Mrs. Murchison pulled her needles out right side out with finality. "I don't deny the girl's talented in her own way, but it's no way to marry on. She'd much better make up her mind just to be a happy independent old maid; any woman might do worse. And take no responsibilities."

"There would always be you, mother, for them to fall back on." It was as near as John Murchison ever got to flattery.

"No thank you, then! I've brought up six of my own, as well as I was able, which isn't saying much, and a hard life I've had of it. Now I'm done with it; they'll have to find somebody else to fall back on. If they get themselves into such a mess"—Mrs. Murchison stopped to laugh with sincere enjoyment—"they needn't look to me to get them out."

"I guess you'd have a hand, mother."

"Not I. But the man isn't thinking of any such folly. What do you suppose his salary is?"

"Eight hundred and fifty dollars a year. They raised it last month."

"And how far would Advena be able to make that go, with servants getting the money they do and expecting the washing put out as a matter of course? Do you remember Eliza, John, that we had when we were first married? Seven dollars a month she got; she would split wood at a pinch, and I've never had one since that could do up shirts like her. Three years and a half she was with me, and did everything, everything I didn't do. But that was management, and Advena's no manager. It would be me that would tell him, if I had the chance. Then he couldn't say he hadn't been warned. But I don't think he has any such idea."

"Advena," pronounced Mr. Murchison, "might do worse."

"Well, I don't know whether she might. The creature is well enough to preach before a congregation. But what she can see in him out of the pulpit is more than I know. A great gawk of a fellow, with eyes that always look as if he were in the middle of next week! He may be able to talk to Advena, but he's no hand at general conversation; I know he finds precious little to say to me. But he's got no such notion. He comes here because, being human, he's got to open his mouth some time or other, I suppose; but it's my opinion he has neither Advena nor anybody else in his mind's eye at present. He doesn't go the right way about it."

"H'm!" said John Murchison.

"He brought her a book the last time he came—what do you think the name of it was? The something or other of Plato! Do you call that a natural thing from a young man who is thinking seriously of a girl? Besides, if I know anything about Plato he was a Greek heathen, and no writer for a Presbyterian minister to go lending around. I'd Plato him to the rightabout if it was me!"

"She might read worse than Plato," remarked John.

"Oh, well, she read it fast enough. She's your own daughter for outlandish books. Mercy on us, here comes the man! We'll just say 'How d'ye do?' to him, and then start for Abby's, John. I'm not easy in my mind about the baby, and I haven't been over since the morning. Harry says it's nothing but stomach, but I think I know whooping-cough when I hear it. And if it is whooping-cough the boy will have to come here and rampage, I suppose, till they're clear of it. There's some use in grandmothers, if I do say it myself!"

FOURTEEN

If any one had told Mr. Hugh Finlay, while he was pursuing his rigorous path to the ideals of the University of Edinburgh, that the first notable interest of his life in the calling and the country to which even then he had given his future would lie in his relations with any woman, he would have treated the prediction as mere folly. To go far enough back in accounting for this, one would arrive at the female sort, sterling and arid, that had presided over his childhood and represented the sex to his youth, the Aunt Lizzie, widowed and frugal and spare, who had brought him up; the Janet Wilson, who had washed and mended him from babyhood, good gaunt creature, half servant and half friend—the mature respectable women and impossible blowsy girls of the Dumfriesshire village whence he came. With such as these, relations, actual or imagined, could only be of the most practical kind, matters to be arranged on grounds of expediency, and certainly not of the first importance. The things of first importance—what you could do with your energy and your brains to beat out some microscopic good for the world, and what you could see and feel and realize in it of value to yourself—left little room for the feminine consideration in Finlay's eyes; it was not a thing, simply, that existed there with any significance. Woman, in her more attractive presentment, was a daughter of the poets, with an esoteric, or perhaps only a symbolic, or perhaps a merely decorative function; in any case, a creature that required an initiation to perceive her—a process to which Finlay would have been as unwilling as he was unlikely to submit. Not that he was destitute of ideals about women—they would have formed in that case a strange exception to his general outlook—but he saw them on a plane detached and impersonal, concerned with the preservation of society, the maintenance of the home, the noble devotions of motherhood. Women had been known, historically, to be capable of lofty sentiments and fine actions: he would have been the last to withhold their due from women. But they were removed from the scope of his imagination, partly by the accidents I have mentioned, and partly, no doubt, by a simple lack in him of the inclination to seek and to know them.

So that Christie Cameron, when she came to stay with his aunt in Bross during the few weeks after his ordination and before his departure for Canada, found a fair light for judgment and more than a reasonable disposition to acquiesce in the scale of her merits, as a woman, on the part of Hugh Finlay. He was familiar with the scale of her merits before she came; his Aunt Lizzie did little but run them up and down. When she arrived she answered to every item: she was a good height, but not too tall; a nice figure of a woman, but not what you would call stout; a fresh-faced body whose excellent principles were written in every feature she had. She was five years older than Hugh, but even that he came to accept in Aunt Lizzie's skilful exhibition as something to the total of her advantages. A pleasant independent creature with a hundred a year of her own, sensible and vigorous and good-tempered, belonging as well to the pre-eminently right denomination, she had virtues that might have figured handsomely in an advertisement had Aunt Lizzie, in the plenitude of her good-will, thought fit to take that measure on Christie's behalf. But nothing was farther from Aunt Lizzie's mind. We must, in fairness, add Christie Cameron to the sum of Finlay's acquaintance with the sex; but even then the total is slender, little to go upon.

Yet the fact which Mr. Finlay would in those days have considered so unimaginable remained; it had come into being and it remained. The chief interest of his life, the chief human interest, did lie in his relations with Advena Murchison. He might challenge it, but he could not move it; he might explain, but he could not alter it. And there had come no point at which it would have occurred to him to do either. When at last he had seen how simple and possible it was to enjoy Miss Murchison's companionship upon unoccupied evenings he had begun to do it with eagerness and zest, the greater because Elgin offered him practically no other. Dr. Drummond lived, for purposes of intellectual contact, at the other end of the century, the other clergy and professional men of the town were separated from Finlay by all the mental predispositions that rose from the virgin soil. He was, as Mrs. Murchison said, a great gawk of a fellow; he had little adaptability; he was not of those who spend a year or two in the New World and go back with a trans-Atlantic accent, either of tongue or of mind. Where he saw a lack of dignity, of consideration, or of restraint, he did not insensibly become less dignified or considerate or restrained to smooth out perceptible differences; nor was he constituted to absorb the qualities of those defects, and enrich his nature by the geniality, the shrewdness, the quick mental movement that stood on the other side of the account. He cherished in secret an admiration for the young men of Elgin, with their unappeasable energy and their indomitable optimism, but he could not translate it in any language of sympathy; and but for Advena his soul would have gone uncomforted and alone.

Advena, as we know, was his companion. Seeing herself just that, constantly content to be just that, she walked beside him closer than he knew. She had her woman's prescience and trusted it. Her own heart, all sweetly alive, counselled her to patience; her instincts laid her in bonds to concealment. She knew, she was sure; so sure that she could play sometimes, smiling, with her living heart—

The nightingale was not yet heard
For the rose was not yet blown,[1]

she could say of his; and what was that but play, and tender laughter, at the expense of her own? And then, perhaps, looking up from the same book, she would whisper, alone in her room—

Oh, speed the day, thou dear, dear May,[2]

and gaze humbly through tears at her own face in the glass, loving it on his behalf. She took her passion with the weight of a thing ordained; she had come upon it where it waited for her, and they had gone on together, carrying the secret. There might be farther to go, but the way could never be long.

Finlay said when he came in that the heat for May was extraordinary; and Advena reminded him that he was in a country where everything was accomplished quickly, even summer.

"Except perhaps civilization," she added. They were both young enough to be pleased with cleverness for its specious self.

---

1 From Edward Fitzgerald (1809-83), from the notes to the fourth stanza of his translation of *The Rubaiyat of Omar Khayyam* (1859).
2 From "Day after Day of this Azure May," a poem by James Thomson (1834-82, not to be confused with the eighteenth-century English poet of the same name).

"Oh, that is slow everywhere," he observed; "but how you can say so, with every modern improvement staring you in the face—"

"Electric cars and telephones! Oh, I didn't say we hadn't the products," and she laughed. "But the thing itself, the precious thing, that never comes just by wishing, does it? The art of indifference, the art of choice—"

"If you had refinements in the beginning what would the end be?" he demanded. "Anaemia."

"Oh, I don't quarrel with the logic of it. I only point out the fact. To do that is to acquiesce, really. I acquiesce; I have to. But one may long for the more delicate appreciations that seem to flower where life has gone on longer."

"I imagine," Finlay said, "that to wish truly and ardently for such things is to possess them. If you didn't possess them you wouldn't desire them! As they say, as they say—"

"As they say?"

"About love. Some novelist does. To be conscious in any way toward it is to be fatally infected."

"What novelist?" Advena asked, with shining interest.

"Some novelist. I—I can't have invented it," he replied, somewhat confounded. He got up and walked to the window, where it stood open upon the verandah. "I don't write novels," he said.

"Perhaps you live them," suggested Advena. "I mean, of course," she added, laughing, "the highest class of fiction."

"Heaven forbid!"

"Why Heaven forbid? You are sensitive to life, and a great deal of it comes into your scope. You can't see a thing truly without feeling it; you can't feel it without living it. I don't write novels either, but I experience—whole publishers' lists."

"That means," he said, smiling, "that your vision is up to date. You see the things, the kind of things that you read of next day. The modern moral sophistications—?"

"Don't make me out boastful," she replied; "I often do."

"Mine would be old-fashioned, I am afraid. Old stories of pain"—he looked out upon the lawn, white where the chestnut blossoms were dropping, and his eyes were just wistful enough to stir her adoration—"and of heroism that is quite dateless in the history of the human heart. At least one likes to hope so."

"I somehow think," she ventured timidly, "that yours would be classic."

Finlay withdrew his glance abruptly from the falling blossoms as if they had tempted him to an expansion he could not justify. He was impatient always of the personal note, and in his intercourse with Miss Murchison he seemed of late to be constantly sounding it.

"Oh, I don't know," he said, almost irritably. "I only meant that I see the obvious things, while you seem to have an eye for the subtle. There's reward, I suppose, in seeing anything. But about those more delicate appreciations of societies longer evolved, I sometimes think that you don't half realize, in a country like this, how much there is to make up."

"Is there anything really to make up?" she asked.

"Oh, so much! Freedom from old habits, inherited problems: look at the absurd difficulty they have in England in handling such a matter as education! Here you can't even conceive it— the schools have been on logical lines from the beginning, or almost. Political activity over there is half strangled at this moment by the secular arm of religion; here it doesn't even impede the circulation! Conceive any Church, or the united Churches, for the matter of that, asking a place in the conduct of the common schools of Ontario! How would the people take it? With anger, or with laughter, but certainly with sense. 'By all means let the ministers serve education on the School Boards,' they would say, 'by election like other people'—an opportunity, by the way, which has just been offered to me. I'm nominated for East Elgin in place of Leverett, the tanner, who is leaving the town. I shall do my best to get in, too; there are several matters that want seeing to over there. The girls' playground, for one thing, is practically under water in the spring."

"You should get in without the least difficulty. Oh, yes, there is something in a fresh start: we're on the straight road as a nation, in most respects; we haven't any picturesque old prescribed lanes to travel. So you think that makes up?"

"It's one thing. You might put down space—elbow-room."

"An empty horizon," Advena murmured.

"For faith and the future. An empty horizon is better than none. England has filled hers up. She has now—these," and he nodded at a window open to the yellow west. Advena looked with him.

"Oh, if you have a creative imagination," she said, "like Wallingham's. But even then your visions must be only political, economic, material. You can't conceive the—flowers—that will come out of all that. And if you could, it wouldn't be like having them."

"And the scope of the individual, his chance of self-respect, unhampered by the traditions of class, which either deaden it or irritate it in England! His chance of significance and success! And the splendid, buoyant, unused air to breathe, and the simplicity of life, and the plenty of things!"

"I am to be consoled because apples are cheap."

"You are to be consoled for a hundred reasons. Doesn't it console you to feel under your very feet the forces that are working to the immense amelioration of a not altogether undeserving people?"

"No," said Advena, rebelliously; and indeed he had been a trifle didactic to her grievance. They laughed together, and then with a look at her in which observation seemed suddenly to awake, Finlay said—

"And those things aren't all, or nearly all. I sometimes think that the human spirit, as it is set free in these wide unblemished spaces, may be something more pure and sensitive, more sincerely curious about what is good and beautiful—"

He broke off, still gazing at her, as if she had been an idea and no more. How much more she was she showed him by a vivid and beautiful blush.

"I am glad you are so well satisfied," she said, and then, as if her words had carried beyond their intention, she blushed again.

Upon which Hugh Finlay saw his idea incarnate.

FIFTEEN

If it were fair or adequate to so quote, I should be very much tempted to draw the history of Lorne Murchison's sojourn in England from his letters home. He put his whole heart into these, his discoveries and his recognitions and his young enthusiasm, all his claimed inheritance, all that he found to criticize and to love. His mother said, half jealously when she read them, that he seemed tremendously taken up with the old country; and of course she expressed the thing exactly, as she always did: he was tremendously taken up with it. The old country fell into the lines of his imagination, from the towers of Westminster to the shops in the Strand; from the Right Hon. Fawcett Wallingham, who laid great issues before the public, to the man who sang melancholy hymns to the same public up and down the benevolent streets. It was naturally London that filled his view; his business was in

London and his time was short; the country he saw from the train, whence it made a low cloudy frame for London, with decorations of hedges and sheep. How he saw London, how he carried away all he did in the time and under the circumstances, may be thought a mystery; there are doubtless people who would consider his opportunities too limited to gather anything essential. Cruickshank was the only one of the deputation who had been "over" before; and they all followed him unquestioningly to the temperance hotel of his preference in Bloomsbury, where bedrooms were three and six[1] and tea was understood as a solid meal and the last in the day. Bates would have voted for the Metropole, and McGill had been advised that you saw a good deal of life at the Cecil, but they bowed to Cruickshank's experience. None of them were total abstainers, but neither had any of them the wine habit; they were not inconvenienced, therefore, in taking advantage of the cheapness with which total abstinence made itself attractive, and they took it, though they were substantial men. As one of them put it, they weren't over there to make a splash, a thing that was pretty hard to do in London, anyhow; and home comforts came before anything. The conviction about the splash was perhaps a little the teaching of circumstances. They were influential fellows at home, who had lived for years in the atmosphere of appreciation that surrounds success; their movements were observed in the newspapers; their names stood for wide interests, big concerns. They had known the satisfaction of a positive importance, not only in their community but in their country; and they had come to England invested as well with the weight that is attached to a public mission. It may very well be that they looked for some echo of what they were accustomed to, and were a little dashed not to find it—to find the merest published announcement of their arrival, and their introduction by Lord Selkirk[2] to the Colonial Secretary;[3] and no heads turned in the temperance hotel when they came into the dining-room. It

---

1 Three shillings and sixpence.
2 In the novel, the High Commissioner of Canada to Britain: Canada's diplomatic representative. In 1903, Canada's High Commissioner in London was Lord Strathcona.
3 The position in the British Cabinet responsible for "the colonies" including Canada, India, and Australia. In the novel, the post is held by Wallingham; in history, the post was held by Joseph Chamberlain from 1895 until his resignation in 1903.

may very well be. It is even more certain, however, that they took the lesson as they found it, with the quick eye for things as they are which seems to come of looking at things as they will be, and with just that humorous comment about the splash. It would be misleading to say that they were humbled; I doubt whether they even felt their relativity, whether they ever dropped consciously, there in the Bloomsbury hotel, into their places in the great scale of London. Observing the scale, recognizing it, they held themselves unaffected by it; they kept, in a curious, positive way, the integrity of what they were and what they had come for; they maintained their point of view. So much must be conceded. The Empire produces a family resemblance, but here and there, when oceans intervene, a different mould of the spirit.

Wallingham certainly invited them to dinner one Sunday, in a body, an occasion which gave one or two of them some anxiety until they found that it was not to be adorned by the ladies of the family. Tricorne was there, President of the Board of Trade, and Fleming, who held the purse-strings of the United Kingdom, two Ministers whom Wallingham had asked because they were supposed to have open minds—open, that is to say, for purposes of assimilation. Wallingham considered, and rightly, that he had done very well for the deputation in getting these two. There were other "colleagues" whose attendance he would have liked to compel; but one of them, deep in the country, was devoting his week-ends to his new French motor, and the other to the proofs of a book upon Neglected Periods of Mahomedan History, and both were at the breaking strain with overwork. Wallingham asked the deputation to dinner. Lord Selkirk, who took them to Wallingham, dined them too, and invited them to one of those garden parties for the sumptuous scale of which he was so justly famed; the occasion we have already heard about, upon which royalty was present in two generations. They travelled to it by special train, a circumstance which made them grave, receptive, and even slightly ceremonious with one another. Lord Selkirk, with royalty on his hands, naturally could not give them much of his time, and they moved about in a cluster, avoiding the ladies' trains and advising one another that it was a good thing the High Commissioner was a man of large private means; it wasn't everybody that could afford to take the job. Yet they were not wholly detached from the occasion; they looked at it, after they had taken it in, with an air half amused, half proprietary. All this had, in a manner, come out of Canada, and Canada was theirs. One of them—

Bates it was—responding to a lady who was effusive about the strawberries, even took the modestly depreciatory attitude of the host. "They're a fair size for this country, ma'am, but if you want berries with a flavour we'll do better for you in the Niagara district."

It must be added that Cruickshank lunched with Wallingham at his club, and with Tricorne at his; and on both occasions the quiet and attentive young secretary went with him, for purposes of reference, his pocket bulging with memoranda. The young secretary felt a little embarrassed to justify his presence at Tricorne's lunch, as the Right Honourable gentleman seemed to have forgotten what his guests had come for beyond it, and talked exclusively and exhaustively about the new possibilities for fruit-farming in England. Cruickshank fairly shook himself into his overcoat with irritation afterwards. "It's the sort of thing we must expect," he said, as they merged upon Pall Mall. It was not the sort of thing Lorne expected; but we know him unsophisticated and a stranger to the heart of the Empire, which beats through such impediment of accumulated tissue. Nor was it the sort of thing they got from Wallingham, the keen-eyed and probing, whose skill in adjusting conflicting interests could astonish even their expectation, and whose vision of the essentials of the future could lift even their enthusiasm. One would like to linger over their touch with Wallingham, that fusion of energy with energy, that straight, satisfying, accomplishing dart. There is more drama here, no doubt, than in all the pages that are to come. But I am explaining now how little, not how much, the Cruickshank deputation, and especially Lorne Murchison, had the opportunity of feeling and learning in London, in order to show how wonderful it was that Lorne felt and learned so widely. That, what he absorbed and took back with him is, after all, what we have to do with; his actual adventures are of no great importance.

The deputation to urge improved communications within the Empire had few points of contact with the great world, but its members were drawn into engagements of their own, more, indeed, than some of them could conveniently overtake. Mr. Bates never saw his niece in the post-office, and regrets it to this day. The engagements arose partly out of business relations. Poulton, who was a dyspeptic, complained that nothing could be got through in London without eating and drinking; for his part he would concede a point any time not to eat and drink, but you could not do it; you just had to suffer. Poulton was a principal in one of the railway companies that were competing to open up the country south of Hudson's Bay to the Pacific, but having dealt with that circumstance in the course of the day he desired only to be allowed to go to bed on bread and butter and a little stewed fruit. Bates, whose name was a nightmare to every other dry-goods man in Toronto, naturally had to see a good many of the wholesale people; he, too, complained of the number of courses and the variety of the wines, but only to disguise his gratification. McGill, of the Great Bear Line, had big proposals to make in connection with southern railway freights from Liverpool: and Cameron, for private reasons of magnitude, proposed to ascertain the real probability of a duty to foreigners on certain forms of manufactured leather—he turned out in Toronto a very good class of suit-case. Cruickshank had private connections to which they were all respectful. Nobody but Cruickshank found it expedient to look up the lost leader of the Canadian House of Commons,[1] contributed to a cause still more completely lost in home politics; nobody but Cruickshank was likely to be asked to dine by a former Governor-General of the Dominion, an invitation which nobody but Cruickshank would be likely to refuse.

"It used to be a 'command' in Ottawa," said Cruickshank, who had got on badly with his sovereign's representative there, "but here it's only a privilege. There's no business in it, and I haven't time for pleasure."

The nobleman in question had, in effect, dropped back into the Lords. So far as the Empire was concerned, he was in the impressive rearguard, and this was a little company of fighting men.

The entertainments arising out of business were usually on a scale more or less sumptuous. They took place in big, well-known restaurants, and included a look at many of the people who seem to lend themselves so willingly to the great buzzing show that anybody can pay for in London, their names in the paper in the morning, their faces at Prince's[2] in the evening, their personali-

---

1 Thomas Tausky suggests that this is a reference to Edward Blake, leader of the Liberal Party in the Canadian Parliament from 1880 to 1887 (see Tausky, ed. *The Imperialist*, Ottawa: Tecumseh Press, 1996). Blake left Canada in 1891 and moved to Britain, where he was elected the House of Commons in 1891. He returned to Canada in 1906, where he died in 1912.

2 "Prince's Sporting Club," located in Knightsbridge, a fashionable area of London.

ties no doubt advantageously exposed in various places during the day. But there were others, humbler ones in Earl's Court Road or Maida Vale, where the members of the deputation had relatives whom it was natural to hunt up. Long years and many billows had rolled between, and more effective separations had arisen in the whole difference of life; still, it was natural to hunt them up, to seek in their eyes and their hands the old subtle bond of kin, and perhaps—such is our vanity in the new lands—to show them what the stock had come to overseas. They tended to be depressing, these visits: the married sister was living in a small way; the first cousin seemed to have got into a rut; the uncle and aunt were failing, with a stooping, trembling, old-fashioned kind of decrepitude, a rigidity of body and mind, which somehow one didn't see much over home.

"England," said Poulton, the Canadian born, "is a dangerous country to live in; you run such risks of growing old." They agreed, I fear, for more reasons than this that England was a good country to leave early; and you cannot blame them—there was not one of them who did not offer in his actual person proof of what he said. Their own dividing chance grew dramatic in their eyes.

"I was offered a clerkship with the Cunards[1] the day before I sailed," said McGill. "Great Scott, if I'd taken that clerkship!" He saw all his glorious past, I suppose, in a suburban aspect.

"I was kicked out," said Cameron, "and it was the kindest attention my father ever paid me;" and Bates remarked that it was worth coming out second-class, as he did, to go back in the best cabin in the ship.

The appearance and opinions of those they had left behind them prompted them to this kind of congratulation, with just a thought of compunction at the back of it for their own better fortunes. In the further spectacle of England most of them saw the repository of singularly old-fashioned ideas, the storehouse of a good deal of money, and the market for unlimited produce. They looked cautiously at imperial sentiment; they were full of the terms of their bargain, and had, as they would have said, little use for schemes that did not commend themselves on a basis of common profit. Cruickshank was the biggest and the best of them;

---

1 The "Cunard Line" was the first trans-Atlantic steamship line. Its founder, Samuel Cunard, was born in Halifax in 1787.

but even Cruickshank submitted the common formulas; submitted them and submitted to them.

Only Lorne Murchison among them looked higher and further, only he was alive to the inrush of the essential; he only lifted up his heart.

SIXTEEN

Lorne was thus an atom in the surge of London. The members of the deputation, as their business progressed, began to feel less like atoms and more like a body exerting an influence, however obscurely hid in a temperance hotel, upon the tide of international affairs; but their secretary had naturally no initiative that appeared, no importance that was taken account of. In these respects, no less than in the others, he justified Mr. Cruickshank's selection. He did his work as unobtrusively as he did it admirably well; and for the rest he was just washed about, carried hither and thither, generally on the tops of omnibuses, receptive, absorbent, mostly silent. He did try once or twice to talk to the 'bus drivers— he had been told it was a thing to do if you wanted to get hold of the point of view of a particular class; but the thick London idiom defeated him, and he found they grew surly when he asked them too often to repeat their replies. He felt a little surly himself after a while, when they asked him, as they nearly always did, if he wasn't an American. "Yes," he would say in the end, "but not the United States kind," resenting the necessity of explaining to the Briton beside him that there were other kinds. The imperial idea goes so quickly from the heart to the head. He felt compelled, nevertheless, to mitigate his denial to the 'bus drivers.

"I expect it's the next best thing," he would say, "but it's only the next best."

It was as if he felt charged to vindicate the race, the whole of Anglo-Saxondom,[1] there in his supreme moment, his splendid position, on the top of an omnibus lumbering west out of Trafalgar Square.

One introduction of his own he had. Mrs. Milburn had got it for him from the rector, Mr. Emmett, to his wife's brother, Mr.

---

1   The community of Anglo-Saxons; deriving from the fiction that the British constituted a unique race, "the Anglo-Saxon race," directly descended from the ancient Germanic peoples that settled in England.

Charles Chafe, who had interests in Chiswick and a house in War-wick Gardens. Lorne put off presenting the letter—did not know, indeed, quite how to present it, till his stay in London was half over. Finally he presented himself with it, as the quickest way, at the office of Mr. Chafe's works at Chiswick. He was cordially received, both there and in Warwick Gardens, where he also met Mr. Alfred Hesketh. Lorne went several times to the house in Warwick Gardens, and Hesketh—a nephew—was there on the very first occasion. It was an encounter interesting on both sides. He—Hesketh—was a young man with a good public school and a university behind him, where his very moderate degree, howev-er, failed to represent the activity of his mind or the capacity of his energy. He had a little money of his own, and no present occu-pation; he belonged to the surplus. He was not content to belong to it; he cast about him a good deal for something to do. There was always the Bar, but only the best fellows get on there, and he was not quite one of the best fellows; he knew that. He had not money enough for politics or interest enough for the higher departments of the public service, nor had he those ready arts of expression that lead naturally into journalism. Anything involving further examinations he rejected on that account; and the future of glassware, in view of what they were doing in Germany, did not entice him to join his uncle in Chiswick. Still he was aware of enterprise, convinced that he had loafed long enough.

Lorne Murchison had never met any one of Hesketh's age in Hesketh's condition before. Affluence and age he knew, in hon-ourable retirement; poverty and youth he knew, embarked in the struggle; indolence and youth he also knew, as it cumbered the ground; but youth and a competence, equipped with education, industry, and vigour, searching vainly in fields empty of opportu-nity, was to him a new spectacle. He himself had intended to be a lawyer since he was fourteen. There never had been any imped-iment to his intention, any qualification to his desire. He was still under his father's roof, but that was for the general happiness; any time within the last eighteen months, if he had chosen to hurry fate, he might have selected another. He was younger than Hes-keth by a year, yet we may say that he had arrived, while Hesketh was still fidgeting at the starting-point.

"Why don't you farm?" he asked once.

"Farming in England may pay in a quarter of a century, not before. I can't wait for it. Besides, why should I farm? Why didn't you?"

"Well," said Lorne, "in your case it seems about the only thing left. I? Oh, it doesn't attract us over there. We're getting away from it—leaving it to the new-comers from this side. Curious circle, that. I wonder, when our place gets overcrowded, where we shall go to plough?"

Hesketh's situation occupied them a good deal; but their great topic had a wider drift, embracing nothing less than the Empire, pausing nowhere short of the flag. The imperial idea[1] was very much at the moment in the public mind; it hung heavily, like a banner, in every newspaper, it was filtering through the slow British consciousness, solidifying as it travelled. In the end it might be expected to arrive at a shape in which the British consciousness must either assimilate it or cast it forth. They were saying in the suburbs that they wanted it explained; at Hatfield[2] they were saying, some of them, with folded arms, that it was self-evident; other members of that great house, swinging their arms, called it blackness of darkness and ruin, so had a prophet divided it against itself. Wallingham, still in the Cabinet, was going up and down the country trying not to explain too much. There was division in the Cabinet, sore travail among private members. The conception being ministerial, the Opposition applied itself to the task of abortion, fearing the worst if it should be presented to the country fully formed and featured, the smiling offspring of progress and imagination. Travellers to Greater Britain returned waving joyous torches in the insular fog; they shed a brilliance and an infectious enthusiasm, but there were not enough to do more than make the fog visible. Many persons found such torches irritating. They pointed out that as England had groped to her present greatness she might be trusted to feel her way further. "Free trade," they said, "has made us what we are. Put out these lights!"

Mr. Chafe was one of these. He was a cautious, heavy fellow, full of Burgundy and distrust. The basis of the imperial idea inspired him with suspicion and hostility. He could accept the

---

1 Sometimes referred to simply as "The Idea." The idea that the British Empire should be restructured under a single federal government with common economic, political and military policies. See Introduction, pp. 18-23.
2 Hatfield House is the home of the Marquis of Salisbury, who was Prime Minister of Great Britain from 1895 to 1902; Joseph Chamberlain served as his Colonial Secretary.

American tariff on English manufactures; that was a plain position, simple damage, a blow full in the face, not to be dodged. But the offer of better business in the English colonies in exchange for a duty on the corn and meat of foreign countries—he could see too deep for that. The colonials might or might not be good customers: he knew how many decanters he sold in the United States, in spite of the tariff. He saw that the tax on food-stuffs was being commended to the working man with the argument of higher wages. Higher wages, with the competition of foreign labour, spelt only one word to English manufacturers, and that was ruin. The bugbear of higher wages, immediate, threatening, near, the terror of the last thirty years, closed the prospect for Charles Chafe; he could see nothing beyond. He did not say so, but to him the prosperity of the British manufacturer was bound up in the indigence of the operative. Thriving workmen, doing well, and looking to do better, rose before him in terms of menace, though their prosperity might be rooted in his own. "Give them cheap food and keep them poor," was the sum of his advice. His opinions had the emphasis of the unexpected, the unnatural: he was one of the people whom Wallingham's scheme in its legitimate development of a tariff on foreign manufactures might be expected to enrich. This fact, which he constantly insisted on, did give them weight; it made him look like a cunning fellow not to be caught with chaff. He and his business had survived free trade—though he would not say this either—and he preferred to go on surviving it rather than take the chances of any zollverein.[1] The name of the thing was enough for him, a word made in Germany, thick and mucky, like their tumblers. As to the colonies— Mr. Chafe had been told of a certain spider who devoured her young ones. He reversed the figure, and it stood, in the imperial connection, for all the argument he wanted.

Alfred Hesketh had lived always in the hearing of such doctrine; it had stood to him for political gospel by mere force of repetition. But he was young, with the curiosity and enterprise and impatience of dogma of youth; he belonged by temperament and situation to those plastic thousands in whom Wallingham hoped to find the leaven that should leaven the whole lump. His own

---

1 A union, originally between certain states of the German empire, for the maintenance of a uniform rate of customs duties on goods from other countries and of free trade among themselves; something like the free-trade treaty currently in force among North American countries.

blood stirred with the desire to accomplish, to carry further; and as the scope of the philanthropist did not attract him, he was vaguely conscious of having been born too late in England. The new political appeal of the colonies, clashing suddenly upon old insular harmonies, brought him a sense of wider fields and chances; his own case he freely translated into his country's, and offered an open mind to politics that would help either of them. He looked at the new countries with interest, an interest evoked by their sudden dramatic leap into the forefront of public concern. He looked at them with what nature intended to be the eye of a practical business man. He looked at Lorne Murchison, too, and listened to him, with steady, critical attention. Lorne seemed in a way to sum it all up in his person, all the better opportunity a man had out there; and he handled large matters of the future with a confidence and a grip that quickened the circulation. Hesketh's open mind gradually became filled with the imperial view as he had the capacity to take it; and we need not be surprised if Lorne Murchison, gazing in the same direction, supposed that they saw the same thing.

Hesketh confessed, declared, that Murchison had brought him round; and Lorne surveyed this achievement with a thrill of the happiest triumph. Hesketh stood, to him, a product of that best which he was so occupied in admiring and pursuing. Perhaps he more properly represented the second best; but we must allow something for the confusion of early impressions. Hesketh had lived always in the presence of ideals disengaged in England as nowhere else in the world; in Oxford, Lorne knew, they clustered thick. There is no doubt that his manners were good, and his ideas unimpeachable in the letter; the young Canadian read the rest into him and loved him for what he might have been.

"As an Englishman," said Hesketh one evening as they walked together back from the Chafes' along Knightsbridge, talking of the policy urged by the Colonial representatives at the last Conference, "I could wish the idea were more our own—that we were pressing it on the colonies instead of the colonies pressing it on us."

"Doesn't there come a time in the history of most families," Lorne replied, "when the old folks look to the sons and daughters to keep them in touch with the times? Why shouldn't a vigorous policy of Empire be conceived by its younger nations—who have the ultimate resources to carry it out? We've got them and we know it—the iron and the coal and the gold, and the wheat-bearing areas. I dare say it makes us seem cheeky, but I tell you the last argument lies in the soil and what you can get out of it. What has this country got in comparison? A market of forty million people, whom she can't feed, and is less and less able to find work for. Do you call that a resource? I call it an impediment—a penalty. It's something to exploit, for the immediate profit in it, something to bargain with; but even as a market it can't preponderate always, and I can't see why it should make such tremendous claims."

"England isn't superannuated yet, Murchison."

"Not yet. Please God she never will be. But she isn't as young as she was, and it does seem to me—"

"What seems to you?"

"Well, I'm no economist, and I don't know how far to trust my impressions, and you needn't tell me I'm a rank outsider, for I know that; but coming here as an outsider, it does seem to me that it's from the outside that any sort of helpful change in the conditions of this country has got to come. England still has military initiative, though it's hard to see how she's going to keep that unless she does something to stop the degeneration of the class she draws her army from; but what other kind do we hear about? Company promoting, beekeeping, asparagus growing, poultry farming for ladies, the opening of a new Oriental Tea-Pot in Regent Street, with samisen-players between four and six, and Japanese attendants, who take the change on their hands and knees. London's one great stomach—how many eating places have we passed in the last ten minutes? The place seems all taken up with inventing new ways of making rich people more comfortable and better amused—I'm fed up with the sight of shiny carriages with cockaded flunkeys on 'em, wooden smart, rolling about with an elderly woman and a parasol and a dog. England seems to have fallen back on itself, got content to spend the money there is in the country already; and about the only line of commercial activity the stranger sees is the onslaught on that accumulation. London isn't the headquarters for big new developing enterprises any more. If you take out Westminster and Wallingham, London is a collection of traditions and great houses, and newspaper offices, and shops. That sort of thing can't go on for ever. Already capital is drawing away to conditions it can find a profit in—steel works in Canada, woollen factories in Australia, jute mills in India. Do you know where the boots came from that shod the troops in South

Africa? Cawnpore.[1] The money will go, you know, and that's a fact; the money will go, and the people will go, anyhow. It's only a case of whether England sends them with blessing and profit and greater glory, or whether she lets them slip away in spite of her."

"I dare say it will," replied Hesketh; "I've got precious little, but what there is I'd take out fast enough, if I saw a decent chance of investing it. I sometimes think of trying my luck in the States. Two or three fellows in my year went over there and aren't making half a bad thing of it."

"Oh, come," said Lorne, half swinging round upon the other, with his hands in his pockets, "it isn't exactly the time, is it, to talk about chucking the Empire?"

"Well, no, it isn't," Hesketh admitted. "One might do better to wait, I dare say. At all events, till we see what the country says to Wallingham."

They walked on for a moment or two in silence; then Lorne broke out again.

"I suppose it's unreasonable, but there's nothing I hate so much as to hear Englishmen talk of settling in the United States."

"It's risky, I admit. And I've never heard anybody yet say it was comfortable."

"In a few years, fifty maybe, it won't matter. Things will have taken their direction by then; but now it's a question of the lead. The Americans think they've got it, and unless we get imperial federation of course they have. It's their plain intention to capture England commercially."

"We're a long way from that," said Hesketh.

"Yes, but it's in the line of fate. Industrial energy is deserting this country; and you have no large movement, no counter-advance, to make against the increasing forces that are driving this way from over there—nothing to oppose to assault. England is in a state of siege, and doesn't seem to know it. She's so great—Hesketh, it's pathetic!—she offers an undefended shore to attack, and a stupid confidence, a kindly blindness, above all to Americans, whom she patronizes in the gate."

"I believe we do patronize them," said Hesketh. "It's rotten bad form."

---

1 A reference to the recently concluded Boer War (1899-1901) between Great Britain and the Boer republics in South Africa. Cawnpore [Kanpur] is in India.

"Oh, form! I may be mad, but one seems to see in politics over here a lack of definition and purpose, a tendency to cling to the abstract and to precedent—'the mainstay of the mandarin' one of the papers calls it; that's a good word—that give one the feeling that this kingdom is beginning to be aware of some influence stronger than its own. It lies, of course, in the great West, where the corn and the cattle grow; and between Winnipeg and Chicago choose quickly, England!"

His companion laughed. "Oh, I'm with you," he said, "but you take a pessimistic view of this country, Murchison."

"It depends on what you call pessimism," Lorne rejoined. "I see England down the future the heart of the Empire, the conscience of the world, and the Mecca of the race."

SEVENTEEN

The Cruickshank deputation returned across that North Atlantic which it was their desire to see so much more than ever the track of the flag, toward the middle of July. The shiny carriages were still rolling about in great numbers when they left; London's air of luxury had thickened with the advancing season and hung heavily in the streets; people had begun to picnic in the Park on Sundays. They had been from the beginning a source of wonder and of depression to Lorne Murchison, the people in the Park, those, I mean, who walked and sat and stood there for the refreshment of their lives, for whom the place has a lyrical value as real as it is unconscious. He noted them ranged on formal benches, quiet, respectable, absorptive, or gathered heavily, shoulder to shoulder, docile under the tutelage of policemen, listening to any one who would lift a voice to speak to them. London, beating on all borders, hemmed them in; England outside seemed hardly to contain for them a wider space. Lorne, with his soul full of free airs and forest depths, never failed to respond to a note in the Park that left him heavy-hearted, longing for an automatic distributing system for the Empire. When he saw them bring their spirit-lamps and kettles and sit down in little companies on four square yards of turf, under the blackened branches, in the roar of the traffic, he went back to Bloomsbury to pack his trunk, glad that it was not his lot to live with that enduring spectacle.

They were all glad, every one of them, to turn their faces to the West again. The unready conception of things, the political concentration upon parish affairs, the cumbrous social machinery, oppressed them with its dull anachronism in a marching world; the problems of sluggish over-population clouded their eager out-look. These conditions might have been their inheritance. Perhaps Lorne Murchison was the only one who thanked Heaven con-sciously that it was not so; but there was no man among them whose pulse did not mark a heart rejoiced as he paced the deck of the Allan liner the first morning out of Liverpool, because he had leave to refuse them. None dreamed of staying, of "settling," though such a course was practicable to any of them except Lorne. They were all rich enough to take the advantages that money brings in England, the comfort, the importance, the state; they had only to add their wealth to the sumptuous side of the dramatic contrast. I doubt whether the idea even presented itself. It is the American who takes up his appreciative residence in Eng-land. He comes as a foreigner, observant, amused, having dis-claimed responsibility for a hundred years. His detachment is as complete as it would be in Italy, with the added pleasure of easy comprehension. But home-comers from Greater Britain[1] have never been cut off, still feel their uneasy share in all that is, and draw a long breath of relief as they turn again to their life in the lands where they found wider scope and different opportunities, and that new quality in the blood which made them different men.

The deputation had accomplished a good deal; less, Cruick-shank said, than he had hoped, but more than he had expected. They had obtained the promise of concessions for Atlantic ser-vices, both mail and certain classes of freight, by being able to demonstrate a generous policy on their own side. Pacific com-munications the home Government were more chary[2] of, there were matters to be fought out with Australia. The Pacific was fur-ther away, as Cruickshank said, and you naturally can't get fel-lows who have never been there to see the country under the Selkirks and south of the Bay—any of them except Wallingham, who had never been there either, but whose imagination took views of the falcon. They were reinforced by news of a shipping combination in Montreal to lower freights to South Africa against the Americans; it wasn't news to them, some of them were in it;

---

1 A common expression at the turn of the century for British possessions outside of Britain; British colonies.
2 Cautiously or suspiciously reluctant.

but it was to the public, and it helped the sentiment of their aim, the feather on the arrow. They had secured something, both financially and morally; what best pleased them, perhaps, was the extent to which they got their scheme discussed. Here Lorne had been invaluable; Murchison had done more with the newspapers, they agreed, than any of them with Cabinet Ministers. The journalist everywhere is perhaps more accessible to ideas, more susceptible to enthusiasm, than his fellows, and Lorne was charged with the object of his deputation in its most communicable, most captivating form. At all events, he came to excellent understanding, whether of agreement or opposition, with the newspaper men he met—Cruickshank knew a good many of them, and these occasions were more fruitful than the official ones—and there is no doubt that the guarded approval of certain leading columns had fewer ifs and buts and other qualifications in consequence, while the disapproval of others was marked by a kind of unwilling sympathy and a freely accorded respect. Lorne found London editors surprisingly unbiassed, London newspapers surprisingly untrammelled. They seemed to him to suffer from no dictated views, no interests in the background or special local circumstances. They had open minds, most of them, and when a cloud appeared it was seldom more than a prejudice. It was only his impression, and perhaps it would not stand cynical inquiry; but he had a grateful conviction that the English Press occupied in the main a lofty and impartial ground of opinion, from which it desired only a view of the facts in their true proportion. On his return he confided it to Horace Williams, who scoffed, and ran the national politics of the *Express* in the local interests of Fox County as hard as ever; but it had fallen in with Lorne's beautiful beliefs about England, and he clung to it for years.

The Williamses had come over the second evening following Lorne's arrival, after tea. Rawlins had gone to the station, just to see that the *Express* would make no mistake in announcing that Mr. L. Murchison had "Returned to the Paternal Roof," and the *Express* had announced it, with due congratulation. Family feeling demanded that for the first twenty-four hours he should be left to his immediate circle, but people had been dropping in all the next day at the office, and now came the Williamses, "trapesing," as Mrs. Murchison said, across the grass, though she was too content to make it more than a private grievance, to where they all sat on the verandah.

"What I don't understand," Horace Williams said to Mr.

Murchison, "was why you didn't give him a blow on the whistle. You and Milburn and a few others might have got up quite a toot. You don't get the secretary to a deputation for tying up the Empire home every day."

"You did that for him in the *Express*" said John Murchison, smiling as he pressed down, with an accustomed thumb, the tobacco into his pipe.

"Oh, we said nothing at all! Wait till he's returned for South Fox," Williams responded jocularly.

"Why not the Imperial Council[1]—of the future—at Westminster, while you're about it?" remarked Lorne, flipping a pebble back upon the gravel path.

"That will keep, my son. But one of these days, mark my words, Mr. L. Murchison will travel to Elgin Station with flags on his engine, and he'll be very much surprised to find the band there, and a large number of his fellow citizens, all able-bodied shouting men, and every factory whistle in Elgin let off at once, to say nothing of kids with tin ones. And if the Murchison Stove and Furnace Works siren stands out of that occasion I'll break in and pull it myself."

"It won't stand out," Stella assured him. "I'll attend to it. Don't you worry."

"I suppose you had a lovely time, Mr. Murchison?" said Mrs. Williams, gently tilting to and fro in a rocking chair, with her pretty feet in their American shoes well in evidence. It is a fact, or perhaps a parable, that should be interesting to political economists, the adaptability of Canadian feet to American shoes; but fortunately it is not our present business. Though I must add that the "rocker" was also American, and the hammock in which Stella reposed came from New York, and upon John Murchison's knee, with the local journal, lay a pink evening paper published in Buffalo.

"Better than I can tell you, Mrs. Williams, in all sorts of ways. But it's good to be back, too. Very good!" Lorne threw up his head and drew in the pleasant evening air of midsummer with infinite relish, while his eye travelled contentedly past the chestnuts on

---

1 Supporters of Imperial Federation proposed that the federated empire would be governed by a council of representatives from all of the former British colonies—they felt this would be an improvement over government by the Colonial Secretary, a British Cabinet minister with no formal responsibility to the colonies themselves.

the lawn, down the vista of the quiet tree-bordered street. It lay empty in the solace of the evening, a blue hill crossed it in the distance, and gave it an unfettered look, the wind stirred in the maples. A pair of schoolgirls strolled up and down bareheaded; now and then a buggy passed.

"There's room here," he said.

"Find it kind of crowded up over there?" asked Mr. Williams. "Worse than New York?"

"Oh, yes. Crowded in a patient sort of way— it's enough to break your heart—that you don't see in New York! The poor of New York—well, they've got the idea of not being poor. In England they're resigned, they've got callous. My goodness! the fellows out of work over there— you can *see* they're used to it, see it in the way they slope along and the look in their eyes, poor dumb dogs. They don't understand it, but they've just got to take it! Crowded? Rather!"

"We don't say 'rather' in this country, mister," observed Stella.

"Well, you can say it now, kiddie."

They laughed at the little passage—the traveller's importation of one or two Briticisms had been the subject of skirmish before—but silence fell among them for a moment afterward. They all had in the blood the remembrance of what Lorne had seen.

"Well, you've been doing big business," said Horace Williams.

Lorne shook his head. "We haven't done any harm," he said, "but our scheme's away out of sight now. At least it ought to be."

"Lost in the bigger issue,"[1] said Williams, and Lorne nodded.

The bigger issue had indeed in the meantime obscured the political horizon, and was widely spreading. A mere colonial project might well disappear in it. England was absorbed in a single contemplation. Wallingham, though he still supported the disabilities of a right honourable evangelist with a gospel of his own, was making astonishing conversions; the edifice of the national economic creed seemed coming over at the top. It was a question of the resistance of the base, and the world was watching.

---

1 In May and June 1903, Joseph Chamberlain gave a series of speeches that advocated "Imperial Unity" through the mechanisms of a common tariff policy, a common military, and a governing council with representatives from each of the self-governing colonies. This was "the bigger issue" that lay behind the lobbying of Lorne's deputation for "improved communications."

"Cruickshank says if the main question had been sprung a month ago we wouldn't have gone over. As it is, on several points we've got to wait. If they reject the preferential trade idea over there we shall have done a little good, for any government would be disposed to try to patch up something to take the place of imperial union in that case; and a few thousands more for shipping subsidies and cheap cablegrams would have a great look of strengthening the ties with the colonies. But if they commit themselves to a zollverein with us and the rest of the family you won't hear much more about the need to foster communications. Communications will foster themselves."

"Just so," remarked John Murchison. "They'll save their money."

"I wouldn't think so before—I couldn't," Lorne went on, "but I'm afraid it's rather futile, the kind of thing we've been trying to do. It's fiddling at a superstructure without a foundation. What we want is the common interest. Common interest, common taxation for defence, common representation, domestic management of domestic affairs, and you've got a working Empire."

"Just as easy as slippin' off a log," remarked Horace Williams.

"Common interest, yes," said his father; "common taxation, no, for defence or any other purpose. The colonies will never send money to be squandered by the London War Office. We'll defend ourselves, as soon as we can manage it, and buy our own guns and our own cruisers. We're better business people than they are, and we know it."

"I guess that's right, Mr. Murchison," said Horace Williams. "Our own army and navy—in the sweet bye and bye. And let 'em understand they'll be welcome to the use of it, but quite in a family way—no sort of compulsion."

"Well, said Lorne, "that's compatible enough."

"And your domestic affairs must include the tariff," Mr. Murchison went on. "There's no such possibility as a tariff that will go round. And tariffs are kittle cattle to shoo behind."[1]

"Has anybody got a Scotch dictionary?" inquired Stella. "This conversation is making me tired."

"Suppose you run away and play with your hoop," suggested

---

1 According to the Oxford English Dictionary, Duncan has this expression wrong: it should be "kittle cattle to shoe behind." "Kittle cattle" are difficult, capricious, unpredictable beasts; they would be difficult to "shoe behind," for a blacksmith who did not want to risk injury

her brother. "I can't see that as an insuperable difficulty, father. Tariffs could be made adaptable, relative to the common interest as well as to the individual one. We could do it if we liked."

"Your adaptability might easily lead to other things. What's to prevent retaliation among ourselves? There's a slump in textiles, and the home Government is forced to let in foreign wool cheaper. Up goes the Australian tax on the output of every mill in Lancashire. The last state of the Empire might be worse than the first."

"It wouldn't be serious. If I pinched Stella's leg as I'm going to in a minute, she will no doubt kick me; and her instincts are such that she will probably kick me with the leg I pinched, but that won't prevent our going to the football match together tomorrow and presenting a united front to the world."

They all laughed, and Stella pulled down her lengthening petticoats with an air of great offence, but John Murchison shook his head.

"If they manage it, they will be clever," he said.

"Talking of Lancashire," said Williams, "there are some funny fellows over there writing in the Press against a tax on foreign cotton because it's going to ruin Lancashire. And at this very minute thousands of looms are shut down in Lancashire because of the high price of cotton produced by an American combine—and worse coming, sevenpence a pound I hear they're going to have it, against the fourpence ha'penny they've got it up to already. That's the sort of thing they're afraid to discourage by a duty."

"Would a duty discourage it?" asked John Murchison.

"Why not—if they let British-grown cotton in free? They won't discourage the combine much—that form of enterprise has got to be tackled where it grows; but the Yankee isn't the only person in the world that can get to understand it. What's to prevent preferential conditions creating British combines, to compete with the American article, and what's to prevent Lancashire getting cheaper cotton in consequence? Two combines are better than one monopoly any day."

"Maybe so. It would want looking into. We won't see a duty on cotton though, or wool either for that matter. The manufacturers would be pleased enough to get it on the stuff they make, but there would be a fine outcry against taxing the stuff they use."

"Did you see much of the aristocracy, Mr. Murchison?" asked Mrs. Williams.

"No," replied Lorne, "but I saw Wallingham."

"You saw the whole House of Lords," interposed Stella, "and you were introduced to three."

"Well, yes, that's so. Fine-looking set of old chaps they are, too. We're a little too funny over here about the Lords—we haven't had to make any."

"What were they doing the day you were there, Lorne?" asked Williams.

"Motor-car legislation," replied Lorne. "Considerably excited about it, too. One of them had had three dogs killed on his estate. I saw a letter about it in the *Times*."

' "I don't see anything to laugh at in that," declared Stella. "Dogs are dogs."

"They are, sister, especially in England."

"Laundresses aren't washerwomen there," observed Mrs. Murchison. "I'd like you to see the colour of the things he's brought home with him, Mrs. Williams. Clean or dirty, to the laundry they go—weeks it will take to get them right again— ingrained London smut, and nothing else."

"In this preference business they've got to lead the way," Williams reverted. "We're not so grown up but what grandma's got to march in front. Now, from your exhaustive observation of Great Britain, extending over a period of six weeks, is she going to?"

"My exhaustive observation," said Lorne, smiling, "enables me to tell you one thing with absolute accuracy; and that is that nobody knows. They adore Wallingham over there—he's pretty nearly a god—and they'd like to do as he tells them, and they're ·dead sick of theoretic politics; but they're afraid—oh, they're afraid!"

"They'll do well to ca' canny,"[1] said John Murchison.

"There's two things in the way, at a glance," Lorne went on. "The conservatism of the people—it isn't a name, it's a fact—the hostility and suspicion; natural enough: they know they're stupid, and they half suspect they're fair game. I suppose the Americans have taught them that. Slow—oh, slow! More interested in the back-garden fence than anything else. Pick up a paper, at the moment when things are being done, mind, all over the world, done against them—when their shipping is being captured, and their industries destroyed, and their goods undersold beneath

---

1 A Scottish expression meaning to go wisely, be cautious.

their very noses—and the thing they want to know is—'Why Are the Swallows Late?' I read it myself, in a ha'penny morning paper, too, that they think rather dangerously go-ahead—a whole column, leaded, to inquire what's the matter with the swallows. The *Times* the same week had a useful leader on Alterations in the Church Service, and a special contribution on Prayers for the Dead. Lord, they need 'em! Those are the things they *think* about! The session's nearly over, and there's two Church Discipline Bills, and five Church Bills—bishoprics and benefices, and Lord knows what—still to get through.[1] Lot of anxiety about 'em, apparently! As to a business view of politics, I expect the climate's against it. They'll see over a thing—they're fond of doing that—or under it, or round one side of it, but they don't seem to have any way of seeing *through* it. What they just love is a good round catchword; they've only got to hear themselves say it often enough, and they'll take it for gospel. They're convinced out of their own mouths. There was the driver of a 'bus I used to ride on pretty often, and if he felt like talking, he'd always begin, 'As I was a-sayin' of yesterday—' Well, that's the general idea—to repeat what they were a-sayin' of yesterday; and it doesn't matter two cents that the rest of the world has changed the subject. They've been a-sayin' a long time that they object to import duties of any sort or kind, and you won't get them to *see* the business in changing. If they do this it won't be because they want to, it will be because Wallingham wants them to."

"I guess that's so," said Williams. "And if Wallingham gets them to he ought to have a statue in every capital in the Empire. He will, too. Good cigar this, Lorne! Where'd you get it?"

"They are Indian cheroots—'Planters' they call 'em—made in Madras. I got some through a man named Hesketh, who has friends out there, at a price you wouldn't believe for as decent a smoke. You can't buy 'em in London; but you will all right, and here, too, as soon as we've got the sense to favour British-grown tobacco."

"Lorne appreciates his family better than he did before," remarked his youngest sister, "because we're British grown."

"You were saying you noticed two things specially in the way?" said his father.

---

1 Prior to 1919, major changes to the laws of the Church of England required a Bill in the British Parliament.

"Oh, the other's of course the awful poverty—the twelve millions that haven't got enough to do with. I expect it's an outside figure and it covers all sorts of qualifying circumstances; but it's the one the Free Fooders[1] quote, and it's the one Wallingham will have to handle.[2] They've muddled along until they've *got* twelve million people in that condition, and now they have to carry on with the handicap. We ask them to put a tax on foreign food to develop our wheat areas and cattle ranges. We say, 'Give us a chance and we'll feed you and take your surplus population.' What is to be done with the twelve million while we are growing the wheat? The colonies offer to create prosperity for everybody concerned at a certain outlay—we've got the raw materials—and they can't afford the investment because of the twelve millions, and what may happen meanwhile. They can't face the meanwhile—that's what it comes to."

"Fine old crop of catchwords in that situation," Mr. Williams remarked; and his eye had the spark of the practical politician. "Can't you hear 'em at it, eh?"

"It scares them out of everything but hand-to-mouth politics. Any other remedy is too heroic. They go on pointing out and contemplating and grieving, with their percentages of misery and degeneration; and they go on poulticing the cancer with benevolence—there are people over there who want the State to feed the school children! Oh, they're kind, good, big-hearted people; and they've got the idea that if they can only give enough away everything will come right. I was talking with a man one day, and I asked him whether the existence of any class justified governing a great country on the principle of an almshouse. He asked me who the alms-givers ought to be, in any country. Of course it was tampering with my figure—in an almshouse there aren't any; but that's the way it presents itself to the best of them. Another fellow was frantic at the idea of a tax on foreign food—he nearly cried—but would be very glad to see Government do more to assist emigration to the colonies. I tried to show him it would be better to make it profitable to emigrate first, but I couldn't make him see it.

---

1 The Free Food league was founded in 1903, specifically to oppose Chamberlain's Tariff Reform league.

2 On 5 June 1903, Henry Campbell-Bannerman, leader of the Liberal Party and the free trade movement in England, gave a speech in which he quoted a study by "Mr. Rowntree and Mr. Charles Booth" that argued "there is about 30% of our population underfed, on the verge of hunger ... 30% of 41 millions comes to something over twelve millions."

"Oh, and there's the old thing against them, of course—the handling of imperial and local affairs by one body. Anybody's good enough to attend to the Baghdad Railway, and nobody's too good to attend to the town pump. Is it any wonder the Germans beat them in their own shops and Russia walks into Thibet?[1] The eternal marvel is that they stand where they do."

"At the top," said Mr. Williams.

"Oh—at the top! Think of what you mean when you say 'England.'"

"I see that the demand for a tariff on manufactured goods is growing," Williams remarked, "even the anti-food-tax organs are beginning to shout for that."

"If they had put it on twenty years ago," said Lorne, "there would be no twelve million people making a problem for want of work, and it would be a good deal easier to do imperial business to-day."

"You'll find," said John Murchison, removing his pipe, "that protection'll have to come first over there. They'll put up a fence and save their trade—in their own good time, not next week or next year—and when they've done that they'll talk to us about our big ideas—not before. And if Wallingham hadn't frightened them with the imperial job, he never would have got them to take up the other. It's just his way of getting both done."

"I hope you're right, father," said Lorne, with a covert glance at his watch. "Horace—Mrs. Williams—I'll have to get you to excuse me. I have an engagement at eight."

He left them with a happy spring in his step, left them looking after him, talking of him, with pride and congratulation. Only Stella, with a severe lip and a disapproving eye, noted the direction he took as he left the house.

EIGHTEEN

Peter Macfarlane had carried the big Bible up the pulpit steps of Knox Church, and arranged the glass of water and the notices to be given out beside it, twice every Sunday for twenty years. He was a small spare man, with thin grey hair that fell back from the

---

1 Britain regarded Russia as a rival for power in Asia, and during the period from 1900-07 engaged in military and diplomatic disputes with Russia over its influence in Tibet. The British invaded Tibet in 1904.

narrow dome of his forehead to his coat collar, decent and severe. He ascended the pulpit exactly three minutes before the minister did; and the dignity with which he put one foot before the other made his appearance a ceremonious feature of the service and a thing quoted. "I was there before Peter" was a triumphant evidence of punctuality. Dr. Drummond would have liked to make it a test. It seemed to him no great thing to expect the people of Knox Church to be there before Peter.

Macfarlane was also in attendance in the vestry to help the minister off with his gown and hang it up. Dr. Drummond's gown needed neither helping nor hanging; the Doctor was deftness and neatness and impatience itself, and would have it on the hook with his own hands, and never a fold crooked. After Mr. Finlay, on the contrary, Peter would have to pick up and smooth out— ten to one the garment would be flung on a chair. Still, he was invariably standing by to see it flung, and to hand Mr. Finlay his hat and stick. He was surprised and put about to find himself one Sunday evening too late for this attendance. The vestry was empty, the gown was on the floor. Peter gathered it up with as perturbed an air as if Mr. Finlay had omitted a point of church observance. "I doubt they get into slack ways in these missions," said Peter. He had been unable, with Dr. Drummond, to see the necessity for such extensions.

Meanwhile Hugh Finlay, in secular attire, had left the church by the vestry door, and was rapidly overtaking groups of his hearers as they walked homeward. He was unusually aware of his change of dress because of a letter in the inside pocket of his coat. The letter, in that intimate place, spread a region of consciousness round it which hastened his blood and step. There was purpose in his whole bearing; Advena Murchison, looking back at some suggestion of Lorne's, caught it, and lost for a moment the meaning of what she said. When he overtook them, with plain intention, she walked beside the two men, withdrawn and silent, like a child. It was unexpected and overwhelming, his joining them after the service, accompanying them, as it were, in the flesh after having led them so far in the spirit; he had never done it before. She felt her heart confronted with a new, an immediate issue, and suddenly afraid. It shrank from the charge for which it longed, and would have fled; yet, paralysed with delight, it kept time with her sauntering feet.

They talked of the sermon, which had been strongly tinged with the issue of the day. Dreamer as he was by temperament,

Finlay held to the wisdom of informing great public questions with the religious idea, vigorously disclaimed that it was anywhere inadmissible.

"You'll have to settle with the Doctor, Mr. Finlay," Lorne warned him gaily, "if you talk politics in Knox Church. He thinks he never does."

"Do you think," said Finlay, "that he would object to—to one's going as far afield as I did to-night?"

"He oughtn't to," said Lorne. "You should have heard him when old Sir John Macdonald gerrymandered the electoral districts[1] and gave votes to the Moneida Indians.[2] The way he put it, the Tories in the congregation couldn't say a word, but it was a treat for his fellow Grits."

Finlay smiled gravely. "Political convictions are a man's birthright," he said. "Any man or any minister is a poor creature without them. But of course there are limits beyond which pulpit influence should not go, and I am sure Dr. Drummond has the clearest perception of them. He seems to have been a wonderful fellow, Macdonald, a man with extraordinary power of imaginative enterprise. I wonder whether he would have seen his way to linking up the Empire as he linked up your Provinces here?"

"He'd have hated uncommonly to be in opposition, but I don't see how he could have helped it," Lorne said. "He was the godfather of Canadian manufactures,[3] you know—the Tories have always been the industrial party. He couldn't have gone for letting English stuff in free, or cheap; and yet he was genuinely loyal and attached to England. He would discriminate against Manchester with tears in his eyes! Imperialist in his time spelled Conservative, now it spells Liberal. The Conservatives have always talked the loudest about the British bond, but when it lately came to doing

---

1 To gerrymander is to adjust the borders of an electoral district in order to gain an unfair advantage.

2 Some indigenous peoples in eastern Canada were granted a vote in federal elections by the Dominion Franchise Act of 1885, which was supported by the Conservative government of Sir John A. Macdonald; the Liberals opposed the original legislation and rescinded this provision of the act in 1898, when they came to power. See Introduction, p. 28.

3 The "National Policy" introduced by the Macdonald government in 1879 consisted of three parts: tariff protection for Canadian manufacturers, the building of the trans-Canada railway, and the promotion of immigration to the prairies. This policy united the nation, and created a captive (western) market for Ontario manufacturers.

we're on record on the right side, and they're on record on the wrong. But it must make the old man's ghost sick to see—"

"To see his court suit stolen," Advena finished for him. "As Disraeli said—wasn't it Disraeli?"[1] She heard, and hated the note of constraint in her voice. "Am I reduced," she thought, indignantly, "to falsetto?" and chose, since she must choose, the betrayal of silence.

"It did one good to hear the question discussed on the higher level," said Lorne. "You would think, to read the papers, that all its merits could be put into dollars and cents."

"I've noticed some of them in terms of sentiment—affection for the mother country—"

"Yes, that's lugged in. But it doesn't cover the moral aspect," Lorne returned. "It's too easy and obvious, as well; it gives the enemy cause to offend."

"Well, there's a tremendous moral aspect," Finlay said, "tremendous moral potentialities hidden in the issue. England has more to lose than she dreams."

"That's just where I felt, as a practical politician, a little restless while you were preaching," said Lorne, laughing. "You seemed to think the advantage of imperialism was all with England. You mustn't press that view on us, you know. We shall get harder to bargain with. Besides, from the point of your sermon, it's all the other way."

"Oh, I don't agree! The younger nations can work out their own salvation unaided; but can England alone? Isn't she too heavily weighted?"

"Oh, materially, very likely! But morally, no," said Lorne, stoutly. "There, if you like, she has accumulations that won't depreciate. Money isn't the only capital the colonies offer investment for."

"I'm afraid I see it in the shadow of the degeneration of age and poverty," said Finlay, smiling—"or age and wealth, if you prefer it."

"And we in the disadvantage of youth and easy success," Lorne retorted. "We're all very well, but we're not the men our fathers were: we need a lot of licking into shape. Look at that disgraceful business of ours in the Ontario legislature the other

---

1   Benjamin Disraeli, Lord Beaconsfield (1804-81), was a novelist and a
    leader of the British Conservative Party. He served as Prime Minister of
    England in 1868, and from 1874 to 1880.

day,[1] and look at that fellow of yours walking out of office at West-minster last session because of a disastrous business connection which he was morally as clear of as you or I! I tell you we've got to hang on to the things that make us ashamed; and I guess we've got sense enough to know it. But this is my corner. I am going to look in at the Milburns', Advena. Good-night, Mr. Finlay."

Advena, walking on with Finlay, became suddenly aware that he had not once addressed her. She had the quick impression that Lorne left him bereft of a refuge; his plight heartened her.

"If the politicians on both sides were only as mutually appre-ciative," she said, "the Empire would soon be knit."

For a moment he did not answer. "I am afraid the economic situation is not quite analogous," he said, stiffly and absently, when the moment had passed.

"Why does your brother always call me 'Mr.' Finlay?" he demanded presently. "It isn't friendly."

The note of irritation in his voice puzzled her. "I think the form is commoner with us," she said, "even among men who know each other fairly well." Her secret glance flashed over the gulf that nevertheless divided Finlay and her brother, that would always divide them. She saw it with something like pain, which struggled through her pride in both. "And then, you know—your calling—"

"I suppose it is that," he replied, ill content.

"I've noticed Dr. Drummond's way," she told him, with ris-ing spirits. "It's delightful. He drops the 'Mr.' with fellow min-isters of his own denomination only—never with Wesleyans or Baptists, for a moment. He always comes back very genial from the General Assembly, and full of stories. 'I said to Grant,' or 'Macdonald said to me'—and he always calls you 'Finlay,'" she added shyly. "By the way, I suppose you know he's to be the new Moderator?"[2]

"Is he, indeed? Yes—yes, of course, I knew! We couldn't have a better."

They walked on through the early autumn night. It was just not raining. The damp air was cool and pungent with the smell of

1 Robert Gamey, a Conservative Member of the Legislative Assembly in Ontario, claimed to have been bribed to switch parties in March 1903. See Darlene Kelly, "Rewriting *The Imperialist*," 34.
2 The elected head of the Presbyterian Church in Canada and chair of the General Assembly.

fallen leaves, which lay thick under their feet. Advena speared the dropped horse-chestnut husks with the point of her umbrella as they went along. She had picked up half a dozen when he spoke again. "I want to tell you—I have to tell you—something—about myself, Miss Murchison."

"I should like," said Advena steadily, "to hear."

"It is a matter that has, I am ashamed to confess, curiously gone out of my mind of late—I should say until lately. There was little until lately—I am so poor a letter writer—to remind me of it. I am engaged to be married!"

"But how interesting!" exclaimed Advena.

He looked at her, taken aback. His own mood was heavy; it failed to answer this lightness from her. It is hard to know what he expected, what his unconscious blood expected for him; but it was not this. If he had little wisdom about the hearts of women, he had less about their behaviour. She said nothing more, but inclined her head in an angle of deference and expectation toward what he should further communicate.

"I don't know that I have ever told you much about my life in Scotland," he went on. "It has always seemed to me so remote and—disconnected with everything here. I could not suppose it would interest any one. I was cared for and educated by my father's only sister, a good woman. It was as if she had whole charge of the part of my life that was not absorbed in work. I don't know that I can make you understand. She was identified with all the rest—I left it to her. Shortly before I sailed for Canada she spoke to me of marriage in connection with my work and—welfare, and with—a niece of her husband's who was staying with us at the time, a person suitable in every way. Apart from my aunt, I do not know— However, I owed everything to her, and I—took her advice in the matter. I left it to her. She is a managing woman; but she can nearly always prove herself right. Her mind ran a great deal, a little too much perhaps, upon creature comforts, and I suppose she thought that in emigrating a man might do well to companion himself."

"That was prudent of her," said Advena.

He turned a look upon her. "You are not—making a mock of it?" he said.

"I am not making a mock of it."

"My aunt now writes to me that Miss Christie's home has been broken up by the death of her mother, and that if it can be arranged she is willing to come to me here. My aunt talks of bringing her. I am to write."

He said the last words slowly, as if he weighed them. They had passed the turning to the Murchisons', walking on with the single consciousness of a path under them, and space before them. Once or twice before that had happened, but Advena had always been aware. This time she did not know.

"You are to write," she said. She sought in vain for more words; he also, throwing back his head, appeared to search the firmament for phrases without result. Silence seemed enforced between them, and walked with them, on into the murky landscape, over the fallen leaves. Passing a street lamp, they quickened their steps, looking furtively at the light, which seemed leagued against them with silence.

"It seems so extraordinarily—far away," said Hugh Finlay, of Bross, Dumfries, at length.

"But it will come near," Advena replied.

"I don't think it ever can."

She looked at him with a sudden leap of the heart, a wild, sweet dismay.

"They, of course, will come. But the life of which they are a part, and the man whom I remember to have been me—there is a gulf fixed—"

"It is only the Atlantic," Advena said. She had recovered her vision; in spite of the stone in her breast she could look. The weight and the hurt she would reckon with later. What was there, after all, to do? Meanwhile she could look, and already she saw with passion what had only begun to form itself in his consciousness, his strange, ironical, pitiful plight.

He shook his head. "It is not marked in any geography," he said, and gave her a troubled smile. "How can I make it clear to you? I have come here into a new world, of interests unknown and scope unguessed before. I know what you would say, but you have no way of learning the beauty and charm of mere vitality— you have always been so alive. One finds a physical freedom in which one's very soul seems to expand; one hears the happiest calls of fancy. And the most wonderful, most delightful thing of all is to discover that one is oneself, strangely enough, able to respond—"

The words reached the woman beside him like some cool dropping balm, healing, inconceivably precious. She knew her share in all this that he recounted. He might not dream of it, might well confound her with the general pulse; but she knew the sweet and separate subcurrent that her life had been in his, felt herself underlying all these new joys of his, could tell him how dear she was. But it seemed that he must not guess.

It came to her with force that his dim perception of his case was grotesque, that it humiliated him. She had a quick desire that he should at least know that civilized, sentient beings did not lend themselves to such outrageous comedies as this which he had confessed; it had somehow the air of a confession. She could not let him fall so lamentably short of man's dignity, of man's estate, for his own sake.

"It is a curious history," she said. "You are right in thinking I should not find it quite easy to understand. We make those—arrangements—so much more for ourselves over here. Perhaps we think them more important than they are."

"But they are of the highest importance." He stopped short, confounded.

"I shall try to consecrate my marriage," he said presently, more to himself than to Advena.

Her thought told him bitterly: "I am afraid it is the only thing you can do with it," but something else came to her lips.

"I have not congratulated you. I am not sure," she went on, with astonishing candour, "whether I can. But I wish you happiness with all my heart. Are you happy now?"

He turned his great dark eyes on her.

"I am as happy, I dare say, as I have any need to be."

"But you are happier since your letter came?"

"No," he said. The simple word fell on her heart, and she forebore.

They went on again in silence until they arrived at a place from which they saw the gleam of the river and the line of the hills beyond. Advena stopped.

"We came here once before together—in the spring. Do you remember?" she asked.

"I remember very well." She had turned, and he with her. They stood together with darkness about them, through which they could just see each other's faces.

"It was spring, then, and I went back alone. You are still living up that street? Good-night, then, please. I wish again—to go back—alone."

He looked at her for an instant in dumb bewilderment, though her words were simple enough. Then as she made a step away from him he caught her hand.

"Advena," he faltered, "what has happened to us? This time I cannot let you."

NINETEEN

"Lorne," said Dora Milburn, in her most animated manner, "who do you think is coming to Elgin? Your London friend, Mr. Hesketh! He's going to stay with the Emmetts, and Mrs. Emmett is perfectly distracted; she says he's accustomed to so much, she doesn't know how he will put up with their plain way of living. Though what she means by that, with late dinner and afternoon tea every day of her life, is more than I know."

"Why, that's splendid!" replied Lorne. "Good old Hesketh! I knew he thought of coming across this fall, but the brute hasn't written to me. We'll have to get him over to our place. When he gets tired of the Emmetts' plain ways he can try ours—they're plainer. You'll like Hesketh; he's a good fellow, and more go-ahead than most of them."

"I don't think I should ask him to stay if I were you, Lorne. Your mother will never consent to change her hours for meals. I wouldn't dream of asking an Englishman to stay if I couldn't give him late dinner; they think so much of it. It's the trial of mother's life that father will not submit to it. As a girl she was used to nothing else. Afternoon tea we do have, he can't prevent that, but father kicks at anything but one o'clock dinner and meat tea at six, and I suppose he always will."

"Doesn't one tea spoil the other?" Lorne inquired. "I find it does when I go to your minister's and peck at a cress sandwich at five. You haven't any appetite for a reasonable meal at six. But I guess it won't matter to Hesketh; he's got a lot of sense about things of that sort. Why he served out in South Africa—volunteered. Mrs. Emmett needn't worry. And if we find him pining for afternoon tea we can send him over here."

"Well, if he's nice. But I suppose he's pretty sure to be nice. Any friend of the Emmetts—What is he like, Lorne?"

"Oh, he's just a young man with a moustache! You seem to see a good many over there. They're all alike while they're at school in round coats, and after they leave school they get moustaches, and then they're all alike again."

"I wish you wouldn't tease. How tall is he? Is he fair or dark? What colour are his eyes?"

Lorne buried his head in his hands in a pretended agony of recollection.

"So far as I remember, not exactly tall, but you wouldn't call him short. Complexion— well, don't you know?—that kind of middling complexion. Colour of his eyes—does anybody ever notice a thing like that? You needn't take my word for it, but I should say they were a kind of average coloured eyes."

"Lorne! You *are*—I suppose I'll just have to wait till I see him. But the girls are wild to know, and I said I'd ask you. He'll be here in about two weeks anyhow, and I dare say we won't find him so much to make a fuss about. The best sort of Englishmen don't come over such a very great deal, as you say. I expect they have a better time at home."

"Hesketh's a very good sort of Englishman," said Lorne.

"He's awfully well off, isn't he?"

"According to our ideas I suppose he is," said Lorne. "Not according to English ideas."

"Still less according to New York ones, then," asserted Dora. "They wouldn't think much of it there even if he passed for rich in England." It was a little as if she resented Lorne's comparison of standards, and claimed the American one as at least cis-Atlantic.[1]

"He has a settled income," said Lorne, "and he's never had to work for it, whatever luck there is in that. That's all I know. Dora—"

"Now Lorne, you're not to be troublesome."

"Your mother hasn't come in at all this evening. Don't you think it's a good sign?"

"She isn't quite so silly as she was," remarked Dora. "Why I should not have the same freedom as other girls in entertaining my gentleman friends I never could quite see."

"I believe if we told her we had made up our minds it would be all right," he pleaded.

"I'm not so sure, Lorne. Mother's so deep. You can't always tell just by what she *does*. She thinks Stephen Stuart likes me—it's too perfectly idiotic; we are the merest friends—when it's any question of you and Stephen—well, she doesn't say anything, but she lets me see! She thinks such a lot of the Stuarts because Stephen's father was Ontario Premier once, and got knighted."

"I might try for that myself if you think it would please her," said the lover.

"Please her! And I should be Lady Murchison!" she let fall upon his ravished ears. "Why, Lorne, she'd just worship us both! But you'll never do it."

---

1 On this side of the Atlantic; opposite of trans-Atlantic.

"Why not?"

Dora looked at him with pretty speculation. She had reasons for supposing that she did admire the young man.

"You're too nice," she said.

"That isn't good enough," he responded, and drew her nearer.

"Then why did you ask me?—No, Lorne, you are not to. Suppose father came in?"

"I shouldn't mind—father's on my side, I think."

"Father isn't on anybody's side," said his daughter, wisely.

"Dora, let me speak to him!"

Miss Milburn gave a clever imitation of a little scream of horror.

"*Indeed* I won't! Lorne, you are never, *never* to do that! As if we were in a ridiculous English novel!"

"That's the part of an English novel I always like," said Lorne. "The going and asking. It must about scare the hero out of a year's growth; but it's a glorious thing to do—it would be the next day, anyhow."

"It's just the sort of thing to please mother," Dora meditated, "but she can't be indulged all the time. No, Lorne, you'll have to leave it to me—when there's anything to tell."

"There's everything to tell now," said he, who had indeed nothing to keep back.

"But you know what Mother is, Lorne. Suppose they hadn't any objection, she would never keep it to herself! She'd want to go announcing it all over the place; she'd think it was the proper thing to do."

"But, Dora, why not? If you knew how I want to announce it! I should like to publish it in the sunrise—and the wind—so that I couldn't go out of doors without seeing it myself."

"I shouldn't mind having it in *Toronto Society*, when the time comes. But not yet, Lorne—not for ages. I'm only twenty-two—nobody thinks of settling down nowadays before she's twenty-five at the very earliest. I don't know a single girl in this town that has—among my friends, anyway. That's three years off, and you *can't* expect me to be engaged for three years."

"No," said Lorne, "engaged six months, married the rest of the time. Or the periods might run concurrently if you preferred—I shouldn't mind."

"An engaged girl has the very worst time. She gets hardly any attention, and as to dances—well, it's a good thing for her if the person she's engaged to *can* dance," she added, teasingly.

Lorne coloured. "You said I was improving, Dora," he said, and then laughed at the childish claim. "But that isn't really a thing that counts, is it? If our lives only keep step it won't matter much about the 'Washington Post.' And so far as attention goes, you'll get it as long as you live, you little princess. Besides, isn't it better to wear the love of one man than the admiration of half a dozen?"

"And be teased and worried half out of your life by everybody you meet? Now, Lorne, you're getting serious and sentimental, and you know I hate that. It isn't any good either—mother always used to say it made me more stubborn to appeal to me. Horrid nature to have, isn't it?"

Lorne's hand went to his waistcoat pocket and came back with a tiny packet. "It's come, Dora—by this morning's English mail."

Her eyes sparkled, and then rested with guarded excitement upon the little case. "Oh, Lorne!"

She said nothing more, but watched intently while he found the spring, and disclosed the ring within. Then she drew a long breath. "Lorne Murchison, what a lovely one!"

"Doesn't it look," said he, "just a little serious and sentimental?"

"But *such* good style, too," she declared, bending over it. "And quite new—I haven't seen anything a bit like it. I do love a design when it's graceful. Solitaires are so old-fashioned."

He kept his eyes upon her face, feeding upon the delight in it. Exultation rose up in him: he knew the primitive guile of man, indifferent to such things, alluring with them the other creature. He did not stop to condone her weakness; rather he seized it in ecstasy; it was all part of the glad scheme to help the lover. He turned the diamonds so that they flashed and flashed again before her. Then, trusting his happy instinct, he sought for her hand. But she held that back. "I want to *see* it," she declared, and he was obliged to let her take the ring in her own way and examine it, and place it in every light, and compare it with others worn by her friends, and make little tentative charges of extravagance in his purchase of it, while he sat elated and adoring, the simple fellow.

Reluctantly at last she gave up her hand.

"But it's only trying on—not putting on," she told him. He said nothing till it flashed upon her finger, and in her eyes he saw a spark from below of that instinctive cupidity toward jewels that man can never recognize as it deserves in woman, because of his desire to gratify it.

"You'll wear it, Dora?" he pleaded.

"Lorne, you are the dearest fellow! But how could I? Everybody would guess!"

Her gaze, nevertheless, rested fascinated on the ring, which she posed as it pleased her.

"Let them guess! I'd rather they knew, but—it does look well on your finger, dear."

She held it up once more to the light, then slipped it decisively off and gave it back to him. "I can't, you know, Lorne. I didn't really say you might get it; and now you'll have to keep it till—till the time comes. But this much I will say—it's the sweetest thing, and you've shown the loveliest taste, and if it weren't such a dreadful give-away I'd like to wear it awfully."

They discussed it with argument, with endearment, with humour, and reproach, but her inflexible basis soon showed through their talk: she would not wear the ring. So far he prevailed, that it was she, not he, who kept it. Her insistence that he should take it back brought something like anger out of him; and in the surprise of this she yielded so much. She did it unwillingly at the time, but afterward, when she tried on the thing again in the privacy of her own room, she was rather satisfied to have it, safe under lock and key, a flashing, smiling mystery to visit when she liked and reveal when she would.

"Lorne could never get me such a beauty again if he lost it," she advised herself, "and he's awfully careless. And I'm not sure that I won't tell Eva Delarue, just to show it to her. She's as close as wax."

One feels a certain sorrow for the lover on his homeward way, squaring his shoulders against the foolish perversity of the feminine mind, resolutely guarding his heart from any hint of real reprobation. Through the sweetness of her lips and the affection of her pretty eyes, through all his half-possession of all her charms and graces, must have come dully the sense of his great occasion *manqué*,[1] that dear day of love when it leaves the mark of its claim. And in one's regret there is perhaps some alloy of pity, that less respectful thing. We know him elsewhere capable of essaying heights, yet we seem to look down upon the drama of his heart. It may be well to remember that the level is not everything in love. He who carefully adjusts an intellectual machine may descry a

---

1 Lost.

higher mark; he can construct nothing in a mistress; he is, therefore, able to see the facts and to discriminate the desirable. But Lorne loved with all his imagination. This way dares the imitation of the gods, by which it improves the quality of the passion, so that such a love stands by itself to be considered, apart from the object, one may say. A strong and beautiful wave lifted Lorne Murchison along to his destiny, since it was the pulse of his own life, though Dora Milburn played moon to it.

TWENTY

Alfred Hesketh had, after all, written to young Murchison about his immediate intention of sailing for Canada and visiting Elgin; the letter arrived a day or two later. It was brief and business-like, but it gave Lorne to understand that since his departure the imperial idea had been steadily fermenting, not only in the national mind, but particularly in Hesketh's; that it produced in his case a condition only to be properly treated by personal experience. Hesketh was coming over to prove whatever advantage there was in seeing for yourself. That he was coming with the right bias Lorne might infer, he said, from the fact that he had waited a fortnight to get his passage by the only big line to New York that stood out for our mercantile supremacy against American combination.

"He needn't bother to bring any bias," Lorne remarked when he had read this, "but he'll have to pay a lot of extra luggage on the one he takes back with him."

He felt a little irritation at being offered the testimony of the Cunard ticket.[1] Back on his native soil, its independence ran again like sap in him: nobody wanted a present of goodwill; the matter stood on its merits.

He was glad, nevertheless, that Hesketh was coming, gratified that it would now be his turn to show prospects, and turn figures into facts, and make plain the imperial profit from the further side. Hesketh was such an intelligent fellow, there would be the

---

1   Hesketh has taken his passage on a ship owned by the Cunard
    steamship line as a demonstration of his allegiance to Lorne's ideas,
    because it is "the only big line to New York that stood out for our mer-
    cantile supremacy against American combination." Lorne thinks Hes-
    keth is perhaps protesting too much.

keenest sort of pleasure in demonstrating things, big things, to him, little things, too, ways of living, differences of habit. Already in the happy exercise of his hospitable instinct he saw how Hesketh would get on with his mother, with Stella, with Dr. Drummond. He saw Hesketh interested, domiciled, remaining—the ranch life this side of the Rockies, Lorne thought, would tempt him, or something new and sound in Winnipeg. He kept his eye open for chances, and noted one or two likely things. "We want labour mostly," he said to Advena, "but nobody is refused leave to land because he has a little money."

"I should think not, indeed," remarked Mrs. Murchison, who was present. "I often wish your father and I had had a little more when we began. That whole Gregory block was going for three thousand dollars then. I wonder what it's worth now?"

"Yes, but you and father are worth more, too," remarked Stella acutely.

"In fact, all the elder members of the family have approximated in value, Stella," said her brother, "and you may too, in time."

"I'll take my chance with the country," she retorted. They were all permeated with the question of the day; even Stella, after holding haughtily aloof for some time, had been obliged to get into step, as she described it, with the silly old Empire. Whatever it was in England, here it was a family affair; I mean in the town of Elgin, in the shops and the offices, up and down the tree-bordered streets as men went to and from their business, atomic creatures building the reef of the future, but conscious, and wanting to know what they were about. Political parties had long declared themselves, the Hampden Debating Society had had several grand field nights. Prospective lifelong friendships, male and female, in every form of "the Collegiate," had been put to this touchstone, sometimes with shattering effect. If you would not serve with Wallingham the greatness of Britain you were held to favour going over to the United States; there was no middle course. It became a personal matter in the ward schools, and small boys pursued small boys with hateful cries of "Annexationist!"[1] The subject even trickled about the apple-barrels and potato-bags of the market square. Here it should have raged, pregnant

1 A person in favour of the "annexation" of Canada by the United States. Duncan's acquaintance Erastus Wiman and her friend Goldwin Smith were accused of being "annexationists" for advocating what they called "commercial union" with the United States.

as it was with bucolic[1] blessing; but our agricultural friends expect nothing readily except adverse weather, least of all a measure of economic benefit to themselves. Those of Fox County thought it looked very well, but it was pretty sure to work out some other way. Elmore Crow failed heavily to catch a light even from Lorne Murchison.

"You keep your hair on, Lorne," he advised. "We ain't going to get such big chances yet. An' if we do the blooming syndicates'll spoil 'em for us."

There were even dissentients among the farmers. The voice of one was raised who had lived laborious years, and many of them, in the hope of seeing his butter and cheese go unimpeded across the American line. It must be said, however, that still less attention was paid to him, and it was generally conceded that he would die without the sight.

It was the great topic. The day Wallingham went his defiant furthest in the House and every colonial newspaper set it up in acclaiming headlines, Horace Williams, enterprising fellow, remembered that Lorne had seen the great man under circumstances that would probably pan out, and sent round Rawlins. Rawlins was to get something that would do to call "Wallingham in the Bosom of his Family," and as much as Lorne cared to pour into him about his own view of the probable issue. Rawlins failed to get the interview, came back to say that Lorne didn't seem to think himself a big enough boy for that, but he did not return empty-handed. Mr. Murchison sent Mr. Williams the promise of some contributions upon the question of the hour which he had no objection to sign, and which Horace should have for the good of the cause. Horace duly had them, the *Express* duly published them, and they were copied in full by the *Dominion* and several other leading journals, with an amount of comment which every one but Mrs. Murchison thought remarkable.

"I don't pretend to understand it," she said, "but anybody can see that he knows what he's talking about." John Murchison read them with a critical eye and a pursed-out lip.

"He takes too much for granted."

"What does he take for granted?" asked Mrs. Murchison.

"Other folks being like himself," said the father.

That, no doubt, was succinct and true; nevertheless, the arti-

---

1 Of the country; rural, pastoral.

cles had competence as well as confidence. The writer treated facts with restraint and conditions with sympathy. He summoned ideas from the obscurity of men's minds, and marshalled them in the light, so that many recognized what they had been trying to think. He wrote with homeliness as well as force, wishing much more to make the issue recognizable than to create fine phrases, with the result that one or two of his sentences passed into the language of the discussion, which, as any of its standard-bearers would have told you, had little use for rhetoric. The articles were competent: if you listened to Horace Williams you would have been obliged to accept them as the last, or latest, word of economic truth, though it must be left to history to endorse Mr. Williams. It was their enthusiasm, however, that gave them the wing on which they travelled. People naturally took different views, even of this quality. "Young Murchison's working the imperial idea for all it's worth," was Walter Winter's; and Octavius Milburn humorously summed up the series as "tall talk."

Alfred Hesketh came, it was felt, rather opportunely into the midst of this. Plenty of people, the whole of Market Square and East Elgin, a good part, too, probably, of the Town Ward, were unaware of his arrival; but for the little world he penetrated he was clothed with all the interest of the great contingency. His decorous head in the Emmetts' pew on Sunday morning stood for a symbol as well as for a stranger. The nation was on the eve of a great far-reaching transaction with the mother country, and thrilling with the terms of the bargain. Hesketh was regarded by people in Elgin who knew who he was with the mingled cordiality and distrust that might have met a principal. They did not perhaps say it, but it was in their minds. "There's one of them," was what they thought when they met him in the street. At any other time he would have been just an Englishman; now he was invested with the very romance of destiny. The perception was obscure, but it was there. Hesketh, on the other hand, found these good people a very well-dressed, well-conditioned, decent lot, rather sallower than he expected, perhaps, who seemed to live in a fair-sized town in a great deal of comfort, and was wholly unconscious of anything special in his relation to them or theirs to him.

He met Lorne just outside the office of Warner, Fulke, and Murchison the following day. They greeted heartily. "Now this *is* good!" said Lorne, and he thought so. Hesketh confided his first impression. "It's not unlike an English country town," he said, "only the streets are wider, and the people don't look so much in earnest."

"Oh, they're just as much in earnest some of the time," Lorne laughed, "but maybe not all the time!"

The sun shone crisply round them; there was a brisk October market; on the other side of the road Elmore Crow dangled his long legs over a cart flap and chewed a cheroot. Elgin was abroad, doing business on its wide margin of opportunity. Lorne cast a backward glance at conditions he had seen.

"I know what you mean," he said. "Sharp of you to spot it so soon, old chap! You're staying with the English Church minister, aren't you—Mr. Emmett? Some connection of yours, aren't they?"

"Mrs. Emmett is Chafe's sister—Mrs. Chafe, you know, is my aunt," Hesketh reminded him. "I say, Murchison, I left old Chafe wilder than ever. Wallingham's committee keep sending him leaflets and things. They take it for granted he's on the right side, since his interests are. The other day they asked him for a sub-scription! The old boy sent his reply to the *Daily News* and car-ried it about for a week. I think that gave him real satisfaction; but he hates the things by post."

Lorne laughed delightedly. "I expect he's snowed under with them. I sent him my own valuable views last week."

"I'm afraid they'll only stiffen him. That got to be his great argument after you left, the fact that you fellows over here want it. He doesn't approve of a bargain if the other side see a profit. Curiously enough, his foremen and people out in Chiswick are all for it. I was talking to one of them just before I left—'Stands to reason, sir,' he said, 'we don't want to pay more for a loaf than we do now. But we'll do it, sir, if it means downing them Germans,' he said."

Lorne's eyebrows half perceptibly twitched. "They do 'sir' you a lot over there, don't they?" he said. "It was as much as I could do to get at what a fellow of that sort meant, tumbling over the 'sirs' he propped it up with. Well, all kinds of people, all kinds of argument, I suppose, when it comes to trying to get 'em solid! But I was going to say we are all hoping you'll give us a part of your time while you're in Elgin. My family are looking forward to meeting you. Come along and let me introduce you to my father now—he's only round the corner."

"By all means!" said Hesketh, and they fell into step together. As Lorne said, it was only a short distance, but far enough to communicate a briskness, an alertness, from the step of one young man to that of the other. "I wish it were five miles," Hesketh said, all his stall-fed muscles responding to the new call of his heart and lungs. "Any good walks about here? I asked Emmett, but he didn't know—supposed you could walk to Clayfield if you didn't take the car. He seems to have lost his legs. I suppose parsons do."

"Not all of them," said Lorne. "There's a fellow that has a church over in East Elgin, Finlay his name is, that beats the record of anything around here. He just about ranges the county in the course of a week."

"The place is too big for one parish, no doubt," Hesketh remarked.

"Oh, he's a Presbyterian! The Episcopalians haven't got any hold to speak of over there. Here we are," said Lorne, and turned in at the door. The old wooden sign was long gone. "John Murchison and Sons" glittered instead in the plate-glass windows, but Hesketh did not see it.

"Why do you think he'll be in here?" he asked, on young Murchison's heels.

"Because he always is when he isn't over at the shop," replied Lorne. "It's his place of business—his store, you know. There he is! Hard luck—he's got a customer. We'll have to wait."

He went on ahead with his impetuous step; he did not perceive the instant's paralysis that seemed to overtake Hesketh's, whose foot dragged, however, no longer than that. It was an initiation; he had been told he might expect some. He checked his impulse to be amused, and guarded his look round, not to show unseemly curiosity. His face, when he was introduced to Alec, who was sorting some odd dozens of tablespoons, was neutral and pleasant. He reflected afterward that he had been quite equal to the occasion. He thought, too, that he had shown some adaptability. Alec was not a person of fluent discourse, and when he had inquired whether Hesketh was going to make a long stay, the conversation might have languished but for this.

"Is that Birmingham?" he asked, nodding kindly at the spoons.

"Came to us through a house in Liverpool," Alec responded. "I expect you had a stormy crossing, Mr. Hesketh."

"It was a bit choppy. We had the fiddles[1] on most of the time,"

---

1 Fiddles are a device to keep objects from falling off tables in a heavy sea.

Hesketh replied. "Most of the time. Now, how do you find the bicycle trade over here? Languishing, as it is with us?"

"Oh, it keeps up pretty well," said Alec, "but we sell more spoons. N' what do you think of this country, far as you've seen it?"

"Oh, come now, it's a little soon to ask, isn't it? Yes—I suppose bicycles go out of fashion, and spoons never do. I was thinking," added Hesketh, casting his eyes over a serried rank, "of buying a bicycle."

Alec had turned to put the spoons in their place on the shelves. "Better take your friend across to Cox's," he advised Lorne over his shoulder. "He'll be able to get a motorbike there," a suggestion which gave Mr. Hesketh to reflect later that if that was the general idea of doing business it must be an easy country to make money in.

The customer was satisfied at last, and Mr. Murchison walked sociably to the door with him; it was the secretary of the local Oddfellows' Lodge, who had come in about a furnace.

"Now's our chance," said Lorne. "Father, this is Mr. Hesketh, from London—my father, Hesketh. He can tell you all you want to know about Canada—this part of it, anyway. Over thirty years, isn't it, father, since you came out?"

"Glad to meet you," said John Murchison, "glad to meet you, Mr. Hesketh. We've heard much about you."

"You must have been quite among the pioneers of Elgin, Mr. Murchison," said Hesketh as they shook hands. Alec hadn't seemed to think of that; Hesketh put it down to the counter.

"Not quite," said John. "We'll say among the early arrivals."

"Have you ever been back in your native Scotland?" asked Hesketh.

"Aye, twice."

"But you prefer the land of your adoption?"

"I do. But I think by now it'll be kin," said Mr. Murchison. "It was good to see the heather again, but a man lives best where he's taken root."

"Yes, yes. You seem to do a large business here, Mr. Murchison."

"Pretty well for the size of the place. You must get Lorne here to take you over Elgin. It's a fair sample of our rising manufacturing towns."

"I hope he will. I understand you manufacture to some extent yourself?"

"We make our own stoves and a few odd things."

"You don't send any across the Atlantic yet?" queried Hesketh jocularly.

"Not yet. No, sir!"

Then did Mr. Hesketh show himself in true sympathy with the novel and independent conditions of the commonwealth he found himself in.

"I beg you won't use that form with me," he said, "I know it isn't the custom of the country, and I am a friend of your son's, you see."

The iron merchant looked at him, just an instant's regard, in which astonishment struggled with the usual deliberation. Then his considering hand went to his chin.

"I see. I must remember," he said.

The son, Lorne, glanced in the pause beyond John Murchison's broad shoulders, through the store door and out into the moderate commerce of Main Street, which had carried the significance and the success of his father's life. His eye came back and moved over the contents of the place, taking stock of it, one might say, and adjusting the balance with pride. He had said very little since they had been in the store. Now he turned to Hesketh quietly.

"I wouldn't bother about that if I were you," he said. "My father spoke quite—colloquially."

"Oh!" said Hesketh.

They parted on the pavement outside. "I hope you understand," said Lorne, with an effort of heartiness, "how glad my parents will be to have you if you find yourself able to spare us any of your time?"

"Thanks very much," said Hesketh; "I shall certainly give myself the pleasure of calling as soon as possible."

TWENTY-ONE

"Dear me!" said Dr. Drummond. "Dear me! Well! And what does Advena Murchison say to all this?"

He and Hugh Finlay were sitting in the Doctor's study, the pleasantest room in the house. It was lined with standard religious philosophy, standard poets, standard fiction, all that was standard, and nothing that was not; and the shelves included several volumes of the Doctor's own sermons, published in black morocco through a local firm that did business by the subscription method, with "Drummond" in gold letters on the back. There were more copies of these, perhaps, than it would be quite thoughtful to count, though a good many were annually disposed of at the church bazaar, where the Doctor presented them with a generous hand. A sumptuous desk, and luxurious leather-covered armchairs furnished the room; a beautiful little Parian copy of a famous Cupid and Psyche[1] decorated the mantelpiece, and betrayed the touch of pagan in the Presbyterian. A bright fire burned in the grate, and there was not a speck of dust anywhere.

Dr. Drummond, lost in his chair, with one knee dropped on the other, joined his fingers at the tips, and drew his forehead into a web of wrinkles. Over it his militant grey crest curled up; under it his eyes darted two shrewd points of interrogation.

"What does Miss Murchison say to it?" he repeated with craft and courage, as Finlay's eyes dropped and his face slowly flushed under the question. It was in this room that Dr. Drummond examined "intending communicants" and cases likely to come before the Session;[2] he never shirked a leading question.

"Miss Murchison," said Finlay, after a moment, "was good enough to say that she thought her father's house would be open to Miss—to my friends when they arrived; but I thought it would be more suitable to ask your hospitality, sir."

"Did she so?" asked Dr. Drummond gravely. It was more a comment than an inquiry. "Did she so?" Infinite kindness was in it.

The young man assented with an awkward gesture, half bend, half nod, and neither for a moment spoke again. It was one of those silences with a character, conscious, tentative. Half veiled, disavowed thoughts rose up in it, awakened by Advena's name, turning away their heads. The ticking of the Doctor's old-fashioned watch came through it from his waistcoat pocket. It was he who spoke first.

"I christened Advena Murchison," he said. "Her father was one of those who called me, as a young man, to this ministry. The names of both her parents are on my first communion roll. Aye!"

The fire snapped and the watch went on ticking.

---

1 A small white marble sculpture of the God of Love from classical mythology and his beloved, Psyche.
2 A local judicial body in the Presbyterian church, composed of the minister and elders of the parish or congregation.

"So Advena thought well of it all. Did she so?"

The young man raised his heavy eyes and looked unflinchingly at Dr. Drummond.

"Miss Murchison," he said, "is the only other person to whom I have confided the matter. I have written, fixing that date, with her approval—at her desire. Not immediately. I took time to—think it over. Then it seemed better to arrange for the ladies' reception first, so before posting I have come to you."

"Then the letter has not gone?"

"It is in my pocket."

"Finlay, you will have a cigar? I don't smoke myself; my throat won't stand it; but I understand these are passable. Grant left them here. He's a chimney, that man Grant. At it day and night."

This was a sacrifice. Dr. Drummond hated tobacco, the smell of it, the ash of it, the time consumed in it. There was no need at all to offer Finlay one of the Reverend Grant's cigars. Propitiation must indeed be desired when the incense is abhorred. But Finlay declined to smoke. The Doctor, with his hands buried deep in his trousers pockets, where something metallic clinked in them, began to pace and turn. His mouth had the set it wore when he handled a difficult motion in the General Assembly.[1]

"I'm surprised to hear that, Finlay; though it may be well not to be surprised at what a woman will say—or won't say."

"Surprised?" said the younger man confusedly. "Why should any one be surprised?"

"I know her well. I've watched her grow up. I remember her mother's trouble because she would scratch the paint on the pew in front of her with the nails in her little boots. John Murchison sang in the choir in those days. He had a fine bass voice; he has it still. And Mrs. Murchison had to keep the family in order by herself. It was sometimes as much as she could do, poor woman. They sat near the front, and many a good hard look I used to give them while I was preaching. Knox Church was a different place then. The choir sat in the back gallery, and we had a precentor,[2]

---

1 Annual general meeting of elders, ministers and members of the Presbyterian Church, for the purpose of adjudicating cases and making Church law.

2 Early in the nineteenth century, Presbyterians in Canada did not allow musical instruments in church. The singing was led by a precentor, a man who had an expert knowledge of hymn tunes and a good singing voice, who determined the correct pitch by means of a tuning fork.

a fine fellow—he lost an arm at Ridgway in the Fenian raid.[1] Well I mind him and the frown he would put on when he took up the fork. But, for that matter, every man Jack in the choir had a frown on in the singing, though the bass fellows would be the fiercest. We've been twice enlarged since, and the organist has long been a salaried professional. But I doubt whether the praise of God is any heartier than it was when it followed Peter Craig's tuning-fork. Aye. You'd always hear John Murchison's note in the finish."

Finlay was listening with the look of a charmed animal. Dr. Drummond's voice was never more vibrant, more moving, more compelling than when he called up the past; and here to Finlay the past was itself enchanted.

"She always had those wonderful dark eyes. She's pale enough now, but as a child she was rosy. Taking her place of winter evening, with the snow on her fur cap and her hair, I often thought her a picture. I liked to have her attention while I was preaching, even as a child; and when she was absent I missed her. It was through my ministrations that she saw her way to professing the Church of Christ, and under my heartfelt benediction that she first broke bread in her Father's house. I hold the girl in great affection, Finlay; and I grieve to hear this."

The other drew a long breath, and his hand tightened on the arm of his chair. He was, as we know, blind to many of the world's aspects, even to those in which he himself figured; and Dr. Drummond's plain hypothesis of his relations with Advena came before him in forced illumination, flash by tragic flash. This kind of revelation is more discomforting than darkness, since it carries the surprise of assault, and Finlay groped in it, helpless and silent.

"You are grieved, sir?" he said mechanically.

"Man, she loves you!" exclaimed the Doctor, in a tone that would no longer forbear.

Hugh Finlay seemed to take the words just where they were levelled, in his breast. He half leaped from his chair; the lower part of his face had the rigidity of iron.

"I am not obliged to discuss such a matter as that," he said hoarsely, "with you or with any man."

---

1   In the mid-nineteenth century, groups of Irish men and their sympathisers based in the United States staged raids on Canada in an attempt to pressure the British government to grant Irish independence. The Fenian raid on Ridgway, a town in the Niagara Peninsula in Ontario, took place in 1866.

He looked confusedly about him for his hat, which he had left in the hall; and Dr. Drummond profited by the instant. He stepped across and laid a hand on the younger man's shoulder. Had they both been standing the gesture would have been impossible to Dr. Drummond with dignity; as it was, it had not only that, but benignance, a kind of tender good-will, rare in expression with the minister, rare, for that matter, in feeling with him too, though the chord was always there to be sounded.

"Finlay," he said; "Finlay!"

Between two such temperaments the touch and the tone together made an extraordinary demonstration. Finlay, with an obvious effort, let it lie upon him. The tension of his body relaxed, that of his soul he covered, leaning forward and burying his head in his hands.

"Will you say I have no claim to speak?" asked Dr. Drummond, and met silence. "It is upon my lips to beg you not to send that letter, Finlay." He took his hand from the young man's shoulder, inserted a thumb in each of his waistcoat pockets, and resumed his walk.

"On my own account I must send it," said Finlay. "On Miss Murchison's—she bids me to. We have gone into the matter together."

"I can imagine what you made of it together. There's a good deal of her father in Advena. He would be the last man to say a word for himself. You told her this tale you have told me, and she told you to get Miss Christie out and marry her without delay, eh? And what would you expect her to tell you—a girl of that spirit?"

"I cannot see why pride should influence her."

"Then you know little about women. It was pride, pure and simple, Finlay, that made her tell you that—and she'll be a sorry woman if you act on it."

"No," said Finlay, suddenly looking up, "I may know little about women, but I know more about Advena Murchison than that. She advised me in the sense she thought right and honourable, and her advice was sincere. And, Dr. Drummond, deeply as I feel the bearing of Miss Murchison's view of the matter, I could not, in any case, allow my decision to rest upon it. It must stand by itself."

"You mean that your decision to marry to oblige your aunt should not be influenced by the fact that it means the wrecking of your own happiness and that of another person. I can't agree,

Finlay. I spoke first of Advena Murchison because her part and lot in it are most upon my heart. I feel, too, that some one should put her case. Her own father would never open his lips. If you're to be hauled over the coals about this I'm the only man to do it. And I'm going to."

A look of sharp determination came into the minister's eyes; he had the momentary air of a small Scotch terrier with a bidding. Finlay looked at him in startled recognition of another possible phase of his dilemma; he thought he knew it in every wretched aspect. It was a bold reference of Dr. Drummond's; it threw down the last possibility of withdrawal for Finlay; they must have it out now, man to man, with a little, perhaps, even in that unlikely place, of penitent to confessor. It was an exigency, it helped Finlay to pull himself together, and there was something in his voice, when he spoke, like the vibration of relief.

"I am pained and distressed more than I have any way of telling you, sir," he said, "that—the state of feeling—between Miss Murchison and myself should have been so plain to you. It is incomprehensible to me that it should be so, since it is only very lately that I have understood it truly myself. I hope you will believe that it was the strangest, most unexpected, most sudden revelation."

He paused and looked timidly at the Doctor; he, the great fellow, in straining bondage to his heart, leaning forward with embarrassed tension in every muscle, Dr. Drummond alert, poised, critical, balancing his little figure on the hearthrug.

"I preach faith in miracles," he said. "I dare say between you and her it would be just that."

"I have been deeply culpable. Common sense, common knowledge of men and women should have warned me that there might be danger. But I looked upon the matter as our own—as between us only. I confess that I have not till now thought of that part of it, but surely—You cannot mean to tell me that what I have always supposed my sincere and devoted friendship for Miss Murchison has been in any way prejudicial—"

"To her in the ordinary sense? To her prospects of marriage and her standing in the eyes of the community? No, Finlay. No. I have not heard the matter much referred to. You seem to have taken none of the ordinary means—you have not distinguished her in the eye of gossip. If you had it would be by no means the gravest thing to consider. Such tokens are quickly forgotten, especially here, where attentions of the kind often, I've noticed, lead to nothing. It is the fact, and not the appearance of it, that I speak of—that I am concerned with."

"The fact is beyond mending," said Finlay, dully.

"Aye, the fact is beyond mending. It is beyond mending that Advena Murchison belongs to you and you to her in no common sense. It's beyond mending that you cannot now be separated without such injury to you both as I would not like to look upon. It's beyond mending, Finlay, because it is one of those things that God has made. But it is not beyond marring, and I charge you to look well what you are about in connection with it."

A flash of happiness, of simple delight, lit the young man's sombre eyes as the phrases fell. To the minister they were mere forcible words; to Finlay they were soft rain in a famished land. Then he looked again heavily at the pattern of the carpet.

"Would you have me marry Advena Murchison?" he said, with a kind of shamed yielding to the words.

"I would—and no other. Man, I saw it from the beginning!" exclaimed the Doctor. "I don't say it isn't an awkward business. But at least there'll be no heartbreak in Scotland. I gather you never said a word to the Bross lady on the subject, and very few on any other. You tell me you left it all with that good woman, your aunt, to arrange after you left. Do you think a creature of any sentiment would have accepted you on those terms? Not she. So far as I can make out, Miss Cameron is just a sensible, wise woman that would be the first to see the folly in this business if she knew the rights of it. Come, Finlay, you're not such a great man with the ladies— you can't pretend she has any affection for you."

The note of raillery in the Doctor's voice drew Finlay's brows together.

"I don't know," he said, "whether I have to think of her affections, but I do know I have to think of her dignity, her confidence, and her belief in the honourable dealing of a man whom she met under the sanction of a trusted roof. The matter may look light here; it is serious there. She has her circle of friends; they are acquainted with her engagement. She has made all her arrangements to carry it out; she has disposed of her life. I cannot ask her to reconsider her lot because I have found a happier adjustment for mine."

"Finlay," said Dr. Drummond, "you will not be known in Bross or anywhere else as a man who has jilted a woman. Is that it?"

"I will not be a man who has jilted a woman."

"There is no sophist like pride. Look at the case on its merits. On the one side a disappointment for Miss Cameron. I don't doubt she's counting on coming, but at worst a worldly disappointment. And the very grievous humiliation for you of writing to tell her that you have made a mistake. You deserve that, Finlay. If you wouldn't be a man who has jilted a woman you have no business to lend yourself to such matters with the capacity of a blind kitten. That is the damage on the one side. On the other—"

"I know all that there is to be said," interrupted Finlay, "on the other."

"Then face it, man. Go home and write the whole truth to Bross. I'll do it for you—no, I won't, either. Stand up to it yourself. You must hurt one of two women; choose the one that will suffer only in her vanity. I tell you that Scotch entanglement of yours is pure cardboard farce—it won't stand examination. It's appalling to think that out of an extravagant, hypersensitive conception of honour, egged on by that poor girl, you could be capable of turning it into the reality of your life."

"I've taken all these points of view, sir, and I can't throw the woman over. The objection to it isn't in reason—it's somehow in the past and the blood. It would mean the sacrifice of all that I hold most valuable in myself. I should expect myself after that to stick at nothing—why should I?"

"There is one point of view that perhaps you have not taken," said Dr. Drummond, in his gravest manner. "You are settled here in your charge. In all human probability you will remain here in East Elgin, as I have remained here, building and fortifying the place you have won for the Lord in the hearts of the people. Advena Murchison's life will also go on here—there is nothing to take it away. You have both strong natures. Are you prepared for that?"

"We are both prepared for it. We shall both be equal to it. I count upon her, and she counts upon me, to furnish in our friendship the greater part of whatever happiness life may have in store for us."

"Then you must be a pair of born lunatics!" said Dr. Drummond, his jaw grim, his eyes snapping. "What you propose is little less than a crime, Finlay. It can come to nothing but grief, if no worse. And your wife, poor woman, whatever she deserves, it is better than that! My word, if she could choose her prospect, think you she would hesitate? Finlay, I entreat you as a matter of ordinary prudence, go home and break it off. Leave Advena out of it—you have no business to make this marriage whether or no. Leave other considerations to God and to the future. I beseech you, bring it to an end!"

Finlay got up and held out his hand. "I tell you from my heart it is impossible," he said.

"I can't move you?" said Dr. Drummond. "Then let us see if the Lord can. You will not object, Finlay, to bring the matter before Him, here and now, in a few words of prayer? I should find it hard to let you go without them."

They went down upon their knees where they stood; and Dr. Drummond did little less than order Divine interference; but the prayer that was inaudible was to the opposite purpose.

Ten minutes later the minister himself opened the door to let Finlay out into the night. "You will remember," he said as they shook hands, "that what I think of your position in this matter makes no difference whatever to the question of your aunt's coming here with Miss Cameron when they arrive. You will bring them to this house as a matter of course. I wish you could be guided to a different conclusion, but, after all, it is your own conscience that must be satisfied. They will be better here than at the Murchisons'," he added with a last shaft of reproach, "and they will be very welcome."

It said much for Dr. Drummond that Finlay was able to fall in with the arrangement. He went back to his boarding-house, and added a postscript embodying it to his letter to Bross. Then he walked out upon the midnight two feverish miles to the town, and posted the letter. The way back was longer and colder.

TWENTY-TWO

"Well, Winter," said Octavius Milburn, "I expect there's business in this for you."

Mr. Milburn and Mr. Winter had met in the act of unlocking their boxes at the post-office. Elgin had enjoyed postal delivery for several years, but not so much as to induce men of business to abandon the post-office box that had been the great convenience succeeding window inquiry. In time the boxes would go, but the habit of dropping in for your own noonday mail on the way home to dinner was deep-rooted, and undoubtedly you got it earlier. Moreover, it takes time to engender confidence in a postman when he is drawn from your midst, and when you know perfectly well that he would otherwise be driving the mere watering-cart, or delivering the mere ice, as he was last year.

"Looks like it," responded Mr. Winter, cheerfully. "The boys have been round as usual. I told them they'd better try another shop this time, but they seemed to think the old reliable was good enough to go on with."

This exchange, to any one in Elgin, would have been patently simple. On that day there was only one serious topic in Elgin, and there could have been only one reference to business for Walter Winter. The *Dominion* had come up the day before with the announcement that Mr. Robert Farquharson, who, for an aggregate of eleven years, had represented the Liberals of South Fox in the Canadian House of Commons, had been compelled under medical advice to withdraw from public life. The news was unexpected, and there was rather a feeling among Mr. Farquharson's local support in Elgin that it shouldn't have come from Toronto. It will be gathered that Horace Williams, as he himself acknowledged, was wild. The general feeling, and to some extent Mr. Williams's, was appeased by the further information that Mr. Farquharson had been obliged to go to Toronto to see a specialist, whose report he had naturally enough taken to party headquarters, whence the *Dominion* would get it, as Mr. Williams said, by telephone or any quicker way there was. Williams, it should be added, was well ahead with the details, as considerate as was consistent with public enterprise, of the retiring member's malady, its duration, the date of the earliest symptoms, and the growth of anxiety in Mrs. Farquharson, who had finally insisted—and how right she was!—on the visit to the specialist, upon which she had accompanied Mr. Farquharson. He sent round Rawlins. So that Elgin was in possession of all the facts, and Walter Winter, who had every pretension to contest the seat again, and every satisfaction that it wouldn't be against Farquharson, might naturally be expected to be taken up with them sufficiently to understand a man who slapped him on the shoulder in the post-office with the remark I have quoted.

"I guess they know what they're about," returned Mr. Milburn. "It's a bad knock for the Grits, old Farquharson having to drop out. He's getting up in years, but he's got a great hold here. He'll be a dead loss in votes to his party. I always said our side wouldn't have a chance till the old man was out of the way."

Mr. Winter twisted the watch-chain across his protuberant waistcoat, and his chin sank in reflective folds above his necktie. Above that again his nose drooped over his moustache, and his eyelids over his eyes, which sought the floor. Altogether he looked sunk, like an overfed bird, in deferential contemplation of what Mr. Milburn was saying.

"They've nobody to touch him, certainly, in either ability or experience," he replied, looking up to do it, with a handsome air of concession. "Now that Martin's dead, and Jim Fawkes come that howler over Pink River, they'll have their work cut out for them to find a man. I hear Fawkes takes it hard, after all he's done for 'em, not to get the nomination, but they won't hear of it. Quite right, too; he's let too many people in over that concession of his to be popular, even among his friends."

"I suppose he has. Dropped anything there yourself?—No? Nor I. When a thing gets to the boom stage I say let it alone, even if there's gold in it and you've got a School of Mines man to tell you so. Fawkes came out of it at the small end himself, I expect, but that doesn't help him any in the eyes of business men."

"I hear," said Walter Winter, stroking his nose, "that old man Parsons has come right over since the bosses at Ottawa have put so much money on preference trade with the old country. He says he was a Liberal once, and may be a Liberal again, but he doesn't see his way to voting to give his customers blankets cheaper than he can make them, and he'll wait till the clouds roll by."

"He won't be the only one, either," said Milburn. "Take my word for it, they'll be dead sick and sorry over this imperial craze in a year's time, every Government that's taken it up. The people won't have it. The Empire looks nice on the map, but when it comes to practical politics their bread and butter's in the home industries. There's a great principle at stake, Winter; I must say I envy you standing up for it under such favourable conditions. Liberals like Young and Windle may talk big, but when it comes to the ballot-box you'll have the whole manufacturing interest of the place behind you, and nobody the wiser. It's a great thing to carry the standard on an issue above and beyond party politics— it's a purer air, my boy."

Walter Winter's nod confirmed the sagacity of this, and appreciated the highmindedness. It was a parting nod; Mr. Winter had too much on hand that morning to waste time upon Octavius Milburn; but it was full of the qualities that ensure the success of a man's relation with his fellows. Consideration was in it, and understanding, and that kind of geniality that offers itself on a plain business footing, a commercial heartiness that has no nonsense about it. He had half a dozen casual chats like this with Mr. Milburn on his way up Main Street, and his manner expanded in cordiality and respect with each, as if his growing confidence in himself increased his confidence in his fellow men. The same assurance greeted him several times over. Every friend wanted to remind him of the enemy's exigency, and to assure him that the enemy's new policy was enough by itself to bring him romping in at last; and to every assurance he presented the same acceptable attitude of desiring for particular reasons to take special note of such valuable views. At the end he had neither elicited nor imparted a single opinion of any importance; nevertheless, he was quite entitled to his glow of satisfaction.

Among Mr. Winter's qualifications for political life was his capacity to arrive at an estimate of the position of the enemy. He was never persuaded to his own advantage; he never stepped ahead of the facts. It was one of the things that made him popular with the other side, his readiness to do justice to their equipment, to acknowledge their chances. There is gratification of a special sort in hearing your points of vantage confessed by the foe; the vanity is soothed by his open admission that you are worthy of his steel. It makes you a little less keen, somehow, about defeating him. It may be that Mr. Winter had an instinct for this, or perhaps he thought such discourse more profitable, if less pleasant, than derisive talk in the opposite sense. At all events, he gained something and lost nothing by it, even in his own camp, where swagger might be expected to breed admiration. He was thought a level-headed fellow who didn't expect miracles; his forecast in most matters was quoted, and his defeats at the polls had been to some extent neutralized by his sagacity in computing the returns in advance.

So that we may safely follow Mr. Winter to the conclusion that the Liberals of South Fox were somewhat put to it to select a successor to Robert Farquharson who could be depended upon to keep the party credit exactly where he found it. The need was unexpected, and the two men who would have stepped most naturally into Farquharson's shoes were disqualified as Winter described. The retirement came at a calculating moment. South Fox still declared itself with pride an unhealthy division for Conservatives; but new considerations had thrust themselves among Liberal counsels, and nobody yet knew what the country would say to them. The place was a "Grit" stronghold, but its steady growth as an industrial centre would give a new significance to the figures of the next returns. The Conservative was the manufacturers' party, and had been ever since the veteran Sir John Macdonald declared for a protective "National Policy," and placed the plain issue before the country which divided the industrial and the agricultural interests. A certain number of millowners—Mr. Milburn mentioned Young and Windle—belonged to the Liberals, as if to illustrate the fact that you inherit your party in Canada as you inherit your "denomination," or your nose; it accompanies you, simply, to the grave. But they were exceptions, and there was no doubt that the other side had been considerably strengthened by the addition of two or three thriving and highly capitalized concerns during the past five years. Upon the top of this had come the possibility of a great and dramatic change of trade relations with Great Britain, which the Liberal Government at Ottawa had given every sign of willingness to adopt—had, indeed, initiated, and were bound by word and letter to follow up. Though the moment had not yet come, might never come, for its acceptance or rejection by the country as a whole, there could be no doubt that every bye-election would be concerned with the policy involved, and that every Liberal candidate must be prepared to stand by it in so far as the leaders had conceived and pushed it. Party feeling was by no means unanimous in favour of the change; many Liberals saw commercial salvation closer in improved trade relations with the United States. On the other hand, the new policy, clothed as it was in the attractive sentiment of loyalty, and making for the solidarity of the British race, might be depended upon to capture votes which had been hitherto Conservative mainly because these professions were supposed to be an indissoluble part of Conservatism. It was a thing to split the vote sufficiently to bring an unusual amount of anxiety and calculation into Liberal counsels. The other side were in no doubt or difficulty: Walter Winter was good enough for them, and it was their cheerful conviction that Walter Winter would put a large number of people wise on the subject of preference trade bye-and-bye who at present only knew enough to vote for it.

The great question was the practicability of the new idea, and how much further it could safely be carried in a loyal Dominion which was just getting on its industrial legs. It was debated with anxiety at Ottawa, and made the subject of special instruction to

South Fox, where the bye-election would have all the importance of an early test. "It's a clear issue," wrote an influential person at Ottawa to the local party leaders at Elgin, "we don't want any tendency to hedge or double. It's straight business with us, the thing we want, and it will be till Wallingham either gets it through over there, or finds he can't deal with us. Meanwhile it might be as well to ascertain just how much there is in it for platform purposes in a safe spot like South Fox, and how much the fresh opposition will cost us where we can afford it. We can't lose the seat, and the returns will be worth anything in their bearing on the General Election next year. The objection to Carter is that he's only half convinced; he couldn't talk straight if he wanted to, and that lecture tour of his in the United States ten years ago pushing reciprocity with the Americans would make awkward literature."

The rejection of Carter practically exhausted the list of men available whose standing in the town and experience of its suffrages brought them naturally into the field of selection; and at this point Cruickshank wrote to Farquharson suggesting the dramatic departure involved in the name of Lorne Murchison. Cruickshank wrote judiciously, leaving the main arguments in Lorne's favour to form themselves in Farquharson's mind, but countering the objections that would rise there by the suggestion that after a long period of confidence and steady going, in fact of the orthodox and expected, the party should profit by the swing of the pendulum toward novelty and tentative, rather than bring forward a candidate who would represent, possibly misrepresent, the same beliefs and intentions on a lower personal level. As there was no first-rate man of the same sort to succeed Farquharson, Cruickshank suggested the undesirability of a second-rate man; and he did it so adroitly that the old fellow found himself in a good deal of sympathy with the idea. He had small opinion of the lot that was left for selection, and smaller relish for the prospect of turning his honourable activity over to any one of them. Force of habit and training made him smile at Cruickshank's proposition as impracticable, but he felt its attraction, even while he dismissed it to an inside pocket. Young Murchison's name would be so unlooked-for that if he, Farquharson, could succeed in imposing it upon the party it would be almost like making a personal choice of his successor, a grateful idea in abdication. Farquharson wished regretfully that Lorne had another five years to his credit in the Liberal record of South Fox. By the time the young fellow had earned them, he, the retiring member, would be quite on the shelf, if in no completer oblivion; he could not expect much of a voice in any nomination five years hence. He sighed to think of it.

It was at that point of his meditations that Mr. Farquharson met Squire Ormiston on the steps of the Bank of British North America, an old-fashioned building with an appearance of dignity and probity, a look of having been founded long ago upon principles which raised it above fluctuation, exactly the place in which Mr. Farquharson and Squire Ormiston might be expected to meet. The two men, though politically opposed, were excellent friends; they greeted cordially.

"So you're ordered out of politics, Farquharson?" said the squire. "We're all sorry for that, you know."

"I'm afraid so; I'm afraid so. Thanks for your letter—very friendly of you, squire. I don't like it—no use pretending I do—but it seems I've got to take a rest if I want to be known as a going concern."

"A fellow with so much influence in committee ought to have more control of his nerve centres," Ormiston told him. The squire belonged to that order of elderly gentlemen who will have their little joke. "Well, have you and Bingham and Horace Williams made up your minds who's to have the seat?"

Farquharson shook his head. "I only know what I see in the papers," he said. "The *Dominion* is away out with Fawkes, and the *Express* is about as lukewarm with Carter as he is with federated trade."

"Your Government won't be obliged to you for Carter," said Mr. Ormiston; "a more slack-kneed, double-jointed scoundrel was never offered a commission in a respectable cause. He'll be the first to rat if things begin to look queer for this new policy of yours and Wallingham's."

"He hasn't got it yet," Farquharson admitted, "and he won't with my good-will. So you're with us for preference trade, Ormiston?"

"It's a thing I'd like to see. It's a thing I'm sorry we're not in a position to take up practically ourselves. But you won't get it, you know. You'll be defeated by the senior partner. It's too much of a doctrine for the people of England. They're listening to Wallingham just now because they admire him, but they won't listen to you. I doubt whether it will ever come to an issue over there. This time next year Wallingham will be sucking his thumbs and thinking of something else. No, it's not a thing to worry about politically, for it won't come through."

The squire's words suggested so much relief in that conviction that Farquharson, sharp on the flair of the experienced nose for waverers, looked at him observantly.

"I'm not so sure. It's a doctrine with a fine practical application for them as well as for us, if they can be got to see it, and they're bound to see it in time. It's a thing I never expected to live to believe, never thought would be practicable until lately, but now I think there's a very good chance of it. And, hang it all," he added, "it may be unreasonable, but the more I notice the Yankees making propositions to get us away from it, the more I want to see it come through."

"I have very much the same feeling," the squire acknowledged. "I've been turning the matter over a good deal since that last Conference[1] showed which way the wind was blowing. And the fellows in your Government gave them a fine lead. But such a proposition was bound to come from your side. The whole political history of the country shows it. We're pledged to take care of the damned industries."

Farquharson smiled at the note of depression. "Well, we want a bigger market somewhere," he said with detachment, "and it looks as if we could get it now Uncle Sam has had a fright. If the question comes to be fought out at the polls, I don't see how your party could do better than go in for a wide scheme of reciprocity with the Americans—in raw products, of course, with a tariff to match theirs on manufactured goods. That would shut a pretty tight door on British connection though."

"They'll not get my vote if they do," said the squire, thrusting his hands fiercely into his breeches pockets.

"As you say, it's most important to put up a man who will show the constituency all the credit and benefit there is in it, anyhow," Farquharson observed. "I've had a letter this morning," he added, laughing, "from a fellow—one of the bosses, too—who wants us to nominate young Murchison."

"The lawyer?"

"That's the man. He's too young, of course—not thirty. But he's well known in the country districts; I don't know a man of his age with a more useful service record. He's got a lot of friends, and he's come a good deal to the front lately through that inter-

---

1 The Colonial Conference of 1902, a meeting of representatives of the self-governing colonies of Great Britain and the British Government, at which Wilfrid Laurier guardedly supported Imperial Preference.

imperial communications business—we might do worse. And upon my word, we're in such a hole—"

"Farquharson," said old Squire Ormiston, the red creeping over features that had not lost in three generations the lines of the old breed, "I've voted in the Conservative interest for forty years, and my father before me. We were Whigs when we settled in Massachusetts, and Whigs when we pulled up stakes and came North rather than take up arms against the King; but it seemed decent to support the Government that gave us a chance again under the flag, and my grandfather changed his politics. Now, confound it! the flag seems to be with the Whigs again, for fighting purposes, anyhow; and I don't seem to have any choice. I've been debating the thing for some time now, and your talk of making that fine young fellow your candidate settles it. If you can get your committee to accept young Murchison, you can count on my vote, and I don't want to brag, but I think you can count on Moneida too, though it's never sent in a Grit majority yet."

The men were standing on the steps of the bank, and the crisp air of autumn brought them both an agreeable tingle of enterprise. Farquharson's buggy was tied to the nearest maple.

"I'm going over to East Elgin to look at my brick-kilns," he said. "Get in with me, will you?"

As they drove up Main Street they encountered Walter Winter, who looked after them with a deeply considering eye.

"Old Ormiston always had the Imperial bee in his bonnet," said he.

TWENTY-THREE

Alfred Hesketh was among the first to hear of Lorne's nomination to represent the constituency of South Fox in the Dominion Parliament. The Milburns told him; it was Dora who actually made the communication. The occasion was high tea;[1] Miss Milburn's apprehension about Englishmen and late dinner had been dissipated in great amusement. Mr. Hesketh liked nothing better than high tea, liked nothing so much. He came often to the Milburns' after Mrs. Milburn said she hoped he would, and pleased her extremely by the alacrity with which he accepted her first

---

1 A tea at which meat is served; the last meal of the day.

invitation to stay to what she described as their very simple and unconventional meal. Later he won her approval entirely by saying boldly that he hoped he was going to be allowed to stay. It was only in good English society, Mrs. Milburn declared, that you found such freedom and confidence; it reminded her of Mrs. Emmett's saying that her sister-in-law in London was always at home to lunch. Mrs. Milburn considered a vague project of informing a select number of her acquaintances that she was always at home to high tea, but on reflection dismissed it, in case an inconvenient number should come at once. She would never have gone into detail, but since a tin of sardines will only hold so many, I may say for her that it was the part of wisdom.

Mr. Hesketh, however, wore the safe and attractive aspect of a single exceptional instance; there were always sardines enough for him. It will be imagined what pleasure Mrs. Milburn and Miss Filkin took in his visits, how he propped up their standard of behaviour in all things unessential, which was too likely to be growing limp, so far from approved examples. I think it was a real aesthetic satisfaction; I know they would talk of it afterward for hours, with sighing comparisons of the "form" of the young men of Elgin, which they called beside Hesketh's quite *outré*. It was a favourite word with Mrs. Milburn—*outré*. She used it like a lorgnette, and felt her familiarity with it a differentiating mark. Mr. Milburn, never so susceptible to delicate distinctions, looked upon the young Englishman with benevolent neutrality. Dora wished it to be understood that she reserved her opinion. He might be all that he seemed, and again he might not. Englishmen were so deep. They might have nice manners, but they didn't always act up to them, so far as she had noticed. There was that Honourable Somebody, who was in jail even then for trying to borrow money under false pretences from the Governor-General. Lorne, when she expressed these views to him, reassured her, but she continued to maintain a guarded attitude upon Mr. Hesketh, to everybody except Mr. Hesketh himself.

It was Dora, as I have said, who imparted the news. Lorne had come over with it in the afternoon, still a little dazed and unbelieving in the face of his tremendous luck, helped by finding her so readily credulous to thinking it reasonably possible himself. He could not have done better than come to Dora for a correction of any undue exaltation that he might have felt, however. She supplied it in ten minutes by reminding him of their wisdom in keeping the secret of their relations. His engagement to the daughter of a prominent Conservative would not indeed have told in his favour with his party, to say nothing of the anomaly of Mr. Milburn's unyielding opposition to the new policy. "I never knew father so nearly bitter about anything," Dora said, a statement which left her lover thoughtful, but undaunted.

"We'll bring him round," said Lorne, "when he sees that the British manufacturer can't possibly get the better of men on the spot, who know to a nut the local requirements."

To which she had responded, "Oh, Lorne, don't begin *that* again," and he had gone away hot-foot for the first step of preparation.

"It's exactly what I should have expected," said Hesketh, when she told him. "Murchison is the very man they want. He's cut out for a political success. I saw that when he was in England."

"You haven't been very long in the country, Mr. Hesketh, or we shouldn't hear you saying that," said Mr. Milburn, amicably. "It's a very remarkable thing with us, a political party putting forward so young a man. Now with you I expect a young fellow might get it on his rank or his wealth—your principle of nonpayment of members confines your selection more or less. I don't say you're not right, but over here we do pay, you see, and it makes a lot of difference in the competition. It isn't a greater honour, but it's more sought for. I expect there'll be a good many sore heads over this business."

"It's all the more creditable to Murchison," said Hesketh.

"Of course it is—a great feather in his cap. Oh, I don't say young Murchison isn't a rising fellow, but it's foolishness for his party—I can't think who is responsible for it. However, they've got a pretty foolish platform just now—they couldn't win this seat on it with any man. A lesson will be good for them."

"Father, don't you think Lorne will get in?" asked Dora, in a tone of injury and slight resentment.

"Not by a handful," said her father. "Mr. Walter Winter will represent South Fox in the next session of Parliament, if you ask my opinion."

"But, father," returned his daughter, with an outraged inflection, "you'll vote for Lorne?"

A smile went round the table, discreetest in Mrs. Milburn.

"I'm afraid not," said Mr. Milburn, "I'm afraid not. Sorry to disoblige, but principles are principles."

Dora perceptibly pouted. Mrs. Milburn created a diversion

with green-gage preserves. Under cover of it Hesketh asked, "Is he a great friend of yours?"

"One of my very greatest," Dora replied. "I know he'll expect father to vote for him. It makes it awfully embarrassing for me."

"Oh, I fancy he'll understand!" said Hesketh, easily. "Political convictions are serious things, you know. Friendship isn't supposed to interfere with them. I wonder," he went on, meditatively, "whether I could be of any use to Murchison. Now that I've made up my mind to stop till after Christmas I'll be on hand for the fight. I've had some experience. I used to canvass now and then from Oxford; it was always a tremendous lark."

"Oh, Mr. Hesketh, *do!* Really and truly he is one of my oldest friends, and I should love to see him get in. I know his sister, too. They're a very clever family. Quite self-made, you know, but highly respected. Promise me you will."

"I promise with pleasure. And I wish it were something it would give me more trouble to perform. I like Murchison," said Hesketh.

All this transpiring while they were supposed to be eating green-gage preserves, and Mrs. Milburn and Miss Filkin endeavoured to engage the head of the house in the kind of easy allusion to affairs of the moment to which Mr. Hesketh would be accustomed as a form of conversation—the accident to the German Empress, the marriage of one of the Rothschilds.[1] The ladies were compelled to supply most of the facts and all of the interest, but they kept up a gallant line of attack; and the young man, taking gratified possession of Dora's eyes, was extremely obliged to them.

Hesketh lost no time in communicating his willingness to be of use to Murchison, and Lorne felt all his old friendliness rise up in him as he cordially accepted the offer. It was made with British heartiness, it was thoroughly meant. Lorne was half ashamed in his recognition of its quality. A certain aloofness had grown in him against his will since Hesketh had prolonged his stay in the town, difficult to justify, impossible to define. Hesketh as Hesketh was worthily admirable as ever, wholesome and agreeable, as well turned out by his conscience as he was by his tailor; it was Hes-

---

1 Incidents in the personal lives of the rich and the royal would have been familiar to Miss Filkin and Mrs. Milburn only from society papers and gossip columns, but they assume that Hesketh is familiar with this kind of conversation.

keth in his relation to his new environment that seemed vaguely to come short. This in spite of an enthusiasm which was genuine enough; he found plenty of things to like about the country. It was perhaps in some manifestation of sensitiveness that he failed; he had the adaptability of the pioneer among rugged conditions, but he could not mingle quite immediately with the essence of them; he did not perceive the *genius loci*.[1] Lorne had been conscious of this as a kind of undefined grievance; now he specified it and put it down to Hesketh's isolation among ways that were different from the ways he knew. You were bound to notice that Hesketh as a stranger had his own point of view, his own training to retreat upon.

"I certainly liked him better over there," Lorne told Advena, "but then he was a part of it—he wasn't separated out as he is here. He was just one sort of fellow that you admired, and there were lots of sorts that you admired more. Over here you seem to see round him somehow."

"I shouldn't have thought it difficult," said his sister.

"Besides," Lorne confessed, "I expect it was easier to like him when you were inclined to like everybody. A person feels more critical of a visitor, especially when he's had advantages," he added, honestly. "I expect we don't care about having to acknowledge 'em so very much—that's what it comes to."

"I don't see them," said Advena. "Mr. Hesketh seems well enough in his way, fairly intelligent and anxious to be pleasant. But I can't say I find him a specially interesting or valuable type."

"Interesting, you wouldn't. But valuable—well, you see, you haven't been in England— you haven't seen them over there, crowds of 'em, piling up the national character. Hesketh's an average, and for an average he's high. Oh, he's a good sort—and he just *smells* of England."

"He seems all right in his politics," said John Murchison, filling his pipe from the tobacco-jar on the mantelpiece. "But I doubt whether you'll find him much assistance the way he talks of. Folks over here know their own business—they've had to learn it. I doubt if they'll take showing from Hesketh."

"They might be a good deal worse advised."

"That may be," said Mr. Murchison, and settled down in his armchair behind the *Dominion*.

---

1 Spirit of place; the associations and values of a place.

"I agree with father," said Advena. "He won't be any good, Lorne."

"Advena prefers Scotch," remarked Stella.

"I don't know. He's full of the subject," said Lorne. "He can present it from the other side."

"The side of the British exporter?" inquired his father, looking over the top of the *Dominion* with unexpected humour.

"No, sir. Though there are places where we might talk cheap overcoats and tablecloths and a few odds and ends like that. The side of the all-British loaf and the lot of people there are to eat it," said Lorne. "That ought to make a friendly feeling. And if there's anything in the sentiment of the scheme," he added, "it shouldn't do any harm to have a good specimen of the English people advocating it. Hesketh ought to be an object-lesson."

"I wouldn't put too much faith in the object-lesson," said John Murchison.

"Neither would I," said Stella emphatically. "Mister Alfred Hesketh may pass in an English crowd, but over here he's just an ignorant young man, and you'd better not have him talking with his mouth at any of your meetings. Tell him to go and play with Walter Winter."

"I heard he was asking at Volunteer Headquarters the other night," remarked Alec, "how long it would be before a man like himself, if he threw in his lot with the country, could expect to get nominated for a provincial seat."

"What did they tell him?" asked Mr. Murchison, when they had finished their laugh.

"I heard they said it would depend a good deal on the size of the lot."

"And a little on the size of the man," remarked Advena.

"He said he would be willing to take a seat in a Legislature and work up," Alec went on. "Ontario for choice, because he thought the people of this Province more advanced."

"There's a representative committee being formed to give the inhabitants of the poor-house a turkey dinner on Thanksgiving Day," said Advena. "He might begin with that."

"I dare say he would if anybody told him. He's just dying to be taken into the public service," Alec said. "He's in dead earnest about it. He thinks this country's a great place because it gives a man the chance of a public career."

"Why is it," asked Advena, "that when people have no capacity for private usefulness they should be so anxious to serve the public?"

"Oh, come," said Lorne, "Hesketh has an income of his own. Why should he sweat for his living? We needn't pride ourselves on being so taken up with getting ours. A man like that is in a position to do some good, and I hope Hesketh will get a chance if he stays over here. We'll soon see how he speaks. He's going to follow Farquharson at Jordanville on Thursday week."

"I wonder at Farquharson," said his father.

By this time the candidature of Mr. Lorne Murchison was well in the public eye. The *Express* announced it in a burst of beaming headlines, with a biographical sketch and a "cut"[1] of its young fellow townsman. Horace Williams, whose hand was plain in every line, apologized for the brevity of the biography— quality rather than quantity, he said; it was all good, and time would make it better. This did not prevent the *Mercury* observing, the next evening, that the Liberal organ had omitted to state the age at which the new candidate was weaned. The Toronto papers commented according to their party bias, but so far as the candidate was concerned there was lack of the material of criticism. If he had achieved little for praise he had achieved nothing for detraction. There was no inconsistent public utterance, no doubtful transaction, no scandalous paper to bring forward to his detriment. When the fact that he was but twenty-eight years of age had been exhausted in elaborate ridicule, little more was available. The policy he championed, however, lent itself to the widest discussion, and it was instructive to note how the Opposition press, while continuing to approve the great principle involved, found material for gravest criticism in the Government's projected application of it. Interest increased in the South Fox bye-election as its first touchstone, and gathered almost romantically about Lorne Murchison as its spirited advocate. It was commonly said that whether he was returned or not on this occasion, his political future was assured; and his name was carried up and down the Dominion with every new wind of imperial doctrine that blew across the Atlantic. He himself felt splendidly that he rode upon the crest of a wave of history. However the event appeared which was hidden beyond the horizon, the great luck of that buoyant emotion, of that thrilling suspense, would be his in a very special way. He was exhilarated by the sense of crisis, and among all the conferences and calculations that armed him for his personal struggle,

---

1 An illustration; an engraving.

he would now and then breathe in his private soul, "Choose quickly, England," like a prayer.

Elgin rose to its liking for the fellow, and even his political enemies felt a half-humorous pride that the town had produced a candidate whose natural parts were held to eclipse the age and experience of party hacks. Plenty of them were found to declare that Lorne Murchison would poll more votes for the Grits than any other man they could lay their hands on, with the saving clause that neither he nor any other man could poll quite enough this time. They professed to be content to let the issue have it; meanwhile they congratulated Lorne on his chance, telling him that a knock or two wouldn't do him any harm at his age. Walter Winter, who hadn't been on speaking terms with Farquharson, made a point of shaking hands with Murchison in the publicity of the post-office, and assuring him that he, Winter, never went into a contest more confident of the straight thing on the part of the other side. Such cavilling as there was came from the organized support of his own party, and had little importance because it did. The grumblers fell into line almost as soon as Horace Williams said they would; a little oil, one small appointment wrung from the Ontario Government—Fawkes, I believe, got it— and the machine was again in good working order. Lorne even profited, in the opinion of many, by the fact of his youth, with its promise of energy and initiative, since Mr. Farquharson had lately been showing the defects as well as the qualities of age and experience, and the charge of servile timidity was already in the mouths of his critics.

The agricultural community took it, as usual, with phlegm; but there was a distinct tendency in the bar at Barker's, on market-days, to lay money on the colt.

TWENTY-FOUR

Mr. Farquharson was to retain his seat until the early spring, for the double purpose of maintaining his influence upon an important commission of which he was chairman until the work should be done, and of giving the imperial departure championed by his successor as good a chance as possible of becoming understood in the constituency. It was understood that the new writ would issue for a date in March; Elgin referred all interest to that point, and prophesied for itself a lively winter. Another event, of importance less general, was arranged for the end of February—the arrival of Miss Cameron and Mrs. Kilbannon from Scotland. Finlay had proposed an earlier date, but matters of business connected with her mother's estate would delay Miss Cameron's departure. Her arrival would be the decisive point of another campaign. He and Advena faced it without misgiving, but there were moments when Finlay greatly wished the moment past.

Their intimacy had never been conspicuous, and their determination to make no change in it could be carried out without attracting attention. It was very dear to them, that determination. They saw it as a test, as an ideal. Last of all, perhaps, as an alleviation. They were both too much encumbered with ideas to move simply, quickly, on the impulse of passion. They looked at it through the wrong end of the glass, and thought they put it farther away. They believed that their relation comprised, would always comprise, the best of life. It was matter for discussion singularly attractive; they allowed themselves upon it wide scope in theory. They could speak of it in the heroic temper, without sadness or bitterness; the thing was to tear away the veil and look fate in the face. The great thing, perhaps, was to speak of it while still they could give themselves leave; a day would arrive, they acknowledged with averted eyes, when dumbness would be more becoming. Meanwhile, Mrs. Murchison would have found it hard to sustain her charge against them that they talked of nothing but books and authors; the philosophy of life, as they were intensely creating it, was more entrancing than any book or any author. Simply and definitely, and to their own satisfaction, they had abandoned the natural demands of their state; they lived in its exaltation and were far from accidents. Deep in both of them was a kind of protective nobility; I will not say it cost them nothing, but it turned the scenes between them into comedy of the better sort, the kind that deserves the relief of stone or bronze. Advena, had she heard it, would have repelled Dr. Drummond's warning with indignation. If it were so possible to keep their friendship on an unfaltering level then, with the latitude they had, what danger could attend them later, when the social law would support them, divide them, protect them? Dr. Drummond, suspecting all, looked grimly on, and from November to March found no need to invite Mr. Finlay to occupy the pulpit of Knox Church.

They had come to full knowledge that night of their long walk in the dark together; but even then, in the rush and shock and glory of it, they had held apart; and their broken avowals had crossed with difficulty from one to the other. The whole fabric of circumstance was between them, to realize and to explore; later surveys, as we know, had not reduced it. They gave it great credit as a barrier; I suppose because it kept them out of each other's arms. It had done that.

It was Advena, I fear, who insisted most that they should continue upon terms of happy debt to one another, the balance always changing, the account never closed and rendered. She no doubt felt that she might impose the terms; she had unconsciously the sense of greater sacrifice, and knew that she had been mistress of the situation long before he was aware of it. He agreed with joy and with misgiving; he saw with enthusiasm her high conception of their alliance, but sometimes wondered, poor fellow, whether he was right in letting it cover him. He came to the house as he had done before, as often as he could, and reproached himself that he could not, after all, come very often.

That they should discuss their relation as candidly as they sustained it was perhaps a little peculiar to them, so I have laid stress on it; but it was not by any means their sole preoccupation. They talked like tried friends of their every-day affairs. Indeed, after the trouble and intoxication of their great understanding had spent itself, it was the small practical interests of life that seemed to hold them most. One might think that Nature, having made them her invitation upon the higher plane, abandoned them in the very scorn of her success to the warm human commonplaces that do her work well enough with the common type. Mrs. Murchison would have thought better of them if she had chanced again to overhear.

"I wouldn't advise you to have it lined with fur," Advena was saying. The winter had sharply announced itself, and Finlay, to her reproach about his light overcoat, had declared his intention of ordering a buffalo-skin the following day. "And the buffaloes are all gone, you know—thirty years ago," she laughed. "You really are not modern in practical matters. Does it ever surprise you that you get no pemmican for dinner, and hardly ever meet an Indian in his feathers?"

He looked at her with delight in his sombre eyes. It was a new discovery, her capacity for happily chaffing[1] him, only revealed since she had come out of her bonds to love; it was hard to say which of them took the greater pleasure in it.

---

1 Teasing.

"What is the use of living in Canada if you can't have fur on your clothes?" he demanded.

"You may have a little—astrakhan,[1] I would—on the collar and cuffs," she said. "A fur lining is too hot if there happens to be a thaw, and then you would leave it off and take cold. You have all the look," she added, with a gravely considering glance at him, "of a person who ought to take care of his chest."

He withdrew his eyes hurriedly, and fixed them instead on his pipe. He always brought it with him, by her order, and Advena usually sewed. He thought as he watched her that it made the silences enjoyable.

"And expensive, I dare say, too," he said.

"Yes, more or less. Alec paid fifty dollars for his, and never liked it."

"Fifty dollars—ten pounds! No vair for me!"[2] he declared. "By the way, Mrs. Firmin is threatening to turn me out of house and home. A married daughter is coming to live with her, and she wants my rooms."

"When does she come—the married daughter?"

"Oh, not till the early spring! There's no immediate despair," said Finlay, "but it is dislocating. My books and I had just succeeded in making room for one another."

"But you will have to move, in any case, in the early spring."

"I suppose I will. I had—I might have remembered that."

"Have you found a house yet?" Advena asked him.

"No."

"Have you been looking?" It was a gentle, sensible reminder.

"I'm afraid I haven't." He moved in his chair as if in physical discomfort. "Do you think I ought—so soon? There are always plenty of—houses, aren't there?"

"Not plenty of desirable ones. Do you think you must live in East Elgin?"

"It would be rather more convenient."

"Because there are two semi-detached in River Street, just finished, that look very pretty and roomy. I thought when I saw them that one of them might be what you would like."

---

1 The fur of very young lambs from Astrakhan in Russia, or cloth made to resemble it.

2 Vair is the fur of particular kind of squirrel, used for trim of the garments of lords in medieval England, and represented in heraldry. Finlay is commenting ruefully on his poverty.

"Thank you," he said, and tried not to say it curtly.

"They belong to White, the grocer. River Street isn't East Elgin, but it is that way, and it would be a great deal pleasanter for—for her."

"I must consider that, of course. You haven't been in them? I should hope for a bright sitting-room, and a very private study."

If Advena was aware of any unconscious implication, the pair of eyes she turned upon him showed no trace of satisfaction in it.

"No, I haven't. But if I could be of any use I should be very glad to go over them with you, and—"

She stopped involuntarily, checked by the embarrassment in his face, though she had to wait for his words to explain it.

"I should be most grateful. But—but might it not be misunderstood?"

She bent her head over her work, and one of those instants passed between them which he had learned to dread. They were so completely the human pair as they sat together, withdrawn in comfort and shelter, absorbed in homely matters and in each other; it was easy to forget that they were only a picture, a sham, and that the reality lay farther on, in the early spring. It must have been hard for him to hear without resentment that she was ready to help him to make a home for that reality. He was fast growing instructed in women, although by a post-graduate course.

Advena looked up. "Possibly," she said, calmly, and their agitation lay still between them. He was silently angry; the thing that stirred without their leave had been sweet.

"No," said Advena, "I can't go, I suppose. I'm sorry. I should have liked so much to be of use." She looked up at him appealingly, and sudden tears came and stood in her eyes, and would perhaps have undone his hurt but that he was staring into the fire.

"How can you be of use," he said, almost irritably, "in such ways as those? They are not important, and I am not sure that for us they are legitimate. If you were about to be—married"— he seemed to plunge at the word—"I should not wish either to hasten you or to house you. I should turn my back on it all. You should have nothing from me," he went on, with a forced smile, "but my blessing, delivered over my shoulder."

"I am sure they are not important," she said humbly—privately all unwilling to give up her martyrdom, "but surely they are legitimate. I would like to help you in every little way I can. Don't you like me in your life? You have said that I may stay."

"I believe you think that by taking strong measures one can

exorcise things," he said. "That if we could only write out this history of ours in our hearts' blood it would somehow vanish."

"No," she said, "but I should like to do it all the same."

"You must bear with me if I refuse the heroic in little. It is even harder than the other." He broke off, leaning back and looking at her from under his shading hand as if that might protect him from too complete a vision. The firelight was warm on her cheek and hair, her needle once again completed the dear delusion: she sat there his wife. This was an aspect he forbade, but it would return; here it was again.

"It is good to have you in my life," he said. "It is also good to recognize one's possibilities."

"How can you definitely lose me?" she asked, and he shook his head.

"I don't know. Now that I have found you it is as if you and I had been rocked together on the tide of that inconceivable ocean that casts us half awake upon life," he said dreamily. "It isn't a friendship of ideas, it's a friendship of spirit. Indeed, I hope and pray never wholly to lose that."

"You never will," she told him. "How many worlds one lives in as the day goes by with the different people one cares for— one beyond the other, concentric, ringing from the heart! Yours comprises all the others; it lies the farthest out—and alas! at present, the closest in," she added irresistibly to the asking of his eyes.

"But," she hurried on, taking high ground to remedy her indiscretion, "I look forward to the time when this—other feeling of ours will become just an idea, as it is now just an emotion, at which we should try to smile. It is the attitude of the gods."

"And therefore not becoming to men. Why should we, not being gods, borrow their attitude?" said Finlay.

"I could never kill it," she put her work in her lap to say, "by any sudden act of violence. It would seem a kind of suicide. While it rules it is like one's life—absolute. But to isolate it—to place it beyond the currents from the heart— to look at it, and realize it, and conquer it for what it is—I don't think it need take so very long. And then our friendship will be beautiful without reproach."

"I sometimes fear there may not be time enough in life," he said. "And if I find that I must simply go—to British Columbia, I think—those mining missions would give a man his chance against himself. There is splendid work to be done there, of a rough-and-ready kind that would make it puerile to spend time in self-questioning."

She smiled as if at a violent boy. "We can do it. We can do it here," she said. "May I quote another religion to you? 'From purification there arises in the Yogi a thorough discernment of the cause and nature of the body, whereupon he loses that regard which others have for the bodily form.'[1] Then, if he loves, he loves in spirit and in truth. I look forward to the time," she went on calmly, "when the best that I can give you or you can give me will ride upon a glance."

"I used to feel more drawn to the ascetic achievement and its rewards," he remarked thoughtfully, "than I do now."

"If I were not a Presbyterian in Canada," she told him, "I would be a Buddhist in Burma. But I have inherited the Shorter Catechism; I must remain without the Law."

Finlay smiled. "They are the simple," he said. "Our Law makes wise the simple."

Advena looked for a moment into the fire. She was listening, with admiration, to her heart; she would not be led to consider esoteric contrasts of East and West.

"Isn't there something that appeals to you," she said, "in the thought of just leaving it, all unsaid and all undone, a dear and tender projection upon the future that faded—a lovely thing we turned away from, until one day it was no longer there?"

"Charming," he said, averting his eyes so that she should not see the hunger in them. "Charming—literature!"

She smiled and sighed, and he wrenched his mind to the consideration of the Buddhism of Browning. She followed him obediently, but the lines they wanted did not come easily; they were compelled to search and verify. Something lately seemed lost to them of that kind of glad activity; he was more aware of it than she, since he was less occupied in the aesthetic ecstasy of self-torture. In the old time before the sun rose they had been so conscious of realms of idea lying just beyond the achievement of

---

1 Number Forty of *The Yoga Sutras of Patanjali*, the founding text of the Yoga system of Indian philosophy. The complete aphorism reads: "From purification of the mind and body there arises in the Yogi a thorough discernment of the cause and nature of the body, whereupon he loses that regard which others have for the bodily form; and he also ceases to feel the desire of, or necessity for, association with his fellow-beings that is common among other men."

thought, approachable, visible by phrases, brokenly, realms which they could see closer when they essayed together. He constantly struggled to reach those enchanted areas again, but they seemed to have gone down behind the horizon; and the only inspiration that carried them far drew its impetus from the poetry of their plight. They looked for verses to prove that Browning's imagination carried him bravely through lives and lives to come, and found them to speculate whether in such chances they might hope to meet again.

And the talk came back to his difficulties with his Board of Management, and to her choice of a frame for the etching he had given her, by his friend the Glasgow impressionist, and to their opinion of a common acquaintance, and to Lorne and his prospects. He told her how little she resembled her brother, and where they diverged, and how; and she listened with submission and delight, enchanted to feel his hand upon her intimate nature. She lingered in the hall while he got into his overcoat, and saw that a glove was the worse for wear. "Would it be the heroic-in-little," she begged, "to let me mend that?"

As he went out alone into the winter streets he too drew upon a pagan for his admonition. "'What then art thou doing here, O imagination?'"[1] he groaned in his private heart. "'Go away, I entreat thee by the gods, for I want thee not. But thou art come again according to thy old fashion. I am not angry with thee, only go away!'"

TWENTY-FIVE

Miss Milburn pressed her contention that the suspicion of his desire would be bad for her lover's political prospects till she made him feel his honest passion almost a form of treachery to his party. She also hinted that, for the time being, it did not make particularly for her own comfort in the family circle, Mr. Milburn having grown by this time quite bitter. She herself drew the excitement of intrigue from the situation, which she hid behind her pretty, pale, decorous features, and never betrayed by the least of her graceful gestures. She told herself that she had never been

---

1 Taken from Book Seven of *The Meditations of Marcus Aurelius*, translated by George Long, first published in 1862.

so right about anything as about that affair of the ring—imagine, for an instant, if she had been wearing it now! She would have banished Lorne altogether if she could. As he insisted on an occasional meeting, she clothed it in mystery, appointing it for an evening when her mother and aunt were out, and answering his ring at the door herself. To her family she remarked with detachment that you saw hardly anything of Lorne Murchison now, he was so taken up with his old election; and to Hesketh she confided her fear that politics did interfere with friendship, whatever he might say. He said a good deal, he cited lofty examples; but the only agreement he could get from her was the hope that the estrangement wouldn't be permanent.

"But you are going to say something, Lorne," she insisted, talking of the Jordanville meeting.

"Not much," he told her. "It's the safest district we've got, and they adore old Farquharson. He'll do most of the talking—they wouldn't thank me for taking up the time. Farquharson is going to tell them I'm a first-class man, and they couldn't do better, and I'm practically only to show my face and tell them I think so too."

"But Mr. Hesketh will speak?"

"Yes; we thought it would be a good chance of testing him. He may interest them, and he can't do much harm, anyhow."

"Lorne, I should simply love to go. It's your first meeting."

"I'll take you."

"Mr. Murchison, *have* you taken leave of your senses? Really, you are—"

"All right, I'll send you. Farquharson and I are going out to the Crow place to supper, but Hesketh is driving straight there. He'll be delighted to bring you—who wouldn't?"

"I shouldn't be allowed to go with him alone," said Dora, thoughtfully.

"Well, no. I don't know that I'd approve of that myself," laughed the confident young man. "Hesketh is driving Mrs. Farquharson, and the cutter will easily hold three. Isn't it lucky there's sleighing?"

"Mother couldn't object to that," said Dora. "Lorne, I always said you were the dearest fellow! I'll wear a thick veil, and not a soul will know me."

"Not a soul would in any case," said Lorne. "It'll be a Jordanville crowd, you know— nobody from Elgin."

"We don't visit much in Jordanville, certainly. Well, mother mayn't object. She has a great idea of Mrs. Farquharson, because she has attended eleven Drawing-Rooms[1] at Ottawa, and one of them was given—held, I should say—by the Princess Louise."

"I won't promise you eleven," said Lorne, "but there seems to be a pretty fair chance of one or two."

At this she had a tale for him which charmed his ears. "I didn't know where to look," she said. "Aunt Emmie, you know, has a very bad trick of coming into my room without knocking. Well, in she walked last night, and found me before the glass *practising my curtsey!* I could have killed her. Pretended she thought I was out."

"Dora, would you like *me* to promise something?" he asked, with a mischievous look.

"Of course, I would. I don't care how much *you* promise. What?"

But already he repented of his daring, and sat beside her suddenly conscious and abashed. Nor could any teasing prevail to draw from him what had been on his audacious lips to say.

Social precedents are easily established in the country. The accident that sent the first Liberal canvasser for Jordanville votes to the Crow place for his supper would be hard to discover now; the fact remains that he has been going there ever since. It made a greater occasion than Mrs. Crow would ever have dreamed of acknowledging. She saw to it that they had a good meal of victuals, and affected indifference to the rest; they must say their say, she supposed. If the occasion had one satisfaction which she came nearer to confessing than another, it was that the two or three substantial neighbours who usually came to meet the politicians left their wives at home, and that she herself, to avoid giving any offence on this score, never sat down with the men. Quite enough to do it was, she would explain later, for her and the hired girl to wait on them and to clear up after them. She and Bella had their bite afterward when the men had hitched up, and when they could exchange comments of proud congratulation upon the inroads on the johnny-cake or the pies. So there was no ill feeling, and Mrs. Crow, having vindicated her dignity by shaking hands with the guests of the evening in the parlour, solaced it further by maintaining the masculine state of the occasion, in spite

<hr>

1 Formal evening social gatherings at which invitees would be presented to Royalty, or its Canadian representatives; in this case Princess Louise, Queen Victoria's fourth daughter, the wife of the Marquis of Lorne, who was Governor General of Canada from 1878 to 1883.

of protests or entreaties. To sit down opposite Mr. Crow would have made it ordinary "company"; she passed the plates and turned it into a function.

She was waiting for them on the parlour sofa when Crow brought them in out of the nipping early dark of December, Elmore staying behind in the yard with the horses. She sat on the sofa in her best black dress with the bead trimming on the neck and sleeves, a good deal pushed up and wrinkled across the bosom, which had done all that would ever be required of it when it gave Elmore and Abe their start in life. Her wiry hands were crossed in her lap in the moment of waiting: you could tell by the look of them that they were not often crossed there. They were strenuous hands; the whole worn figure was strenuous, and the narrow set mouth, and the eyes which had looked after so many matters for so long, and even the way the hair was drawn back into a knot in a fashion that would have given a phrenologist his opportunity. It was a different Mrs. Crow from the one that sat in the midst of her poultry and garden-stuff in the Elgin market square; but it was even more the same Mrs. Crow, the sum of a certain measure of opportunity and service, an imperial figure in her bead trimming, if the truth were known.

The room was heated to express the geniality that was harder to put in words. The window was shut; there was a smell of varnish and whatever was inside the "suite" of which Mrs. Crow occupied the sofa. Enlarged photographs—very much enlarged— of Mr. and Mrs. Crow hung upon the walls, and one other of a young girl done in that process which tells you at once that she was an only daughter and that she is dead. There had been other bereavements; they were written upon the silver coffin-plates which, framed and glazed, also contributed to the decoration of the room; but you would have had to look close, and you might feel a delicacy.

Mrs. Crow made her greetings with precision, and sat down again upon the sofa for a few minutes' conversation.

"I'm telling them," said her husband, "that the sleighin's just held out for them. If it 'ud been to-morrow they'd have had to come on wheels. Pretty soft travellin' as it was, some places, I guess."

"Snow's come early this year," said Mrs. Crow. "It was an open fall, too."

"It has certainly," Mr. Farquharson backed her up. "About as early as I remember it. I don't know how much you got out here; we had a good foot in Elgin."

"'Bout the same, 'bout the same," Mr. Crow deliberated, "but it's been layin' light all along over Clayfield way—ain't had a pair of runners out, them folks."

"Makes a more cheerful winter, Mrs. Crow, don't you think, when it comes early?" remarked Lorne. "Or would you rather not get it till after Christmas?"

"I don't know as it matters much, out here in the country. We don't get a great many folks passin', best of times. An' it's more of a job to take care of the stock."

"That's so," Mr. Crow told them. "Chores come heavier when there's snow on the ground, a great sight, especially if there's drifts."

And for an instant, with his knotted hands hanging between his knees, he pondered this unvarying aspect of his yearly experience. They all pondered it, sympathetic.

"Well, now, Mr. Farquharson," Mrs. Crow turned to him. "An' how reely *be* ye? We've heard better, an' worse, an middlin'—there's ben such contradictory reports."

"Oh, very well, Mrs. Crow! Never better. I'm going to give a lot more trouble yet. I can't do it in politics, that's the worst of it. But here's the man that's going to do it for me. Here's the man!"

The Crows looked at the pretendant, as in duty bound, but not any longer than they could help.

"Why, I guess you were at school with Elmore?" said Crow, as if the idea had just struck him.

"He may be right peart, for all that," said Elmore's mother, and Elmore, himself, entering with two leading Liberals of Jordanville, effected a diversion, under cover of which Mrs. Crow escaped, to superintend, with Bella, the last touches to the supper in the kitchen.

Politics in and about Jordanville were accepted as a purely masculine interest. If you had asked Mrs. Crow to take a hand in them she would have thanked you with sarcasm, and said she thought she had about enough to do as it was. The schoolhouse, on the night of such a meeting as this, was recognized to be no place for ladies. It was a man's affair, left to the men, and the appearance there of the other sex would have been greeted with remark and levity. Elgin, as we know, was more sophisticated in every way, plenty of ladies attended political meetings in the Drill Shed, where seats as likely as not would be reserved for them; plenty of handkerchiefs waved there for the encouragement of the hero of the evening. They did not kiss him; British phlegm, so far, had stayed that demonstration at the southern border.

The ladies of Elgin, however, drew the line somewhere, drew it at country meetings. Mrs. Farquharson went with her husband because, since his state of health had handed him over to her more than ever, she saw it a part of her wifely duty. His retirement had been decided upon for the spring, but she would be on hand to retire him at any earlier moment should the necessity arise. "We'll be the only female creatures there, my dear," she had said to Dora on the way out, and Hesketh had praised them both for public spirit. He didn't know, he said, how anybody would get elected in England without the ladies, especially in the villages, where the people were obliged to listen respectfully.

"I wonder you can afford to throw away all the influence you get in the rural districts with soup and blankets," he said; "but this is an extravagant country in many ways." Dora kept silence, not being sure of the social prestige bound up with the distribution of soup and blankets, but Mrs. Farquharson set him sharply right.

"I guess we'd rather do without our influence if it came to that," she said.

Hesketh listened with deference to her account of the rural district which had as yet produced no Ladies Bountiful,[1] made mental notes of several points, and placed her privately as a woman of more than ordinary intelligence. I have always claimed for Hesketh an open mind; he was filling it now, to its capacity, with care and satisfaction.

The schoolroom was full and waiting when they arrived. Jordanville had been well billed,[2] and the posters held, in addition to the conspicuous names of Farquharson and Murchison, that of Mr. Alfred Hesketh (of London, England). There was a "send-off" to give to the retiring member, there was a critical inspection to make of the new candidate, and there was Mr. Alfred Hesketh, of London, England, and whatever he might signify. They were big, quiet, expectant fellows, with less sophistication and polemic than their American counterparts, less stolid aggressiveness than their parallels in England, if they have parallels there. They stood, indeed, for the development between the two; they came of the

---

1 "Lady Bountiful" is a derogatory expression meaning a rich woman who hypocritically gives charity.
2 Covered with posters (hand-bills).

new country but not of the new light; they were democrats who had never thrown off the monarch—what harm did he do there overseas? They had the air of being prosperous, but not prosperous enough for theories and doctrines. The Liberal vote of South Fox had yet to be split by Socialism or Labour. Life was a decent rough business that required all their attention; there was time enough for sleep but not much for speculation. They sat leaning forward with their hats dropped between their knees, more with the air of big schoolboys expecting an entertainment than responsible electors come together to approve their party's choice. They had the uncomplaining bucolic look, but they wore it with a difference; the difference, by this time, was enough to mark them of another nation. Most of them had driven to the meeting; it was not an adjournment from the public-house. Nor did the air hold any hint of beer. Where it had an alcoholic drift the flavour was of whisky; but the stimulant of the occasion had been tea or cider, and the room was full of patient good-will.

The preliminaries were gone through with promptness; the Chair had supped with the speakers, and Mr. Crow had given him a friendly hint that the boys wouldn't be expecting much in the way of trimmings from *him*. Stamping and clapping from the back benches greeted Mr. Farquharson. It diminished, grew more subdued, as it reached the front. The young fellows were mostly at the back, and the power of demonstration had somehow ebbed in the old ones. The retiring member addressed his constituents for half an hour. He was standing before them as their representative for the last time, and it was natural to look back and note the milestones behind, the changes for the better with which he could fairly claim association. They were matters of Federal business chiefly, beyond the immediate horizon of Jordanville, but Farquharson made them a personal interest for that hour at all events, and there were one or two points of educational policy which he could illustrate by their own schoolhouse. He approached them, as he had always done, on the level of mutual friendly interest, and in the hope of doing mutual friendly business. "You know and I know," he said more than once; they and he knew a number of things together.

He was afraid, he said, that if the doctors hadn't chased him out of politics, he never would have gone. Now, however, that they gave him no choice, he was glad to think that though times had been pretty good for the farmers of South Fox all through the eleven years of his appearance in the political arena, he was leaving it at a moment when they promised to be better still. Already, he was sure, they were familiar with the main heads of that attractive prospect, and, agreeable as the subject, great as the policy was to him, he would leave it to be further unfolded by the gentleman whom they all hoped to enlist in the cause, as his successor for this constituency, Mr. Lorne Murchison, and by his friend from the old country, Mr. Alfred Hesketh. He, Farquharson, would not take the words out of the mouths of these gentlemen, much as he envied them the opportunity of uttering them. The French Academy, he told them, that illustrious body of literary and scientific men, had a custom, on the death of a member and the selection of his successor, of appointing one of their number to eulogize the new-comer. The person upon whom the task would most appropriately fall, did circumstances permit, would be the departing academician. In this case, he was happy to say, circumstances did permit—his political funeral was still far enough off to enable him to express his profound confidence in and his hearty admiration of the young and vigorous political heir whom the Liberals of South Fox had selected to stand in his shoes. Mr. Farquharson proceeded to give his grounds for this confidence and admiration, reminding the Jordanville electors that they had met Mr. Murchison as a Liberal standard-bearer in the last general election, when he, Farquharson, had to acknowledge very valuable services on Mr. Murchison's part. The retiring member then thanked his audience for the kind attention and support they had given him for so many years, made a final cheerful joke about a Pagan divinity known as Anno Domini,[1] and took his seat.

They applauded him, and it was plain that they regretted him, the tried friend, the man there was never any doubt about, whose convictions they had repeated, and whose speeches in Parliament they had read with a kind of proprietorship for so long. The Chair had to wait, before introducing Mr. Alfred Hesketh, until the back benchers had got through with a double rendering of "For He's a Jolly Good Fellow," which bolder spirits, from the anteroom where the little girls kept their hats and comforters, interspersed with whoops. Hesketh, it had been arranged, should speak next, and Lorne last.

Mr. Hesketh left his wooden chair with smiling ease, the ease which is intended to level distinctions and put everybody con-

---

1   A roundabout way of saying his time was up.

cerned on the best of terms. He said that though he was no stranger to the work of political campaigns, this was the first time that he had had the privilege of addressing a colonial audience. "I consider," said he handsomely, "that it is a privilege." He clasped his hands behind his back and threw out his chest.

"Opinions have differed in England as to the value of the colonies, and the consequence of colonials. I say here with pride that I have ever been among those who insist that the value is very high and the consequence very great. The fault is common to humanity, but we are, I fear, in England, too prone to be led away by appearances, and to forget that under a rough unpolished exterior may beat virtues which are the brightest ornaments of civilization, that in the virgin fields of the possessions which the good swords of our ancestors wrung for us from the Algonquins and the—and the other savages—may be hidden the most glorious period of the British race."

Mr. Hesketh paused and coughed. His audience neglected the opportunity for applause, but he had their undivided attention. They were looking at him and listening to him, these Canadian farmers, with curious interest in his attitude, his appearance, his inflection, his whole personality as it offered itself to them—it was a thing new and strange. Far out in the North-West, where the emigrant trains had been unloading all the summer, Hesketh's would have been a voice from home; but here, in long-settled Ontario, men had forgotten the sound of it, with many other things. They listened in silence, weighing with folded arms, appraising with chin in hand; they were slow, equitable men.

"If we in England," Hesketh proceeded, "required a lesson—as perhaps we did—in the importance of the colonies, we had it, need I remind you? in the course of the late protracted campaign in South Africa. Then did the mother country indeed prove the loyalty and devotion of her colonial sons. Then were envious nations compelled to see the spectacle of Canadians and Australians rallying about the common flag, eager to attest their affection for it with their life-blood, and to demonstrate that they, too, were worthy to add deeds to British traditions and victories to the British cause."

Still no mark of appreciation. Hesketh began to think them an unhandsome lot. He stood bravely, however, by the note he had sounded. He dilated on the pleasure and satisfaction it had been to the people of England to receive this mark of attachment from far-away dominions and dependencies, on the cementing of the bonds of brotherhood by the blood of the fallen, on the impossibility that the mother country should ever forget such voluntary sacrifices for her sake, when, unexpectedly and irrelevantly, from the direction of the cloakroom, came the expressive comment— "Yah!"

Though brief, nothing could have been more to the purpose, and Hesketh sacrificed several effective points to hurry to the quotation—

What should they know of England
Who only England know?[1]

which he could not, perhaps, have been expected to forbear. His audience, however, were plainly not in the vein for compliment. The same voice from the ante-room inquired ironically, "That so?" and the speaker felt advised to turn to more immediate considerations.

He said he had had the great pleasure on his arrival in this country to find a political party, the party in power, their Canadian Liberal party, taking initiative in a cause which he was sure they all had at heart—the strengthening of the bonds between the colonies and the mother country. He congratulated the Liberal party warmly upon having shown themselves capable of this great function—a point at which he was again interrupted; and he recapitulated some of the familiar arguments about the desirability of closer union from the point of view of the army, of the Admiralty, and from one which would come home, he knew, to all of them, the necessity of a dependable food supply for the mother country in time of war. Here he quoted a noble lord. He said that he believed no definite proposals had been made, and he did not understand how any definite proposals could be made; for his part, if the new arrangement was to be in the nature of a bargain, he would prefer to have nothing to do with it.

"England," he said, loftily, "has no wish to buy the loyalty of her colonies, nor, I hope, has any colony the desire to offer her allegiance at the price of preference in British markets. Even proposals for mutual commercial benefit may be underpinned, I am glad to say, by loftier principles than those of the market-place and the counting-house."

---

1 From "The English Flag" by Rudyard Kipling (1865-1936).

At this one of his hearers, unacquainted with the higher commercial plane, exclaimed, "How be ye goin' to get 'em kept to, then?"

Hesketh took up the question. He said a friend in the audience asked how they were to ensure that such arrangements would be adhered to. His answer was in the words of the Duke of Dartmoor, "By the mutual esteem, the inherent integrity, and the willing compromise of the British race."

Here someone on the back benches, impatient, doubtless, at his own incapacity to follow this high doctrine, exclaimed intemperately, "Oh, shut up!" and the gathering, remembering that this, after all, was not what it had come for, began to hint that it had had enough in intermittent stamps and uncompromising shouts for "Murchison!"

Hesketh kept on his legs, however, a few minutes longer. He had a trenchant sentence to repeat to them which he thought they would take as a direct message from the distinguished nobleman who had uttered it. The Marquis of Aldeburgh was the father of the pithy thing, which he had presented, as it happened, to Hesketh himself. The audience received it with respect— Hesketh's own respect was so marked—but with misapprehension; there had been too many allusions to the nobility for a community so far removed from its soothing influence. "Had ye no friends among the commoners?" suddenly spoke up a dry old fellow, stroking a long white beard; and the roar that greeted this showed the sense of the meeting. Hesketh closed with assurances of the admiration and confidence he felt towards the candidate proposed to their suffrages by the Liberal party that were quite inaudible, and sought his yellow pinewood schoolroom chair with rather a forced smile. It had been used once before that day to isolate conspicuous stupidity.

They were at bottom a good-natured and a loyal crowd, and they had not, after all, come there to make trouble, or Mr. Alfred Hesketh might have carried away a worse opinion of them. As it was, young Murchison, whose address occupied the rest of the evening, succeeded in making an impression upon them distinct enough, happily for his personal influence, to efface that of his friend. He did it by the simple expedient of talking business, and as high prices for produce and low ones for agricultural implements would be more interesting there than here, I will not report him. He and Mr. Farquharson waited, after the meeting, for a personal word with a good many of those present, but it was suggested to Hesketh that the ladies might be tired, and that he had better get them home without unnecessary delay. Mrs. Farquharson had less comment to offer during the drive home than Hesketh thought might be expected from a woman of her intelligence, but Miss Milburn was very enthusiastic. She said he had made a lovely speech, and she wished her father could have heard it.

A personal impression, during a time of political excitement, travels unexpectedly far. A week later Mr. Hesketh was concernedly accosted in Main Street by a boy on a bicycle.

"Say, mister, how's the dook?"[1]

"What duke?" asked Hesketh, puzzled.

"Oh, any dook," responded the boy, and bicycled cheerfully away.

TWENTY-SIX

Christmas came and went. Dr. Drummond had long accepted the innovation of a service on Christmas Day, as he agreed to the anthem while the collection was being taken up, to flowers about the pulpit, and to the habit of sitting at prayer. He was a progressive by his business instinct, in everything but theology, where perhaps his business instinct also operated the other way, in favour of the sure thing. The Christmas Day service soon became one of those "special" occasions so dear to his heart, which made a demand upon him out of the ordinary way. He rose to these on the wing of the eagle, and his congregation never lacked the lesson that could be most dramatically drawn from them. His Christmas Day discourse gathered everything into it that could emphasize the anniversary, including a vigorous attack upon the saints' days and ceremonies of the Church of England calculated to correct the concession of the service, and pull up sharply any who thought that Presbyterianism was giving way to the spurious attractions of sentimentality or ritual. The special Easter service, with every appropriate feature of hymn and invocation, was apt to be marked by an unsparing denunciation of the pageants and practices of the Church of Rome. Balance was thus preserved, and principle relentlessly indicated.

---

1 The text draws attention to the difference in pronunciation between American and British "u": "dook" [duk] vs. "duke" [djuk], respectively.

Dr. Drummond loved, as I have said, all that asked for notable comment; the poet and the tragedian in him caught at the opportunity, and revelled in it. Public events carried him far, especially if they were disastrous, but what he most profited by was the dealing of Providence with members of his own congregation. Of all the occasions that inspired him, the funeral sermon was his happiest opportunity, nor was it, in his hands, by any means unstinted eulogy. Candid was his summing-up, behind the decent veil, the accepted apology of death; he was not afraid to refer to the follies of youth or the weaknesses of age in terms as unmistakable as they were kindly.

"Grace," he said once, of an estimable plain spinster who had passed away, "did more for her than ever nature had done." He repeated it, too. "She was far more indebted, I say, to grace, than to nature," and before his sharp earnestness none were seen to smile. Nor could you forget the note in his voice when the loss he deplored was that of a youth of virtue and promise, or that of a personal friend. His very text would be a blow upon the heart; the eyes filled from the beginning. People would often say that they were "sorry for the family," sitting through Dr. Drummond's celebration of their bereavement; and the sympathy was probably well founded. But how fine he was when he paid the last tribute to that upright man, his elder and office-bearer, David Davidson! How his words marched, sorrowing to the close! "Much I have said of him, and more than he would have had me say." Will it not stay with those who heard it till the very end, the trenchant, mournful fall of that "more than he would have had me say"?

It was a thing that Hugh Finlay could not abide in Dr. Drummond.

As the winter passed, the little Doctor was hard put to it to keep his hands off the great political issue of the year, bound up as it was in the tenets of his own politics, which he held only less uncompromisingly than those of the Shorter Catechism. It was, unfortunately for him, a gradual and peaceful progress of opinion, marked by no dramatic incidents; and analogy was hard to find in either Testament for a change of fiscal policy based on imperial advantage. Dr. Drummond liked a pretty definite parallel; he had small opinion of the practice of drawing a pint out of a thimble, as he considered Finlay must have done when he preached the gospel of imperialism from Deuteronomy 30:14: "For the word is very nigh unto thee, in thy mouth and in thy heart, that thou mayest do it." Moreover, to preach politics in Knox Church was a liberty in Finlay.

The fact that Finlay had been beforehand with him operated perhaps to reconcile the Doctor to his difficulty; and the candidature of one of his own members in what was practically the imperial interest no doubt increased his embarrassment. Nevertheless, he would not lose sight of the matter for more than two or three weeks together. Many an odd blow he delivered for its furtherance by way of illustrating higher things, and he kept it always, so to speak, in the practical politics of the long prayer.

It was Sunday evening, and Abby and her husband, as usual, had come to tea. The family was complete with the exception of Lorne, who had driven out to Clayfield with Horace Williams, to talk over some urgent matters with persons whom he would meet at supper at the Metropole Hotel at Clayfield. It was a thing Mrs. Murchison thought little short of scandalous— supper to talk business on the Sabbath day, and in an hotel, a place of which the smell about the door was enough to knock you down, even on a weekday. Mrs. Murchison considered, and did not scruple to say so, that politics should be let alone on Sundays. Clayfield votes might be very important, but there were such things as commandments, she supposed. "It'll bring no blessing," she declared severely, eyeing Lorne's empty place.

The talk about the lamplit table was, nevertheless, all of the election, blessed or unblessed. It was not in human nature that it shouldn't be, as Mrs. Murchison would have very quickly told you if you had found her inconsistent. There was reason in all things, as she frequently said.

"I hear," Alec had told them, "that Octavius Milburn is going around bragging he's got the Elgin Chamber of Commerce consolidated this time."

"Against us?" exclaimed Stella; and her brother said, "Of course!"

"Those Milburns," remarked Mrs. Murchison, "are enough to make one's blood boil. I met Mrs. Milburn in the market yesterday; she'd been pricing Mrs. Crow's ducks, and they were just five cents too dear for her, and she stopped—wonderful thing for her—and had *such* an amount to say about Lorne, and the honour it was, and the dear only knows what! Butter wouldn't melt in her mouth—and Octavius Milburn doing all he knew against him the whole time! That's the Milburns! I cut her remarkably short," Mrs. Murchison added, with satisfaction, "and when she'd made up her mind she'd have to give that extra five cents for the ducks because there weren't any others to be had, she went back and found I'd bought them."

"Well done, mother!" said Alec, and Oliver remarked that if those were to-day's ducks they were too good for the Milburn crowd, a lot.

"I expect she wanted them, too," remarked Stella. "They've got the only Mr. Hesketh staying with them now. Miss Filkin's in a great state of excitement."

"I guess we can spare them Hesketh," said John Murchison.

"He's a lobster," said Stella with fervour.

"He seems to bring a frost where he goes," continued Abby's husband, "in politics, anyhow. I hear Lorne wants to make a present of him to the other side, for use wherever they'll let him speak longest. Is it true he began his speech out at Jordanville— 'Gentlemen—and those of you who are not gentlemen'?"

"Could he have meant Mrs. Farquharson and Miss Milburn?" asked Mr. Murchison quietly, when the derision subsided; and they laughed again.

"He told me," said Advena, "that he proposed to convert Mr. Milburn to the imperial policy."

"He'll have his job cut out for him," said her father.

"For my part," Abby told them, "I think the Milburns are beneath contempt. You don't know exactly what it is, but there's something *about* them—not that we ever come in contact with them," she continued with dignity. "I believe they used to be patients of Dr. Henry's till he got up in years, but they don't call in Harry."

"Maybe that's what there is about them," said Mr. Murchison, innocently.

"Father's made up his mind," announced Dr. Harry, and they waited breathless. There could be only one point upon which Dr. Henry could be dubitating[1] at that moment.

"He's going to vote for Lorne."

"He's a lovely old darling!" cried Stella. "Good for Dr. Henry Johnson! I knew he would."

The rest were silent with independence and gratification. Dr. Henry's Conservatism had been supposed to be invincible. Dr. Harry they thought a fair prey to Murchison influence, and he

---

1 Hesitating over, wavering over.

had capitulated early, but he had never promised to answer for his father.

"Yes, he's taken his time about it, and he's consulted about all the known authorities," said his son, humorously. "Went right back to the Manchester school[1] to begin with—sat out on the verandah reading Cobden and Bright[2] the whole summer; if anybody came for advice sent 'em in to me. I did a trade, I tell you! He thought they talked an awful lot of sense, those fellows—from the English point of view. 'D'ye mean to tell me,' he'd say, 'that a generation born and bred in political doctrine of that sort is going to hold on to the colonies at a sacrifice? They'd rather let 'em go at a sacrifice!' Well, then he got to reading the other side of the question, and old Ormiston lent him Parkin,[3] and he lent old Ormiston Goldwin Smith,[4] and then he subscribed to the *Times* for six months—the bill must have nearly bust him; and then the squire went over without waiting for him and without any assistance from the *Times* either; and finally—well, he says that if it's good enough business for the people of England it's good enough business for him. Only he keeps on worrying about the people of England, and whether they'll make enough by it to keep them contented, till he can't half enjoy his meals. And though he's going to vote for Lorne next month all right, he wants it to be distinctly understood that family connection has nothing to do with it."

"Of course it hasn't," Advena said.

"But we're just as much obliged," remarked Stella.

"A lot of our church people are going to stay at home election day," declared Abby; "they won't vote for Lorne, and they won't vote against imperialism, so they'll just sulk. Silly, I call it."

---

1 A term used to refer to the group of British economists and politicians who favoured free trade, and were associated with the "Anti-Corn Law league" that lobbied for the repeal of tariffs on "corn" (grains) in 1846.

2 Richard Cobden (1804-65) and John Bright (1811-89), ardent supporters of free trade in Britain, founded the Anti-Corn law league and campaigned against British Imperialism on the grounds that it hurt British economic self-interest.

3 George Parkin was the author of *Imperial Federation: the Problem of National Unity* (1892), an influential book arguing in favour of imperial federation.

4 Author of *Canada and the Canadian Question* (1891), a book arguing that Canada should become part of the United States. See Appendix B.4.

"Good enough business for us," said Alec.

"Well, what I want to know is," said Mrs. Murchison "whether you are coming to the church you were born and brought up in, Abby, or not, to-night? There's the first bell."

"I'm not going to any church," said Abby. "I went this morning. I'm going home to my baby."

"Your father and mother," said Mrs. Murchison, "can go twice a day, and be none the worse for it. By the way, father, did you know old Mrs. Parr was dead? Died this morning at four o'clock. They telephoned for Dr. Drummond, and I think they had little to do, for he had been up with her half the night already, Mrs. Forsyth told me."

"Did he go?" asked Mr. Murchison.

"He did not, for the very good reason that he knew nothing about it. Mrs. Forsyth answered the telephone, and told them he hadn't been two hours in his bed, and she wouldn't get him out again for an unconscious deathbed, and him with bronchitis on him and two sermons to preach to-day."

"I'll warrant Mrs. Forsyth caught it in the morning," said John Murchison.

"That she did. The doctor was as cross as two sticks that she hadn't had him out to answer the 'phone. 'I just spoke up,' she said, 'and told him I didn't see how he was going to do any good to the poor soul over a telephone wire.' 'It isn't that,' he said, 'but I might have put them on to Peter Fratch for the funeral. We've never had an undertaker in the church before,' he said; 'he's just come, and he ought to be supported. Now I expect it's too late, they'll have gone to Liscombe.' He rang them up right away, but they had."

"Dr. Drummond can't stand Liscombe," said Alec, as they all laughed a little at the Doctor's foible, all except Advena, who laughed a great deal. She laughed wildly, then weakly. "I wouldn't—think it a pleasure—to be buried by Liscombe myself!" she cried hysterically, and then laughed again until the tears ran down her face, and she lay back in her chair and moaned, still laughing.

Mr. and Mrs. Murchison, Alec, Stella, and Advena made up the family party; Oliver, for reasons of his own, would attend the River Avenue Methodist Church that evening. They slipped out presently into the crisp white winter night. The snow was banked on both sides of the street. Spreading garden fir-trees huddled together weighted down with it; ragged icicles hung from the eaves or lay in long broken fingers on the trodden paths. The snow snapped and tore under their feet; there was a glorious moon that observed every tattered weed sticking up through the whiteness, and etched it with its shadow. The town lay under the moon almost dramatic, almost mysterious, so withdrawn it was out of the cold, so turned in upon its own soul of the fireplace. It might have stood, in the snow and the silence, for a shell and a symbol of the humanity within, for angels or other strangers to mark with curiosity. Mr. and Mrs. Murchison were neither angels nor strangers; they looked at it and saw that the Peterson place was still standing empty, and that old Mr. Fisher hadn't finished his new porch before zero weather came to stop him.

The young people were well ahead; Mrs. Murchison, on her husband's arm, stepped along with the spring of an impetus undisclosed.

"Is it to be the Doctor to-night?" asked John Murchison. "He was so hoarse this morning I wouldn't be surprised to see Finlay in the pulpit. They're getting only morning services in East Elgin just now, while they're changing the lighting arrangements."

"Are they, indeed? Well, I hope they'll change them and be done with it, for I can't say I'm anxious for too much of their Mr. Finlay in Knox Church."

"Oh you like the man well enough for a change, mother!" John assured her.

"I've nothing to say against his preaching. It's the fellow himself. And I hope we won't get him to-night, for, the way I feel now, if I see him gawking up the pulpit steps it'll be as much as I can do to keep in my seat, and so I just tell you, John."

"You're a little out of patience with him, I see," said Mr. Murchison.

"And it would be a good thing if more than me were out of patience with him. There's such a thing as too much patience, I've noticed."

"I dare say," replied her husband, cheerfully.

"If Advena were any daughter of mine she'd have less patience with him."

"She's not much like you," assented the father.

"I must say I like a girl to have a little spirit if a man has none. And before I'd have him coming to the house week after week the way he has, I'd see him far enough."

"He might as well come there as anywhere," Mr. Murchison replied, ambiguously. "I suppose he has now and then time on his hands?"

"Well, he won't have it on his hands much longer."

"He won't, eh?"

"No, he won't," Mrs. Murchison almost shook the arms he was attached to. "John, I think you might show a little interest! The man's going to be married."

"You don't say that?" John Murchison's tone expressed not only astonishment but concern. Mrs. Murchison was almost mollified.

"But I do say it. His future wife is coming here to Elgin next month, she and her aunt, or her grandmother, or somebody, and they're to stay at Dr. Drummond's and be married as soon as possible."

"Nonsense," said Mr. Murchison, which was his way of expressing simple astonishment.

"There's no nonsense about it. Advena told me herself this afternoon."

"Did she seem put out about it?"

"She's not a girl to show it," Mrs. Murchison hedged, "if she was. I just looked at her. 'Well,' I said, 'that's a piece of news. When did you hear it?' I said. 'Oh, I've known it all the winter!' says my lady. What I wanted to say was that for an engaged man he had been pretty liberal with his visits, but she had such a queer look in her eyes I couldn't express myself, somehow."

"It was just as well left unsaid," her husband told her, thoughtfully.

"I'm not so sure," Mrs. Murchison retorted. "You're a great man, John, for letting everything alone. When he's been coming here regularly for more than a year, putting ideas into the girl's head—"

"He seems to have told her how things were."

"That's all very well—if he had kept himself to himself at the same time."

"Well, mother, you know you never thought much of the prospect."

"No, I didn't," Mrs. Murchison said. "It wouldn't be me that would be married to him, and I've always said so. But I'd got more or less used to it," she confessed. "The man's well enough in some ways. Dear knows there would be a pair of them—one's as much of a muddler as the other! And anybody can see with half an eye that Advena likes him. It hasn't turned out as I expected, that's a fact, John, and I'm just very much annoyed."

"I'm not best pleased about it myself," said John Murchison, expressing, as usual, a very small proportion of the regret that he felt, "but I suppose they know their own business."

Thus, in their different ways, did these elder ones also acknowledge their helplessness before the advancing event. They could talk of it in private and express their dissatisfaction with it, and that was all they could do. It would not be a matter much further turned over between them at best. They would be shy of any affair of sentiment in terms of speech, and from one that affected a member of the family self-respect would help to pull them the other way. Mrs. Murchison might remember it in the list of things which roused her vain indignation; John Murchison would put it away in the limbo of irremediables that were better forgotten. For the present they had reached the church door.

Mrs. Murchison saw with relief that Dr. Drummond occupied his own pulpit, but if her glance had gone the length of three pews behind her she would have discovered that Hugh Finlay made one of the congregation. Fortunately, perhaps, for her enjoyment of the service, she did not look round. Dr. Drummond was more observing, but his was a position of advantage. In the accustomed sea of faces two, heavy shadowed and obstinately facing fate, swam together before Dr. Drummond, and after he had lifted his hands and closed his eyes for the long prayer he saw them still. So that these words occurred, near the end, in the long prayer—

"O Thou Searcher of hearts, who hast known man from the beginning, to whom his highest desires and his loftiest intentions are but as the desires and intentions of a little child, look with Thine own compassion, we beseech Thee, upon souls before Thee in any peculiar difficulty. Our mortal life is full of sin, it is also full of the misconception of virtue. Do Thou clear the understanding, O Lord, of such as would interpret Thy will to their own undoing; do Thou teach them that as happiness may reside in chastening, so chastening may reside in happiness. And though such stand fast to their hurt, do Thou grant to them in Thine own way, which may not be our way, a safe issue out of the dangers that beset them."

Dr. Drummond had his own method of reconciling foreordination and free will. To Advena his supplication came with that mysterious double emphasis of chance words that fit. Her thought played upon them all through the sermon, rejecting and rejecting again their application and their argument and the spring of hope in them. She, too, knew that Finlay was in church, and, half timidly, she looked back for him, as the congregation filed out again into the winter streets. But he, furious, and more resolved than ever, had gone home by another way.

TWENTY-SEVEN

Octavius Milburn was not far beyond the facts when he said that the Elgin Chamber of Commerce was practically solid this time against the Liberal platform, though to what extent this state of things was due to his personal influence might be a matter of opinion. Mr. Milburn was President of the Chamber of Commerce, and his name stood for one of the most thriving of Elgin's industries, but he was not a person of influence except as it might be represented in a draft on the Bank of British North America. He had never converted anybody to anything, and never would, possibly because the governing principle of his life was the terror of being converted to anything himself. If an important nonentity is an imaginable thing, perhaps it would stand for Mr. Milburn; and he found it a more valuable combination than it may appear, since his importance gave him position and opportunity, and his nonentity saved him from their risks. Certainly he had not imposed his view upon his fellow members—they would have blown it off like a feather—yet they found themselves much of his mind. Most of them were manufacturing men of the Conservative party, whose factories had been nursed by high duties upon the goods of outsiders, and few even of the Liberals among them felt inclined to abandon this immediate safeguard for a benefit more or less remote, and more or less disputable. John Murchison thought otherwise, and put it in few words as usual. He said he was more concerned to see big prices in British markets for Canadian crops than he was to put big prices on ironware he couldn't sell. He was more afraid of hard times among the farmers of Canada than he was of competition by the manufacturers of England. That is what he said when he was asked if it didn't go against the grain a little to have to support a son who advocated low duties on British ranges; and when he was not asked he said nothing, disliking the discount that was naturally put upon his opinion. Parsons, of the Blanket Mills, bolted at the first hint of the new policy and justified it by reminding people that he always said he would if it ever looked like business.

"We give their woollen goods a pull of a third as it is," he said, "which is just a third more than I approve of. I don't propose to vote to make it any bigger—can't afford it."

He had some followers, but there were also some, like Young, of the Plough Works, and Windle, who made bicycles, who announced that there was no need to change their politics to defeat a measure that had no existence, and never would have. What sickened them, they declared, was to see young Murchison allowed to give it so much prominence as Liberal doctrine. The party had been strong enough to hold South Fox for the best part of the last twenty years on the old principles, and this British boot-licking feature wasn't going to do it any good. It was fool politics in the opinion of Mr. Young and Mr. Windle.

Then remained the retail trades, the professions, and the farmers. Both sides could leave out of their counsels the interests of the leisured class, since the leisured class in Elgin consisted almost entirely of persons who were too old to work, and therefore not influential. The landed proprietors were the farmers, when they weren't, alas! the banks. As to the retail men, the prosperity of the stores of Main Street and Market Street was bound up about equally with that of Fox County and the Elgin factories. The lawyers and doctors, the odd surveyors and engineers, were inclined, by their greater detachment, to theories and prejudices, delightful luxuries where a certain rigidity of opinion is dictated by considerations of bread and butter. They made a factor debatable, but small. The farmers had everything to win, nothing to lose. The prospect offered them more for what they had to sell, and less for what they had to buy, and most of them were Liberals already; but the rest had to be convinced, and a political change of heart in a bosom of South Fox was as difficult as any other. Industrial, commercial, professional, agricultural, Lorne Murchison scanned them all hopefully, but Walter Winter felt them his garnered sheaves.

It will be imagined how Mr. Winter, as a practical politician, rejoiced in the aspect of things. The fundamental change, with its incalculable chances to play upon, the opening of the gate to admit plain detriment in the first instance for the sake of benefit, easily beclouded, in the second, the effective arm, in the hands of a satirist, of sentiment in politics—and if there was a weapon Mr. Winter owned a weakness for it was satire—the whole situation, as he often confessed, suited him down to the ground. He professed himself, though no optimist under any circumstances, very well pleased. Only in one other place, he declared, would he have preferred to conduct a campaign at the present moment on the issue involved, though he would have to change his politics to do it there, and that place was England. He cast an envious eye across the ocean at the trenchant argument of the dear loaf; he had no such straight road to the public stomach and grand arbitrator of the fate of empires. If the Liberals in England failed to turn out the Government over this business, they would lose in his eyes all the respect he ever had for them, which wasn't much, he acknowledged. When his opponents twitted him with discrepancy here, since a bargain so bad for one side could hardly fail to favour the other, he poured all his contempt on the scheme as concocted by damned enthusiasts for the ruin of business men of both countries. Such persons, Mr. Winter said, if they could have their way, would be happy and satisfied; but in his opinion neither England nor the colonies could afford to please them as much as that. He professed loud contempt for the opinions of the Conservative party organs at Toronto, and stood boldly for his own views. That was what would happen, he declared, in every manufacturing division in the country, if the issue came to be fought in a general election. He was against the scheme, root and branch.

Mr. Winter was skilled, practised, and indefatigable. We need not follow him in all his ways and works; a good many of his arguments, I fear, must also escape us. The Elgin *Mercury*, if consulted, would produce them in daily disclosure; so would the Clayfield *Standard*. One of these offered a good deal of sympathy to Mayor Winter, the veteran of so many good fights, in being asked to contest South Fox with an opponent who had not so much as a village reeveship to his public credit. If the Conservative candidate felt the damage to his dignity, however, he concealed it.

In Elgin and Clayfield, where factory chimneys had also begun to point the way to enterprise, Winter had a clear field. Official reports gave him figures to prove the great and increasing prosperity of the country, astonishing figures of capital coming in, of emigrants landing, of new lands broken, new mineral regions exploited, new railways projected, of stocks and shares normal, safe, assured. He could ask the manufacturers of Elgin to look no farther than themselves, which they were quite willing to do, for illustration of the plenty and the promise which reigned in the land from one end to the other. He could tell them that in their own Province more than one hundred new industries had been established in the last year. He could ask them, and he did ask them, whether this was a state of things to disturb with an inrush from British looms and rolling mills, and they told him with applause that it was not.

Country audiences were not open to arguments like these; they were slow in the country, as the *Mercury* complained, to understand that agricultural prospects were bound up with the prosperity of the towns and cities; they had been especially slow in the country in England, as the *Express* ironically pointed out, to understand it. So Winter and his supporters asked the farmers of South Fox if they were prepared to believe all they heard of the good-will of England to the colonies, with the flattering assumption that they were by no means prepared to believe it. Was it a likely thing, Mr. Winter inquired, that the people of Great Britain were going to pay more for their flour and their bacon, their butter and their cheese, than they had any need to do, simply out of a desire to benefit countries which most of them had never seen, and never would see? No, said Mr. Winter, they might take it from him, that was not the idea. But Mr. Winter thought there was an idea, and that they and he together would not have much trouble in deciphering it. He did not claim to be longer-sighted in politics than any other man, but he thought the present British idea was pretty plain. It was, in two words, to secure the Canadian market for British goods, and a handsome contribution from the Canadian taxpayer toward the expense of the British army and navy, in return for the offer of favours to food supplies from Canada. But this, as they all knew, was not the first time favours had been offered by the British Government to food supplies from Canada. Just sixty years ago the British Government had felt one of these spasms of benevolence to Canada, and there were men sitting before him who could remember the good-will and the gratitude, the hope and the confidence, that greeted Stanley's bill[1] of that year, which admitted Canadian wheat and flour at a nominal duty. Some could remember, and those who could not remember could read, how the farmers and the millers of Ontario took heart and laid out capital, and how money was easy and enterprise was everywhere, and how agricultural towns such as Elgin was at that time sent up streets of shops to accommodate the trade that was to pour in under the new and generous "preference" granted to the Dominion by the mother country. And

---

1   The "Canada Corn Bill" proposed by the Colonial Secretary Lord Stanley (Earl of Derby), and passed by the government of Sir Robert Peel in 1843.

how long, Mr. Winter demanded, swinging round in that pivotal manner which seems assisted by thumbs in the armholes of the waistcoat, how long did the golden illusion last? Precisely three years. In precisely three years the British nation compelled the British Government to adopt the Free Trade Act of '46. The wheat of the world flowed into every port in England, and the hopes of Canada, especially the hopes of Ontario, based then, as now, on "preferential" treatment, were blasted to the root. Enterprise was laid flat, mortgages were foreclosed, shops were left empty, the milling and forwarding interests were temporarily ruined, and the Governor-General actually wrote to the Secretary of State in England that things were so bad that not a shilling could be raised on the credit of the Province.

Now Mr. Winter did not blame the people of England for insisting on free food. It was the policy that suited their interests, and they had just as good a right to look after their interests, he conceded handsomely, as anybody else. But he did blame the British Government for holding out hopes, for making definite pledges, to a young and struggling nation, which they must have known they would not be able to redeem. He blamed their action then, and he would blame it now, if the opportunity were given to them to repeat it, for the opportunity would pass and the pledge would pass into the happy hunting ground of unrealizable politics, but not—and Mr. Winter asked his listeners to mark this very carefully—not until Canada was committed to such relations of trade and taxes with the Imperial Government as would require the most heroic efforts—it might run to a war—to extricate herself from. In plain words, Mr. Winter assured his country audiences, Great Britain had sold them before, and she would sell them again. He stood there before them as loyal to British connection as any man. He addressed a public as loyal to British connection as any public. *But*—once bitten twice shy.

Horace Williams might riddle such arguments from end to end in the next day's *Express*, but if there is a thing that we enjoy in the country, it is having the dodges of Government shown up with ignominy, and Mr. Winter found his account in this historic parallel.

Nothing could have been more serious in public than his line of defence against the danger that menaced, but in friendly ears Mr. Winter derided it as a practical possibility, like the Liberals, Young and Windle.

"It seems to me," he said, talking to Octavius Milburn, "that the important thing at present is the party attitude to the disposition of Crown lands and to Government-made railways. As for this racket of Wallingham's, it has about as much in it as an empty bun-bag. He's running round taking a lot of satisfaction blowing it out just now, and the swells over there are clapping like anything, but the first knock will show that it's just a bun-bag, with a hole in it."

"Folks in the old country are solid on the buns, though," said Milburn as they parted, and Alfred Hesketh, who was walking with his host, said—"It's bound in the end to get down to that, isn't it?"

Presently Hesketh came back to it.

"Quaint idea, that—describing Wallingham's policy as a bun-bag," he said, and laughed. "Winter is an amusing fellow."

"Wallingham's policy won't even be a bun-bag much longer," said Milburn. "It won't be anything at all. Imperial union is very nice to talk about, but when you come down to hard fact it's Australia for the Australians, Canada for the Canadians, Africa for the Africans, every time."

"Each for himself, and devil take the hindmost," said Hesketh; "and when the hindmost is England, as our friend Murchison declares it will be—"

"So much the worse for England," said Milburn, amiably. "But we should all be sorry to see it, and, for my part, I don't believe such a thing is at all likely. And you may be certain of one thing," he continued, impressively: "No flag but the Union Jack will ever wave over Canada."

"Oh, I'm sure of that!" Hesketh responded. "Since I have heard more of your side of the question I am quite convinced that loyalty to England and complete commercial independence—I might say even commercial antagonism—may exist together in the colonies. It seems paradoxical, but it is true."

Mr. Hesketh had naturally been hearing a good deal more of Mr. Milburn's side of the question, staying as he was under Mr. Milburn's hospitable roof. It had taken the least persuasion in the world to induce him to make the Milburns a visit. He found them delightful people. He described them in his letters home as the most typically Canadian family he had met, quite simple and unconventional, but thoroughly warm-hearted, and touchingly devoted to far-away England. Politically he could not see eye to eye with Mr. Milburn, but he could quite perceive Mr. Milburn's grounds for the view he held. One thing, he explained to his correspondents, you learned at once by visiting the colonies, and that was to make allowance for local conditions, both social and economic.

He and Mr. Milburn had long serious discussions, staying behind in the dining-room to have them after tea, when the ladies took their fancy work into the drawing-room, and Dora's light touch was heard upon the piano. It may be supposed that Hesketh brought every argument forward in favour of the great departure that had been conceived in England; he certainly succeeded in interesting his host very deeply in the English point of view. He had, however, to encounter one that was made in Canada—it resided in Mr. Milburn as a stone might reside in a bag of wool. Mr. Milburn wouldn't say that this preference trade idea, if practicable, might not work out for the benefit of the Empire as a whole. That was a thing he didn't pretend to know. But it wouldn't work out for his benefit—that was a thing he did know. When a man was confronted with a big political change the question he naturally asked himself was, "Is it going to be worth my while?" and he acted on the answer to that question. He was able to explain to Hesketh, by a variety of facts and figures, of fascinating interest to the inquiring mind, just how and where such a concern as the Milburn Boiler Company would be "hit" by the new policy, after which he asked his guest fairly, "Now, if you were in my shoes, would you see your way to voting for any such thing?"

"If I were in your shoes," said Hesketh, thoughtfully, "I can't say I would."

On grounds of sentiment, Octavius assured him, they were absolutely at one, but in practical matters a man had to proceed on business principles. He went about at this time expressing great esteem for Hesketh's capacity to assimilate facts. His opportunity to assimilate them was not curtailed by any further demand for his services in the South Fox campaign. He was as willing as ever, he told Lorne Murchison, to enlist under the flag, and not for the first time; but Murchison and Farquharson, and that lot, while grateful for the offer, seemed never quite able to avail themselves of it: the fact was all the dates were pretty well taken up. No doubt, Hesketh acknowledged, the work could be done best by men familiar with the local conditions, but he could not avoid the conviction that this attitude toward proffered help was very like dangerous trifling. Possibly these circumstances gave him an added impartiality for Mr. Milburn's facts. As the winter advanced his enthusiasm for the country increased with his intelligent appreciation of the possibilities of the Elgin boiler. The Elgin boiler was his object-lesson in the development of the colonies; he paid several visits to the works to study it, and several times he thanked Mr. Milburn for the opportunity of familiarizing himself with such an important and promising branch of Canadian industry.

"It looks," said Octavius one evening in early February, "as if the Grits were getting a little anxious about South Fox—high time, too. I see Cruickshank is down to speak at Clayfield on the seventh, and Tellier is to be here for the big meeting at the opera-house on the eleventh."

"Tellier is Minister of Public Works, isn't he?" asked Hesketh.

"Yes—and Cruickshank is an ex-Minister," replied Mr. Milburn. "Looks pretty shaky when they've got to take men like that away from their work in the middle of the session."

"I shall be glad," remarked his daughter Dora, "when this horrid election is over. It spoils everything."

She spoke a little fretfully. The election and the matters it involved did interfere a good deal with her interest in life. As an occupation it absorbed Lorne Murchison even more completely than she occasionally desired; and as a topic it took up a larger share of the attention of Mr. Alfred Hesketh than she thought either reasonable or pleasing. Between politics and boilers Miss Milburn almost felt at times that the world held a second place for her.

TWENTY-EIGHT

The progress of Mrs. Kilbannon and Miss Christie Cameron up the river to Montreal, and so west to Elgin, was one series of surprises, most of them pleasant and instructive to such a pair of intelligent Scotch-women, if we leave out the number of Roman Catholic churches that lift their special symbol along the banks of the St. Lawrence and the fact that Hugh Finlay was not in Elgin to meet them upon their arrival. Dr. Drummond, of course, was there at the station to explain. Finlay had been obliged to leave for Winnipeg only the day before, to attend a mission conference in place of a delegate who had been suddenly laid aside by serious illness. Finlay, he said, had been very loth to go, but there were many reasons why it was imperative that he should; Dr. Drummond explained them all. "I insisted on it," he assured them, frankly. "I told him I would take the responsibility."

He seemed very capable of taking it, both the ladies must have thought, with his quick orders about the luggage and his waiting cab. Mrs. Kilbannon said so. "I'm sure," she told him, "we are better off with you than with Hugh. He was always a daft dependence[1] at a railway station."

They both—Mrs. Kilbannon and Dr. Drummond—looked out of the corners of their eyes, so to speak, at Christie, the only one who might be expected to show any sensitiveness; but Miss Cameron accepted the explanation with readiness. Indeed, she said, she would have been real vexed if Mr. Finlay had stayed behind on her account—she showed herself well aware of the importance of a nomination, and the desirability of responding to it.

"It will just give me an opportunity of seeing the town," she said, looking at it through the cab windows as they drove; and Dr. Drummond had to admit that she seemed a sensible creature. Other things being equal, Finlay might be doing very well for himself. As they talked of Scotland —it transpired that Dr. Drummond knew all the braes[2] about Bross as a boy—he found himself more than ever annoyed with Finlay about the inequality of other things; and when they passed Knox Church and Miss Cameron told him she hadn't realized it was so imposing an edifice, he felt downright sorry for the woman.

Dr. Drummond had persuaded Finlay to go to Winnipeg with a vague hope that something, in the fortnight's grace thus provided, might be induced to happen. The form it oftenest took to his imagination was Miss Christie's announcement, when she set foot upon the station platform, that she had become engaged, on the way over, to somebody else—some fellow-traveller. Such things, Dr. Drummond knew, did come about, usually bringing distress and discomfiture in their train. Why, then, should they not happen when all the consequences would be rejoiceful?

It was plain enough, however, that nothing of the kind had come to pass. Miss Christie had arrived in Elgin, bringing her affections intact; they might have been in any one of her portmanteaux. She had come with definite calm intention, precisely in the guise in which she should have been expected. At the very hour, in the very clothes, she was there. Robust and pleasant, with

---

1 Not reliable, not to be depended on.
2 Hillsides.

a practical eye on her promising future, she had arrived, the ful-
filment of despair. Dr. Drummond looked at her with acquiescence, half cowed, half comic, wondering at his own folly in
dreaming of anything else. Miss Cameron brought the situation,
as it were, with her; it had to be faced, and Dr. Drummond faced
it like a philosopher. She was the material necessity, the fact in the
case, the substantiation of her own legend; and Dr. Drummond
promptly gave her all the consideration she demanded in this
aspect. Already he heard himself pronouncing a blessing over the
pair—and they would make the best of it. With characteristic dispatch he decided that the marriage should take place the first
Monday after Finlay's return. That would give them time to take
a day or two in Toronto, perhaps, and get back for Finlay's
Wednesday prayer meeting. "Or I could take it off his hands," said
Dr. Drummond to himself. "That would free them till the end of
the week." Solicitude increased in him that the best should be
made of it; after all, for a long time they had been making the
worst. Mrs. Forsyth, whom it had been necessary to inform when
Mrs. Kilbannon and Miss Cameron became actually imminent,
saw plainly that the future Mrs. Finlay had made a very good
impression on the Doctor; and as nature, in Mrs. Forsyth's case,
was more powerful than grace, she became critical accordingly.
Still, she was an honest soul: she found more fault with what she
called Miss Cameron's "shirtwaists"[1] than with Miss Cameron
herself, whom she didn't doubt to be a good woman though she
would never see thirty-five again. Time and observation would no
doubt mend or remodel the shirt-waists; and meanwhile both
they and Miss Cameron would do very well for East Elgin, Mrs.
Forsyth avowed. Mrs. Kilbannon, definitely given over to caps
and curls as they still wear them in Bross, Mrs. Forsyth at once
formed a great opinion of. She might be something, Mrs. Forsyth
thought, out of a novel by Mr. Crockett,[2] and made you long to
go to Scotland, where presumably every one was like her. On the
whole the ladies from Bross profited rather than lost by the new
frame they stepped into in the house of Dr. Drummond, of Elgin,
Ontario. Their special virtues, of dignity and solidity and frugali-
ty, stood out saliently against the ease and unconstraint about

1 Blouses.
2 Samuel Rutherford Crockett (1860-1914), popular novelist of the "Kailyard" school, was known for his depiction of uniquely Scottish culture
   and characters.

them; in the profusion of the table it was little less than edifying to hear Mrs. Kilbannon, invited to preserves, say, "Thank you, I have butter." It was the pleasantest spectacle, happily common enough, of the world's greatest inheritance. We see it in immigrants of all degrees, and we may perceive it in Miss Cameron and Mrs. Kilbannon. They come in couples and in companies from those little imperial islands, bringing the crusted qualities of the old blood bottled there so long, and sink with grateful absorption into the wide bountiful stretches of the further countries. They have much to take, but they give themselves; and so it comes about that the Empire is summed up in the race, and the flag flies for its ideals.

Mrs. Forsyth had been told of the approaching event; but neither Dr. Drummond, who was not fond of making communications he did not approve of, nor the Murchisons, who were shy of the matter as a queer business which Advena seemed too much mixed up with, had mentioned it to any one else. Finlay himself had no intimates, and moved into his new house in River Street under little comment. His doings excited small surprise, because the town knew too little about him to expect him to do one thing more than another. He was very significant among his people, very important in their lives, but not, somehow, at any expense to his private self. He knew them, but they did not know him; and it is high praise of him that this was no grievance among them. They would tell you without resentment that the minister was a "very reserved" man; there might be even a touch of proper pride in it. The worshippers of Knox Church mission were rather a reserved lot themselves. It was different with the Methodists; plenty of expansion there.

Elgin, therefore, knew nothing, beyond the fact that Dr. Drummond had two ladies from the old country staying with him, about whom particular curiosity would hardly be expected outside of Knox Church. In view of Finlay's absence, Dr. Drummond, consulting with Mrs. Kilbannon, decided that for the present Elgin need not be further informed. There was no need, they agreed, to give people occasion to talk; and it would just be a nuisance to have to make so many explanations. Both Mrs. Kilbannon and her niece belonged to the race that takes great satisfaction in keeping its own counsel. Their situation gained for them the further interest that nothing need be said about it; and the added importance of caution was plainly to be discerned in their bearing, even toward one another. It was a portentous business, this of marrying a minister, under the most ordinary circumstances, not to be lightly dealt with, and even more of an undertaking in a far new country where the very wind blew differently, and the extraordinary freedom of conversation made it more than ever necessary to take heed to what you were saying. So far as Miss Cameron and Mrs. Kilbannon were aware, the matter had not been "spoken of" elsewhere at all. Dr. Drummond, remembering Advena Murchison's acquaintance with it, had felt the weight of a complication, and had discreetly held his tongue. Mrs. Kilbannon approved her nephew in this connection. "Hugh," she said, "was never one to let on more than necessary." It was a fine secret between Hugh, in Winnipeg, whence he had written all that was lawful or desirable, and themselves at Dr. Drummond's. Miss Cameron said it would give her more freedom to look about her.

In the midst of all this security, and on the very first day after their arrival, it was disconcerting to be told that a lady, whose name they had never heard before, had called to see Miss Cameron and Mrs. Kilbannon. They had not even appeared at church, as they told one another with dubious glances. They had no reason whatever to expect visitors. Dr. Drummond was in the cemetery burying a member; Mrs. Forsyth was also abroad. "Now who in the world," asked Mrs. Kilbannon of Miss Cameron, "is Miss Murchison?"

"They come to our church," said Sarah, in the door. "They've got the foundry. It's the oldest one. She teaches."

Sarah in the door was even more disconcerting than an unexpected visitor. Sarah invariably took them off their guard, in the door or anywhere. She freely invited their criticism, but they would not have known how to mend her. They looked at her now helplessly, and Mrs. Kilbannon said, "Very well. We will be down directly."

"It may be just some friendly body," she said, as they descended the stairs together, "or it may be common curiosity. In that case we'll disappoint it."

Whatever they expected, therefore, it was not Advena. It was not a tall young woman with expressive eyes, a manner which was at once abrupt and easy, and rather a lounging way of occupying the corner of a sofa. "When she sat down," as Mrs. Kilbannon said afterward, "she seemed to untie and fling herself as you might a parcel." Neither Mrs. Kilbannon nor Christie Cameron could possibly be untied or flung, so perhaps they gave this capacity in Advena more importance than it had. But it was only a part of what was to them a new human demonstration, something to inspect very carefully and accept very cautiously—the product, like themselves, yet so suspiciously different, of these free airs and these astonishingly large ideas. In some ways, as she sat there in her graceful dress and careless attitude, asking them direct smiling questions about their voyage, she imposed herself as of the class whom both these ladies of Bross would acknowledge unquestioningly to be "above" them; in others she seemed to be of no class at all; so far she came short of small standards of speech and behaviour. The ladies from Bross, more and more confused, grew more and more reticent, when suddenly, out of a simple remark of Miss Cameron's about missing in the train the hot-water cans they gave you "to your feet" in Scotland, reticence descended upon Miss Murchison also. She sat in an odd silence, looking at Miss Cameron, absorbed apparently in the need of looking at her, finding nothing to say, her flow of pleasant inquiry dried up, and all her soul at work, instead, to perceive the woman. Mrs. Kilbannon was beginning to think better of her—it was so much more natural to be a little backward with strangers—when the moment passed. Their visitor drew herself out of it with almost a perceptible effort, and seemed to glance consideringly at them in their aloofness, their incommunicativeness, their plain odds with her. I don't know what she expected; but we may assume that she was there simply to offer herself up, and the impulse of sacrifice seldom considers whether or not it may be understood. It was to her a normal, natural thing that a friend of Hugh Finlay's should bring an early welcome to his bride; and to do the normal, natural thing at keen personal cost was to sound that depth, or rise to that height of the spirit where pain sustains. We know of Advena that she was prone to this form of exaltation. Those who feel themselves capable may pronounce whether she would have been better at home crying in her bedroom.

She decided badly—how could she decide well?—on what she would say to explain herself.

"I am so sorry," she told them, "that Mr. Finlay is obliged to be away."

It was quite wrong; it assumed too much, her knowledge and their confidence, and the propriety of discussing Mr. Finlay's absence. There was even an unconscious hint of another kind of assumption in it—a suggestion of apology for Mr. Finlay. Advena was aware of it even as it left her lips, and the perception covered her with a damning blush. She had a sudden terrified misgiving that her *rôle* was too high for her, that she had already cracked her mask. But she looked quietly at Miss Cameron and smiled across the tide that surged in her as she added, "He was very distressed at having to go."

They looked at her in an instant's blank astonishment. Miss Cameron opened her lips and closed them again, glancing at Mrs. Kilbannon. They fell back together, but not in disorder. This was something much more formidable than common curiosity. Just what it was they would consider later; meanwhile Mrs. Kilbannon responded with what she would have called cool civility.

"Perhaps you have heard that Mr. Finlay is my nephew?" she said.

"Indeed I have. Mr. Finlay has told me a great deal about you, Mrs. Kilbannon, and about his life at Bross," Advena replied. "And he has told me about you, too," she went on, turning to Christie Cameron.

"Indeed?" said she.

"Oh, a long time ago. He has been looking forward to your arrival for some months, hasn't he?"

"We took our passages in December," said Miss Cameron.

"And you are to be married almost immediately, are you not?" Miss Murchison continued, pleasantly.

Mrs. Kilbannon had an inspiration. "Could he by any means have had the banns cried?"[1] she demanded of Christie, who looked piercingly at their visitor for the answer.

"Oh, no," Advena laughed softly. "Presbyterians haven't that custom over here—does it still exist anywhere? Mr. Finlay told me himself."

"Has he informed all his acquaintances?" asked Mrs. Kilbannon. "We thought maybe his elders would be expecting to hear, or his Board of Management. Or he might have just dropped a word to his Sessions Clerk. But—"

Advena shook her head. "I think it unlikely," she said.

"Then why would he be telling you?" inquired the elder lady, bluntly.

"He told me, I suppose, because I have the honour to be a friend of his," Advena said, smiling. "But he is not a man, is he? who makes many friends. It is possible, I dare say, that he has mentioned it to no one else."

---

1 Given notice in church of an intention to be married, according to an ancient Christian tradition. The banns were cried three weeks prior to a wedding, in order to allow anyone opposed to the match to register their objection.

Poor Advena! She had indeed uttered her ideal to unsympathetic ears—brought her pig, as her father would have said, to the wrong market. She sat before the ladies from Bross, Hugh Finlay's only confidante. She sat handsome and upheld and not altogether penetrable, a kind of gipsy to their understanding, though indeed the Rommany strain in her was beyond any divining of theirs. They, on their part, reposed in their clothes with all their bristles out—what else could have been expected of them?—convinced in their own minds that they had come not only to a growing but to a forward country.

Mrs. Kilbannon was perhaps a little severe. "I wonder that we have not heard of you, Miss Murchison," said she, "but we are happy to make the acquaintance of any of my nephew's friends. You will have heard him preach, perhaps?"

"Often," said Advena, rising. "We have no one here who can compare with him in preaching. There was very little reason why you should have heard of me. I am—of no importance." She hesitated and fought for an instant with a trembling of the lip. "But now that you have been persuaded to be a part of our life here," she said to Christie, "I thought I would like to come and offer you my friendship because it is his already. I hope—so much—that you will be happy here. It is a nice little place. And I want you to let me help you—about your house, and in every way that is possible. I am sure I can be of use." She paused and looked at their still half-hostile faces. "I hope," she faltered, "you don't mind my—having come?"

"Not at all," said Christie, and Mrs. Kilbannon added, "I'm sure you mean it very kindly."

A flash of the comedy of it shot up in Advena's eyes. "Yes," she said, "I do. Good-bye."

If they had followed her departure they would have been further confounded to see her walk not quite steadily away, shaken with fantastic laughter. They looked instead at one another, as if to find the solution of the mystery where indeed it lay, in themselves.

"She doesn't even belong to his congregation," said Christie. "Just a friend, she said."

"I expect the friendship's mostly upon her side," remarked Mrs. Kilbannon. "She seemed frank enough about it. But I would see no necessity for encouraging her friendship on my own account, if I were in your place, Christie."

"I think I'll manage without it," said Christie.

TWENTY-NINE

The South Fox fight was almost over. Three days only remained before the polling booths would be open, and the voters of the towns of Elgin and Clayfield and the surrounding townships would once again be invited to make their choice between a Liberal and a Conservative representative of the district in the Dominion House of Commons. The ground had never been more completely covered, every inch of advantage more stubbornly held, by either side, in the political history of the riding. There was no doubt of the hope that sat behind the deprecation in Walter Winter's eye, nor of the anxiety that showed through the confidence freely expressed by the Liberal leaders. The issue would be no foregone conclusion, as it had been practically any time within the last eleven years; and as Horace Williams remarked to the select lot that met pretty frequently at the *Express* office for consultation and rally, they had "no use for any sort of carelessness."

It was undeniably felt that the new idea, the great idea whose putative fatherhood in Canada certainly lay at the door of the Liberal party, had drawn in fewer supporters than might have been expected. In England Wallingham, wearing it like a medal, seemed to be courting political excommunication with it, except that Wallingham was so hard to effectively curse. The ex-Minister[1] deserved, clearly, any ban that could be put upon him. No sort of remonstrance could hold him from going about openly and persistently exhorting people to "think imperially," a liberty which, as is well known, the Holy Cobdenite Church, supreme in those islands, expressly forbids. Wallingham appeared to think that by teaching and explaining he could help his fellow islanders to see further than the length of their fists, and exorcise from them the spirit, only a century and a quarter older and a trifle more sophisticated, that lost them the American colonies. But so far little had transpired to show that Wallingham was stronger than nature and destiny. There had been Wallingham meetings of remarkable enthusiasm; his supporters called them epoch-making, as if epochs were made of cheers. But the working man of Great Britain was declaring stolidly in the bye-elections against

---

1 Joseph Chamberlain resigned from the Salisbury cabinet in September 1903, over disagreements with his cabinet colleagues on the issue of Imperial Preference trade.

any favour to colonial produce at his expense, thereby showing himself one of those humble instruments that Providence uses for the downfall of arrogant empires. It will be thus, no doubt, that the working man will explain in the future his eminent usefulness to the government of his country, and it will be in these terms that the cost of educating him by means of the ballot will be demonstrated. Meanwhile we may look on and cultivate philosophy; or we may make war upon the gods with Mr. Wallingham, which is, perhaps, the better part.

That, to turn from recrimination, was what they saw in Canada looking across;—the queerest thing of all was the recalcitrance of the farm labourer; they could only stare at that—and it may be that the spectacle was depressing to hopeful initiative. At all events, it was plain that the new policy was suffering from a certain flatness on the further side. As a *ballon d'essai*[1] it lacked buoyancy; and no doubt Mr. Farquharson was right in declaring that above all things it lacked actuality, business—the proposition, in good set terms, for men to turn over, to accept or reject. Nothing could be done with it, Mr. Farquharson averred, as a mere prospect; it was useful only to its enemies. We of the young countries must be invited to deeds, not theories, of which we have a restless impatience; and this particular theory, though of golden promise, was beginning to recoil to some extent, upon the cause which had been confident enough to adopt it before it could be translated into action and its hard equivalent. The Elgin *Mercury* probably overstated the matter when it said that the Grits were dead sick of the preference they would never get; but Horace Williams was quite within the mark when he advised Lorne to stick to old Reform principles—clean administration, generous railway policy, sympathetic labour legislation, and freeze himself a little on imperial love and attachment.

"They're not so sweet on it in Ottawa as they were, by a long chalk," he said. "Look at the Premier's speech to the Chambers of Commerce in Montreal. Pretty plain statement that, of a few things the British Government needn't expect."

"Oh, I don't know," said Lorne. "He was talking to manufacturers, you know, a pretty skittish lot anywhere. It sounded independent, but if you look into it you won't find it gave the cause away any."

---

1   Trial balloon.

"The old man's got to think of Quebec, where his fat little majority lives," remarked Bingham, chairman of the most difficult subdivision in the town. "The Premier of this country drives a team, you know."

"Yes," said Lorne, "but he drives it tandem,[1] and Johnny François is the second horse."

"Maybe so," returned Mr. Williams, "but the organ's singing pretty small, too. Look at this." He picked up the *Dominion* from the office table and read aloud: "'If Great Britain wishes to do a deal with the colonies she will find them willing to meet her in a spirit of fairness and enthusiasm. But it is for her to decide, and Canada would be the last to force her bread down the throat of the British labourer at a higher price than he can afford to pay for it.' What's that, my boy? Is it high-mindedness? No, sir, it's lukewarmness."

"The *Dominion* makes me sick," said young Murchison. "It's so scared of the Tory source of the scheme in England that it's handing the whole boom of the biggest chance this country ever had over to the Tories here. If anything will help us to lose it that will. No Conservative Government in Canada can put through a cent of preference on English goods when it comes to the touch, and they know it. They're full of loyalty just now—baying the moon—but if anybody opens a window they'll turn tail fast enough."

"I guess the *Dominion* knows it, too," said Mr. Williams. "When Great Britain is quite sure she's ready to do business on preference lines it's the Liberal party on this side she'll have to talk to. No use showing ourselves too anxious, you know. Besides, it might do harm over there. We're all right; we're on record. Wallingham knows as well as we do the lines we're open on—he's heard them from Canadian Liberals more than once. When they get good and ready they can let us know."

"Jolly them up with it at your meetings by all means," advised Bingham, "but use it as a kind of superfluous taffy; don't make it your main lay-out."

The Reform Association[2] of South Fox had no more energetic officer than Bingham, though as he sat on the edge of the editorial table chewing portions of the margin of that afternoon's

---

1 Hitched together in single file, one in front of the other. See Introduction (p. 30) for a discussion of Duncan's attitude to French Canada.
2 An association of Liberal supporters.

Express, and drawling out maxims to the Liberal candidate, you might not have thought so. He was explaining that he had been in this business for years, and had never had a job that gave him so much trouble.

"We'll win out," he said, "but the canvass isn't any Christmas joy—not this time. There's Jim Whelan," he told them. "We all know what Jim is—a Tory from way back, where they make 'em so they last, and a soaker from way back, too, one day on his job and two days sleepin' off his whisky. Now we don't need Jim Whelan's vote, never did need it, but the boys have generally been able to see that one of those two days was election day. There's no necessity for Jim's putting in his paper—a character like that—no necessity at all—he'd much better be comfortable in bed. This time, I'm darned if the old boozer hasn't sworn off! Tells the boys he's on to their game, and there's no liquor in this town that's good enough to get him to lose his vote —wouldn't get drunk on champagne. He's held out for ten days already, and it looks like Winter'd take his cross all right on Thursday."

"I guess I'd let him have it, Bingham," said Lorne Murchison with a kind of tolerant deprecation, void of offence, the only manner in which he knew how to convey disapproval to the older man. "The boys in your division are a pretty tough lot, anyhow. We don't want the other side getting hold of any monkey tricks."

"It's necessary to win this election, young man," said Bingham, "lawfully. You won't have any trouble with my bunch."

It was not, as will be imagined, the first discussion, so late in the day, of the value of the preference trade argument to the Liberal campaign. They had all realized, after the first few weeks, that their young candidate was a trifle overbitten with it, though remonstrance had been a good deal curbed by Murchison's treatment of it. When he had brought it forward at the late fall fairs and in the lonely country schoolhouses, his talk had been so trenchant, so vivid and pictorial, that the gathered farmers listened with open mouths, like children, pathetically used with life, to a grown-up fairy tale. As Horace Williams said, if a dead horse. could be made to go this one would have brought Murchison romping in. And Lorne had taken heed to the counsel of his party leaders. At joint meetings, which offered the enemy his best opportunity for travesty and derision, he had left it in the background of debate, devoting himself to arguments of more immediate utility. In the literature of the campaign it glowed with prospective benefit, but vaguely, like a halo of Liberal conception and possible achievement, waiting for the word from overseas. The *Express* still approved it, but not in headlines, and wished the fact to be widely understood that while the imperial idea was a very big idea, the Liberals of South Fox were going to win this election without any assistance from it.

Lorne submitted. After all, victory was the thing. There could be no conquest for the idea without the party triumph first. He submitted, but his heart rebelled. He looked over the subdivisional reports with Williams and Farquharson, and gave ear to their warning interpretations; but his heart was an optimist, and turned always to the splendid projection upon the future that was so incomparably the title to success of those who would unite to further it. His mind accepted the old working formulas for dealing with an average electorate, but to his eager apprehending heart it seemed unbelievable that the great imperial possibility, the dramatic chance for the race that hung even now, in the history of the world, between the rising and the setting of the sun, should fail to be perceived and acknowledged as the paramount issue, the contingency which made the bye-election of South Fox an extraordinary and momentous affair. He believed in the Idea; he saw it, with Wallingham, not only a glorious prospect, but an educative force; and never had he a moment of such despondency that it confounded him upon his horizon in the faded colours of some old Elizabethan mirage.

The opera-house, the night of Mr. Murchison's final address to the electors of South Fox, was packed from floor to ceiling, and a large and patient overflow made the best of the hearing accommodation of the corridors and the foyer. A Minister was to speak, Sir Matthew Tellier, who held the portfolio of Public Works; and for drawing a crowd in Elgin there was nothing to compare with a member of the Government. He was the sum of all ambition and the centre of all importance; he was held to have achieved in the loftiest sense, and probably because he deserved to; a kind of afflatus sat upon him. They paid him real deference and they flocked to hear him. Cruickshank was a second attraction; and Lorne himself, even at this stage of the proceedings, "drew" without abatement. They knew young Murchison well enough; he had gone in and out among them all his life; yet since he had come before them in this new capacity a curious interest had gathered about him. People looked at him as if he had developed something they did not understand, and perhaps he had; he was in touch with the Idea. They listened with an intense personal interest in him which, no doubt, went to obscure what he said: perhaps a less absorbing personality would have carried the Idea further. However, they did look and listen—that was the main point, and on their last opportunity they were in the opera-house in great numbers.

Lorne faced them with an enviable security; the friendliness of the meeting was in the air. The gathering was almost entirely of one political complexion: the Conservatives of the town would have been glad enough to turn out to hear Minister Tellier; but the Liberals were of no mind to gratify them at the cost of having to stand themselves, and were on hand early to assert a prior moral claim to chairs. In the seated throng Lorne could pick out the fine head of his father, and his mother's face, bright with anticipation, beside. Advena was there, too, and Stella; and the boys would have a perch, not too conspicuous, somewhere in the gallery. Dr. Drummond was in the second row, and a couple of strange ladies with him: he was chuckling with uncommon humour at some remark of the younger one when Lorne noted him. Old Sandy MacQuhot was in a good place; had been since six o'clock, and Peter Macfarlane, too, for that matter, though Peter sat away back as beseemed a modest functionary whose business was with the book and the bell. Altogether, as Horace Williams leaned over to tell him, it was like a Knox Church sociable—he could feel completely at home; and though the audience was by no means confined to Knox Church, Lorne did feel at home. Dora Milburn's countenance he might perhaps have missed, but Dora was absent by arrangement. Mr. Milburn, as the fight went on, had shown himself so increasingly bitter, to the point of writing letters in the *Mercury* attacking Wallingham and the Liberal leaders of South Fox, that his daughter felt an insurmountable delicacy in attending even Lorne's "big meeting." Alfred Hesketh meant to have gone, but it was ten by the Milburns' drawing-room clock before he remembered. Miss Filkin actually did go, and brought home a great report of it. Miss Filkin would no more have missed a Minister than she would a bishop, but she was the only one.

Lorne had prepared for this occasion for a long time. It was certain to come, the day of the supreme effort, when he should make his final appeal under the most favourable circumstances that could be devised, when the harassing work of the campaign would be behind him, and nothing would remain but the luxury of one last strenuous call to arms. The glory of that anticipation had been with him from the beginning; and in the beginning he saw his great moment only in one character. For weeks, while he plodded through the details of the benefits South Fox had received and might expect to receive at the hands of the Liberal party, he privately stored argument on argument, piled phrase on phrase, still further to advance and defend the imperial unity of his vision on this certain and special opportunity. His jehad[1] it would be, for the faith and purpose of his race; so he scanned it and heard it, with conviction hot in him, and impulse strong, and intention noble. Then uneasiness had arisen, as we know; and under steady pressure he had daily drawn himself from these high intentions, persuaded by Bingham and the rest that they were not yet "in shape" to talk about. So that his address on this memorable evening would have a different stamp from the one he designed in the early burning hours of his candidature. He had postponed those matters, under advice, to the hour of practical dealing, when a Government which it would be his privilege to support would consider and carry them. He put the notes of his original speech away in his office desk with solicitude—it was indeed very thorough, a grand marshalling of the facts and review of the principles involved—and pigeonholed it in the chambers of his mind, with the good hope to bring it forth another day. Then he devoted his attention to the history of Liberalism in Fox County—both ridings were solid—and it was upon the history of Liberalism in Fox County, its triumphs and its fruits, that he embarked so easily and so assuredly, when he opened his address in the opera-house that Tuesday night.

Who knows at what suggestion, or even precisely at what moment, the fabric of his sincere intention fell away? Bingham does not; Mr. Farquharson has the vaguest idea; Dr. Drummond declares that he expected it from the beginning, but is totally unable to say why. I can get nothing more out of them, though they were all there, though they all saw him, indeed a dramatic figure, standing for the youth and energy of the old blood, and heard him, as he slipped away into his great preoccupation, as he made what Bingham called his "bad break." His very confidence may have accounted for it; he was off guard against the enemy, and the more completely off guard against himself. The history of Liberalism in Fox County offered, no doubt, some inlet to the

---

1 Also jihad; a war to gain religious converts.

rush of the Idea; for suddenly, Mr. Farquharson says, he was "off." Mr. Farquharson was on the platform, and "I can tell you," said he, "I pricked up my ears." They all did; the Idea came in upon such a personal note.

"I claim it my great good fortune," the young man was suddenly telling them, in a note of curious gravity and concentration, "and however the fight goes, I shall always claim it my great good fortune to have been identified, at a critical moment, with the political principles that are ennobled in this country by the imperialistic aim. An intention, a great purpose in the endless construction and reconstruction of the world, will choose its own agency; and the imperial design in Canada has chosen the Liberal party, because the Liberal party in this country is the party of the soil, the land, the nation as it springs from that which makes it a nation; and imperialism is intensely and supremely a national affair. Ours is the policy of the fields. We stand for the wheat-belt and the stock-yard, the forest and the mine, as the basic interests of the country. We stand for the principles that make for nation-building by the slow sweet processes of the earth, cultivating the individual rooted man who draws his essence and his tissues from the soil, and so, by unhurried, natural, healthy growth, labour sweating his vices out of him, forms the character of the commonwealth, the foundation of the State. So the imperial idea seeks its Canadian home in Liberal councils. The imperial idea is far-sighted. England has outlived her own body. Apart from her heart and her history, England is an area where certain trades are carried on—still carried on. In the scrolls of the future it is already written that the centre of the Empire must shift—and where, if not to Canada?"

There was a half-comprehending burst of applause, Dr. Drummond's the first clap. It was a curious change from the simple colloquial manner in which young Murchison had begun and to which the audience were accustomed; and on this account probably they stamped the harder. They applauded Lorne himself; something from him infected them; they applauded being made to feel like that. They would clap first and consider afterwards. John Murchison smiled with pleasure, but shook his head. Bingham, doubled up and clapping like a repeating rifle, groaned aloud under cover of it to Horace Williams: "Oh, the darned kid!"

"A certain Liberal peer of blessed political memory," Lorne continued, with a humorous twist of his mouth, "on one of those graceful, elegant, academic occasions which offer political peers such happy opportunities of getting in their work over there, had lately a vision, which he described to his university audience, of what might have happened if the American colonies had remained faithful to Great Britain—a vision of monarch and Ministers, Government and Parliament, departing solemnly for the other hemisphere. They did not so remain; so the noble peer may conjure up his vision or dismiss his nightmare as he chooses; and it is safe to prophesy that no port of the United States will see that entry. But, remembering that the greater half of the continent did remain faithful, the northern and strenuous half, destined to move with sure steps and steady mind to greater growth and higher place among the nations than any of us can now imagine—would it be as safe to prophesy that such a momentous sailing-day will never be more than the after-dinner fantasy of aristocratic rhetoric? Is it not at least as easy to imagine that even now, while the people of England send their viceroys to the ends of the earth, and vote careless millions for a reconstructed army, and sit in the wrecks of Cabinets disputing whether they will eat our bread or the stranger's, the sails may be filling, in the far harbour of time, which will bear their descendants to a representative share of the duties and responsibilities of Empire in the capital of the Dominion of Canada?"

It was the boldest proposition, and the Liberal voters of the town of Elgin blinked a little, looking at it. Still they applauded, hurriedly, to get it over and hear what more might be coming. Bingham, on the platform, laughed heartily and conspicuously, as if anybody could see that it was all an excellent joke. Lorne half turned to him with a gesture of protest. Then he went on— "If that transport ever left the shores of England we would go far, some of us, to meet it; but for all the purposes that matter most it sailed long ago. British statesmen could bring us nothing better than the ideals of British government; and those we have had since we levied our first tax and made our first law. That precious cargo was our heritage, and we never threw it overboard, but chose rather to render what impost it brought; and there are those who say that the impost has been heavy, though never a dollar was paid."

He paused for an instant and seemed to review and take account of what he had said. He was hopelessly adrift from the subject he had proposed to himself, launched for better or for worse upon the theme that was subliminal in him and had flowed up, on which he was launched, and almost rudderless, without

construction and without control. The speech of his first intention, orderly, developed, was as far from him as the history of Liberalism in Fox County. For an instant he hesitated; and then,
under the suggestion, no doubt, of that ancient misbehaviour in
Boston Harbour at which he had hinted, he took up another
argument.[1] I will quote him a little.

"Let us hold," he said simply, "to the Empire. Let us keep this
patrimony that has been ours for three hundred years. Let us not
forget the flag. We believe ourselves, at this moment, in no danger of forgetting it. The day after Paardeburg,[2] that still winter
day, did not our hearts rise within us to see it shaken out with its
message everywhere, shaken out against the snow? How it spoke
to us, and lifted us, the silent flag in the new fallen snow! Theirs—
and ours.... That was but a little while ago, and there is not a man
here who will not bear me out in saying that we were never more
loyal, in word and deed, than we are now. And that very state of
things has created for us an undermining alternative ...

"So long as no force appeared to improve the trade relations
between England and this country Canada sought in vain to
make commercial bargains with the United States. They would
have none of us or our produce; they kept their wall just as high
against us as against the rest of the world: not a pine plank or a
bushel of barley could we get over under a reciprocal arrangement. But the imperial trade idea has changed the attitude of our
friends to the south. They have small liking for any scheme which
will improve trade between Great Britain and Canada, because
trade between Great Britain and Canada must be improved at
their expense. And now you cannot take up an American paper
without finding the report of some commercial association
demanding closer trade relations with Canada, or an American
magazine in which some far-sighted economist is not urging the
same thing. They see us thinking about keeping the business in
the family; with that hard American common sense that has made
them what they are, they accept the situation; and at this moment
they are ready to offer us better terms to keep our trade."

---

1 A reference to the Boston Tea Party (1773), when a party of American
   colonists dressed as "Indians" threw a cargo of tea overboard from a
   ship in Boston Harbour to protest the import duties imposed by the
   British Government.
2 The first big battle of the Boer War that involved Canadian troops, in
   1900.

Bingham, Horace Williams, and Mr. Farquharson applauded loudly. Their young man frowned a little and squared his chin. He was past hints of that kind.

"And that," he went on to say, "is, on the surface, a very satisfactory state of things. No doubt a bargain between the Americans and ourselves could be devised which would be a very good bargain on both sides. In the absence of certain pressing family affairs, it might be as well worth our consideration as we used to think it before we were invited to the family council. But if any one imagines that any degree of reciprocity with the United States could be entered upon without killing the idea of British preference trade for all time, let him consider what Canada's attitude toward that idea would be to-day if the Americans had consented to our proposals twenty-five years ago, and we were invited to make an imperial sacrifice of the American trade that had prospered, as it would have prospered, for a quarter of a century! I doubt whether the proposition would even be made to us....

"But the alternative before Canada is not a mere choice of markets; we are confronted with a much graver issue. In this matter of dealing with our neighbour our very existence is involved. If we would preserve ourselves as a nation, it has become our business, not only to reject American overtures in favour of the overtures of our own great England, but to keenly watch and actively resist American influence, as it already threatens us through the common channels of life and energy. We often say that we fear no invasion from the south, but the armies of the south have already crossed the border. American enterprise, American capital, is taking rapid possession of our mines and our water-power, our oil areas and our timber limits. In to-day's *Dominion*, one paper alone, you may read of charters granted to five industrial concerns with headquarters in the United States. The trades unions of the two countries are already international. American settlers are pouring into the wheat-belt of the Northwest, and when the Dominion of Canada has paid the hundred million dollars she has just voted for a railway to open up the great lone northern lands between Quebec and the Pacific, it will be the American farmer and the American capitalist who will reap the benefit. They approach us to-day with all the arts of peace, commercial missionaries to the ungathered harvests of neglected territories; but the day may come when they will menace our coasts to protect their markets—unless, by firm, resolved, whole-hearted action now, we keep our opportunities for our own people."

They cheered him promptly, and a gathered intensity came into his face at the note of praise.

"Nothing on earth can hold him now," said Bingham, as he crossed his arms upon a breast seething with practical politics, and waited for the worst.

"The question of the hour for us," said Lorne Murchison to his fellow townsmen, curbing the strenuous note in his voice, "is deeper than any balance of trade can indicate, wider than any department of statistics can prove. We cannot calculate it in terms of pig-iron, or reduce it to any formula of consumption. The question that underlies this decision for Canada is that of the whole stamp and character of her future existence. Is that stamp and character to be impressed by the American Republic effacing"—he smiled a little—"the old Queen's head and the new King's oath? Or is it to be our own stamp and character, acquired in the rugged discipline of our colonial youth, and developed in the national usage of the British Empire?..."

Dr. Drummond clapped alone; everybody else was listening.

"It is ours," he told them, "in this greater half of the continent, to evolve a nobler ideal. The Americans from the beginning went in a spirit of revolt; the seed of disaffection was in every Puritan bosom. We from the beginning went in a spirit of amity, forgetting nothing, disavowing nothing, to plant the flag with our fortunes. We took our very Constitution, our very chart of national life, from England—her laws, her liberty, her equity were good enough for us. We have lived by them, some of us have died by them ... and, thank God, we were long poor...."

"And this Republic," he went on hotly, "this Republic that menaces our national life with commercial extinction, what past has she that is comparable? The daughter who left the old stock to be the light woman among nations, welcoming all comers, mingling her pure blood, polluting her lofty ideals until it is hard indeed to recognize the features and the aims of her honourable youth...."

Allowance will be made for the intemperance of his figure. He believed himself, you see, at the bar for the life of a nation.

"... Let us not hesitate to announce ourselves for the Empire, to throw all we are and all we have into the balance for that great decision. The seers of political economy tell us that if the stars continue to be propitious, it is certain that a day will come which will usher in a union of the Anglo-Saxon nations of the world. As between England and the United States the predominant partner in that firm will be the one that brings Canada. So that the imperial movement of the hour may mean even more than the future of the mother land, may reach even further than the boundaries of Greater Britain...."

Again he paused, and his eye ranged over their listening faces. He had them all with him, his words were vivid in their minds; the truth of them stood about him like an atmosphere. Even Bingham looked at him without reproach. But he had done.

"Ladies and gentlemen," he said, his voice dropping, with a hint of tiredness, to another level, "I have the honour to stand for your suffrages as candidate in the Liberal interest for the riding of South Fox in the Dominion House of Commons the day after to-morrow. I solicit your support, and I hereby pledge myself to justify it by every means in my power. But it would be idle to disguise from you that while I attach all importance to the immediate interests in charge of the Liberal party, and if elected shall use my best efforts to further them, the great task before that party, in my opinion, the overshadowing task to which, I shall hope, in my place and degree to stand committed from the beginning, is the one which I have endeavoured to bring before your consideration this evening."

They gave him a great appreciation, and Mr. Cruickshank, following, spoke in complimentary terms of the eloquent appeal made by the "young and vigorous protagonist" of the imperial cause, but proceeded to a number of quite other and apparently more important grounds why he should be elected. The Hon. Mr. Tellier's speech—the Minister was always kept to the last—was a defence of the recent dramatic development of the Government's railway policy, and a reminder of the generous treatment Elgin was receiving in the Estimates for the following year—thirty thousand dollars for a new Drill Hall, and fifteen thousand for improvements to the post-office. It was a telling speech, with the chink of hard cash in every sentence, a kind of audit by a chartered accountant of the Liberal books of South Fox, showing good sound reason why the Liberal candidate should be returned on Thursday, if only to keep the balance right. The audience listened with practical satisfaction. "That's Tellier all over," they said to one another....

The effect in committee of what, in spite of the Hon. Mr. Tellier's participation, I must continue to call the speech of the evening, may be gathered from a brief colloquy between Mr. Bingham and Mr. Williams, in the act of separating at the door of the opera-house.

"I don't know what it was worth to preference trade," said Bingham, "but it wasn't worth a hill o' beans to his own election."

"He had as soft a snap," returned Horace Williams, on the brink of tears—"as soft a snap as anybody ever had in this town. And he's monkeyed it all away. All away."

Both the local papers published the speech in full the following day. "If there's anything in Manchester or Birmingham that Mr. Lorne Murchison would like," commented the *Mercury* editorially, "we understand he has only to call for it."

THIRTY

The Milburns' door-bell rang very early the morning of the election. The family and Alfred Hesketh were just sitting down to breakfast. Mr. Hesketh was again the guest of the house. He had taken a run out to Vancouver with Mr. Milburn's partner, who had gone to settle a point or two in connection with the establishment of a branch there. The points had been settled, and Hesketh, having learned more than ever, had returned to Elgin.

The maid came back into the room with a conscious air, and said something in a low voice to Dora, who flushed and frowned a little, and asked to be excused. As she left the room a glance of intelligence passed between her and her mother. While Miss Milburn was generally thought to be "most like" her father both in appearance and disposition, there were points upon which she could count on an excellent understanding with her other parent.

"Oh, Lorne," she said, having carefully closed the drawing-room door, "what in the world have you come here for? To-day of all days! Did anybody see you?"

The young man, standing tall and broad-shouldered before the mantelpiece, had yet a look of expecting reproach.

"I don't know," he said humbly.

"I don't think father would like it," Dora told him, "if he knew you were here. Why, we're having an early breakfast on purpose to let him get out and work for Winter. I never saw him so excited over an election. To think of your coming to-day!"

He made a step toward her. "I came because it is to-day," he said. "Only for a minute, dear. It's a great day for me, you know— whether we win or lose. I wanted you to be in it. I wanted you to wish me good luck."

"But you know I always do," she objected.

"Yes, I know. But a fellow likes to hear it, Dora—on the day, you know. And I've seen so little of you lately."

She looked at him measuringly. "You're looking awfully thin," she exclaimed, with sudden compunction. "I wish you had never gone into this horrid campaign. I wish they had nominated somebody else."

Lorne smiled half bitterly. "I shouldn't wonder if a few other people wished the same thing," he said. "But I'm afraid they'll have to make the best of it now."

Dora had not sanctioned his visit by sitting down; and as he came nearer to her she drew a step away, moving by instinct from the capture of the lover. But he had made little of that, and almost as he spoke was at her side. She had to yield her hands to him.

"Well, you'll win it for them if anybody could," she assured him.

"Say 'win it for us,' dear."

She shook her head. "I'm not a Liberal—yet," she said, laughing.

"It's only a question of time."

"I'll never be converted to Grit politics."

"No, but you'll be converted to me," he told her, and drew her nearer. "I'm going now, Dora. I dare say I shouldn't have come. Every minute counts to-day. Good-bye."

She could not withhold her face from his asking lips, and he had bent to take his privilege when a step in the hall threatened and divided them.

"It's only Mr. Hesketh going upstairs," said Dora, with relief. "I thought it was father. Oh, Lorne—fly!"

"Hesketh!" Young Murchison's face clouded. "Is he working for Winter, too?"

"Lorne! What a thing to ask when you know he believes in your ideas. But he's a Conservative at home, you see, so he says he's in an awkward position, and he has been taking perfectly neutral ground lately. He hasn't a vote, any way."

"No," said Lorne. "He's of no consequence."

The familiar easy step in the house of his beloved, the house he was being entreated to leave with all speed, struck upon his heart and his nerves. She, with her dull surface to the more delicate vibrations of things, failed to perceive this, or perhaps she would have thought it worth while to find some word to bring back his peace. She disliked seeing people unhappy. When she was five years old and her kitten broke its leg, she had given it to a servant to drown.

He took his hat, making no further attempt to caress her, and opened the door. "I hope you *will* win, Lorne," she said, half resentfully, and he, with forced cheerfulness, replied, "Oh, we'll have a shot at it." Then with a little silent nod at her, which, notwithstanding her provocations, conveyed his love and trust, he went out into the struggle of the day.

In spite of Squire Ormiston's confident prediction, it was known that the fight would be hottest, among the townships, in Moneida Reservation. Elgin itself, of course, would lead the van for excitement, would be the real theatre for the arts of practical politics; but things would be pretty warm in Moneida, too. It was for that reason that Bingham and the rest strongly advised Lorne not to spend too much of the day in the town, but to get out to Moneida early, and drive around with Ormiston—stick to him like a fly to poison-paper.

"You leave Elgin to your friends," said Bingham. "Just show your face here and there wearing a smile of triumph, to encourage the crowd; but don't worry about the details—we'll attend to them."

"We can't have him upsettin' his own election by any interference with the boys," said Bingham to Horace Williams. "He's got too long a nose for all kinds of things to be comfortable in town to-day. He'll do a great deal less harm trotting round the Reserve braced up against old Ormiston."

So Elgin was left to the capable hands of the boys, for the furtherance of the Liberal interest and the sacred cause of imperialism. Mr. Farquharson, whose experience was longer and whose nose presumably shorter than the candidate's, never abandoned the Town Ward. Bingham skirmished between the polling-booths and the committee-room. Horace Williams was out all day— Rawlins edited the paper. The returns wouldn't be ready in time for anything but an extra anyhow, and the "Stand to Arms, South Fox," leader had been written two days ago. The rest was millinery, or might be for all anybody would read it. The other side had a better idea of the value of their candidate than to send him into the country. Walter Winter remained where he was most effective and most at home. He had a neat little livery outfit, and he seemed to spend the whole day in it accompanied by intimate personal friends who had never spoken to him, much less driven with him, before. Two or three strangers arrived the previous night at the leading hotels. Their business was various, but they had one point in common: they were very solicitous about their personal luggage. I should be sorry to assign their politics, and none of them seemed to know much about the merits of the candidates, so they are not perhaps very pertinent, except for the curiosity shown by the public at the spectacle of gentlemen carrying their own bags when there were porters to do it.

It was a day long remembered and long quoted. The weather was spring-like, sun after a week's thaw; it was pleasant to be abroad in the relaxed air and the drying streets, that here and there sent up threads of steam after the winter house-cleaning of their wooden sidewalks. Voting was a privilege never unappreciated in Elgin; and to-day the weather brought out every soul to the polls; the ladies of his family waiting, in many instances, on the verandah, with shawls over their heads, to hear the report of how the fight was going. Abby saw Dr. Harry back in his consulting-room, and Dr. Henry safely off to vote, and then took the two children and went over to her father's house because she simply could not endure the suspense anywhere else. The adventurous Stella picketed herself at a corner near the empty grocery which served as a polling-booth for Subdivision Eleven, one of the most doubtful, but was forced to retire at the sight of the first carryall full of men from the Milburn Boiler Company flaunting a banner inscribed "We are Solid for W.W." Met in the hall by her sister, she protested that she hadn't cried till she got inside the gate, anyhow. Abby lectured her soundly on her want of proper pride: she was much too big a girl to be "seen around" on a day when her brother was "running," if it were only for school trustee. The other ladies of the family, having acquired proper pride, kept in the back of the house so as not to be tempted to look out of the front windows. Mrs. Murchison assumed a stoical demeanour and made a pudding; though there was no reason to help Eliza, who was sufficiently lacking in proper pride to ask the milkman whether Mr. Lorne wasn't sure to be elected down there now. The milkman said he guessed the best man 'ud get in, but in a manner which roused general suspicion as to which he had himself favoured.

"We'll finish the month," said Mrs. Murchison, "and then not another quart do we take from *him*—a gentleman that's so uncertain when he's asked a simple question."

The butcher came, and brought a jovial report without being asked for it; said he was the first man to hand in a paper at his place, but they were piling up there in great shape for Mr. Murchison when he left.

"If he gets in, he gets in," said Mrs. Murchison. "And if he doesn't it won't be because of not deserving to. Those were real nice cutlets yesterday, Mr. Price, and you had better send us a sirloin for to-morrow, about six pounds; but it doesn't matter to an ounce. And you can save us sweetbreads for Sunday; I like yours better than Luff's."

John Murchison, Alec, and Oliver came shortly up to dinner, bringing stirring tales from the field. There was the personator[1] in Subdivision Six of a dead man—a dead Grit—wanted by the bloodhounds of the other side and tracked to the Reform committee-room, where he was ostensibly and publicly taking refuge.

"Why did he go there?" asked Stella, breathlessly.

"Why, to make it look like a put-up job of ours, of course," said her brother. "And it was a put-up job, a good old Tory fake. But they didn't calculate on Bingham and Bingham's memory. Bingham happened to be in the committee-room, and he recognized this fellow for a regular political tough from up Muskoka[2] way, where they get six for a bottle of Canadian and ten if it's Scotch.[3] 'Why, good morning,' says Bingham, 'thought you were in jail,' and just then he catches sight of a couple of trailers of Winter's from the window. Well, Bingham isn't just lightning smart, but then he isn't *slow*, you know. 'Well,' he says, 'you can't stop here,' and in another second he was throwing the fellow out. Threw him out pretty hard, too, I guess; right down the stairs, and Bingham on top. Met Winter's men at the door. 'The next time you want information from the headquarters of this association, gentlemen,' Bingham said, 'send somebody respectable.' Bingham thought the man was just any kind of low spy at first, but when they claimed him for personation, Bingham just laughed. 'Don't be so hard on your friends,' he said. I don't think we'll hear much more about that little racket."

"Can't anything be done to any of them?" asked Stella. "Not to-day, of course, but when there's time."

"We'll have to see about it, Stella," said Alec. "When there's time."

---

1 Someone who is pretending to be someone else, usually for the purposes of fraud—in this case, election fraud.
2 A rural county in central Ontario.
3 This is a reference to buying votes with whiskey.

"Talking about Bingham," Oliver told them; "you know Bingham's story about Jim Whelan keeping sober for two weeks, for the first time in twenty years, to vote for Winter? Wouldn't touch a thing—no, he was going to do it this time, if he died for it; it was disagreeable to refuse drinks, but it was going to be worth his while. Been boasting about the post-office janitorship Winter was to give him if he got in. Well, in he came to Number Eleven this morning all dressed up, with a clean collar, looking thirstier than any man you ever saw, and gets his paper. Young Charlie Bingham is deputy-returning officer at Number Eleven. In a second back comes Whelan. 'This ballot's marked,' he says; 'you don't fool me.' 'Is it?' says Charlie, taking it out of his hand. 'That's very wrong, Jim; you shouldn't have marked it,' and drops it into the ballot-box. Oh, Jim was wild! The paper had gone in blank, you see, and he'd lost all those good drunks and his vote too! He was going to have Charlie's blood right away. But there it was— done. He'd handed in his ballot—he couldn't have another."

They all laughed, I fear, at the unfortunate plight of the too suspicious Whelan. "Why did he think the ballot was marked?" asked Advena.

"Oh, there was a little smudge on it—a fly-spot or something, Charlie says. But you couldn't fool Whelan."

"I hope," said Stella meditatively, "that Lorne will get in by more than one. He wouldn't like to owe his election to a low-down trick like that."

"Don't you be at all alarmed, you little girlish thing," replied her brother. "Lorne will get in by five hundred."

John Murchison had listened to their excited talk, mostly in silence, going on with his dinner as if that and nothing else were the important matter of the moment. Mrs. Murchison had had this idiosyncrasy of his "to put up with" for over thirty years. She bore it now as long as she could.

"*Father!*" she exploded at last. "Do you think Lorne will get in by five hundred?"

Mr. Murchison shook his head, and bestowed his whole attention upon the paring of an apple. If he kept his hopes to himself, he also kept his doubts. "That remains to be seen," he said.

"Well, considering it's your own son, I think you might show a little more confidence," said Mrs. Murchison. "No thank you; no dessert for me. With a member of the family being elected—or not—for a seat in Parliament, I'm not the one to want dessert."

Between Mr. Murchison and the milkman that morning, Mrs. Murchison felt almost too much tried by the superior capacity for reticence.

It was seven in the evening before the ballot-boxes were all in the hands of the sheriff, and nine before that officer found it necessary to let the town know that it had piled up a majority of three hundred for Walter Winter. He was not a supporter of Walter Winter, and he preferred to wait until the returns began to come in from Clayfield and the townships, in the hope that they would make the serious difference that was required of them. The results were flashed one after the other to the total from the windows of the *Express* and the *Mercury* upon the cheering crowd that gathered in Market Square. There were moments of wild elation, moments of deep suspense upon both sides, but when the final addition and subtraction was made the enthusiastic voters of South Fox, including Jim Whelan, who had neglected no further opportunity, read, with yells and groans, hurrahs and catcalls, that they had elected Mr. Lorne Murchison to the Dominion House of Commons by a majority of seventy.

Then the band began to play and all the tin whistles to rejoice. Young and Windle had the grace to blow their sirens, and across the excited darkness of the town came the long familiar boom of the Murchison Stove Works. Every Liberal in Elgin who had any means of making a noise made it. From the window of the Association committee-room their young fellow-townsman thanked them for the honour they had done him, while his mother sat in the cab he had brought her down in and applauded vigorously between tears, and his father took congratulations from a hundred friendly hands. They all went home in a torchlight procession, the band always playing, the tin whistles always performing; and it was two in the morning before the occasion could in any sense be said to be over.

Lights burned quite as late, however, in the Conservative committee-room, where matters were being arranged to bark threateningly at the heels of victory next day. Victory looked like something that might be made to turn and parley. A majority of seventy was too small for finality. Her attention was called without twenty-four hours' delay to a paragraph in the Elgin *Mercury*, plainly authoritative, to the effect that the election of Mr. Murchison would be immediately challenged, on the ground of the infringement in the electoral district of Moneida of certain provisions of the Ontario Elections Act with the knowledge and consent of the candidate, whose claim to the contested seat, it was confidently expected, would be rendered within a very short time null and void.

THIRTY-ONE

"You can never trust an Indian," said Mrs. Murchison at the anxious family council. "Well do I remember them when you were a little thing, Advena, hanging round the town on a market-day; and the squaws coming to the back door with their tin pails of raspberries to sell, and just knowing English enough to ask a big price for them. But it was on the squaws we depended in those days, or go without raspberry preserves for the winter. Slovenly-looking things they were with their three or four coloured petticoats and their papooses on their backs. And for dirt—! But I thought they were all gone long ago."

"There are enough of them left to make trouble all right," said Alec. "They don't dress up like they used to, and I guess they send the papooses to kindergarten now; but you'll find plenty of them lying around any time there's nothing to do but vote and get drunk."

Allowing for the natural exaggeration of partisanship, the facts about the remaining red man of Moneida were much as Alec described them. On market-days he slid easily, unless you looked twice, into what the *Express* continues to call the farming community. Invariably, if you did look twice, you would note that his stiff felt hat was an inch taller in the crown than those worn generally by the farming community, the pathetic assertion, perhaps, of an old sovereignty; invariably, too, his coat and trousers betrayed a form within, which, in the effort at adaptation, had become high-shouldered and lank of leg. And the brown skin was there to be noticed, though you might pass it by, and the high cheek-bones and the liquidly muddy eye. He had taken on the signs of civilization at the level which he occupied; the farming community had lent him its look of shrewdness in small bargains and its rakish sophistication in garments, nor could you always assume with certainty, except at Fox County fairs and elections, that he was intoxicated. So much Government had done for him in Fox County, where the "Reservation," nursing the dying fragment of his race, testified that there is such a thing as political compunction. Out in the wide spaces of the West he still protects his savagery; they know an Indian there to-day as far as they can see him, without a second glance.

And in Moneida, upon polling-days, he still, as Alec said, "made trouble." Perhaps it would be more to the fact to say that he presented the elements of which trouble is made. Civilization had given him a vote,[1] not with his coat and trousers, but shortly after; and he had not yet learned to keep it anywhere but in his pocket, whence the transfer was easy, and could be made in different ways. The law contemplated only one, the straight drop into the ballot-box; but the "boys" had other views. The law represented one level of political sentiment, the boys represented another; both parties represented the law, both parties were represented by the boys; and on the occasion of the South Fox election the boys had been active in Moneida. There are, as we know, two kinds of activity on these occasions, one being set to observe the other; and Walter Winter's boys, while presumably neglecting no legitimate opportunity of their own, claimed to have been highly successful in detecting the methods of the other side.

The Indians owed their holdings, their allowances, their school, and their protecting superintendent, Squire Ormiston, to a Conservative Government. It made a grateful bond of which a later Conservative Government was not, perhaps, unaware, when it added the ballot to its previous benefits. The Indians, therefore, on election-days, were supposed to "go solid" for the candidate in whom they had been taught to see good-will. If they did not go quite solid, the other side might point to the evolution of the political idea in every dissentient—a gladdening spectacle, indeed, on which, however, the other side seldom showed any desire to dwell.

Hitherto the desires and intentions of the "Reserve" had been exemplified in its superintendent. Squire Ormiston had never led his wards to the polls—there were strong reasons against that. But the squire made no secret of his politics, either before or, unluckily, after he changed them. The Indians had always known that they were voting on the same side as "de boss." They were likely, the friends of Mr. Winter thought, to know now that they were voting on a different side. This was the secret of Mr. Winter's friends' unusual diligence on voting-day in Moneida. The mere

---

1   Members of First Nations who lived in "old Canada" (Ontario, Quebec, and the Atlantic Provinces) were granted the right to vote in the Dominion Franchise Act of 1885. This right was rescinded in 1898.

indication of a wish on the part of the superintendent would constitute undue influence in the eye of the law. The squire was not the most discreet of men—often before it had been the joke of Conservative councils how near the old man had come to making a case for the Grits in connection with this chief or that. I will not say that he was acquainted with the famous letter from Queen Victoria, affectionately bidding her Indian children to vote for the Conservative candidate. But perhaps he had not adhered to the strictest interpretation of the law which gave him fatherly influence in everything pertaining to his red-skinned charges' interests, temporal and spiritual, excepting only their sacred privilege of the ballot. He may even have held it in some genial derision, their sacred privilege; it would be natural, he had been there among them in unquestioned authority so long. Now it had assumed an importance. The squire looked at it with the ardour of a converted eye. When he told Mr. Farquharson that he could bring Moneida with him to a Liberal victory, he thought and spoke of the farmers of the township, not of his wards of the Reserve. Yet as the day approached these would infallibly become voters in his eyes, to swell or to diminish the sum of Moneida's loyalty to the Empire. They remembered all this in the committee-room of his old party. "The squire," they said to one another, "will give himself away this time if ever he did." Then young Murchison hadn't known any better than to spend the best part of the day out there, and there were a dozen witnesses to swear that old Ormiston introduced him to three or four of the chiefs. That was basis enough for the boys detailed to watch Moneida, basis enough in the end for a petition constructed to travel to the High Court at Toronto for the purpose of rendering null and void the election of Mr. Lorne Murchison, and transferring the South Fox seat to the candidate of the opposite party.

That possibility had been promptly frustrated by a cross petition. There was enough evidence in Subdivision Eleven, according to Bingham, to void the Tory returns on six different counts; but the house-cat sold by Peter Finnigan to Mr. Winter for five dollars[1] would answer all practical purposes. It was a first-rate mouser, Bingham said, and it would settle Winter. They would have plenty of other charges "good and ready" if Finnigan's cat

---

1 Five dollars was much too much to pay for a cat, even if it was a good mouser. Mr. Winter was paying for Peter Finnegan's vote.

should fail them, but Bingham didn't think the court would get to anything else; he had great confidence in the cat.

The petitions had been lodged with promptness. "Evidence," as Mr. Winter remarked, "is like a good many other things—better when it's hot, especially the kind you get on the Reserve." To which, when he heard it, Bingham observed sarcastically that the cat would keep. The necessary thousand dollars were ready on each side the day after the election, lodged in court the next. Counsel were as promptly engaged—the Liberals selected Cruickshank—and the suit against the elected candidate, beginning with charges against his agents in the town, was shortly in full hearing before the judges sent from Toronto to try it. Meanwhile the Elgin *Mercury* had shown enterprise in getting hold of Moneida evidence, and foolhardiness, as the *Express* pointed out, in publishing it before the matter was reached in court. There was no foolhardiness in printing what the *Express* knew about Finnigan's cat; it was just a common cat, and Walter Winter paid five dollars for it, Finnigan declaring that if Mr. Winter hadn't filled him up with bad whisky before the bargain, he wouldn't have let her go under ten, he was that fond of the creature. The *Express* pointed out that this was grasping of Finnigan, as the cat had never left him, and Mr. Winter showed no intention of taking her away; but there was nothing *sub judice* about the cat. Finnigan, before he sobered up, had let her completely out of the bag. It was otherwise with the charges that were to be made, according to the *Mercury*, on the evidence of Chief Joseph Fry and another member of his tribe, to the effect that he and his Conservative friends had been instructed by Squire Ormiston and Mr. Murchison to vote on this occasion for both the candidates, thereby producing, when the box was opened, eleven ballot-papers inscribed with two crosses instead of one, and valueless. Here, should the charges against a distinguished and highly respected Government official fail, as in the opinion of the *Express* they undoubtedly would fail, of substantiation, was a big libel case all dressed and ready and looking for the *Mercury* office. "Foolish—foolish," wrote Mr. Williams at the close of his editorial comments. "Very ill-advised."

"They've made no case so far," Mr. Murchison assured the family. "I saw Williams on my way up, and he says the evidence of that corner grocery fellow—what's his name?—went all to pieces this morning. Oliver was in court. He says one of the judges—Hooke—lost his patience altogether."

"They won't do anything with the town charges," Alec said, "and they know it. They're saving themselves for Moneida and old man Ormiston."

"Well, I heartily wish," said Mrs. Murchison, in a tone of grievance with the world at large, and if you were not responsible you might keep out of the way—"I heartily wish that Lorne had stayed at home that day and not got mixed up with old man Ormiston."

"They'll find it pretty hard to fix anything on Lorne," said Alec. "But I guess the squire did go off his head a little."

"Have they anything more than Indian evidence?" asked Advena.

"We don't know what they've got," said her brother darkly, "and we won't till Wednesday, when they expect to get round to it."

"Indian evidence will be a poor dependence[1] in Cruickshank's hands," Mr. Murchison told them, with a chuckle. "They say this Chief Joseph Fry is going about complaining that he always got three dollars for one vote before, and this time he expected six for two, and got nothing!"

"Chief Joseph Fry!" exclaimed Alec. "They make me tired with their Chief Josephs and Chief Henrys! White Clam Shell— that was the name he got when he wasn't christened."

"That's the name," remarked Advena, "that he probably votes under."

"Well," said Mrs. Murchison, "it was very kind of Squire Ormiston to give Lorne his support, but it seems to me that as far as Moneida is concerned he would have done better alone."

"No, I guess he wouldn't, mother," said Alec. "Moneida came right round with the squire, outside the Reserve. If it hadn't been for the majority there we would have lost the election. The old man worked hard, and Lorne is grateful to him, and so he ought to be."

"If they carry the case against Lorne," said Stella, "he'll be disqualified for seven years."

"Only if they prove him personally mixed up in it," said the father. "And that," he added, with a concentration of family sentiment in the emphasis of it, "they'll not do."

---

1 A poor thing to depend upon, not reliable.

THIRTY-TWO

It was late afternoon when the train from the West deposited Hugh Finlay upon the Elgin platform, the close of one of those wide, wet, uncertain February days when the call of spring is on the wind though spring is weeks away. The lights of the town flashed and glimmered down the streets under the bare swaying maple branches. The early evening was full of soft bluster; the air was conscious with an appeal of nature, vague yet poignant. The young man caught at the strange sympathy that seemed to be abroad for his spirit. He walked to his house, courting it, troubled by it. They were expecting him that evening at Dr. Drummond's, and there it was his intention to go. But on his way he would call for a moment to see Advena Murchison. He had something to tell her. It would be news of interest at Dr. Drummond's also; but it was of no consequence, within an hour or so, when they should receive it there, while it was of great consequence that Advena should hear it at the earliest opportunity, and from him. There is no weighing or analysing the burden of such a necessity as this. It simply is important: it makes its own weight; and those whom it concerns must put aside other matters until it has been accomplished. He would tell her: they would accept it for a moment together, a moment during which he would also ascertain whether she was well and strong, with a good chance of happiness —God protect her—in the future that he should not know. Then he would go on to Dr. Drummond's.

The wind had risen when he went out again; it blew a longer blast, and the trees made a steady sonorous rhythm in it. The sky was full of clouds that dashed upon the track of a failing moon; there was portent everywhere, and a hint of tumult at the end of the street. No two ways led from Finlay's house to his first destination. River Street made an angle with that on which the Murchisons lived—half a mile to the corner, and three-quarters the other way. Drops drove in his face as he strode along against the wind, stilling his unquiet heart, that leaped before him to that brief interview. As he took the single turning he came into the full blast of the veering, irresolute storm. The street was solitary and full of the sound of the blown trees, wild and uplifting. Far down the figure of a woman wavered before the wind across the zone of a blurred lamp-post. She was coming toward him. He bent his head and lowered his umbrella and lost sight of her as they approached, she with the storm behind her, driven with hardly more resistance than the last year's blackened leaves that blew with her, he assailed by it and making the best way he could. Certainly the wind was taking her part and his, when in another moment her skirt whipped against him and he saw her face glimmer out. A mere wreck of lines and shadows it seemed in the livid light, with suddenly perceiving eyes and lips that cried his name. She had on a hat and a cloak, but carried no umbrella, and her hands were bare and wet. Pitifully the storm blew her into his arms, a tossed and straying thing that could not speak for sobs; pitifully and with a rough incoherent sound he gathered and held her in that refuge. A rising fear and a great solicitude laid a finger upon his craving embrace of her; he had a sense of something strangely different in her, of the unknown irremediable. Yet she was there, in his arms, as she had never been before; her plight but made her in a manner sweeter; the storm that brought her barricaded them in the empty spaces of the street with a divinely entreating solitude. He had been prepared to meet her in the lighted decorum of her father's house and he knew what he should say. He was not prepared to take her out of the tempest, helpless and weeping and lost for the harbour of his heart, and nothing could he say. He locked his lips against all that came murmuring to them. But his arms tightened about her and he drew her into the shelter of a wall that jutted out in the irregular street; and there they stood and clung together in a long, close, broken silence that covered the downfall of her spirit. It was the moment of their great experience of one another; never again, in whatever crisis, could either know so deep, so wonderful a fathoming of the other soul. Once as it passed, Advena put up her hand and touched his cheek. There were tears on it, and she trembled, and wound her arm about his neck, and held up her face to his. "No," he muttered, and crushed it against his breast. There without complaint she let it lie; she was all submission to him: his blood leaped and his spirit groaned with the knowledge of it.

"Why did you come out? Why did you come, dear?" he said at last.

"I don't know. There was such a wind. I could not stay in the house."

She spoke timidly, in a voice that should have been new to him, but that it was, above all, her voice.

"I was on my way to you."

"I know. I thought you might perhaps come. If you had not— I think I was on my way to you.

It seemed not unnatural.

"Did you find—any message from me when you came?" she asked presently, in a quieted, almost a contented tone.

It shot—the message—before his eyes, though he had seen it no message in the preoccupation of his arrival.

"I found a rose on my dressing-table," he told her; and the rose stood for him in a wonder of tenderness, looking back.

"I smuggled it in," she confessed, "I knew your old servant— she used to be with us. The others—from Dr. Drummond's— have been there all day making it warm and comfortable for you. I had no right to do anything like that, but I had the right, hadn't I, to bring the rose?"

"I don't know," he answered her, hard pressed, "how we are to bear this."

She shrank away from him a little, as if at a glimpse of a surgeon's knife.

"We are not to bear it," she said eagerly. "The rose is to tell you that. I didn't mean it, when I left it, to be anything more—more than a rose; but now I do. I didn't even know when I came out tonight. But now I do. We aren't to bear it, Hugh. I don't want it so—now. I can't—can't have it so."

She came nearer to him again and caught with her two hands the lapels of his coat. He closed his own over them and looked down at her in that half detachment, which still claimed and held her.

"Advena," he whispered, out of the sudden clamour in his mind, "she can't be—she isn't—nothing has happened to her?"

She smiled faintly, but her eyes were again full of fear at his implication of the only way.

"Oh, no!" she said. "But you have been away, and she has come. I have seen her; and oh! she won't care, Hugh—she won't care."

Her asking, straining face seemed to gather and reflect all the light there was in the shifting night about them. The rain had stopped, but the wind still hurtled past, whirling the leaves from one darkness to another. They were as isolated, as outlawed there in the wild wet wind as they were in the confusion of their own souls.

"We must care," he said helplessly, clinging to the sound and form of the words.

"Oh, no!" she cried. "No, no! Indeed I know now what is possible and what is not!"

For an instant her eyes searched the rigid lines of his face in astonishment. In their struggle to establish the impossible she had been so far ahead, so greatly the more confident and daring, had tempted him to such heights, scorning every dizzy verge, that now, when she turned quite back from their adventure, humbly confessing it too hard, she could not understand how he should continue to set himself doggedly toward it. Perhaps, too, she trusted unconsciously in her prerogative. He loved her, and she him: before she would not, now she would. Before she had preferred an ideal to the desire of her heart; now it lay about her; her strenuous heart had pulled it down to foolish ruin, and how should she lie abased with it and see him still erect and full of the deed they had to do?

"Come," he said, "let me take you home, dear," and at that and some accent in it that struck again at hope, she sank at his feet in a torrent of weeping, clasping them and entreating him, "Oh send her away! Send her away!"

He lifted her, and was obliged literally to support her. Her hat had fallen off; he stroked her hair and murmured such comfort to her as we have for children in their extremity, of which the burden is chiefly love and "Don't cry." She grew gradually quieter, drawing one knows not what restitution from the intrinsic in him; but there was no pride in her, and when she said "Let me go home now," it was the broken word of hapless defeat. They struggled together out into the boisterous street, and once or twice she failed and had to stop and turn. Then she would cling to a wall or a tree, putting his help aside with a gesture in which there was again some pitiful trace of renunciation. They went almost without a word, each treading upon the heart of the other toward the gulf that was to come. They reached it at the Murchisons' gate, and there they paused, as briefly as possible, since pause was torture, and he told her what he could not tell her before.

"I have accepted the charge of the White Water Mission Station in Alberta," he said. "I, too, learned very soon after I left you what was possible and what was not. I go as soon as—things can be set in order here. Good-bye, my dear love, and may God help us both."

She looked at him with a pitiful effort at a steady lip. "I must try to believe it," she said. "And afterward, when it comes true for you, remember this—I was ashamed."

Then he saw her pass into her father's house, and he took the road to his duty and Dr. Drummond's.

His extremity was very great. Through it lines came to him from the beautiful archaic inheritance of his Church. He strode along hearing them again and again in the dying storm.

So, I do stretch my hands
To Thee my help alone;
Thou only understands
All my complaint and moan.[1]

He listened to the prayer on the wind, which seemed to offer it for him, listened and was gravely touched. But he himself was far from the throes of supplication. He was looking for the forces of his soul; and by the time he reached Dr. Drummond's door we may suppose that he had found them.

Sarah, who let him in, cried, "How wet you are, Mr. Finlay!" and took his overcoat to dry in the kitchen. The Scotch ladies, she told him, and Mrs. Forsyth, had gone out to tea, but they would be back right away, and meanwhile "the Doctor" was expecting him in the study—he knew the way.

Finlay did know the way, but, as a matter of fact, there had been time for him to forget it; he had not crossed Dr. Drummond's threshold since the night on which the Doctor had done all, as he would have said, that was humanly possible to bring him, Finlay, to reason upon the matter of his incredible entanglement in Bross. The door at the end of the passage was ajar, however, as if impatient; and Dr. Drummond himself, standing in it, heightened that appearance, with his "Come you in, Finlay. Come you in!"

The Doctor looked at the young man in a manner even more acute, more shrewd, and more kindly than was his wont. His eye searched Finlay thoroughly, and his smile seemed to broaden as his glance travelled.

"Man," he said, "you're shivering," and rolled him an armchair near the fire. ("The fellow came into the room," he would say, when he told the story afterward to the person most concerned, "as if he were going to the stake!") "This is extraordinary weather we are having, but I think the storm is passing over."

---

1 Psalm 143 of the Scottish Metrical Psalter of 1650: "Lo, I do stretch my hands / To thee, my help alone; / For thou well understands / All my complaint and moan."

"I hope," said Finlay, "that my aunt and Miss Cameron are well. I understand they are out."

"Oh, very well—finely. They're out at present, but you'll see them bye-and-bye. An excellent voyage over they had—just the eight days. But we'll be doing it in less than that when the new fast line is running to Halifax. But four days of actual ocean travelling they say now it will take. Four days from imperial shore to shore! That should incorporate us—that should bring them out and take us home."

The Doctor had not taken a seat himself, but was pacing the study, his thumbs in his waistcoat pockets; and a touch of embarrassment seemed added to the inveterate habit.

"I hear the ladies had pleasant weather," Finlay remarked.

"Capital—capital! You won't smoke? I know nothing about these cigars; they're some Grant left behind him—a chimney, that man Grant. Well, Finlay"—he threw himself into the armchair on the other side of the hearth—"I don't know what to say to you."

"Surely," said Finlay restively, "it has all been said, sir."

"No, it has not all been said," Dr. Drummond retorted. "No, it has not. There's more to be said, and you must hear it, Finlay, with such patience as you have. But I speak the truth when I say that I don't know how to begin."

The young man gave him opportunity, gazing silently into the fire. He was hardly aware that Dr. Drummond had again left his seat when he started violently at a clap on the shoulder.

"Finlay!" exclaimed the Doctor. "You won't be offended? No—you couldn't be offended!"

It was half jocular, half anxious, wholly inexplicable.

"At what," asked Hugh Finlay, "should I be offended?"

Again, with a deep sigh, the Doctor dropped into his chair. "I see I must begin at the beginning," he said. But Finlay, with sudden intuition, had risen and stood before him trembling, with a hand against the mantelpiece.

"No," he said, "if you have anything to tell me of importance, for God's sake begin at the end."

Some vibration in his voice went straight to the heart of the Doctor, banishing as it travelled, every irrelevant thing that it encountered.

"Then the end is this, Finlay," he said. "The young woman, Miss Christie Cameron, whom you were so wilfully bound and determined to marry, has thrown you over—that is, if you will give her back her word—has jilted you—that is, if you'll let her away. Has thought entirely better of the matter."

("He stared out of his great sockets of eyes as if the sky had fallen," Dr. Drummond would say, recounting it.)

"For—for what reason?" asked Finlay, hardly yet able to distinguish between the sound of disaster and the sense that lay beneath.

"May I begin at the beginning?" asked the Doctor, and Hugh silently nodded.

("He sat there and never took his eyes off me, twisting his fingers. I might have been in a confession-box," Dr. Drummond would explain to her.)

"She came here, Miss Cameron, with that good woman, Mrs. Kilbannon, it will be three weeks next Monday," he said, with all the air of beginning a story that would be well worth hearing. "And I wasn't very well pleased to see her, for reasons that you know. However, that's neither here nor there. I met them both at the station, and I own to you that I thought when I made Miss Cameron's acquaintance that you were getting better than you deserved in the circumstances. You were a thousand miles away—now that was a fortunate thing!—and she and Mrs. Kilbannon just stayed here and made themselves as comfortable as they could. And that was so comfortable that any one could see with half an eye"—the Doctor's own eye twinkled—"so far as Miss Cameron was concerned, that she wasn't pining in any sense of the word. But I wasn't sorry for you, Finlay, on that account." He stopped to laugh enjoyingly, and Finlay blushed like a girl.

"I just let matters bide and went about my own business. Though after poor Mrs. Forsyth here—a good woman enough, but the brains of a rabbit—it was pleasant to find these intelligent ladies at every meal, and wonderful how quick they were at picking up the differences between points of Church administration here and at home. That was a thing I noticed particularly in Miss Cameron.

"Matters went smoothly enough—smoothly enough—till one afternoon that foolish creature Advena Murchison"—Finlay started—"came here to pay a call on Miss Cameron and Mrs. Kilbannon. It was well and kindly meant, but it was not a wise-like thing to do. I didn't exactly make it out, but it seems that she came all because of you and on account of you; and the ladies didn't understand it, and Mrs. Kilbannon came to me. My word, but there was a woman to deal with! Who was this young lady, and what was she to you that she should go anywhere or do anything in your name? Without doubt"—he put up a staying hand—"it was foolish of Advena. And what sort of freedom, and how far, and why, and what way, and I tell you it was no easy matter, to quiet her. 'Is Miss Cameron distressed about it?' said I. 'Not a bit,' said she, 'but I am, and I must have the rights of this matter,' said she, 'if I have to put it to my nephew himself.'

"It was at that point, Finlay, that the idea—just then that the thought came into my mind—well I won't say absolutely, but practically for the first time—'Why can't this matter be arranged on a basis to suit all parties?' So I said to her, 'Mrs. Kilbannon,' I said, 'if you had reasonable grounds for it, do you think you could persuade your niece not to marry Hugh Finlay?' Wait—patience!" He held up his hand, and Finlay gripped the arm of his chair again.

"She just stared at me. 'Are you gone clean daft, Dr. Drummond?' she said. 'There could be no grounds serious enough for that. I will not believe that Hugh Finlay has compromised himself in any way.' I had to stop her; I was obliged to tell her there was nothing of the kind—nothing of the kind; and later on I'll have to settle with my conscience about that. 'I meant,' I said, 'the reasonable grounds of an alternative.' 'An alternative?' said she. To cut a long story short," continued the Doctor, leaning forward, always with the finger in his waistcoat pocket to emphasize what he said, "I represented to Mrs. Kilbannon that Miss Cameron was not in sentimental relations toward you, that she had some reason to suspect you of having placed your affections elsewhere, and that I myself was very much taken up with what I had seen of Miss Cameron. In brief, I said to Mrs. Kilbannon that if Miss Cameron saw no objection to altering the arrangements to admit of it, I should be pleased to marry her myself. The thing was much more suitable in every way. I was fifty-three years of age last week, I told her, 'but,' I said, 'Miss Cameron is thirty-six or seven, if she's a day, and Finlay there would be like nothing but a grown-up son to her. I can offer her a good home and the minister's pew in a church that any woman might be proud of—and though far be it from me,' I said, 'to depreciate mission work, either home or foreign, Miss Cameron in that field would be little less than thrown away. Think it over,' I said.

"Well, she was pleased, I could see that. But she didn't half like the idea of changing the original notion. It was leaving you to your own devices that weighed most with her against it; she'd set her heart on seeing you married with her approval. So I said to her, to make an end of it, 'Well, Mrs. Kilbannon," I said, 'suppose we say no more about it for the present. I think I see the finger of Providence in this matter; but you'll talk it over with Miss Cameron, and we'll all just make it, for the next few days, the subject of quiet and sober reflection. Maybe at the end of that time I'll think better of it myself, though that is not my expectation.'

"'I think,' she said, 'we'll just leave it to Christie.'"

As the Doctor went on with his tale, relaxation had stolen dumbly about Finlay's brow and lips. He dropped from the plane of his own absorption to the humorous common sense of the recital: it claimed and held him with infinite solace. His eyes had something like the light of laughter in them, flashing behind a cloud, as he fixed them on Dr. Drummond, and said, "And did you?"

"We did," said Dr. Drummond, getting up once more from his chair, and playing complacently with his watch-charms as he took another turn about the study. "We left it to Miss Cameron, and the result is"—the Doctor stopped sharply and wheeled round upon Finlay—"the result is—why, the upshot seems to be that I've cut you out, man!"

Finlay measured the little Doctor standing there twisting his watch-chain, beaming with achieved satisfaction, in a consuming desire to know how far chance had been kind to him, and how far he had to be simply, unspeakably grateful. He stared in silence, occupied with his great debt; it was like him that that, and not his liberty, should be first in his mind. We who have not his opportunity may find it more difficult to decide; but from our private knowledge of Dr. Drummond we may remember what poor Finlay probably forgot at the moment, that even when pitted against Providence, the Doctor was a man of great determination.

The young fellow got up, still speechless, and confronted Dr. Drummond. He was troubled for something to say; the chambers of his brain seemed empty or reiterating foolish sounds. He pressed the hand the minister offered him and his lips quivered. Then a light came into his face, and he picked up his hat.

"And I'll say this for myself," chuckled Dr. Drummond. "It was no hard matter."

Finlay looked at him and smiled. "It would not be, sir," he said lamely. Dr. Drummond cast a shrewd glance at him and dropped the tone of banter.

"Aye—I know! It's no joking matter," he said, and with a hand behind the young man's elbow, he half pushed him to the door and took out his watch. He must always be starting somebody, something, in the right direction, the Doctor. "It's not much after half-past nine, Finlay," he said. "I notice the stars are out."

It had the feeling of a colloquial benediction, and Finlay carried it with him all the way.

It was nevertheless nearly ten when he reached her father's house, so late that the family had dispersed for the night. Yet he had the hardihood to ring, and the hour blessed them both, for Advena on the stair, catching who knows what of presage out of the sound, turned, and found him at the threshold herself.

THIRTY-THREE

"I understand how you must feel in the matter, Murchison," said Henry Cruickshank. "It's the most natural thing in the world that you should want to clear yourself definitely, especially, as you say, since the charges have been given such wide publicity. On the other hand, I think it quite possible that you exaggerate the inference that will be drawn from our consenting to saw off[1] with the other side on the two principal counts."

"The inference will be," said Lorne, "that there's not a pin to choose between Winter's political honesty and my own. I'm no Pharisee,[2] but I don't think I can sit down under that. I can't impair my possible usefulness by accepting a slur upon my reputation at the very beginning."

"Politics are very impersonal. It wouldn't be remembered a year."

"Winter, of course," said young Murchison moodily, "doesn't want to take any chances. He knows he's done for if we go on. Seven years for him would put him pretty well out of politics. And it would suit him down to the ground to fight it over again. There's nothing he would like better to see than another writ for South Fox."

---

1 A "saw-off" is a mutual agreement to withdraw equal numbers of contested election petitions in order to avoid going to court.
2 A self-righteous person, taken from the name of an ancient sect in the Bible that strictly observed religious rites and claimed to be holier than other believers.

"That's all right," the lawyer responded, "but Moneida doesn't look altogether pleasant, you know. We may have good grounds for supposing that the court will find you clear of that business; but Ormiston, so far as I can make out, was playing the fool down there for a week before polling-day, and there are three or four Yellow Dogs and Red Feathers only too anxious to pay back a grudge on him. We'll have to fight again, there's no doubt about that. The only question is whether we'll ruin Ormiston first or not. Have you seen Bingham?"

"I know what Bingham thinks," said Lorne, impatiently. "The squire's position is a different consideration. I don't see how I can—However, I'll go across to the committee-room now and talk it over."

It is doubtful whether young Murchison knew all that Bingham thought; Bingham so seldom told it all. There were matters in the back of Bingham's mind that prompted him to urge the course that Cruickshank had been empowered by the opposing counsel to suggest—party considerations that it would serve no useful purpose to talk over with Murchison. Bingham put it darkly when he said he had quite as much hay on his fork as he cared to tackle already, implying that the defence of indiscretions in Moneida was quite an unnecessary addition. Contingencies seemed probable, arising out of the Moneida charges, that might affect the central organization of the party in South Fox to an extent wholly out of proportion with the mere necessity of a second election. Bingham talked it over with Horace Williams, and both of them with Farquharson; they were all there to urge the desirability of "sawing off" upon Lorne when he found them at headquarters. Their most potent argument was, of course, the squire and the immediate dismissal that awaited him under the law if undue influence were proved against him. Other considerations found the newly elected member for South Fox obstinate and troublesome, but to that he was bound to listen, and before that he finally withdrew his objections. The election would come on again, as happened commonly enough. Bingham could point to the opening, in a few days, of a big flour milling industry across the river, which would help; operations on the Drill Hall and the Post Office would be hurried on at once, and the local party organization would be thoroughly overhauled. Bingham had good reason for believing that they could entirely regain their lost ground, and at the same time dissipate the dangerous impression that South

Fox was being undermined. Their candidate gave a reluctant ear to it all, and in the end agreed to everything.

So that Chief Joseph Fry—the White Clam Shell of his own lost fires—was never allowed the chance of making good the election losses of that year, as he had confidently expected to do when the charge came on; nor was it given to any of the Yellow Dogs and Red Feathers of Mr. Cruickshank's citation to boast at the tribal dog-feasts[1] of the future, of the occasion on which they had bested "de boss." Neither was any further part in public affairs, except by way of jocular reference, assigned to Finnigan's cat. The proceedings of the court abruptly terminated, the judges reported the desirability of a second contest, and the public accepted with a wink. The wink in any form was hateful to Lorne Murchison, but he had not to encounter it long.

The young man had changed in none of the aspects he presented to his fellow citizens since the beginning of the campaign. In the public eye he wore the same virtues as he wore the same clothes; he summed up even a greater measure of success; his popularity was unimpaired. He went as keenly about the business of life, handling its details with the same capable old drawl. Only his mother, with the divination of mothers, declared that since the night of the opera-house meeting Lorne had been "all worked up." She watched him with furtive anxious looks, was solicitous about his food, expressed relief when she knew him to be safely in bed and asleep. He himself observed himself with discontent, unable to fathom his extraordinary lapse from self-control on the night of his final address. He charged it to the strain of unavoidable office work on top of the business of the campaign, abused his nerves, talked of a few days' rest when they had settled Winter. He could think of nothing but the points he had forgotten when he had his great chance. "The flag should have come in at the end," he would say to himself, trying vainly to remember where it did come in. He was ill pleased with the issue of that occasion; and it was small compensation to be told by Stella that his speech gave her shivers up and down her back.

Meanwhile the theory of Empire coursed in his blood, fed by the revelation of the future of his country in every newspaper, by the calculated prophecies of American onlookers, and by the

---

1   The white dog feast was a traditional New Year celebration at the Six Nations Reserve in Brantford.

telegrams which repeated the trumpet notes of Wallingham's war upon the mandarinate[1] of Great Britain. It occupied him so that he began to measure and limit what he had to say about it, and to probe the casual eye for sympathy before he would give an inch of rope to his enthusiasm. He found it as hard as ever to understand that the public interest should be otherwise preoccupied, as it plainly was, that the party organ, terrified of Quebec, should shuffle away from the subject with perfunctory and non-committal reference, that among the men he met in the street, nobody's blood seemed stirred, whatever the day's news was from England. He subscribed to the *Toronto Post*, the leading organ of the Tories, because of its fuller reports and more sympathetic treatment of the Idea, due to the fact that the Idea originated in a brain temporarily affiliated to the Conservative party. If the departure to imperial preference had any damage in it for Canadian interests, it would be for those which the *Post* made its special care; but the spirit of party draws the breath of expediency, and the *Post* flaunting the Union Jack every other day, put secondary manufactures aside for future discussion, and tickled the wheat-growers with the two-shilling advantage they were coming into at the hands of the English Conservatives, until Liberal leaders began to be a little anxious about a possible loss of wheat-growing votes. It was, as John Murchison said, a queer position for everybody concerned; queer enough, no doubt, to admit a Tory journal into the house on sufferance and as a special matter; but he had a disapproving look for it as it lay on the hall floor, and seldom was the first to open it.

Nevertheless Lorne found more satisfaction in talking imperialism with his father than with any one else. While the practical half of John Murchison was characteristically alive to the difficulties involved, the sentimental half of him was ready at any time to give out cautious sparks of sympathy with the splendour of Wallingham's scheme; and he liked the feeling that a son of his should hark back in his allegiance to the old land. There was a kind of chivalry in the placing of certain forms of beauty—political honour and public devotion, which blossomed best, it seemed, over there—above the material ease and margin of the new country, and even above the grand chance it offered for a man to make his mark. Mr. Murchison was susceptible to this in any one, and responsive to it in his son.

---

1 The upper echelons of the civil service.

As to the local party leaders, they had little more than a shrug for the subject. So far as they were concerned, there was no Empire and no Idea; Wallingham might as well not have been born. It seemed to Lorne that they maintained toward him personally a special reticence about it. Reticence indeed characterized their behaviour generally during the period between the abandonment of the suits and the arrangement of the second Liberal convention. They had little advice for him about his political attitude, little advice about anything. He noticed that his presence on one or two occasions seemed to embarrass them, and that his arrival would sometimes have a disintegrating effect upon a group in the post-office or at a street corner. He added it, without thinking, to his general heaviness; they held it a good deal against him, he supposed, to have reduced their proud standing majority to a beggarly two figures; he didn't blame them.

I cannot think that the sum of these depressions alone would have been enough to overshadow so buoyant a soul as Lorne Murchison's. The characteristics of him I have tried to convey were grafted on an excellent fund of common sense. He was well aware of the proportions of things; he had no despair of the Idea, nor would he despair should the Idea etherealize and fly away. Neither had he, for his personal honour, any morbid desires toward White Clam Shell or Finnigan's cat. His luck had been a good deal better than it might have been; he recognized that as fully as any sensible young man could, and as for the Great Chance, and the queer grip it had on him, he would have argued that too if any one had approached him curiously about it. There I think we might doubt his conclusions. There is nothing subtler, more elusive to trace than the intercurrents of the emotions. Politics and love are thought of at opposite poles, and Wallingham perhaps would have laughed to know that he owed an exalted allegiance in part to a half-broken heart. Yet the impulse that is beyond our calculation, the thing we know potential in the blood but not to be summoned or conditioned, lies always in the shadow of the ideal; and who can analyze that, and say, "Of this class is the will to believe in the integrity of the beloved and false; of that is the desire to lift a nation to the level of its mountain-ranges"? Both dispositions have a tendency to overwork the heart; and it is easy to imagine that they might interact. Lorne Murchison's wish, which was indeed a burning longing and necessity, to believe in the Dora Milburn of his passion, had been under a strain since the night on which he brought her the pledge which she refused to wear. He had hardly been conscious of it in the beginning, but by constant suggestion it had grown into his knowledge, and for weeks he had taken poignant account of it. His election had brought him no nearer a settlement with her objection to letting the world know of their relations. The immediate announcement that it was to be disputed gave Dora another chance, and once again postponed the assurance that he longed for with a fever which was his own condemnation of her, if he could have read that sign. For months he had seen so little of her, had so altered his constant habit of going to the Milburns', that his family talked of it, wondering among themselves; and Stella indulged in hopeful speculations. They did not wonder or speculate at the Milburns'. It was an axiom there that it is well to do nothing rashly.

Lorne, in the office on Market Street, had been replying to Mr. Fulke to the effect that the convention could hardly be much longer postponed, but that as yet he had no word of the date of it, when the telephone bell rang and Mr. Farquharson's voice at the other end asked him to come over to the committee-room. "They've decided about it now, I imagine," he told his senior, putting on his hat; and something of the wonted fighting elation came upon him as he went down the stairs. He was right in his supposition. They had decided about it, and they were waiting, in a group that made every effort to look casual, to tell him when he arrived.

They had delegated what Horace Williams called "the job" to Mr. Farquharson, and he was actually struggling with the preliminaries of it, when Bingham, uncomfortable under the curious quietude of the young fellow's attention, burst out with the whole thing.

"The fact is, Murchison, you can't poll the vote. There's no man in the Riding we'd be better pleased to send to the House; but we've got to win this election, and we can't win it with you."

"You think you can't?" said Lorne.

"You see, old man," Horace Williams put in, "you didn't get rid of that save-the-Empire-or-die scheme of yours soon enough. People got to think you meant something by it."

"I shall never get rid of it," Lorne returned simply, and the others looked at one another.

"The popular idea seems to be," said Mr. Farquharson judicially, "that you would not hesitate to put Canada to some material loss, or at least to postpone her development in various important directions, for the sake of the imperial connection."

"Wasn't that," Lorne asked him, "what, six months ago, you were all prepared to do?"

"Oh, no," said Bingham, with the air of repudiating for everybody concerned. "Not for a cent. We were willing at one time to work it for what it was worth, but it never was worth that, and if you'd had a little more experience, Murchison, you'd have realized it."

"That's right, Lorne," contributed Horace Williams. "Experience—that's all you want. You've got everything else, and a darned sight more. We'll get you there, all in good time. But this time—"

"You want me to step down and out," said Lorne.

"That's for you to say," Bingham told him. "We can nominate you again all right, but we're afraid we can't get you the convention. Young and Windle have been working like moles for the past ten days—"

"For Carter?" interrupted Lorne. "Carter, of course."

They nodded. Carter stood the admitted fact.

"I'm sorry it's Carter," said Lorne thoughtfully. "However—" And he dropped, staring before him, into silence. The others eyed him from serious, underhung faces. Horace Williams, with an obvious effort, got up and clapped him on the shoulder.

"Brace up, old chap," he said. "You made a blame good fight for us, and we'll do the same for you another day."

"However, gentlemen," the young man gathered himself up to say, "I believe I understand the situation. You are my friends and this is your advice. We must save the seat. I'll see Carter. If I can get anything out of him to make me think he'll go straight on the scheme to save the Empire"—he smiled faintly—"when it comes to a vote, I'll withdraw in his favour at the convention. Horace here will think up something for me—any old lie will do, I suppose? In any case, of course, I withdraw."

He took his hat, and they all got up, startled a little at the quick and simple close of the difficult scene they had anticipated. Horace Williams offered his hand.

"Shake, Lorne," he said, and the other two, coming nearer, followed his example.

"Why, yes," said Lorne.

He left them with a brief excuse, and they stood together in a moment's silence, three practical politicians who had delivered themselves from a dangerous network involving higher things.

"Dash these heart-to-heart talks," said Bingham irritably, "it's the only thing to do, but why the devil didn't he want something out of it? I had that Registrarship in my inside pocket."

"If anybody likes to kick me round the room," remarked Horace Williams with depression, "I have no very strong objection."

"And now," Mr. Farquharson said with a sigh, "we understand it's got to be Carter. I suppose I'm too old a man to do jockey for a three-year-old, but I own I've enjoyed the ride."

Lorne Murchison went out into the companionship of Main Street, the new check in his fortunes hanging before him. We may imagine that it hung heavily; we may suppose that it cut off the view. As Bingham would have said, he was "up against it," and that, when one is confidently treading the straight path to accomplishment, is a dazing experience. He was up against it, yet already he had recoiled far enough to consider it; already he was adapting his heart, his nerves, and his future to it. His heart took it greatly, told him he had not yet force enough for the business he had aspired to, but gave him a secret assurance. Another time he would find more strength and show more cunning; he would not disdain the tools of diplomacy and desirability, he would dream no more of short cuts in great political departures. His heart bowed to its sorry education and took counsel with him, bidding him be of good courage and push on. He was up against it, but he would get round it, and there on the other side lay the same wide prospect, with the Idea shining high. At one point he faltered, but that was a matter of expediency rather than of courage. He searched and selected, as he went along the street, among phrases that would convey his disaster to Dora Milburn.

Just at that point, the turning to his own office, he felt it hard luck that Alfred Hesketh should meet and want a word with him. Hesketh had become tolerable only when other things were equal. Lorne had not seen him since the night of his election, when his felicitations had seemed to stand for very little one way or another. His manner now was more important, charged with other considerations. Lorne waited on the word, uncomfortably putting off the necessity of coming out with his misfortune.

"I haven't come across you, Murchison, but you've had my sympathy, I needn't say, all this time. A man can't go into politics with gloves on, there's no doubt about that. Though, mind you, I never for a moment believed that you let yourself in personally. I mean, I've held you all through, above the faintest suspicion."

"Have you?" said Lorne. "Well, I suppose I ought to be grateful."

"Oh, I have—I assure you! But give me a disputed election for the revelation of a rotten state of things—eh?"

"It does show up pretty low, doesn't it?"

"However, upon my word, I don't know whether it's any better in England. At bottom we've got a lower class to deal with, you know. I'm beginning to have a great respect for the electorate of this country, Murchison—not necessarily the methods, but the rank and file of the people. They know what they want, and they're going to have it."

"Yes," said Lorne, "I guess they are."

"And that brings me to my news, old man. I've given the matter a lot of time and a lot of consideration, and I've decided that I can't do better than drive in a stake for myself in this new country of yours."

"It isn't so very new," Lorne told him, in rather dull response, "but I expect that's a pretty good line to take. Why, yes—first rate."

"As to the line," Hesketh went on, weightily, leading the way through an encumbering group of farmers at a corner, "I've selected that, too. Traction-engines. Milburn has never built them yet, but he says the opportunity is ripe—"

"Milburn!" Lorne wheeled sharply.

"My future partner. He was planning extensions just as I came along, a fortunate moment, I hope it will prove, for us both. I'd like to go into it with you, some time when you have leisure—it's a scheme of extraordinary promise. By the way, there's an idea in it that ought to appeal to you—driving the force that's to subdue this wilderness of yours."

"When you've lived here for a while," said Lorne, painfully preoccupied, "you'll think it quite civilized. So you're going in with Milburn?"

"Oh, I'm proud of it already! I shall make a good Canadian, I trust. And as good an imperialist," he added, "as is consistent with the claims of my adopted country."

"That seems to be the popular view," said Lorne.

"And a very reasonable view, too. But I'm not going to embark on that with you, old fellow—you shan't draw me in. I know where you are on that subject."

"So do I—I'm stranded. But it's all right—the subject isn't," Lorne said quietly; and Hesketh's exclamations and inquiries brought out the morning's reverse. The young Englishman was cordially sorry, full of concern and personal disappointment, abandoning his own absorbing affairs, and devoting his whole attention to the unfortunate exigency which Lorne dragged out of his breast, in pure manfulness, to lay before him.

However, they came to the end of it, arriving at the same time at the door which led up the stairs to the office of Fulke, Warner, and Murchison.

"Thank you," said Lorne. "Thank you. Oh, I dare say it will come all right in the course of time. You return to England, I suppose—or do you?—before you go in with Milburn?"

"I sail next week," said Hesketh, and a great relief shot into the face of his companion. "I have a good deal to see to over there. I shan't get back much before June, I fancy. And—I must tell you—I am doing the thing very thoroughly. This business of naturalizing myself, I mean. I am going to marry that very charming girl—a great friend of yours, by the way, I know her to be—Miss Milburn."

For accepting the strokes of fate we have curiously trivial demonstrations. Lorne met Hesketh's eye with the steadiness of a lion's in his own; the unusual thing he did was to take his hands out of his pockets and let his arms hang loosely by his side. It was as tragic a gesture of helplessness as if he had flung them above his head.

"Dora is going to marry you?"

"I believe she will do me that honour. And I consider it an honour. Miss Milburn will compare with any English girl I ever met. But I half expected you to congratulate me. I know she wrote to you this morning—you were one of the first."

"I shall probably find the letter," said Lorne mechanically, "when I go home."

He still eyed Hesketh narrowly, as if he had somewhere concealed about him the explanation of this final bitter circumstance. He had a desire not to leave him, to stand and parley—to go upstairs to the office would be to plunge into the gulf. He held back from that and leaned against the door frame, crossing his arms and looking over into the market-place for subjects to postpone Hesketh's departure. They talked of various matters in sight, Hesketh showing the zest of his newly-determined citizenship in every observation—the extension of the electric tramway, the pulling down of the old Fire Hall. In one consciousness Lorne made concise and relevant remarks; in another he sat in a spinning dark world and waited for the crash.

It seemed to come when Hesketh said, preparing to go, "I'll

tell Miss Milburn I saw you. I suppose this change in your political prospects won't affect your professional plans in any way—you'll stick on here, at the Bar?"

It was the very shock of calamity, and for the instant he could see nothing in the night of it but one far avenue of escape, a possibility he had never thought of seriously until that moment. The conception seemed to form itself on his lips, to be involuntary.

"I don't know. A college friend has been pressing me for some time to join him in Milwaukee. He offers me plenty of work, and I am thinking seriously of closing with him."

"Go over to the United States? You can't mean that!"

"Oh yes—it's the next best thing!"

Hesketh's face assumed a gravity, a look of feeling and of remonstrance. He came a step nearer and put a hand on his companion's arm.

"Come now, Murchison," he said, "I ask you—is this a time to be thinking of chucking the Empire?"

Lorne moved further into the passage with an abruptness which left his interlocutor staring. He stood there for a moment in silence, and then turned to mount the stair with a reply which a passing dray happily prevented from reaching Hesketh's ears.

"No, damn you," he said. "It's not!"

I cannot let him finish on that uncontrolled phrase, though it will be acknowledged that his provocation was great. Nor must we leave him in heavy captivity to the thought of oblivion in the unregarding welter of the near republic, of plunging into more strenuous activities and abandoning his ideal, in queer inverted analogy to the refuging of weak women in a convent. We know that his ideal was strong enough to reassert itself, under a keen irony of suggestion, in the very depth of his overwhelming: and the thing that could rise in him at that black moment may be trusted, perhaps, to reclaim his fortitude and reconsecrate his energy when these things come again into the full current of his life. The illness that, after two or three lagging days, brought him its merciful physical distraction was laid in the general understanding at the door of his political disappointment; and, among a crowd of sympathizers confined to no party, Horace Williams, as his wife expressed it, was pretty nearly wild during its progress. The power of the press is regrettably small in such emergencies, but what restoration it had Horace anxiously administered; the *Express* published a daily bulletin. The second election passed only half noticed by the Murchison family; Carter very nearly re-established the Liberal majority. The *Dominion* dwelt upon this repeated demonstration of the strength of Reform principles in South Fox, and Mrs. Murchison said they were welcome to Carter.

Many will sympathize with Mrs. Murchison at this point, I hope, and regret to abandon her in such equivocal approval of the circumstances which have arisen round her. Too anxiously occupied at home to take her share in the general pleasant sensation of Dr. Drummond's marriage, she was compelled to give it a hurried consideration and a sanction which was practically wrested from her. She could not be clear as to the course of events that led to it, nor entirely satisfied, as she said, about the ins and outs of that affair; this although she felt she could be clearer, and possibly had better grounds for being satisfied, than other people. As to Advena's simple statement that Miss Cameron had made a second choice of the Doctor, changing her mind, as far as Mrs. Murchison could see, without rhyme or reason, that Mrs. Murchison took leave to find a very poor explanation. Advena's own behaviour toward the rejection is one of the things which her mother declares, probably truly, that she never will understand. To pick up a man in the actual fling of being thrown over, will never, in Mrs. Murchison's eyes, constitute a decorous proceeding. I suppose she thinks the creature might have been made to wait at least until he had found his feet. She professes to cherish no antagonism to her future son-in-law on this account, although, as she says, it's a queer way to come into a family; and she makes no secret of her belief that Miss Cameron showed excellent judgment in doing as she did, however that far-seeing woman came to have the opportunity.

Hesketh had sailed before Lorne left his room, to return in June to those privileges and prospects of citizenship which he so eminently deserves to enjoy. When her brother's convalescence and departure for Florida had untied her tongue, Stella widely proclaimed her opinion that Mr. Hesketh's engagement to Miss Milburn was the most suitable thing that could be imagined or desired. We know the youngest Miss Murchison to be inclined to impulsive views; but it would be safe, I think, to follow her here. Now that the question no longer circles in the actual vortex of Elgin politics Mr. Octavius Milburn's attitude toward the conditions of imperial connection has become almost as mellow as ever. Circumstances may arise any day, however, to stir up that latent bitterness which is so potential in him: and then I fear there will be no restraining him from again attacking Wallingham in the papers.

Henry Cruickshank, growing old in his eminence and less secure, perhaps, in the increasing conflict of loud voices, of his own grasp of the ultimate best, fearing too, no doubt, the approach of that cynicism which, moral or immoral, is the real hoar of age, wrote to young Murchison while he was still examining the problems of the United States with the half heart of the alien, and offered him a partnership. The terms were so simple and advantageous as only to be explicable on the grounds I have mentioned, though no phrase suggested them in the brief formulas of the letter, in which one is tempted to find the individual parallel of certain propositions of a great government also growing old. The offer was accepted, not without emotion, and there, too, it would be good to trace the parallel, were we permitted; but for that it is too soon, or perhaps it is too late. Here, for Lorne and for his country, we lose the thread of destiny. The shuttles fly, weaving the will of the nations, with a skein for ever dipped again; and he goes forth to his share in the task among those by whose hand and direction the pattern and the colours will be made.

Appendix A: Personal and Domestic Contexts

1. Sara Jeannette Duncan, "[North American Indians]." "Other People and I," *The Globe*, 29 July 1885

[Duncan wrote a weekly column in the Toronto *Globe* during the summer of 1885. It often contained commentary on articles published in British or American magazines, from a Canadian point of view.]

The *Glasgow Weekly Herald*, with an eye to the instruction of the masses, amiably recommends that at a forthcoming exhibition miniature American Indian and Esquimaux villages be constructed and "real painted braves, squaws, and papooses be imported to give an air of picturesque reality to the representation." Giving *The Herald* due credit for philanthropic motives and enterprising spirit, we must respectfully beg it to desist from thus thoughtlessly adding fuel to the unappeasable flame of British curiosity about the North American Indian. Introduced to the intelligent Briton some years ago by Mr. Cooper,[1] paint, feathers, wampum and all, he has ever since been impressed upon that usually unimaginative being as forming a predominant and highly interesting element in Canadian society. A wigwam, pitched invariably in the foreground of the Canadian landscapes adorning the said intelligent Briton's walls, he naturally looks around for it when he arrives, and is usually disappointed at not finding it prominent to any extent as an architectural feature. He doesn't seem able to divest himself of the idea that the noble red man still habitually and irrepressibly whoops along our highways, and that scalps are to be had for a shilling or two as curios in some localities. No, it is not desirable further to impress the British mind with the North American Indian. Besides he has been sufficiently conspicuous lately. We really can't have the whole front of our admirable civilization obscured any longer by this flying nomad with his chronic appetite and his unsavoury ideas of housekeeping. We would like to direct public

---

1 James Fenimore Cooper (1789-1851), author of the *Last of the Mohicans* (1826).

attention to a few other features, not quite so picturesque perhaps, but more progressive and infinitely more popular. Put the Collegiate Institute in your American village, and the telephone, and block pavements, and stores with plate glass windows, and elevators—no, by the way, not elevators, the British public wouldn't understand you. With true insular directness and economy of syllables, they say "lift" over there I believe. The Englishwoman who told me that also informed me that upon one occasion she was requested by her American hostess to have some "insertion" with her turkey. She was relieved to find that it was only American for what she had all her life in honest English parlance called "stuffing."

★ ★ ★ ★ ★

But that has nothing to do with the North American Indian, whose feminine counterpart is just now making her unaccustomed appearance at the back doors of some places in our land in quite idyllic guise. The noisy criers of "Straw-berrees! Fine, fresh straw-berrees! Strawbiries ripe! Strawb'r'ees ripe!" have been displaced by these silent vendors whose wares lie in red juicy masses under the broad green leaves of their wooden pails. I'm sorry for you, if you have to buy your raspberries from the fruiterer in little quart boxes, and miss the poetry of bargaining with one of these brown-skinned, liquid-eyed, many-over-skirted berry-peddlers, who, smiling and silent, proffers her leaf-hid burden, turning away, still smiling and silent, if you don't want it.

"How much?"

"Ten shillin'." And she stands there in her red petticoat, and composedly fans herself with her broad straw hat still vacantly smiling and unexpectant. Ten shillings for the long day's picking in the bird-haunted solitudes of the woods, where the sunlight filters down upon the bracken and great grey branches send flickering shadows across mossy logs, and the heavy-headed raspberry sprays flash a shining baptism of dew upon the brown hand that rifles them! It is quite possible that the brown hand needed the baptism, but of this it is not appetizing to discourse at present. The "ten shillin'" are yours, my dusky matron, mine is the feast you robbed great Pan of, and a new kerchief will shortly add its rainbow tints to the feminine fascinations of the reserve.

2. Sara Jeannette Duncan, "[The Old-Time Heroine]." "Saunterings," *The Week*, 28 October 1886

[Duncan's regular column in *The Week* frequently addressed issues related to the arts.]

Has it occurred to nobody, in his struggles to keep abreast of the tide of new activity that sets in fiction, as in every other department of modern thought, to cast one deploring glance over his shoulder at the lovely form of the heroine of old-time, drifting fast and far into oblivion? It would be strange indeed if we did not regret her, this daughter of the lively imagination of a bygone day. By long familiarity, how dear her features grew! Having heard of her blue eyes, with what zestful anticipation we foreknew the golden hair, the rosebud mouth, the faintly-flushed, ethereal cheek, and the pink sea-shell that was privileged to do auricular duty in catching the never-ceasing murmur of adoration that beat about the feet of the blonde maiden! Wotting of her ebon locks, with what subtle prescience we guessed the dark and flashing optics, the alabaster forehead, the lips curved in fine scorn, the regal height, and the very unapproachable demeanour of the brunette! The fact that these startling differences were purely physical, that the lines of their psychical construction ran sweetly parallel, never interfered with our joyous interest in them as we breathlessly followed their varying fortunes from an auspicious beginning, through harrowing vicissitudes, to a blissful close. So that her ringlets were long enough, and her woes deep enough, and her conduct under them marked by a beautiful resignation and the more becoming forms of grief, it never occurred to us to cavil at the object of Algernon's passion, because her capabilities were strictly limited to making love and Oriental landscapes in Berlin wool. Her very feminine attributes were invariably forthcoming; and if the author by any chance forgot to particularise the sweetness of her disposition, the neatness of her *boudoir*—they all had *boudoirs*—or the twining nature of her affections, we unconsciously supplied the deficiency, and thought no less respectfully of Araminta. She was very wooden, this person for whom gallant youths attained remarkable heights of self-sacrifice, and villains intrigued in vain; her virtues and her faults alike might form part of the intricate and expensive interior of a Paris doll; and we loved her perhaps with the unmeaning love of infancy for its toys. She was the painted pivot of the merry-go-round—

it could not possibly revolve, with its exciting episodes, without her; yet her humble presence bore no striking relation to the mimic pageant that went on about her. She vanished with the last page, ceased utterly with the sound of her wedding-bells; and we remembered for a little space, not the maiden, but the duels in her honour, the designs upon her fortune, and the poetic justice that overtook her calumniators.

But extinction in time overtook this amiable damsel. Mere complexion began to be considered an insufficient basis upon which to erect a character worthy of public attention in the capacity of a heroine. So we were introduced to the young creature of "parts"—the parts consisting of an immoderate desire to investigate the wisdom of the ancients, as Plato has expressed it, an insatiable appetite for metaphysical conversation, and a lofty contempt for the frivolities of her sex. To keep the balance between these somewhat laudable peculiarities and proper womanly accomplishments, she was usually invested with a powerful and melodious vocal organ, whose minor notes frequently depressed her frivolous associates of the drawing room to tears, and reduced the hitherto invincible heart of the interesting woman-hater of the volume to instant and abject submission. To preserve the unities, charms of feature and philosophical tendencies being somewhat incompatible, she was given a rather wide mouth, and a forehead too high and thoughtful for beauty's strict requirements; while her dark expressive eyes and straight nose sufficed to secure our regard from an aesthetic standpoint. Then came that daring innovator who gave us a countenance all out of line, with freckles on it, a look of restless intellectuality, and a vague charm that was beyond his power to analyse or ours to conceive. The conduct of this young person was usually characterised by the wildest vagaries. She held communings with herself, which she reluctantly imparted to the interesting youth in whom she recognised her mental superior, and therefore her fate; and the sole end of her existence appeared to be to make his as wretched as possible. The plot, of which this ingenuous maid was the centre, usually turned upon a mood of hers—the various chapters, indeed, were chiefly given over to the elucidation of her moods, and their effect upon her unfortunate admirers.

Just about here, in the development of the heroine, do we begin to see that she is not a fixed quantity in the problems of the novelist, but varies with his day and generation. Araminta was the product of an age that demanded no more of femininity than unlimited affection and embroidery. The advent of the blue-stocking suggested the introduction of brains into her composition, though her personality was not seriously affected by them, as the blue-stocking was but a creature of report in the mind of the story-teller, the feminine intelligence not being popularly cultivated beyond the seminary limit. As dissatisfaction with her opportunities infected the modern young lady, her appearance in fiction with a turned-up nose and freckles, solely relying upon her yearnings after the infinite for popular appreciation, followed as a matter of course.

We are not talking, O captious soul—with a dozen notable heroines of the past at your fingers' ends!—of the great people in the world of fiction, but of the democracy of that populous literary sphere. We are discussing those short-lived Ethels and Irenes who have long since gone over, with their devoted Arthurs and Adolphuses, to that great majority whose fortunes are to be traced only at the second-hand book-stalls now; but whose afflictions formed the solace of many an hour in the dusty seclusion of the garret, while the rain pattered on the roof, and the mice adventured over the floor, and the garments of other days swayed to and fro in dishevelled remembrance of their departed possessors. Ah, Genevieve and Rosabel, Vivien and Belinda, how fare ye now whose yellow-bound vicissitudes were treasured so carefully from the fiery fate that awaited them at the hands of stern authorities diametrically opposed to "light reading!" By what black ingratitude are ye reduced, alas! to the pulp of the base material economy of the age on which, perhaps, the fortunes of damsels less worthy and less fair are typographically set forth for the fickle amusement of a later generation!

Hardly less complete is the evanishment of Rosabel and Belinda than that of their successors in fiction, and the time-honoured functions they performed. A novel without a heroine used to be as absurd an idea as the play of Hamlet with Hamlet left out. But the heroine of to-day's fiction is the exception, not the rule. The levelling process the age is undergoing has reduced women with their own knowledge and consent to very much the same plane of thought and action as men. It has also raised them to it, paradoxical though the statement be. The woman of to-day is no longer an exceptional being surrounded by exceptional circumstances. She bears a translatable relation to the world, and the novelists who translate it correctly have ceased to mark it by unduly exalting one woman by virtue of her sex to a position of interest in their books which dwarfs all the other characters. It has been found that successful novels can be written without her. The woman of to-day understands herself, and is understood in her present and possible worth. The novel of to-day is a reflection of our present social state. The women who enter into its composition are but intelligent agents in this reflection, and show themselves as they are, not as a false ideal would have them

3. A Selection of Duncan's Letters concerning *The Imperialist*

Holcombe, Simla[1]
Sept 18th [1902]

Dear Mr. Willison,[2]

I have taken upon myself to write a Canadian novel, with a political *motif*, and I am rather anxious that none of you shall be ashamed of it. I feel a little helpless so far from my material and I write to ask if you will very kindly send me a little. I want a week's issues of the *Globe*, preferably numbers dealing editorially with the question of *Imperial Federation*, and I want, if they are to be had in pamphlet form, all *Sir W. Laurier's speeches* on the subject, or any others that may be useful. It is asking a good deal of a busy man to look up this sort of thing, I know, but I trust to your interest in the result to excuse me. I am trying very hard to make it my best book, and the ground is practically unbroken. I have Holland's "Imperium et Libertas" which strikes me, admirable as it is, as a little like whipping a dead horse. If you know of anything more closely occupied with the practical intricacies of the question, will you send it to me, and I will pay up by return. Some Canadian must have published a view. I am sending per money order only one miserable dollar to pay for the papers etc but I should be only too glad to afford anything that would be helpful.

I wonder if you have seen "Those Delightful Americans"?[3] I

---

1 J.S. Willison Fonds, MG30 D29, Volume 10, Folder 78, 6653-6600. Reproduced by permission of Library and Archives Canada.
2 J.S. Willison (1856-1927) was in 1902 editor of the Toronto *News* where *The Imperialist* was eventually published. A supporter of the Liberal party, Willison was also author of *Sir Wilfrid Laurier and the Liberal Party* (1903).
3 *Those Delightful Americans* (New York: D. Appleton, 1902) was Duncan's most recently published novel.

have given up as hopeless any attempt to get any books on the market in my own country. They always seem to fall between the two stools of the London & New York publishers. However, I have had the luck lately to place stories with *Scribner* & *The Century*, and a couple of Burmese sketches with *Harpers*, so I should not complain. I am going to England after the big Durbar[1] in January—anybody coming out to represent the *Globe?* All press correspondents to be taken care of by the hospitable Gov't of India. You ought to come. The *Times* is sending a man, also *Daily Mail* and *Morning Post* and Reuter is to have 3,000 words a day!—and expect to be in Canada in June. It will be a pleasure to see you all again in Toronto.

With Kind Regards and many apologies

Yours very sincerely

Sara Jeannette Cotes.

The Ladies' Empire Club[2]

69 Grosvenor Street W.,

Jan 8th [1905]

Dear Lord Lansdowne,[3]

I wonder if I may count upon your affection for Canada and the kind interest you expressed in the beginnings of my literary work there, far enough to send you my Canadian novel *The Imperialist?* The book was published a few months ago, but I was in India at the time, and felt too far out upon the periphery of the Empire to take a very active share in its distribution from the centre.

It seemed to me that among the assumptions and disputes over here as to what the "colonial view" really is, it might be worth while to present the situation as it appears to the average Canadian of the average small town, inarticulate except at election times, but whose view in the end counts for more than that of those pictorial people whose speeches at Toronto banquets go so far to over-colour the British imagination about Canadian senti-

---

1 A public celebration held in Delhi to mark Edward VII's accession to the throne.

2 Letter inserted in the flyleaf of a presentation copy of *The Imperialist*. Reproduced courtesy of the Metropolitan Toronto Reference Library.

3 The Marquess of Lansdowne was Canada's Governor General from 1883 to 1888, and Viceroy of India from 1888 to 1894. Duncan was presented to him in Ottawa and in Calcutta.

ment. I thought it might be useful to bring this practical person forward and let him be seen. I hope I have not made him too prominent, but he is there.

My book offers only a picture of life and opinion, and attempts no argument. I have on this account the better courage in sending it. I should be very happy indeed if it might claim some stray half hour of your leisure time.

and I am
dear Lord Lansdowne
your sincerely
Sara Jeannette Cotes

Red Roof,[1]
Simla S.W.
May 4th [1905]

Dear Dr. MacMechan,[2]

Your two most kind letters and the delightful article in the *Halifax Herald*[3] have at last found me here. I hope, if it has occurred to you to wonder at my tardy acknowledgement of them, that you have remembered how near I live to the Roof of the World, to which the mails climb slowly.

I need not say that I have taken the greatest pleasure in your generous expression of liking for *The Imperialist*. I confess I *had* wondered, a little here on my remote hill top, whether anybody had listened to me in Canada and had come rather to the conclusion that I had been too far away to be well heard, or perhaps I had forgotten my country's note. But that anyone should write like this reassures me quite, and that you alone should feel the book as you do justifies me very happily in having written it. I share with you the conviction of the individuality of the Canadi-

---

1 Reproduced by permission of Dalhousie University Archives (MS-2-82, pp. B1-B2).

2 Archibald MacMechan (1862-1933) was Professor of Literature at Dalhousie University and author of *Headwaters of Canadian Literature* (1924).

3 On 14 June 1904 the *Halifax Herald* published an interview with Mrs. Robert Borden by the well-known feminist journalist Margaret Graham, in which Graham disparagingly compared Mrs. Borden to Dora Milburn: "As I came away I recalled Mrs. Sara Duncan Coates' [sic] description of her heroine in the 'Imperialist' (a Canadian novel of political life by the way). 'She had several kinds of cleverness, one of them being a particularly nice way of doing her hair.' This applies to Mrs. Borden." This article may be the one forwarded by MacMechan; diligent searches have failed to turn up another possibility.

an type. The spirit of place always seems to me strong in the land. I want to come back and work at it from closer range, and soon I think this will be possible. I am especially curious about your Eastern past. My mother is a New Brunswicker—Shediac and all that country has the charm for me of nursery description. I am sure it is as different from Ontario as Massachusetts is from Illinois. We find that we have been almost long enough in India and I hope to sail through the "Ditch" for the last time, westward bound, in November, and be in Canada next summer. The Empire is a big place and interesting everywhere, but ours is by far the best part of it, and the most full of the future.

I rejoice that you enjoyed Dr. Drummond. The dear original was Dr. Wm. Cochrane[1] of Brantford, who christened most of the Presbyterians now there. He has been dead these five or six years—or I would never have dared!

Please accept my best and warmest thanks,
and believe me
Yours very sincerely
Sara Jeannette Cotes

The college magazine has not reached me. If you have another copy might I receive it direct? I should like so much to keep it. SJC

4. From Sara Jeannette Duncan, "[Growing Golden-rod in Simla]." *The Crow's Nest* (1901)

However you do it, there is no more delicious experience in life than to put something beautiful where nothing was before; I mean in any suitable empty space. I have done it; I have had the consummation of this pleasure for a fortnight. There was no golden-rod in Simla till I went to America and got it. I make the lofty statement with confidence, but subject to correction. Some one else may have thought of it long ago, and may be able to confront me with finer plumes than mine. If this should be so I shall accept it with reluctance and mortification, and hereby promise to go and admire the other person's, which is the most anybody can do; but my pride does not expect such a fall.

It is the Queen's golden-rod, not the President's, though he

---

1 William Cochrane (1831-98), Presbyterian minister at Zion United Church in Brantford.

has a great deal of it and makes, I think, rather more fuss about it. A field flower of generous mind, it ignores the political line, and I gathered the seed one splendid autumn afternoon in Canada; so here on the shelf it may claim its humble part in the Imperial idea. A friend of my youth lent herself to the project; she took me in her father's buggy, and as we went along the country roads I saw again, in the light of a long absence, the quiet of the fields and the broad, pebbled stretches of the river, and the bronze and purple of the untrimmed woods that had always been for me the margin of the thought of home. The quiet of after-harvest held it all, nothing was about but a chipmunk that ran along the top of a fence, you could count the apples in the orchards among their scanty leaves; it was time to talk and to remember. And so, not by anything unusual that we did or said, but by the rare and beautiful correspondence that is sometimes to be felt between the sentiment of the hour and the hour itself, this afternoon took its place in the dateless calendar of the heart which is so much more valuable a reference than any other. What a delight it is when old, forgotten things construct themselves again and the years gather into an afternoon! And is there any such curious instance of real usefulness for hidden treasure in the attic?

We found masses of golden-rod, all dry and scattering, principally along the railway embankment, which we took for a good omen that it would be a travelling flower; and in the fulness of time it was given to Atma, with instructions. His excitement was even greater than mine; he nursed it tenderly, but it needed no nursing. It came up in thousands, delighted with itself and the new climate, overrunning its boxes so that Atma pointed to it like a proud father. Then we planted it out along the paling behind the coreopsis, and it immediately—that is to say, in three month's time—grew to be five feet high, with the most thick and lovely yellow sprays, which have been waving there against the fir-trees, as I said before, for the last fortnight. It has quite lost the way to its proper season; at home it blossoms in September, and this is only June, but it appears to be rather the better than the worse for that, though it does seem to look about, as the Princess[1] said when I sent her some, for the red sumach which is its friend and companion at home. It is itself like a little fir-tree with flat,

---

1   Duncan's friends and acquaintances appear in this book of personal
    essays under various pseudonyms; "the Princess" is probably Lady Mary
    Curzon, the American-born wife of the Viceroy Lord Curzon.

spreading branches of blossom, especially when it stands in groups as they do, and the sun slants upon it, giving the sprays an edge of brighter gold, so that it is the most luminous thing in the garden. And the warm scent of it, holding something so far beyond itself and India, something essential, impregnated with the solace that one's youth and its affections are not lost, but only on the other side of the world!

5. Recipes from *The Canadian Home Cook Book* (1887)

[*The Canadian Home Cook Book* was the first fund-raising cookbook in Canada, and included recipes contributed by local women. These recipes have not been tested in a contemporary kitchen.]

Scalloped Oysters

Crush and roll several handfuls of Boston crackers; put a layer in the bottom of a buttered pudding dish. Wet this with a mixture of the oyster liquor and milk slightly warmed. Next a layer of oysters sprinkled with salt, pepper, and small bits of butter; then another layer of the moistened crumbs, then a layer of oysters, and so on till the dish is full. Let the top layer be of crumbs, and beat an egg into the milk, which you pour over them. Stick bits of butter thickly over it, and bake half an hour.

Pickled Peaches [or Pears]

Take five pounds of brown sugar to one gallon of pure cider vinegar; boil it hard for thirty minutes, skimming off the scum till clear; rub off the peaches in the meantime out of boiling water (quickly) with a flannel cloth, sticking four cloves in each peach; and put a bag of cinnamon into the boiling syrup. If the peaches are clingstones, put them into the boiling syrup for fifteen or twenty minutes; if freestones, lay them in the jar in layers, and pour the syrup over them while hot; then put a small plate over to keep them from rising, and cover tightly with cloth or paper. In four days look at them, and if necessary, boil the syrup again, and pour on while hot; keep them in a cool place while the weather is hot to prevent souring. The white Sugar Cling is nice for pickling, and the Blood Peach is very rich, but dark. Small pears can be pickled in the same manner, if the skin is taken off.

Chicken Salad

Boil one chicken tender, then take the meat and chop it up, take two tablespoons of mustard, 3 eggs boiled hard, chop up the whites with the chickens, the yolks rub up fine with the mustard, one tablespoon of salt, three tablespoons melted butter, one tablespoon black pepper, vinegar enough to moisten it, chop three heads of celery to one chicken, mix all together and serve.

Stewed Tongue

Cut square fillets of bacon, which dredge with a mixture of chopped parsley, salt, pepper, and a little allspice. Lard the tongue with the fillets; put in a sauce-pan two ounces of bacon cut in slices, four springs of parsley, two of thyme, a little garlic, two cloves, two carrots cut in small pieces, two small onions, salt and pepper. Lay the tongue on the whole; wet with a glass of white wine and a glass of broth. Set it on a moderate fire and simmer about five hours, keeping it well covered. Put the tongue on a dish and strain the sauce over it.

Tea Biscuits

One quart flour, four teaspoonsful of baking powder, about the size of an egg of butter, one tablespoonful of brown sugar, a teaspoonful of salt, and half cup of currants; grate in a little nutmeg; bake twenty minutes in a quick oven.

6. Twenty-fourth of May Celebration from *The Brantford Expositor*, 22 May 1884

Appendix B: Imperialism and the Tariff Question

1. "A Pertinent Question." *Diogenes*, 19 June 1869

A Pertinent Question.

Mrs. Brittania: "Is it possible, my dear, that you have ever given your cousin Jonathan any Encouragement?"

Miss Canada: "Encouragement? Certainly not, Mamma; I have told him we can *Never* be United."

2. "The Effect of the National Policy." Political pamphlet, c. 1891. CIHM.45881.

(A PICTURE FROM REAL LIFE.)

The original of this picture, called "Mortgaging the Homestead," is a painting by the celebrated Canadian artist, G.A. Reid, and is now in the Art Gallery at Ottawa.

The figures to the right represent the old couple, who as pioneers cleared the farm from the bush, while the son, who has failed to make "both ends meet," is signing the Mortgage Deed of the "Old Homestead." The picture of the old folks is one of hopeless resignation, while that of the young wife is expressive of fierce anger at the sad ending of her husband's labours.

**FARMERS AND FARMERS' WIVES,
LOOK AT THIS PICTURE !**
**Men, Vote for your own welfare—Reform,
Unrestricted Reciprocity and Farmers Rights**

3. Sara Jeannette Duncan, "Imperial Sentiment in Canada." *Indian Daily News*, 7 October 1896

Mr. Chamberlain, whose plain hope it is to identify his name and period of office with the practical Federation of the British Empire, will shortly receive important assistance to this end from a quarter in which he has probably not been taught to look for it—the Liberal party in Canada, which now holds the reins of power in the Dominion. Hitherto, it might almost be supposed by the casual reader of contemporary history, that a monopoly of Canadian loyalty to the mother country was held by the Conservatives of the colony. The late Sir John Macdonald was the head and front of it, and this able politician's eloquence and plausibility were such that he contrived to stand at the head of his party as the personification of impassioned devotion to England for many years. In this he was aided, of course, by its history, which shows it composed in part of the old United Empire Loyalists, who crossed the line with their families from Massachusetts more than a century ago to avoid taking up arms against King George, and to continue to live under the British flag. This has always given a great accent to the loyal professions of Canadian Conservatives and has combined with the aristocratic and monarchical traditions claimed by the party everywhere to establish them very conspicuously. In this connection it is surprising to note how an accustomed way of looking at things will survive much that should conduce to another point of view. Sir John Macdonald's notable "National Policy" was conceived and carried out in plain opposition to British interest as a whole, and many of its tariff provisions were directly aimed at British manufactures. Yet the after-dinner toast and the Queen's Birthday demonstrate it prevailed upon British sentiment, and it was Imperially recognised that for Canada, in the words of the nautical song "It don't matter what you do, if your 'eart be true," and that the heart of the Dominion was still daughterly.

This attitude was successfully adopted by the Conservative party for the eighteen years that began in 1878 and ended two months ago. The history of the Dominion during that time offers valuable instruction to the protectionist. The high tariff national policy was designed, of course, to nourish home manufactures; it was promptly successful in establishing them, and for a time Canada appeared to have entered upon a period of industrial deliverance. Then the new industries began to flicker out, exhausted by their own competition in a narrow market. It became obvious that the resources of the country, in coal and iron and gold, were failing to receive the development freely promised under the new fiscal regime, and in 1891 the fact shouted from an official report that the shipping industry of the maritime provinces, formerly so important and so thriving, had declined in twelve years by nearly a half. In that year, too, the census was republished, which showed that Canada had added only 508,000 to her inhabitants during the foregoing decade, an increase so small that the country might be considered, for those ten years, practically stationary. The explanation lay, not in any diminution of the birth rate, young and healthy Canadians having added themselves to the world's population in quite creditable numbers, but in the steady flow of emigration from the Dominions to the United States. There was no lack of proof of this fatal leakage, by which Canada lost a round million inhabitants, either born in the colony or leaving it after the settling experience of a year or two under tariff regu[la]tions which placed a prohibitive price on the very implements by which the immigrant had to turn the sods of the fields he reclaimed from the wilderness. It was on these sober facts, quite as much as in the revolt against the dictum of the Roman Catholic Church, that the Canadian electorate found their reason for displacing the Conservative party and its policy by the Liberals and a promised tariff for revenue purposes only.

Already the new Canadian Premier, the Hon. Mr. Wilfred Laurier, has found occasion to announce that he and his Liberals looked with favour upon designs for Imperial Federation based on a preferential tariff for the goods of Great Britain and her colonies. This is more than his predecessors would ever have been able to say, since their very being lay in the hands of the manufacturers. Neither, indeed, but for the experiences of the last eighteen years, would any Canadian party have been able to say it; for the innovation requires all the courage that comes of the knowledge that experiments in the opposite direction, at least, have failed.

Neither can it be denied that in recent years, and especially during the past year, the political outlook of the Dominion has been affected by the growth of the Imperial sentiment. Twenty or twenty-five years ago, any scheme of Federation founded thereon would not have been seriously received by the Canadian people; it is utterly beyond the range of practical politics. The views of the Manchester school were then strong in England, and were accepted as the proper interpretation of colonial destiny. All this has been changed; and during the past year or two, Canadian politics has seen the final effacement of ideas which conflict with British connection. The Venezuela embroglio, the South African question, and the progress of Australian Federation, have strongly reinforced Imperial feeling, which is now sanguine of a permanent organisation of the Empire on a federal basis. The weakness of the idea has, hitherto, been the lack of its embodiment in any definite plan; but even its opponents are compelled to admit the vigor of the sentiment behind it; nor are they disposed to belittle the essential foundation which such sentiment supplies.

Not long ago the Canadian Liberals, in despair at the yoke of the national policy, took for a plank in their platform commercial union with the United States. This they have for some time definitely abandoned, being convinced of the political dangers involved; but the theory was sufficiently advertised to give an entirely wrong impression of the attitude towards Great Britain of a great and powerful political party in her most progressive colony. It is, therefore, doubly gratifying that the present Secretary of State should find the first sincere welcome to his scheme for Imperial Federation offered by the Liberals of Canada, with whose economic principles it accords, and who are proud to claim a part in the greatness it prefigures.

4. From Goldwin Smith, "Commercial Union."[1] *Canada and the Canadian Question* (1891). Chapter Ten, Section V

[*Canada and the Canadian Question* was a major contribution on the question of trade relations with the US by Smith, a well-known British historian and journalist who lived in Toronto. Duncan wrote for his magazine, *The Week*, and refers to his views in *The Imperialist*. In this excerpt, Smith argues that Commercial Union with the United States (what we would now call free trade, with mutual free access to shared waterways and resources) would be much more advantageous for Canada than Imperial Preference Trade.]

"I am confident," said Mr. Bayard, the American Secretary of State, to Sir Charles Tupper, "that we both seek to attain a just

---

1 Smith's original footnotes to this chapter have been omitted.

and permanent settlement—and there is but one way to procure it, and that is by a straightforward treatment on a liberal and statesman-like plan of the entire commercial relations of the two countries. I say commercial, because I do not propose to include, however indirectly or by any intendment, however partial and oblique, the political relations of Canada and the United States, nor to affect the legislative independence of either country." The object of the movement now on foot under the name of 'Commercial Union' is to bring Canada within the commercial pale of her own continent, and thereby put an end to the commercial atrophy which her isolation entails. A reciprocal benefit would of course be afforded to the United States in an increase of commercial area and opportunities of opening up new sources of wealth. The name Commercial Union, which has been challenged as suggestive of political union, was adopted in contradistinction to it, and in exact accordance with the intention of Mr. Bayard. The measure would be necessarily accompanied by an assimilation of the excise and of the seaboard tariff, without which there would be smuggling of liquors across the line, and of goods through the ports of one country into the other. Whether there should be a pooling of the seaboard duties is a separate question. Community of Fisheries, the Coasting Trade, and Water-ways is included in Commercial Union.

The movement in Canada originated with a Farmers' Convention in Toronto, and was taken up by the Farmers' Institutes of the Province. On the farmer's mind had dawned the fact that he was the sheep, and the protected manufacturer was the shearer. The special organ of the movement has been the Commercial Union Club, an association independent of political party. The policy of Reciprocity, however, has been embraced by the Liberal Party now in opposition:[1] it forms the main plank in the platform of that party; and will, in all probability, be the issue at the coming elections. On the American side a resolution in Congress authorising the President to treat for Commercial Union with the Canadian Government has been brought forward by Mr. Hitt, of Illinois, and has been passed unanimously by the House of Representatives, while in the Senate it has failed of unanimous consent only by one vote. Another resolution pointing the same way was

---

1 In 1891, Laurier's Liberals were in opposition and supported reciprocity with the US.

brought forward by Mr. Butterworth, the member for Cincinnati, one of the foremost men in the Republican party, and like Mr. Hitt thoroughly friendly both to Canada and to Great Britain. Life has been given to the movement by the public spirit and energy of Mr. Erastus Wiman, a Canadian who has won his way to a high place in American commerce without ceasing to be a Canadian, and has done more than any other man to keep up attachment both to Canada and England and to sustain the honour of the British flag at New York, so that he is well placed for dealing with any question in the interest of all three countries. A word of justice is due to him, since he has not been fairly treated by certain journals in England whose confidence is abused by their correspondents in Canada on this and on other Canadian questions.

That the market of her own continent is the natural market of Canada, both as a seller and a buyer, even so strong an Imperialist as Sir Charles Dilke admits, and no one but a protected manufacturer or a fanatical Tory would attempt to deny. The Conservative leader, Sir John Macdonald, has always professed to be doing his utmost to bring about reciprocity. His motto has been Reciprocity of Trade or Reciprocity of Tariffs, meaning that if he had recourse to reciprocity of tariffs it was only because he could not get reciprocity of trade, and an order to enforce it. His Protectionist Tariff Act contained a standing offer of reciprocity in natural products. This, as has been said before, was illusory, inasmuch as the Americans evidently could not, in common justice to their own interests, allow their manufactures to be excluded while they admitted the natural products of Canada; but it was at all events the homage paid by political strategy to commercial wisdom. If the offer has now been cancelled, this, it may safely be said, is not because conviction has changed on the commercial question, but because the irritation bred by the M'Kinley Act presents an opportunity for an appeal to that feeling against American connection which is the life of the existing system. M. Chapleau, one of Sir John Macdonald's French colleagues, still declares for Reciprocity in the teeth of the declaration of Mr. Colby, another member of the Government, against it, as well as of the general action of the Administration, showing thereby apparently his sense of the fact that Reciprocity is a prime necessity in the French Province. Let any one scan the economical map of the North American continent with its adjacent waters, mark its northern zone abounding in minerals, in bituminous coal, in lumber, in fish, as well as in special farm products, brought in the north to hardier perfection, all of which the southern people have need: then let him look to its southern regions, the natural products of which as well as the manufactures produced in its wealthy centres of industry are needed by the people of the northern zone: he will see that the continent is an economic whole, and that to run a Customs line athwart it and try to sever its members from each other is to wage a desperate war against nature. Each several Province of the Dominion is by nature wedded to a commercial partner on the south, though a perverse policy struggles to divorce them. The Maritime Provinces want to send their lumber, their bituminous coal, and their fish to the markets of New England; Ontario and Quebec want to send their barley, eggs, and other farm products, their horses, their cattle and their lumber to New York and other neighbouring States; Manitoba and the North-West want to send their superior wheat, their barley, their wool, and the fish of their great lakes to St. Paul and Minneapolis; British Columbia wants to send her bituminous coal, her salmon, and the timber of which she is the mighty mother, to California and Oregon. All of them want to get American manufactures as well as the products of a more southern climate in return. It must be long before Canada can produce a first-rate printing press. Even when an article is made in the Dominion, the freight from one of the scattered Provinces to another may be ruinous. British Columbia was paying for nails a price for transit exceeding their first cost at Montreal. Canada is not one market but four, widely separated from each other, and each of them spare in itself.

It is in regard to minerals, perhaps, that the case of Canada is the hardest. She has all the economic minerals except tin. She has vast stores of magnetic and hematatic iron, such as would make the best of iron and steel. In some districts she is rich in copper and nickel. She has valuable veins of silver and gold-bearing quartz, the former in the Lake Superior district, the latter in Nova Scotia and British Columbia. She has abundance of coal, both in British Columbia and in Nova Scotia. Chemical minerals she has also in abundance, and stores of mineral manure. Yet the total value of her mineral exports for 1888, was under $5,000,000, of which nearly a half was for bituminous coal, while she imported hard coal to nearly the same value. What she wants is a free market, free inflow of American capital, free purchase of mining machinery. On the American shore of Lake Superior mining is rife, and its yield is immense; on the Canadian shore, which is not less rich in minerals, it sleeps. Continual appeals are made to the Government by Protectionist patriotism to 'open up' the mines, as though a Government could open up production of any kind otherwise than by giving it fair play. With free trade Port Arthur, in the centre of an immensely rich mining district, instead of being, as it now is, a mere village, might be a mining city. Let the mines be opened and there would be a mining population such as would give the Canadian farmer a home market for which he would not have to pay. For the home market which Protectionism gives him he pays both in the price and quality of the goods. An interest or a country trying to make itself prosperous by such means is, as has been truly said, like a man trying to lift himself up by his boot-straps.

The shipping interest of Canada again pines for the freedom of the coasting trade. Canadian vessels are not allowed to trade between American ports, and have often to return without a cargo. The consequence is that the Canadian marine is fast disappearing from the Lakes. Of the vast trade in ore and grain on the Upper Lakes less than 10 per cent is now carried in Canadian bottoms. The Canadian tonnage passing through the Sault Ste. Marie Canal has fallen to 4 per cent, the rest being American. The new Canadian-built tonnage in the past five years is not over 5 per cent of that launched from Lake shipyards. There is little use in constructing at immense expense a special lock for Canada alongside of the American lock at the "Soo," while Canadian shipping is being made the victim of a policy of extermination. The Dominion *Statistical Abstract*, for 1889, admits a decrease of the amount even of the seagoing trade of the country carried in Canadian bottoms compared with that carried in foreign bottoms. There has also, according to the same authority, been a steady decline in the number and tonnage of the vessels built in the Dominion during the last ten or twelve years, that is since the inauguration of the Protectionist policy of Sir John Macdonald. Protectionists who profess that it is an object of their system by multiplying industries to diversify national character, should consider whether a variety of it will not perish with the mariner.

The Americans, on their side, want to buy things which Canada has to sell; they want an extended market for the products of a more southern climate, such as fruits; they want an extended market for their manufactures. They can manufacture as a rule better and more cheaply because they do it on a larger scale and can specialise; whereas the manufacturer with a small market is obliged to produce several kinds of goods to keep his hands employed. All this is most strongly felt at Detroit, Buffalo, and other commercial cities along the frontier which find themselves cribbed and confined by the Customs line. It has been objected by some American Protectionists that America would be giving a market of 65,000,000 in exchange for one of 5,000,000, as though markets when thrown together were exchanged and not enjoyed in common. According to this reasoning the 60,000,000 of Americans outside the State of New York would be better off without the 6,000,000 of that State. But American capital also wants free access to the natural resources of Canada, her mineral resources especially, which await only the touch of capital, together with the opening of the market, in order to turn them into wealth for the benefit of all the people of the continent. Mr. Blaine, the political leader of the Protectionist party in the United States, has shown himself alive to the need of new markets by declaring in favour of Reciprocity, and he will not be long in finding that the only American community reciprocal trade with which would be of much value is the Dominion of Canada. The half-civilised masses of South America want little except gaudy cottons, with which they are supplied to their satisfaction by England.

It is alleged by Protectionists that there cannot be a profitable trade between Canada and the United States, because the products of the two countries are the same. The products of the two countries, even their natural products, leaving out of sight special manufactures, are not the same. In the United States are included regions and productions almost tropical. Canada, on the other hand, has bituminous coal, for which there are markets in the United States, and plenty of nickel, of which the United States have but little. Canada has lumber to export, and the United States want all they can get. Both countries produce barley, but the Canadian barley is the best for making beer, and its exclusion by the M'Kinley Act brought out a heavy vote at Buffalo against the party of Mr. M'Kinley. This is the first answer. The second and the most decisive is that, in spite of the tariff, Canada has actually been trading with the United States more than with England or any other country in the world, and nearly as much as with all the other countries in the world put together. In 1889 her exports to Great Britain were $38,105,126; her imports from Great Britain were $42,249,555. Her exports to the United States were $48,522,404; her imports from the United States were $56,368,990. Of the total trade of Canada, in the same year, 41.35 per cent was with Great Britain; 49.65 was with the United States; while only 9 per cent was with the rest of the world. To take even the case of farm products, of 18,799 horses which Canada sold in one year, the United States bought 18,225. Of 443,000 sheep, they bought 363,000. Of 116,000 head of cattle, they bought 45,000. Of $107,000 worth of poultry, they bought $99,000 worth. Of $1,825,000 worth of eggs, they bought all. Of $593,000 worth of hides they bought $413,000 worth. Of 1,416,000 pounds of wool, they bought 1,300,000 pounds. Of $9,456,000 worth [of] barley, they bought all. Of $743,000 worth of hay, they bought $670,000 worth. Of $439,000 worth of potatoes, they bought $338,000 worth. Of $83,000 worth of vegetables, they bought $75,000 worth. Of $254,000 worth of miscellaneous agricultural products, they bought $249,000 worth. Manitoba and the North-West believe that, were the tariff wall out of the way, the United States would be their best customer for a great deal of high-class wheat. In spite of the fisheries disputes and taxes, out of $7,000,000 worth of fish, the United States take annually about $3,000,000 worth.

The case is specially strong with regard to some of the smaller Provinces. Prince Edward Island exported in 1889 only $800 worth of agricultural products to Great Britain, while she exported to the United States $466,000 worth. The total export of her own produce to all countries in that year amounted to $974,000, of which $686,000 worth went to the United States. The exports of British Columbia for 1889 amounted to $4,284,000, of which $2,782,000 in value went to the United States, and only $870,000 went to Great Britain. To these Provinces the tariff war is ruinous, and they have some reason for demanding compensation in subsidies from the Dominion.

High as the tariff wall between Canada and the United States is, trade, we see, has climbed over it. Wherever an opening is made in the wall, trade at once rushes through. Before the removal of the duty on eggs, the trade in them was nominal: it rose, when the duty was removed, to over $2,000,000 in 1889. The M'Kinley tariff sends it down again.

Smuggling, as might be expected, is rife along the whole Line, with the usual consequences to popular morality and honest trade. When a border township in which the potato crop is short cannot go to the adjoining township for potatoes, a severe appeal is made to the hamlet's respect for law.

To Manitoba and the North-West, which neither have manufactures, nor, as farm products are their staple, are likely to have them, the tariff is a curse, without even a shadow of compensation. It is difficult to believe that in that region it will be possible for ever to maintain the Custom line, the frontier being merely an imaginary boundary drawn across the prairie for 800 miles, with identically the same population on each side of it, so that a village, even a house, may be placed astride the line, and the housewife with a new kettle may be liable to duty in passing from one room to the other; while the Ottawa Government, for the benefit of which the duties are imposed, is remote and, with too good reason, unbeloved. But the case of Manitoba is hardly worse than that of Nova Scotia and New Brunswick, which get absolutely nothing to make up for their exclusion from the natural market in New England, the attempt to force Ontario, by violent legislative pressure, to buy her coal of Nova Scotia instead of buying it of Pennsylvania having utterly failed.

The assertion that the British market is better for Canada than the American market has already been met by the figures. If for a time the English market was better than the American the reason was that the British market was open, whereas the American market was half closed by the tariff. Remove the Customs line between Canada and the United States and there can be no doubt about the value of the American compared with that of the British market. No people are individually so rich as the Americans, or so ready to pay freely for everything they want or fancy. The American market is always increasing with the rapid growth of population. It is also secure, whereas that of England, or any transmarine country, would become very insecure if England were at war with a maritime power. Canada would then be without any free market at all. But it is needless to discuss this question, because when the American market was opened to Canada that of England would not be closed. Canada would enjoy them both.

The near market must as a rule be the best, not only on account of the difference in freights, but in many cases on account of the perishableness of goods. It must be best for fruits, fish, vegetables, and even for poultry and eggs. It is the best for horses, the breeding of which is a great Canadian industry, and might be a greater. The American comes to Canada and buys the horses on the spot, whereas if the horses are sent to England, unless they at once take the fancy of the market, they may eat up a great part of their value before they are sold. Not till the American market is opened can its full value be understood. Commercial Union between Scotland and England gave a value to black cattle and kelp which could hardly have been foreseen. Production would adapt itself to the new demands, and new roads to wealth would be found. Besides, Canada wants to buy as well as to sell, and the near market, even irrespectively of freights, is preferable as the most convenient and the most likely to produce exactly the kind of goods required. This will be acknowledged by the buyers of farm machines and implements in the North-West.

It has been proposed that rather than succumb to the force of nature, and allow Canada to secure her destined measure of prosperity by trading with her own continent, England should put back the shadow on the dial of economical history, institute an Imperial Zollverein, and restore to the Colonies their former protection against the foreigner in her market. It is hardly necessary to discuss a policy in which Great Britain would have to take the initiative, and which no British statesman has shown the slightest disposition to embrace. The trade, both of imports and exports, of England with the Colonies was, in 1889, £187,000,000; her total trade in the same year with foreign countries was £554,000,000. Is it likely that she will sacrifice a trade of £554,000,000 sterling to a trade of £187,000,000 sterling? The framers of an Imperial Zollverein, moreover, would have some lively work in reconciling the tendencies of strong Protectionist Colonies, such as Victoria and Canada, with the free trade tendencies of Great Britain and New South Wales. The Conservative Prime Minister of England, if he has been correctly reported, holds that the adoption of Protection, on which the Imperialists of Canada insist as a condition of any arrangement, would in England kindle a civil war.

The Canadian Government shows its sense of the situation and of the real effect of its policy by trying to open up new markets in distant countries, in the West Indies, in Brazil, in the Argentine Republic, in France, in Spain, in Australia—in the Moon. It thus hopes to stay the craving of Canadian commerce and industry for their natural market. It has been compared to the father who told his boy that he could not be taken to the circus, but that if he was good he should be taken to see his grandmother's tomb. If the Canadian manufacturer, as the Protectionists aver, is unable to compete in his own market with the American, how can he compete with him in the markets of other countries?

It may safely be said that all the natural interests in Canada, the farming interest—which is much the greatest of all—the lumber interest, the mining interest, and the shipping interest, would vote for a measure which would admit them freely to the American market. On the other side are only the protected manufacturers. But the protected manufacturers are strongly organised, whereas the other interests, notably the farmers', are comparatively unorganised; so that, as was often said in the case of the United States, the fight between Protection and Free Trade is a fight between an army and a mob. The Protectionists have a firm hold upon the present Government, the existence of which is completely bound up with their system, and which looks to them largely for its election fund. It has, however, been already said that they are the hothouse industries which are alarmed. Of the Canadian manufacturers who feel that their business is natural and has a sound basis not a few avow themselves ready for an open market. They would have in some cases to put their production on a new footing, making fewer articles and on a larger scale, but, this being done, they do not fear the competition. They would still have the advantage of somewhat cheaper labour. Sir George Stephen, than whom there can be no higher authority, in a circular addressed in 1875 to the heads of the woollen trade, with which he was then connected, said that if Canada could have free interchange with the United States of all products, whether natural or manufactured, she "would become the Lancashire of the continent and increase in wealth and population to a degree that could hardly be imagined." That some of the weaker houses might suffer is acknowledged, and is to be lamented. All possible consideration is due to those whom Parliament has encouraged to invest. But the whole community cannot be allowed to suffer, nor can commerce and industry be kept for ever on an unsound basis, for the sake of a few. Besides, it will be mercy to shut the door of unsound investment. But this is the bane of the Protectionist policy: when its unwisdom appears, you can hardly draw back from it without doing injury to artificial industries which it has created, and those engaged in them. Not that the artisans will suffer. For them the expansion of natural industries would furnish fresh employment, if not in Canada in the United States, to which they pass with little hesitation when the labour market invites.

Canadian are told, to scare them from Commercial Union, that if the tariff wall were out of the way they would become "hewers of wood and drawers of water for the Yankees." Hewers of wood for the Yankees they are already to their own great profit. It is not obvious why the producer of raw materials should be deemed so much beneath the factory hand; perhaps looking to the effect of manufactures on national character in England we might think that a nation would be wise in contenting itself with so much of factory life as nature had allotted it. Whatever yields most wealth will raise highest the condition of the people, their standard of living, and their general civilisation. Another bugbear is the fear that Canadian cities will be swallowed up by New York, though the cities of the State of New York itself, Buffalo, Rochester, Syracuse, Oswego, and even Albany, which is within four hours' run of New York, are growing all the time. These vague alarms remind us of those raised on commercial grounds by the opponents of the union between England and Scotland. The English were told that their wealth would be devoured by the hungry Scots, the Scotch were told that they would become commercial slaves to the wealthy English, and "with their grain spoiling on their hands, stand cursing the day of their birth, dreading the expense of their burial." The able and eloquent Lord Belhaven formally paused in the middle of his speech that he might shed a tear over the approaching ruin of his country which he foresaw in a vision of woe. Lord Marchmont in reply said that he thought a short answer would suffice. "Behold, he dreamed; but, lo, when he awoke, behold, it was a dream." The reality was what the Duke of Argyll in his work on Scotland calls "The Burst of Industry." It was the works and warehouses of Glasgow, the shipbuilding yards of the Clyde, and the farms of the Lothians.

To make up for the dearth of economical arguments against Reciprocity its opponents appeal to Loyalty and the Old Flag. "Discriminate against the Mother Country! Never!" So with uplifted hands and eyes cry Protectionists who are running to Ottawa to get higher duties laid on British goods, and would not be sorry to shut the gate, if they could, against British importation altogether. Canada does already discriminate against Great Britain, if not on any specific article, on the aggregate trade. It has been shown that she collects about four per cent more in the aggregate on British than on American goods, and admits more American than British products free. When the privileges enjoyed by the Colonies in the British market were withdrawn and the commercial unity of the Empire was broken up, notice was in effect given to each member of the Empire to do the best that it could for itself under its own circumstances. The circumstances of Canada are those of a country commercially bound up with another country much larger than itself and with a high tariff. It is surely too much to expect that all Canada shall remain in a state of commercial atrophy for the sake of a few exporting houses in Great Britain. The British people themselves would never be brought to make such a sacrifice. The discrimination would not, like the duties imposed by Canadian Protectionists on British goods, be directed against British commerce; it would be merely, like the equalisation of excise, a necessity incidental to an arrangement for the benefit of Canada with the United States; so that no breach of good feeling would be involved. Not a penny would be taken from the British Crown. Nor would England be really a loser; she would gain by the enhanced value of her Canadian investments more than she would lose by the reduction of her exports.

It is further alleged that Commercial Union would be Annexation in disguise. When railways were introduced it was thought that a gauge uniform with the American would be annexation in disguise and a difference of gauge was insisted on accordingly. Is there a natural tendency on the part of Canada to political union? If there is, increased intercourse of any kind, whether locomotive or commercial, will no doubt help it; but nothing can help it more than the fusion of population by the exodus which the separatist policy keeps up. The enemies of Reciprocity forget that they are themselves the most active of annexationists, if not in regard to the Canadian territory, in regard to the Canadian people. Canada would be as much as ever mistress of her own political destinies, nor could any step towards political union be taken without the free vote of her citizens. If her nationality is sound what does she require more? That would be a weak nationality indeed which should depend on a Customs line. The German Zollverein, which is pointed out as a warning example, would never have unified Germany or tended much to her unification had not she already been a nation, though in a state of political disruption. Zollvereins are now, it seems, being proposed between other communities of Central Europe without any idea of altering political relations. If the reciprocity in natural products enjoyed under the Elgin treaty did not impair Canada's independence, why should reciprocity in manufactures destroy it? Not only did the Elgin treaty not impair independence but it put an end to the movement in favour of annexation, which commercial distress had generated, and which had led to the Annexationist manifesto of

1849. In entering into any contract, the parties, whether nations or men, must give up their independence to the extent for which they covenant: in no other sense would a commercial treaty, however extensive, if freely made on both sides, be on either side a surrender of independence. Dependent on the Americans for her winter ports Canada already is, and large branches of her railway system are on their soil and in their power. Americans who desire immediate Annexation are always against Commercial Union.

Commercial Union would include mutual participation in the fisheries, in the coasting trade, and in the use of the canals and water-ways. In this it is distinguished from Unrestricted Reciprocity, which would equally involve the complete removal of the Customs line. In regard to the fisheries it would give effect to the policy of British statesmen who desired, as Shelburne and Pitt seem to have desired, that England and her American colonies should not become foreign nations to each other, but divide amicably between them the family heritage. In no other way is the dispute about the fisheries likely to be ended. Even supposing a treaty satisfactory to diplomacy to be made, fishermen are not diplomatists; they are naturally tenacious of the trade by which they live; they will always be prone to deny their rivals the facilities and hospitalities incident to treaty rights, and thus quarrels will be apt to arise.

The main objection to Commercial Union is the difficulty of framing, in concert with the Americans, a uniform seaboard tariff. This difficulty, however, as matters stood before the passing of the M'Kinley Act, was by no means insuperable, the principle of the American and Canadian tariffs being the same, and the difference of rates not very great. The smaller interest in case of disagreement might, as in ordinary bargains, without loss of honour, yield a point. An arrangement would probably have been brought about easily enough by a conference of commercial men, free from the malign influences of party, and unaffected by the appeals to national pride and jealousy which, if the negotiation were in the hands of a party government, the opposite party, in its anxiety to discredit its rivals would be sure to make. Nor need there be any fears of subsequent disturbance of the agreement, from any source, at least, but a quarrel between Great Britain and the United States, such as that by which the Reciprocity Treaty was overturned. Commerce after a little experience would be too sensible of the benefit to renounce it or allow the politicians, whom, by a resolute effort, she can even in the United States control, to wrest it from her. The line of Custom houses built across a continent which nature has forbidden to be divided, once pulled down, will never be built up again. Fresh obstacles and of a serious kind might have been created by the M'Kinley Act. Commercial Unionists did not feel themselves called upon to raise the general questions between Protection and Free Trade, so far as the seaboard tariff was concerned. They confined their aim to the removal of the Customs line across their own continent, which on any rational hypothesis is an evil, unless it would be a good thing to have a Customs line between Pennsylvania and New York, or between York and Lancashire. But there must be limits to the compromise of principle, even for the sake of an immediate advantage so great as Commercial Union will bring. Canada cannot commit treason against civilisation. However, the manifest faults of the measure, combined with the enormous waste of public money incurred in baling out surplus revenue to avert a reform of the tariff, have proved too much for the superstition or the sufferance of the American people. Symptoms of a change of opinion had even before appeared. At the last Presidential election, Mr. Cleveland was defeated more by party than by protection, and more by the manufacturers' money than either, and there was a marked increase of the mechanics' vote in favour of a reduction of the tariff, showing that the fallacious belief in protection as a mode of raising wages was losing its hold. Moreover, protection was being nullified by the extension of its own area, which exposed the protectionist to increased competition, national it might be, but not more welcome to him, in spite of his patriotic professions, than that of the foreigner. New England is now praying for free admission of raw materials. The Republican party in the United States is the war party kept on foot for the sake of maintaining the war tariff in the interest of the protected manufacturers. It has made a desperate effort to retain power and to rivet its policy on the nation by means which have estranged from it the best of its supporters; but in the late elections it has received a signal, and probably decisive, overthrow. What all the preachings of economic science were powerless to effect has been brought about at last by the reduction of the public debt and of the necessity for duties as revenue. A new commercial era has apparently dawned for the United States, and the lead of the United States will be followed in time by the rest of the world.

By the abandonment of the Customs duties on American goods, the Canadian government would lose revenue perhaps to the amount of $7,000,000. This loss might be made up partly by new taxes of such a character as not to press on industry or shackle trade—to begin with, an increase of the excise—partly by economy in subsidies to Provinces, public works undertaken for political purposes, and needless expenditure on legislation and government. To say that such economy is impracticable, would be to admit that a confederation, united by no natural bond of geography, race, language, or commercial interest, can be held together only by corruption.

While these pages are going through the press, Canada is the scene of a general election. Seeing that the tide in favour of free trade with the continent was rising, and, before the constitutional time for the next election came round, might rise to an overwhelming height, the Protectionist Government of Sir John Macdonald has sprung a dissolution on the country, the Governor-General passively lending the prerogative for that purpose. There is not a shadow of constitutional ground for the step, and the reason alleged—that the Government contemplates making overtures on the trade question to the Americans, and cannot do this without a fresh Parliament at its back—was evidently hollow. The Government at first sought to head off the current of opinion and dish the Opposition by declaring for Restricted against Unrestricted Reciprocity. But this strategy has failed of effect, and the appeal on the part of the Government is now to "The Old Flag," with which are coupled "The Old Leader," and "The Old Policy," against American connection. On the issue thus raised the deliverance of the country will be made. The verdict will be greatly confused, not only by local questions, such as that of a Submarine Tunnel for Prince Edward Island, which seems uppermost in the Islander's mind, but by the Equal Right movement against Jesuit and priestly aggression, which is still strong, and cuts across the lines of political and commercial party. The Protected Manufacturers will do their best, and the Government will ply all the engines which it has long had at its command. To ply those engines in Nova Scotia the Canadian High Commissioner has been brought over from England. Nor have party names and shibboleths lost their extraordinary power. Tories, though in favour of Reciprocity, will still vote Tory. To stimulate the enthusiasm of loyalty "Annexation plots" are being discovered, and the discoveries are paraded with all the resources of emotional eloquence and sensation type. What will come out of this chaos is, at the time of our writing, uncertain. But already tidings reach us from the rural districts which seem to show that the farmer, however much he may care for the Old Flag, cares also for his bread. Should the government be beaten or even hard pressed in a pitched battle of its own seeking on the question of relation with the United States, the result will be full of meaning.

5. From Joseph Chamberlain, "Trade and The Empire." *Imperial Union and Tariff Reform: Speeches Delivered from May 15th to Nov. 4 1903 by The Right Hon. Joseph Chamberlain, MP* (London: Grant Richards, 1903)

[This speech by Colonial Secretary Joseph Chamberlain illustrates the kind of rhetoric used by British supporters of Imperialism. Chamberlain was forced to resign from Cabinet when his colleagues refused to endorse his plan for Imperial Preference Trade in the fall of 1903.]

We have something, the importance of which I am trying to impress upon my countrymen, which at present they have not sufficiently appreciated. We have a great reserve in the sons of Britain across the seas (loud cheers). There is nothing we want that they cannot supply; there is nothing we sell that they cannot buy (cheers). One great cause for the prosperity of the United States of America, admitted by every one to be a fact, is that they are a great Empire of over 70,000,000 of people; that the numbers of these people alone, without any assistance from the rest of the world, would ensure a large amount of prosperity. Yes; but the British Empire is even greater than the United States of America. We have a population—it is true, not all a white population—but we have a white population of over 50,000,000 against the 70,000,000—who are not all white, by-the bye—(laughter)— against the 70,000,000 of America. We have, in addition, 350,000,000 or more of people under our protectorate, under our civilisation, sympathising with our rule, grateful for the benefits that we accord to them, and all of them more or less prospective or actual customers of this country (cheers).

In times past we have in some inconceivable way ignored our Colonies. We have not appreciated their greatness. We have not had imagination enough to see that, great as they are, there is no limit to what they may become. We have gone through a time (it is a most significant fact) when the men who advocated Free Trade in this country were at the same time absolutely indifferent to all idea of Empire, and considered the Colonies encumbrances which we should be glad to get rid of. That lasted for thirty years, and in the course of that time we tried the patience of our sons across the seas. We tried hardly their love of us and their devotion to the Mother Country. They began to think that we had no sympathy with their aspirations; that we regarded them as troublesome children and wished to get them out of the house, and therefore that it would be their duty to break with the sentiment which would otherwise have held us together; that it would be their duty to fend for themselves, and to leave out of account everything which concerned the Empire of which they formed a part. That was not their fault; that was our fault, the result of our policy. Although we have done our best to correct that impression, although there is not a man living who thinks, or, if there is one who thinks, there is not one who dares to say, that he would wish to get rid of the Colonies, that he does not desire their closer union with us, yet we have a good deal to make up, for we have to show that, whereas at one time we or our ancestors advocated separation, we are now prepared to do all that in reason can be asked of us in order to promote a greater and a closer union (loud cheers).

The Colonies are no longer in their infancy. They are growing rapidly to a vigorous manhood. Now is the time—the last time—that you can bind them closer to you. If now you disregard their aspirations and wishes, if when they make you an offer not specially in their interests, but in the interests of the Empire of which we are all a portion, you reject this offer or treat it with scorn, you may do an injury which will be irreparable; and, whatever you yourselves may feel in after life, be sure that your descendants will scorn and denounce the cowardly and selfish decision which you will have adopted (cheers). We can if we will make the empire mutually supporting. We can make it one for defence, one for common aid and assistance. We are face to face at this time with complications in which we may find ourselves alone. We have to face the envy of other people who have noted our wonderful success, although I do not think it has ever done them any harm. We have to face their envy, their jealousy, their desire, perhaps, to share the wealth which they think us to possess. I am not afraid. We shall be isolated. Yes; but our isolation will be splendid one if we are fortified, if this country is buttressed by the affection and love of its kinsmen, those sons of Britain throughout the world—(cheers)—and we shall rest secure if we continue to enjoy the affection of all our children.

When I was in South Africa (loud cheers) nothing was more inspiring, nothing more encouraging, to a Briton than to find how the men who had either themselves come from our shores or were the descendants of those who had, still retained the old traditions, still remembered that their forefathers were buried in our churchyards, that they spoke a common language, that they were under a common flag, still in their hearts desired to be remembered above all as British subjects, equally entitled with us to a part in the great Empire which they, as well as we, have contributed to make (cheers). The sentiment is there powerful, vivifying, influential for good. I did not hesitate, however, to preach to them that it was not enough to shout for Empire, that it was not enough to bear this sentiment in their hearts, but that they and we alike must be content to make a common sacrifice, if that were necessary in order to secure the common good (cheers).

To my appeal they rose (renewed cheers). And I cannot believe that here in this country, in the Mother Country, their enthusiasm will not find an echo (cheers). They felt, as I felt, and as you feel, that all history is the history of States once powerful and then decaying. Is Britain to be numbered among the decaying States? Is all the glory of the past to be forgotten? Are we to prove ourselves unregenerate sons of the forefathers who left us so glorious an inheritance? Are the efforts of all our sons to be frittered away? Are all their sacrifices to be vain? Or are we to take up a new youth as members of a great Empire, which will continue for generation after generation, the strength, the power, and the glory of the British race? (Cheers.)

6. "Hon. Geo. E. Foster Answers Sir Wilfrid Laurier: Speech Delivered at St. Paul's Hall, Toronto, Oct. 13th 1904." Political pamphlet (excerpt, CIHM 78702)

[George Eulas Foster (1847-1931) was Minister of Fisheries under Sir John A. Macdonald and subsequently Finance Minister and Trade Minister in a number of Conservative governments between the years 1885 and 1921. He was an accomplished orator and politician, as illustrated in this excerpt in which he ridicules Laurier's economic policies.]

The Good Time at Massey Hall[1]

Now, Mr. Chairman, they had over at Massey Hall last night, as the Boston girl would say, an "elegant" time. (Laughter.) I don't think any happier lot of people seemingly ever got together in any one place before, if you have regard to the demonstrations, to the speeches, and to the reports in the *Globe* of this morning. But there is this thing to be said, they had an equally good time in 1896; they had an equally good time in 1891; and in 1891 and in 1896 the result in the City of Toronto was about the same—they had a good time, but the Conservatives got the votes. (Cheers.) Now, the people of Toronto are a kindly people; they like to give a man a good reception, take him in—in a hospitable kind of way. (Laughter.) They like to hear a man use mellifluous language, be it even somewhat rhetorical, and they have a certain admiration for a picturesque figure. (Laughter.) They enjoy all that, and give a hearty reception to one who gives them all that, but when it comes right down to business the Toronto people are level-headed—(hear, hear)—they size up the position and they make up their minds upon it sensibly and pretty thoroughly. (Hear, hear.) That is the reason why Sir Wilfrid always has had, and always will have, a good reception in the City of Toronto, and that is why, after it is over, the business men in the City of Toronto will go about their own work in their own way without paying very much attention to what he has said. (Hear, hear and laughter.) There is another reason for this.

The Man of Fads

In 1891 and in 1896 Sir Wilfrid Laurier was just as eloquent on the boards at Massey Hall. Each time he had a different set of schemes, a different policy, and for each one he was equally eloquent, in 1891 and in 1896. But time passed after 1891, and when it came up to 1896, lo, and behold, the schemes and policies about which he so eloquently spoke in 1891 had been relegated to the background, had been found impracticable, and had been left with the wreckage on the shore.

---

1 Massey Hall is a four-thousand seat concert hall on Shuter Street in Toronto, built in 1894.

The Unrestricted Reciprocity Fad

In 1891 he stood upon the platform at Massey Hall and argued for a brand-new policy. You remember what it was. It was unrestricted trade with the United States of America, coupled with discrimination against the goods and imports from Great Britain and the British colonies. (Hear, hear.) That was the flag under which he fought; that was the flag that he nailed to the masthead. That is the flag in the advocacy of which he declared that we never could be reasonably prosperous until we had such a treaty with the United States of America; while Sir Richard Cartwright, his lieutenant, declared that the trade with the United States was worth to us more than the trade of all other countries put together, and that we could never work out our commercial salvation until we had unrestricted reciprocity with the United States of America. Now, he could not be more eloquent last night in support of his new scheme than he was in 1891 in support of the then scheme. He met with a fine reception in Toronto in 1891 because of his eloquence. He was given the same last night. But the people do not forget that the thing which he said was all-important and absolutely right in 1891, he and his whole party had been obliged to abandon within five short years. (Cheers.) Therefore it is that the electors of the City of Toronto, though they listen with pleasure, make up their minds in the light of facts that become patent as time rolls round.

The 1896 Platform

In 1896 he appeared again; again he was most rhetorical; again he was picturesque in his language, eloquent in his periods. He had another plan and policy then. What was it? He pleaded with the electors of Toronto to put him into power so that he might relieve the terrible burden of taxation that was weighing down this people, and, as Sir Richard Cartwright remarked, "bleeding the people of this country white." He lifted up his eloquent voice in tremendous strength and vehemence against the outrageous expenditures of this country, and he declared, without reservation, that if he were put in power he would make those expenditures from three to five millions less. He said there was something this country needed and might have, and that he was the very man who could get it if he were put in power. What was that?

Preferential trade relations with Great Britain. Now, I think that is so important I am going to read you exactly what he said in 1896, at London, Ont., and he repeated the substance of it in Toronto:

> Now, the statesmen of Great Britain have thought that the Governments of the colonies have come to a time when a new step can be taken in their development. What is that? That there should be a commercial agreement between England and the colonies. That practical statesman, Mr. Joseph Chamberlain, has come to the conclusion that the time has come when it is possible to have within the bounds of the Empire a new step taken which will give to the colonies in England a preference for their products over the products of other nations.

That is what it was. No one-sided preference; it was a preference in England for the goods of the colonies. And he says:

> What would the possibilities of such a step be if it were taken? We sell our goods in England; we send our wheat, our butter, our cheese, all our natural products, but there we have to compete with similar products from the United States, from Russia, and from other nations. Just see what an advantage it would be to Canada if the wheat, cheese and butter which we would send to England should be met in England with a preference over other products of other nations. The possibilities are immense. England does not expect that we should take her own system of free trade, such as she has it; but I lay it before you that the thing the English people would expect in return is that instead of the principle of protection, we should adopt a form of revenue tariff. Those are the conditions on which we could have that boom.

And then he says:

> My hope is—nay, my conviction is, that on the 23rd of June the Liberal party will be at the head of the polls. Then it will be the Liberal party, with its policy of revenue tariff, that will send commissioners to London to arrange for a basis of preferential trade.

Now, he advocated that with the same rhetorical and picturesque eloquence with which he advocated his new policy, his new child, last night at Massey Hall. Well, sir, he was elected. They had a session of Parliament.

Mutual Preference Performance

They put through a 12 1/2 per cent. preference for British goods in this country. Then he sailed for Great Britain, and every man's ear was open to hear, and every man's eye was fixed to see Sir Wilfrid when he arrived in England to fulfil the pledge he made the people here, namely, arrange for a basis of preferential trade. He landed in Liverpool. His first meeting was in Liverpool, and the first speech that he made upon this matter was as follows:

> I claim for the present Government of Canada that they have passed a resolution by which the products of Great Britain are admitted on the rate of their tariff at 12 1/2 per cent., next year at 25 per cent, reduction. This we have done, not asking any compensation. There is a class of our fellow-citizens who ask that all such concessions should be made for a quid pro quo. The Canadian Government has ignored all such sentiments. We have done it because we owe a debt of gratitude to Great Britain. We have done it because it is no intention of ours to disturb in any way the system of free trade, which has done so much for England. What we give by our tariff, we give you in gratitude for the splendid freedom under which we are prospering. It is a free gift. We ask no compensation. Protection has been the curse of Canada, and we would not wish you and we would not see you come under its baneful influence, for what weakens you must weaken us.

In 1896 they had heard his declarations in Massey Hall. There were his promises; here was his performance. Now, when he spoke to an audience of Toronto people last night, they remembered that in 1896 he was just as thoroughly in earnest about these questions of taxation, of expenditure, of mutual preferential trade, and of the expurgation of every vestige of protection from our tariff as he was last night with reference to his Grand Trunk Pacific scheme. They knew perfectly well how he acted on these since 1896, and as they listened to him last night they said: "Oh, this is a new thing to canvass with, that's all; it will go just as far but no further than his 1891 and his 1896 propaganda went; it is a platform to get in on, but not to stand on after he has got in." (Cheers.)

Appendix C: Selected Reviews of The Imperialist

1. Unsigned. "Canada and Imperial Policy." *New York Times*, 5 March 1904

Mrs. Cotes's[1] new book, which is certainly clever, gives the effect of a sort of Canadian "Cranford"[2] with projections into the field of English imperial politics. The picture of society in the small Canadian town of Elgin, and in the still narrower fold of the Knox Presbyterian Church of that town, is not presented at large, rather in bits and suggestions, but it is presented effectively none the less. The attitude of the ladies of Elgin toward the town, the world, and the proprieties is a thing which the reader can feel fairly bristling from the pages which have to deal with them. Mrs. Cotes, who is Canadian herself, has a humorous eye for provincial marks, and a pleasing fashion of comment on the side. And she is especially happy in the conception she has formed and conveyed of Mrs. Murchison, a lady cast as the mother of several persons who figure conspicuously in the story. It seems to us that Mrs. Murchison is the most natural and delightful mother that we have encountered between the covers of a novel in a long time. There's a queer combination of a certain shrewd humorous drift of mind with an absolutely literal lack of humor in other directions which seems to be the mark of the best kind of mother-women—devoted sensible, proud of their children, but quite aware of the faults of these prodigies. That's a very complex character, as you can see—but Mrs. Murchison seems to come very near filling the bill. It is evident anyhow that Mrs. Cotes has the knack of characterization; there are two studies of parsons in the book, each as different as possible from the other, but both perfectly parson-like, while John Murchison, the husband of the

---

1 Soon after her marriage in 1890, Duncan began to publish her books under both her married and maiden names, as "Mrs. Everard Cotes (Sara Jeanette Duncan)." Contemporary book reviewers usually referred to her as "Mrs. Cotes," the name she used in her private life as well.
2 A novel by Elizabeth Gaskell (1810-65) about small town life in England, published in 1853.

mother-woman mentioned, gives the reader a distinct impression of reality—quiet strength and sound sense in a man of solid flesh and warm blood. For the younger people, these, of course, have love affairs. There are two such affairs for either taste—one lucky, one unlucky—and, in connection several rather shrewd bits of observation of the ways of lover-folk.

As for the other side of the book, that which relates to politics, one is eager to suspect that it is designed to an elaborate satire on the Imperial Zollverein and all that. Yet one cannot be sure how much real enthusiasm for the English imperial idea is hidden in the appearance of satire. One cannot quite be sure even that Mrs. Cotes herself knows at times whether she is preaching Mr. Joseph Chamberlain's doctrine or laughing at it. Mr. Chamberlain, by the way, is figured, afar off, under the name of "Wallingham," and always, it appears, admiringly considered. The author makes her young hero, at all events, a red-hot imperialist, and she has him speak on the question and argue for it in and out of season, and at lengths which tempt the reader to skip. Not that she doesn't present the arguments rather well, and not that she doesn't present at the next opportunity the arguments on the other side equally well—but a story is—a story. It is to be observed that the practical politicians who try to use the young imperialist's enthusiasm for party ends are not themselves convinced imperialists. They rather admire the young man—but they are forced to let him go as an unmanageable political quantity. He is, after all, a young man of strict limitations conceivable enough, considering his youth and upbringing, but not the sort of man for a career as a leader of other men. The truth is that Mrs. Cotes's reputation for grasp of the essentials in humanity had best not rest on her "Imperialist" in his own person. She draws better women and parsons that she does men. Which is natural enough. Her story, for all that, is good reading. Barring the politics, which is interesting, but only so-so, as might be expected, it is a story very far above the average of stories—perhaps the most worth while which has come out in some time.

2. Unsigned. *The Imperialist. Times Literary Supplement*, 22 April 1904

It were scarcely possible to fall a longer interval than the distance between "Love Among the Ruins" and *The Imperialist*, by Sara Jeannette Duncan (Constable, 6s.). The one book is not of to-day or yesterday, the other nothing if not written off the pages of the current newspaper. The crusade of *The Imperialist* is preferential tariffs; allusions to such occurrences as the Cunard line and the Atlantic combination are the tissue of the narrative; Mr. Parkin and Mr. Goldwin Smith appear in their naked titles; Mr. Chamberlain is thinly disguised as Wallingham; the development of the plot is suggested by recent movements among political parties in Canada; pages without the benefit even of a paragraph are devoted to discussions as straight to the fiscal point as the pamphlets of the Tariff Reform League. It may be proof of the width and depth of the new creed that the poets, and now the novelists, must preach it, and there is no reason why preferential trade should not back an essay in fiction as well as the Reform Bill. The Imperialist himself at the first introduction seemed an adequate crusader, and of the right quality; no Union Jackass, blatant and heavy, but a good example of the Canadian—"straight," after the favourite Canadian superlative of praise, and simple. But he proved no Lothair, capable of carrying a great political or religious theme; and even Mr. Chamberlain would hardly wish Mrs. Cotes to quash her habile capacity for the small humours of life under a load of political essay-writing. Politics are not merely an atmosphere, an environment, an accident of life. A particular Bill, and nothing but the Bill, is discussed, and it would be unfair to review the work except as a preferential pamphlet. It is not a bad pamphlet; but one may hope that the moral, which is made very distinct, is not true—that patriotism is not yet enough advanced in England or in Canada to carry through an imperial scheme. Even the young lady is symbolic, and throws over the Imperialist at the very moment when his party does the same. Until the Imperialism dominated it, the theme promised well. The setting demands a good romance. Those good Scotch settlers, many of them staunch Presbyterians, who form so large a part of some of the townships in Ontario, and the U.E. loyalists, still very "stark to traitors" to the imperial sentiment; the busy jealousy of the United States and the strengthened pride in the superiority of Canadian liberty; the keenness, even the corruption, of the elections are new and good material ready to the hand of any novelist of knowledge. Certainly the material is much too good to be used as a vehicle for a fiscal sermon, and to be left behind as soon as the hero is well set on his hobby-horse. The only genuine bit of romance is parallel to the central theme, and so never meets it: and the Imperialist's love affair, in which even he takes a mild and subsidiary interest, is finished off perfunctorily, just to leave no end showing.

3. Unsigned. *The Imperialist*. *The Spectator*, 23 April 1904

(A. Constable and Co. 6s.)—The average reader about halfway through *The Imperialist* will experience all the indignant feelings of the child who finds a powder concealed in a proffered spoonful of jam. Under the disguise of an innocent and lively modern novel, Mrs. Cotes has actually had the perfidy to entice her readers into perusing a fiscal pamphlet. Pages of what is called "the Imperial argument" for the widest development of Mr. Chamberlain's scheme will be found in her story; and the weary political economist who has taken it up for a little rest and oblivion from the problem which is constantly in his mind will find himself most treacherously betrayed. The book gives otherwise an interesting picture of life in modern Canada, though Mrs. Cotes is rather a long time getting her story under way. For about the first hundred pages the reader feels that each new chapter breaks fresh ground, and the result is a little fatiguing. But until the fiscal chapters are reached, Mrs. Cotes charm of writing triumphs over the rather wearisome nature of her materials, and the reader is upheld by the hope of better things later in the book. How that hope is belied has been indicated above.

4. Mary K. Ford,[1] "The Novel of the Month: Mrs. Cotes' *The Imperialist*." *Current Literature*, April 1904

Mrs. Everard Cotes' books, though comparatively few in number, cover a wide expanse of territory, the United States, London, India, and Canada all being in turn the scene of what we feel have been her personal experiences.

In *The Imperialist*, her last book, she has taken for her subject the question that is just now agitating all classes in England, and, placing the scene of her story in Canada, has given us a view of the case from the Colonial standpoint as seen by a set of business-like people, members of a community where everyone is engaged

1 Mary Kingman Ford (1856-1934), author of *Woman's Progress, a Comparison of Centuries* (1909), and reviewer for *The Bookman* and *Vanity Fair*.

in earning a living, and where the question "How will it affect us personally?" is of more importance than a wide view of the British Empire.

The story hangs upon the career of Lorne Murchison, who, after passing through the law school at Toronto with honor, returns to his native town of Elgin, Ontario, to practise his profession. He attracts the attention of one Cruikshank, the greatest criminal lawyer of the province. A deputation from the Canadian Chambers of Commerce is about going to England to press for the encouragement of improved communications within the Empire. Cruikshank is at the head of it, and through him Lorne is asked to become its secretary. He accepts, and his visit to London confirms his view as to the relations of the colonies and the home government. He becomes a strong Imperialist, and takes back to Canada a vivid realization of the great Empire of which his country is a part, and an impatience with those who, while acknowledging the grandeur of the idea, do not see their way to foregoing, for its sake, any present advantage.

Soon after Lorne's return, the Liberal member for South Fox is obliged to give up his seat in the Canadian House of Commons; Lorne is asked to stand, and is elected by a narrow majority. Charges of bribery are made on both sides, an investigation demanded, and a new election is ordered. During the campaign Lorne has spoken frankly on the matter so near his heart, Imperialism, the consolidating into one great power of England and her colonies, and his desire to see a willingness on the part of the latter to forego immediate commercial advantages to further that end. But by this time the business men of the county have come to the conclusion that such a wide view of the Empire is incompatible with their private interests, and so, knowing that Lorne is committed to an Imperialist policy, they realize that he can never carry the second election, and he is asked to resign, for the safety of his party. This he does, disappointed in his hopes and in his countrymen; he has an illness, and upon his recovery accepts a partnership with Mr. Cruikshank, and we are left with the hope that the future may still hold something for him, politically.

Two love stories run through the book: the unfortunate one of Lorne Murchison and Dora Milburn, and the happier one of Lorne's sister and the young minister.

Elgin was settled by the Scotch, and Mrs. Cotes, in describing the little town and its people, has skilfully preserved a Scotch atmosphere, though one somewhat diluted by transplanting; and as no Scotch story can be written without the introduction of a minister, she has portrayed two excellent ones.

Dr. Drummond, the minister of Knox Church, is perhaps the best character in the book, and represents a minister of the old school; one who has personal knowledge of each member of his flock, and who watches assiduously over their church-going. Mrs. Cotes describes the congregation in a few words:

A pew-holder had a distinct status, an 'adherent' enjoyed friendly consideration, especially if he adhered faithfully; and stray attendants from other congregations were treated with punctilious hospitality, places being found for them in the Old Testament, as if they could hardly be expected to discover such things for themselves.

The feeling of Canada for England is touched upon in a few words that would repay the study of the British politician who counts upon an intense affection among Colonials for the mother country. After speaking of the real love of the people for the throne, and their sentiment of affection for the reigning house, Mrs. Cotes goes on to say: "The fall of a British Government would hardly fail to excite comment; and the retirement of a Prime Minister would induce both the Mercury and Express to publish a biographical sketch of him considerably shorter than the leader embodying the editor's views as to who should get the electric-light contract."

The visit of the delegation to London gives Mrs. Cotes an opportunity of describing how the business methods of the older civilization strike the energetic Colonials.

The unready conception of things, the political concentration upon parish affairs, the cumbrous social machinery, oppressed them with its dull anachronism in a marching world.

Lorne meets a young Englishman, Alfred Hesketh, who has been well educated, has a little money of his own, and is anxious for occupation, but can find no opening. This was something new to Lorne. "Affluence and age he knew, in honorable retirement; poverty and youth he knew, embarked in the struggle; indolence and youth he also knew, as it cumbered the ground; but youth and a competence, equipped with education, industry, and vigor, searching vainly in fields empty of opportunity, was to him a new spectacle."

To Lorne, the absorption of the English in trifles is more surprising that anything else. "Pick up a paper," he says, "at the
moment when things are being done, mind, all over the world,
done against them—when their shipping is being captured, and
their industries destroyed: and their goods undersold beneath
their very noses—and the thing they want to know is—'Why are
the Swallows Late?' I read it myself in a ha'penny morning paper,
too, that they think rather dangerously go-ahead—a whole column, leaded, to inquire what's the matter with the swallows. The
Times the same week had a useful leader on Alterations in the
Church Service, and a special contribution on Prayers for the
Dead. Lord, they need'em!"

Alfred Hesketh comes to Elgin to look about him with a view
to settling there, and the author has described admirably, and
without commonplace exaggeration, the effect he produces upon
the Canadian community with its firm conviction of England's
superiority to the provinces and his preconceived ideas of Colonial ways and institutions.

His introduction to Lorne's father takes place in Mr. Murchison's hardware shop, and being his first intimation that the older
man is "in trade," it is a blow to him which he manfully tries to
conceal. When Lorne is stumping the country before election,
Hesketh offers help, and delivers a speech that would have been
proper in England, but is most unsuitable in Canada. His attitude
of lofty appreciation of the virtues of England's colonists, the
assurance, that he had always considered the colonies of the highest value, whatever others might think, his allusion to the "rough,
unpolished exterior" of the Colonials, and his frequent quotations
of titled politicians are all listened to in silence, until one old man
suddenly asks, "Had ye no friends among the commoners?" and
the roars of laughter which greet this question, show the sense of
the meeting. As is natural, the incident does not end there.

A week later Mr. Hesketh was concernedly accosted in Main
Street by a boy on a bicycle:

"Say, mister how's the dook?"

"What duke?" asked Hesketh, puzzled.

"Oh, any dook," responded the boy, and bicycled cheerfully
away.

Upon the political issue that gives its name to the book, the
average reader will hardly be able to give an opinion. Mrs. Cotes
seems to think that to Canadians generally, the question "How
will this affect us personally?" will be more forcible than the ques-

tion of how it will affect the British Empire. As to the merits of the book as a story there need be but one opinion. In the drawing of character, this is the best thing that Mrs. Cotes has done for some time. Dr. Drummond, the Murchisons, Hugh Finlay, Alfred Hesketh—all these characters, though entirely different, are so clearly depicted, without exaggeration and with such quiet humor, that the social atmosphere of Elgin is before us as we read, as distinct, though not as delicate, as that of "Cranford."

5. J[ean] G[raham],[1] *The Imperialist. Saturday Night*, 4 June 1904

It cannot be said that Mrs. Everard Cotes has been without honor among her own people. Her *Globe* articles, signed "Garth Grafton," excited general interest, and when, as Sara Jeannette Duncan, she gave us *A Social Departure*, Canadians felt proud of "a Brantford girl" who had written a book. Since those days she has traveled far, has seen many parts of the Empire, and now regards India as her home. But she will probably be known to the end of the chapter among her Canadian friends as a Brantford girl, and no doubt will be content with the description, since she has not forgotten her Ontario home, and Brantford is no mean city.

Her latest book, *The Imperialist*, appeared as a serial in the Toronto *News*, but there are many who would consider the reading of a serial heavy punishment, and therefore waited for the full publication. Bound in bright red, with the Canadian coat-of-arms patriotically adorning the cover, *The Imperialist*, with its 472 pages of comfortable, large type, is not a book to be taken in hand lightly or undiscerningly. The English critic or the United States reviewer may say what he likes about the book, but we know, before we have finished the first chapter, that it is the very life of our people. It is not "about" us or "concerning" us, but here is an Ontario town, with its every-day trials and triumphs, its local ambitions, and its national significance. Elgin, the town described, is said to be Brantford, but it might be Guelph or

---

1   Jean Graham was women's editor of *Saturday Night* magazine, and later editor of the *Canadian Home Journal*. See Marjory Lang, *The Women who Made the News: Female Journalists in Canada 1880-1945* (Montreal: McGill-Queen's UP, 1999) for more information.

Stratford or Goderich. We all know the Murchisons, the family circle into which Mrs. Cotes so warmly welcomes us; in fact, I know I have had tea at the Murchisons' where "the chicken salad gleamed at one end of the table and the scalloped oysters smoked delicious at the other. Lorne had charge of the cold tongue and Advena was entrusted with the pickled pears."

The Imperialist is not a book to be read in a hammock on a summer afternoon, for it is to be taken seriously, although the charge of dullness may not for a moment be preferred against it. The first chapter introduces us to the town of Elgin and the Murchison household on the twenty-fourth of May, and there isn't a "grownup" in the Province of Ontario whose heart will not recognize the scene. John Murchison is a merchant "in the line of hardware," and, having been born in Scotland, is fast making his way, and is regarded by Dr. Drummond as a pillar of Knox Church. There are six small Murchisons, who are prepared to keep the day right royally, for Elgin is a town which does the proper thing by the sovereign. "Here it was a real holiday, that woke you with bells and cannon—who has forgotten the time the ancient piece of ordnance in 'the Square' blew out all the windows in the Methodist Church?—and went on with squibs and crackers till you didn't know where to step on the sidewalks, and ended up splendidly with rockets and fire-balloons and drunken Indians vociferous on their way to the lock-up." The description of the ice-cream parlor at Snow's is a faithful touch. "Gallantry exacted ten-cent dishes, but for young ladies alone, or family parties, Mrs. Snow would bring five-cent quantities almost without asking, and for very small boys one dish and the requisite number of spoons."

The names of the youthful Murchisons are somewhat significant. The girls are Abby, Advena and Stella, while the boys express both loyalty and political conviction. Lorne's name explains itself. The baptism of the youngest boy is thus described: "Sonorously Dr. Drummond said it: 'Oliver Mowat, I baptize thee in the Name of the Father—' The compliment should have all the impressiveness the rite could give it, while the Murchison brothers and sisters, a-row in the family pew, stood on one foot with excitement as to how Oliver Mowat would take the drops that defined him. The verdict was, on the way home, that he behaved splendidly. Alexander Mackenzie, the year before, had roared." So, we find Elgin and the Murchisons—a prosperous young town and a typical Canadian family with whom it is impossible not to feel at home.

Dr. Drummond, the pastor at Knox Church, is quite worthy of a place beside Ian MacLaren's divines.[1] But there is a difference—the difference that comes of life in a new land among a young people. It is well defined in the attitude of the minister and John Murchison. "They had gone the length of their tether, but the tether was always there. Thus, before a congregation that always stood in the early days, had the minister every Sunday morning for thirty years besought the Almighty, with ardor and humility, on behalf of the Royal Family. It came in the long prayer, about the middle. Not in the perfunctory words of ritual, but in the language of his choice, which varied according to what he believed to be the spiritual needs of the reigning House, and was at one period, touching certain of its members, extremely candid. The General Assembly of the Church of Scotland—was it ever forgotten once? And even the Prime Minister, 'and those who sit in council with him,' with just a hint of extra commendation if it happened to be Mr. Gladstone. The minister of Knox Church, Elgin, Ontario, Canada, kept his eye on them all."

The place of Canada in the British fabric puzzles both English and United States visitors when, from season to season, they condescendingly drop in upon us and make remarks concerning our climate and our politics. Mrs. Cotes has most clearly and even humorously set forth our sentiments without detracting from the individual interests in the novel. The title leads one to expect a political atmosphere, but how could a novel of Ontario affairs be written without hauling in politics? We are a people given to such mild dissipation as is occasioned by a provincial election or a party picnic, and Elgin is not behind the rest of the country in its political ardor. Lorne Murchison is the alert young man who emerges as the "hero" of the novel, although such a term seems too dramatic for so modern and practical a young man. Yet Lorne has his day-dreams. He is the "smart boy" of the town, who has done well at the Collegiate Institute, passed at the top in the Law School's examination, has won local fame by a well-conducted case, and is finally induced to "run for Parliament." In the meantime, Lorne has been to England, a country which is he finds both inspiring and discouraging. Wallingham, who is, being interpreted, Mr. Joseph Chamberlain, is the only statesman at "Home" who has

---

1 Ian MacLaren was the pseudonym of John Watson (1850-1907), Scottish author of *Beside the Bonnie Briar Bush* (1894) and other works of fiction of the "Kailyard" school.

any understanding of the place and importance of the colonies, who has, in fact, grasped the idea that there is a tide in the affairs of the Empire which, taken at the flood, may lead on to something like a British Confederacy. The optimism and crudity of the Canadian is brought sometimes sadly, sometimes amusingly, into contrast with the pessimism and stolidity of John Bull. Lorne pithily voices his consternation at England's seeming indifference to her threatened commercial supremacy. "I may be mad, but one seems to see in politics over here a lack of definition and purpose, a tendency to cling to the abstract and to precedent—'the mainstay of the mandarin' one of the papers calls it: that's a good word—that gives one the feeling that this kingdom is beginning to be aware of some influence stronger that its own. It lies, of course, in the great West, where the corn and cattle grow: and between Winnipeg and Chicago choose quickly, England."

Lorne Murchison is an idealist in both politics and the tender passion, and he comes a sad cropper, both with his party and his lady fair, as many an idealist has done before him. He runs for South Fox in the interests of the Liberals, but he forgets local issues in his stump orations to deliver enthusiastic utterances concerning the Empire which are not "the thing" in the eyes and ears of the local Liberals. He is elected by a majority of seventy, but the election is successfully protested and the "pairty" decides that Lorne is not to be their candidate at the bye-election. In truth, the local leaders distrust a young man who has ideals and theories, and who may not prove a good "working politician." In the meantime, Dora Milburn, who had been betrothed to Lorne Murchison, succumbs to the accent and distinction of a young Englishman, and promises to become his wife, without going to the trouble of formally notifying her old love that she is on with the new. Dora is so like Rosamond Vincy of *Middlemarch* memories that one feels like congratulating Lorne on his escape, although that unfortunate young man falls ill and is away in Florida, in a state of convalescence, at the close of the story. But he has already accepted a partnership with a prominent Canadian lawyer, and it is more than likely that the young man will return to the Land of the Maple with a mended heart and a clearer head for the game of politics.

The other members of the Murchison family are quite subordinate in interest. Oliver Mowat and Alexander Mackenzie, in spite of the names bestowed upon them in baptism, are ordinary young people. Abby is married at an early age to Dr. Harry

Johnson, and accompanies her husband to the Church of England, which is correct conduct on the part of a wife, but poor spirit in a Presbyterian.

The comments occasionally dropped on the evolution of Elgin society will be recognized as altogether just and reasonable. "The 'nicest' of the young men were in the banks. Others might be more substantial, but there was an allure about a young man in a bank as difficult to define as to resist. To say of a certain party-giver that she had 'about every bank clerk in town' was to announce the success of her entertainment in ultimate terms." The changes that have come in almost every Canadian town are tersely set forth. "There came a time when the Sheriff's whist club and the Archdeacon's port became a tradition to the oldest inhabitant. Trade flourished, education improved, politics changed. The original dignified group broke, dissolved, scattered.... Their grandsons married the daughters of well-to-do persons who came from the North of Ireland, the east of Scotland, and the Lord knows where.... Any process of blending implies confusion to begin with: we are here at the making of a nation."

The trade distinctions are to be drawn in the following fashion: "Dry goods were held in respect and chemists in comparative esteem: house-furnishings and hardware made an appreciable claim, and quite a leading family was occupied with seed grains. Groceries, on the other hand, were harder to swallow, possibly on account of the apron, though the grocer's apron, being of linen, had several degrees more consideration than the shoemaker's, which was of leather.... Anything 'wholesale' or manufacturing stood, of course, on its own feet; there was nothing ridiculous in molasses, nothing objectionable in a tannery, nothing amusing in soap."

The case of Advena Murchison is the nearest approach to a "problem" of the morbid modern type that we find, but even Advena seems to draw the line at Ibsen and restricts her heart affair to a member of the Presbyterian clergy, and an imported Scot at that. Advena is a sore trial to her eminently practical mother, who is by no means the least interesting person in the household. "Advena would hide in the hayloft with a novel; she would be off by herself in a canoe at six o'clock in the morning; she would go for walks in the rain of windy October twilights and be met kicking the wet leaves in front of her 'in a dream.' No one could dream with impunity in Elgin, except in bed. Mothers of daughters sympathized in good set terms with Mrs. Murchison ... When she took to passing examinations and teaching, Elgin considered that her parents ought to be thankful in the probability that she had escaped some dramatic end." Then there came to Elgin the young parson from Scotland—Hugh Finlay—who was "a great long fellow, with a shock of black hair and deep dreams in his eyes; his head was what people call a type.... He had the brow of a Covenanter and the mouth of Adonais, the flame of religious ardor in his eyes and the composure of perceived philosophy on his lips. He was fettered by an impenetrable shyness." Mrs. Murchison regards with displeasure his visits to the house, and thus expresses her views to her husband: "A great gawk of a fellow, with eyes that always look as if he were in the middle of next week! He brought her a book the last time he came. What do you think the name of it was? The something or other of Plato! Do you call that a natural thing from a young man who is thinking seriously of a girl? Besides, if I know anything about Plato, he was a Greek heathen, and no writer for a Presbyterian minister to go lending around. I'd Plato him to the rightabout, if it was me!"

But Advena gives her schoolma'am heart completely away to the shy and awkward Mr. Finlay, who, however, has a fiancee in Scotland, a most proper person, who is hardly young, and whom he feels it his duty to send for. On a certain stormy night Advena throws herself (a mere accident, of course) into his arms and at his head. She is, indeed, highly unmaidenly, and her mother would be most indignant could she know of Advena's language. However, the young parson remains firm, although the lady falls at his feet in the rain and weeps copiously over his shoes. It is to be hoped that no pious members of Mr. Finlay's congregation "happen along" at that moment. There is a happy outcome, after all, though the reader shall be left to find out how Mr. Finlay's Scottish fiancee is disposed of. How he and Advena, two persons who have Plato in their brains and dreams in their eyes, are going to live on eight hundred dollars a year is a distressing question.

The Imperialist, although rather long and somewhat given to politics, is a thoroughly readable and stimulating book. It is photographic in his fidelity to local conditions and types, while its subtle humor and literary finish set it far above the average novel. Anyone may read it with interest and satisfaction. But to the Canadian, to the Ontarian especially, it means more than any other Canadian story, for it gives with truth and with art a depiction of our own community as it appears in the "pattern and the colors" of the Empire. There is much that its trivial, much that is amusing, and a great deal to be proud of in the Elgins of Ontario—and as Canadians and Imperialists, in the best sense of that abused word, we owe a debt to Mrs Everard Cotes, who has told our story.

6. Unsigned. *The Imperialist*. *Daily News* [Toronto], 4 June 1904

... Nowhere else but in Canada can the book be entirely understood; and anyone who goes without reading it will miss a part of present Canadian life which in its own way is as useful as it is inspiring. Few political novels have been as much in earnest, or as generous and enthusiastic as *The Imperialist*.

Putting the question of Canadian love for English principles and the fiscal problem—which is a great part of *The Imperialist*—to one side, there is still much left in the book to be considered only as imaginative writing. There are many Canadians, of course, who will feel that they have not been brought up precisely in the same way as the Murchisons. But how charming to everyone are the early chapters, written with the unhasting geniality of one who remembers very well. The Queen's Birthday—the Twenty-fourth of May—in Elgin is one of the prettiest, most humorous and touching things that have been written for our own country. For Mr. and Mrs. Murchison—Lorne's father and mother—Mrs. Cotes has not before ever done quite such good work as this. If she will consent to write another Canadian novel, and has the opportunity to make it purely a domestic one, her audience will be fortunate. The enthusiasm and intensity of *The Imperialist*, however, comes from the development of the problem put in its name; and there can be little doubt that his countrymen will be the better Canadians for having known Lorne Murchison. Advena is another variation of the same elevated type, a very admirable and lovable one. Lorne's lady-love, who adores England after her own fashion, is a type too; and indeed, most of the characters in *The Imperialist* can stand for representatives of real people, individuals, or by classes. It is a book, after all, to be read and not to be analyzed, since those who know best whether it is a true presentation or not cannot have at the same time the advantage of an outsider's point of view....

7. E. Hoyt, *The Imperialist*. *The Lamp*, July 1904

The Imperialist by Mrs. Everard Cotes (Sara Jeannette Duncan), is preeminently a book for Canadians. Except for a brief visit to

England, where the hero goes to be unnecessarily confirmed in his Canadian predilections, the scene of the story does not go outside of the smoke of the chimneys of the little Dominion town of Elgin. It would be impossible for Mrs. Cotes to write a dull book, but if any one else had written this story it would have been desperately dull, except to a Canadian. By her art, the ins and outs of Dominion politics and local happenings are made interesting, and when one reads of Mrs. Murchison and Dr. Drummond, one recalls Barrie and Thrums.[1] After all, perhaps there is no valid reason why one should not be as much interested in the workings of a political ring and how they affected the love story of an estimable young man when the scene is laid in Ontario as one would be if the action took place in the Middle West or Down East. But whether it be the fault of the reader or of the writer, it must be conceded that Mrs. Cotes has failed to halo this story with the charm she threw about her "Mem-Sahib" and her "American Girl in London." There is no character in *The Imperialist* who will live by the side of Orthodocia,—and yet it is a clever book.

8. Unsigned. *The Imperialist. Canadian Magazine*, July 1904

No young Canadian, though willing to go to Parliament to represent a constituency, and though well enough known to be a possible candidate, can be an imperialist and a successful candidate. That is the general proposition upon which Sara Jeannette Cotes has based her arguments in *The Imperialist*. Her definition of an imperialist is one who would not hesitate to put Canada to some material loss, or at least to postpone her development in various important directions, for the sake of the imperial connection. Having thus defined him, she carries him through a political contest to defeat.

Mrs. Cotes may or may not be right. I fancy Lieut.-Col. Dennison would disagree and perhaps one or two others. There are many Imperialists in the country, but most of these place their Canadianism first. This is especially true of the Canadians who speak French; they have steadily refused to sing "God Save the

---

1   J.M. Barrie (1860-1930), best known as the author of *Peter Pan*, wrote about a fictional Scottish town named Thrums in his work *Auld Licht Idylls* (1888).

King." I recently attended a dinner at which about a score of French Canadian women were present; when the national anthem was being sung they contented themselves with a shrug and a smile. The Canadian who speaks English but who was born in this country usually sings the national anthem with vigour, but privately he believes the residents of the British Isles are members of a decadent race. He is willing to shout for the Empire, but does not believe in taxation without representation.

Whether Mrs. Cotes is right or wrong, the story is opportune. It comes at a time when Imperialism is being calmly considered. The intense glorification of Wallingham, who is the Rt. Hon. Joseph Chamberlain in thin disguise, is a fault in the story, perhaps. The Idea would have been just as forcible if less closely associated with one man. Again, the style of the author is extremely bad in many places, showing a lack of close revision. Ungrammatical constructions are common; the improper use of words shows a sad lack of dictionary and classical knowledge; the unnecessary chapters show a mercenary willingness to "pad." Yet, in spite of its glaring faults, one would hesitate to say that the book is not a valuable contribution to Canadian literature.

9. Unsigned. *The Imperialist*. *The Globe*, 13 August 1904

A story with contemporary Canadian life for its materials by Mrs. Everard Cotes is something in which the Canadian reader will undisguisedly be interested. It was natural, therefore, to turn to *The Imperialist* (The Copp, Clark Co., Toronto) with expectations which in most cases, it may be surmised, will be unrealized. Mrs. Cotes has won recognition in more than one branch of literature, but she has essayed in this book one of the hardest tasks that a novelist could undertake. The genius of Jane Austen is manifested in her power to reflect for us in the pages of a book, as in a mirror, the very essence and spirit of the life by which she was surrounded. The judgment of her contemporaries was that she effected this feat with wonderful fidelity and verisimilitude. Nothing short of genius could have acquitted itself so perfectly. Mrs. Cotes has set herself the same elusive task, and it is sound praise to say that there are glimpses here and there of a high range of accomplishment. The possibility of success is unquestionably lessened, however, by the attempt to weave a political theme into the simplicity and commonplaces of the ordinary life of a country town. That half of the population which is disfranchised take but little interest in politics, and it is a rule to which there are few exceptions that even when our sisters and wives make a conscious effort to compass the mystery their success is but partial. This is about all that could be said of the political passages of *The Imperialist*. They are not living and real, and as a picture of Canadian feeling they are not convincing. There is some good characterization. Dr. Drummond is a vital personage. Mr. and Mrs. Murchison are people that we know, and Stella is decidedly recognizable as the Canadian's younger sister.

A word should be said of Mrs. Cotes' mastery of the magic of the English tongue. It is a quality that she revealed in the first of her works and grows with her growth. We know of few writers who have a happier knack of conveying those fleeting moods and modes of our personality which we are all conscious of, but find it so difficult to set down felicitously in black and white. The first few pages of *The Imperialist* display this fine, light illuminating touch in perfection. It is the penalty of success, however, that what we do well and with facility we are apt to do in superabundance, just as the man who tells anecdotes well wearies us with wanting to tell them continuously. There are pages of clever phraseology in *The Imperialist* which could nevertheless be excised to advantage, and when it is employed about the political side of the tale it assumes a vagueness, a talking "about it and about," that is really a little dull and exasperating. It gets us no "forwarder," and getting forward is one of the indispensable merits of a tale that holds the attention.

Select Bibliography

Selected Works by Sara Jeannette Duncan

Cousin Cinderella. Ed. Misao Dean. Ottawa: Tecumseh, 1994.
A Daughter of To-Day. Ed. Misao Dean. Ottawa: Tecumseh, 1988.
On the Other Side of the Latch. London: Methuen, 1901.
Selected Journalism. Ed. Thomas Tausky. Ottawa: Tecumseh, 1978.
Set in Authority. Ed. Germaine Warkentin. Peterborough: Broadview, 1996.
The Simple Adventures of a Memsahib. New York: D. Appleton, 1893.

Secondary Sources

Allen, Peter. "Narrative Uncertainty in Duncan's *The Imperialist*." *Studies in Canadian Literature* 9:1 (Winter 1984): 41-60.

Bailey, Alfred G. "The Historical Setting of Sara Duncan's *The Imperialist*." *Twentieth Century Essays on Confederation Literature*. Ed. Lorraine McMullen. Ottawa: Tecumseh, 1976. 60-76.

Berger, Carl. *The Sense of Power: Studies in the Ideas of Canadian Imperialism 1867-1914*. Toronto: U of Toronto P, 1970.

—. "The True North Strong and Free." *Canadian Culture: An Introductory Reader*. Ed. Elspeth Cameron. Toronto: Canadian Scholars' Press, 1997. 83-102.

Bissell, Claude. "Introduction." *The Imperialist*. New Canadian Library. Ed. Malcolm Ross. Toronto: McClelland and Stewart, 1961. v-ix.

Burgin, G.B. "A Chat with Sara Jeannette Duncan." *The Idler* VIII (1895): 113-18.

Chamberlain, Joseph. *Imperial Union and Tariff Reform: Speeches Delivered from May 15 to Nov. 4, 1903*. London: G. Richards, 1903.

Collu, Gabrielle. "Sara Jeannette Duncan: Portrait of a Colonizer/Colonized." Textual Studies in Canada 5 (1994): 22-31.

Dean, Misao. *A Different Point of View: Sara Jeannette Duncan*. Montreal: McGill-Queen's UP, 1991.

—. "The Process of Definition: Nationality in Sara Jeannette Duncan's Early International Novels." *Journal of Canadian Studies* 20:2 (Summer 1985): 132-49.

—. "Political Change in Sara Jeannette Duncan's Novels." *The Literary Criterion* 29.3-4 (1984): 93-104.

—. *Practising Femininity: Domestic Realism and the Performance of Gender in Early Canadian Fiction.* Toronto: U of Toronto P, 1998.

Devereux, Cecily. "Are We There Yet? Reading the 'Post Colonial' and *The Imperialist* in Canada." *Is Canada Postcolonial?* Ed. Laura Moss. Waterloo, ON: Wilfrid Laurier UP, 2003. 177-89.

Donaldson, Florence. "An Interview with Mrs. Everard Cotes." *The Bookman* 14 (June 1898): 67.

Dooley, D.J. "Sara Jeannette Duncan: Political Morality at the Grass Roots." *Moral Vision in the Canadian Novel.* Toronto: Clarke, Irwin, 1979. 25-35.

Fiamengo, Janice. "'Susceptible to No Common Translation': Language and Idealism in Sara Jeannette Duncan's *The Imperialist.*" *Canadian Literature* 160 (1999): 121-40.

Fowler, Marian. *Redney: A Life of Sara Jeannette Duncan.* Toronto: Anansi, 1983.

Gerson, Carole. "Duncan's Web." Canadian Literature 63 (Winter 1975): 73-80.

—. *A Purer Taste: The Writing and Reading of Fiction in English in Nineteenth-Century Canada.* Toronto: U of Toronto P, 1989.

—. "Speculations." Rev. of *Redney,* by Marian Fowler. *Canadian Literature* 103 (Winter 1984): 78-80.

Goodwin, Rae. "The Early Journalism of Sara Jeannette Duncan, with a Chapter of Biography." M.A. University of Toronto, 1964.

Gray, Kim Heinrich. "Uncovered: The Ultimate Canadian Book(S)." *Globe and Mail* 27 April 1996: E7.

Hammill, Faye. "Sara Jeannette Duncan in the 'Camp of the Philistines.'" *Journal of Canadian Studies* 32.2 (1997): 154-69.

Heble, Ajay. "'This Little Outpost of Empire': Sara Jeannette Duncan and the Decolonization of Canada." *Journal of Commonwealth Literature* 26.1 (1991): 215-28.

Johnston, Anna and Alan Lawson. "Settler Colonies." *A Com-*

panion to *Postcolonial Studies*. Ed. Henry Schwartz and Ray Schwartz. Malden, MA: Blackwell, 2000. 360-76.

Kertzer, Jon. "Destiny into Chance: S.J. Duncan's *The Imperialist* and the Perils of Nation Building." *Studies in Canadian Literature* 24.2 (Summer 1999): 1-34.

Lang, Marjory. *Women Who Made the News: Female Journalists in Canada 1880-1945*. Montreal: McGill-Queen's UP, 1999.

MacMurchy, Marjorie. "Mrs. Everard Cotes (Sara Jeannette Duncan)." *The Bookman* 48 (May 1915): 39-40.

M.E.R. [Ross, Mrs. Sandford]. "Sara Jeannette Duncan: Personal Glimpses." *Canadian Literature* 27 (Winter 1966): 15-19.

Moss, Laura (Ed.). *Is Canada Postcolonial?* Waterloo, ON: Wilfrid Laurier UP, 2003.

"Not Quite the Unchanging East: Sara Jeannette Duncan" (interview) *The Globe* 14 November 1903: 21.

Peterman, Michael. "Humour and Balance in *The Imperialist*." *Journal of Canadian Studies* 11.2 (May 1976): 56-64.

Ready, Kathryn. "Sara Jeannette Duncan's *A Daughter of Today*: Nineteenth-Century Canadian Literary Feminism and the *Fin-De-Siècle* Magic-Picture Story." *Canadian Literature* 173 (2002): 95-112.

Ross, Catherine Sheldrick. "Calling Back the Ghost of the Old-Time Heroine: Duncan, Montgomery, Atwood, Laurence, and Munro." *Studies in Canadian Literature* 4.1 (Winter 1979): 43-57.

Saunders, Rebecca. "Gender, Colonialism, and Exile: Flora Annie Steel and Sara Jeannette Duncan in India." *Women's Writing in Exile*. Ed. Mary Lynn Broe and Angela Ingram. Chapel Hill: U of North Carolina P, 1989. 303-24.

Tausky, Thomas. *Sara Jeannette Duncan, Novelist of Empire*. Port Credit, ON: P.D. Meany, 1980.

Thomas, Clara. "Canadian Social Mythologies in Sara Jeannette Duncan's *The Imperialist*." *Journal of Canadian Studies* 12.2 (Spring 1977): 38-49.

Ward, Peter. *A History of Domestic Space*. Vancouver: U of British Columbia P, 1999.

Willmott, Glenn. *Unreal Country: Modernity in the Canadian Novel in English*. Montreal: McGill-Queen's UP, 2002.

Zezulka, Joseph M. "*The Imperialist*: Imperialism, Provincialism, and Point of View." *Beginnings: A Critical Anthology*. Ed. John Moss. Toronto: NC Press, 1980. 142-91.

Zichy, Francis. "Portrait of the Idealist as Politician: The Individual and Society in *The Imperialist*." *English Studies in Canada* X.3 (1984): 330-42.